SET IN AUTHORITY

Sara Jeannette Duncan

edited by Germaine Warkentin

broadview literary texts

Canadian Cataloguing in Publication Data

Duncan, Sara Jeannette, 1861-1922
    Set in authority

(Broadview literary texts)
Includes bibliographical references.
ISBN 1-55111-080-6

I. Warkentin, Germaine, 1933-   . II. Title. III. Series.
PS8457.08S4 1996   C813'.4   C96-930153-7
PR9199.2.D8S4 1996

Broadview Press, Post Office Box 1243, Peterborough, Ontario, Canada
K9J 7H5

in the United States of America:
3576 California Road, Orchard Park, NY 14127

in the United Kingdom:
B.R.A.D. Book Representation and Distribution Ltd., 244A London
Road, Hadleigh, Essex SS7 2DE

Broadview Press is grateful to Professor Eugene Benson for advice on editorial matters for the Broadview Literary Texts series.

Broadview Press gratefully acknowledges the support of the Canada Council, the Ontario Arts Council, and the Ministry of Canadian Heritage.

PRINTED IN CANADA

Sara Jeannette Duncan in 1909

(Photograph from Putnam's Reader, Vol V, October 1908–March 1909
p. 502. Courtesy of the Metropolitan Toronto Reference Library)

Contents

Acknowledgements

In editing *Set in Authority* – and particularly in devising the annotation – I have incurred debts almost too extensive to acknowledge, though I plan to do so as soon as the many friends I harassed with queries are speaking to me again. My most important debt is to Elaine Zinkhan, who at the urging of Carole Gerson, to whom I am also grateful, contacted me about new and quite unknown material on Duncan which had recently become available in the A. P. Watt Papers at the University of North Carolina. Judith Skelton Grant listened and read attentively as the project developed. Helmut Reichenbächer provided essential research assistance. Andrew Lamb took the photograph of Egerton Crescent, and Ingrid Smith typed portions of the text. Among the many who helped with the annotation I owe specific debts to Joanna Barker, Joseph Black, James W. Cook, James M. Estes, Robin Healey, Jeffrey Heath, Peter Hinchcliffe, Craig Jamieson, Jan Jenkins, Alexandra Johnston, Chelva Kanaganayakam, Bernard L. Karon, Clare Loughlin, Jane Millgate, Michael Millgate, Robert L. Montgomery Jr., Mark Nicholls, Sol Nigosian, Diana Patterson, Dylan Reid, Sanjay Sharma, John Warkentin, and Joan Winearls. I am grateful to the London Library, whose run of Duncan's novels, which I have constantly consulted, is nearly complete. I am also indebted to the Thomas Fisher Rare Book Library, University of Toronto and to the E.J. Pratt Library of Victoria University in the University of Toronto. I am grateful to the Metropolitan Toronto Reference Library and the British Library's India Office collections for permission to reproduce photographs in their possession. And finally I would like to thank the editorial team at Broadview Press, especially Don LePan and Barbara Conolly, for their support as the project transformed itself before our eyes.

Germaine Warkentin
Toronto

Introduction

THE central incident in Sara Jeannette Duncan's novel *Set in Authority* (1906), around which all the other events in the novel revolve, is a trial. In the great Indian city of Calcutta, an English soldier is tried for the murder of a native, and condemned to hang by the appeal court which is reviewing the case. A trial also takes place early in Duncan's Canadian masterpiece *The Imperialist*, which preceded *Set in Authority* by only two years. The first third of *The Imperialist* relates how Lorne Murchison, the earnest and able lawyer son of one of the small town of Elgin's chief citizens, initially makes his name by winning an acquittal for the son of a prominent local landowner charged with complicity in robbing the bank where he works. But in *The Imperialist* the real trial is in Chapter XXIX, when Lorne, who believes he is "at the bar for the life of a nation," makes a passionate but imprudent political speech before the hard-nosed citizens of Elgin, and for the time being destroys the public career for which he is so superbly qualified. In *The Imperialist* we as readers are there in the audience; we hear the speech, recognize the hopelessness of the Presbyterian minister's solitary applause, and eavesdrop on the whispers of Lorne's disillusioned handlers. In *Set in Authority* the trial of Henry Morgan (his second; again there are two trials) takes place off-stage. We witness it only in the agitated gossip that spreads verdict and sentence from courthouse to newspaper and telegraph office, to market stall and English club, to the corridors of the India Office in London and the tea-tables of Bloomsbury and Kensington. And in the novel we never actually meet Henry Morgan himself.

This clinical distance marks an important difference in approach between two of Duncan's attempts, within half a decade, at a single subject central both to her work and the problematics of her imperialist era: the question of how and by what right authority is maintained. Her first book, *A Social Departure: How Orthodocia and I Went Round the World by Ourselves* (1890), had mockingly addressed this question, both in its contrast between the high-spirited, unconventional narrator and her travelling companion, the aptly-named Orthodocia,[1] and in the flouting – in a story about two unmarried young women travelling without a chaperone – of conventional ideas about the rules which ought to govern female behaviour. As Duncan's career progressed she returned, first in light satire and then with increasing depth, to the problem of authority, which by 1906 she had begun to see not just as an aspect of the colonial situation, or as a feminist issue (though it was certainly both), but as a profound source of psychological and social conflict. In *The Imperialist*, the result had been a *Bildungsroman*, an affectionate portrait of a young man discovering the limits within which he must live, and – not incidentally – of a young society at work on the same task. *Set in Authority* is a book of middle age; almost all its characters have long since learned the lesson Lorne Murchison is faced with. Its setting is not a new society, but two very old ones in wary confrontation with each other, and its manner is ruthlessly detached and ironic.

Duncan's preoccupation with authority was an authentically modern one; much of the "decadent" writing of the *fin de siècle* and the Edwardian period had restlessly taken up the same problem, in a style and manner notoriously contemptuous of middle-class orthodoxy. But though Duncan's concerns were progressive for her time, her characters and stories were often drawn from the world of the administrative upper class and the gentry, precisely the class the "decadents" set out to shock.[2] As a novelist she has thus remained a somewhat ambivalent figure. For its original audience (in Britain as well as Canada) *The Imperialist* was too advanced; they resisted the density of social observation, the irony, and the sheer contemporaneity of what has proven to be the first truly modern Canadian novel. The book received bad reviews in both England and North America when it first appeared, and remained virtually unread until the 1960s.[3] In its day *Set in Authority*, which is even more ironic than *The Imperialist* but is set in scenes more attractive to an international audience, was both better known and better received. Nevertheless, for later readers it has often been Duncan's apparent *lack* of the modern, the glossy social surface of her novels with their debt to Trollope and Thackeray, which has led to neglect. Though Canadians today are interested in Duncan, they read her other novels chiefly for the light they throw on what is now viewed as a founding work of Canadian fiction; elsewhere she appears only occasionally in the writings of students of feminism and post-colonialism trawling the backwaters of the Edwardian novel, and almost never in accounts of Anglo-Indian literature.[4]

In the summer of 1906, however, Duncan could content herself with the knowledge she had produced a success; *Set in Authority* had been serialized throughout the spring, and was published in book form by Constable on May 18, 1906. It was fairly widely reviewed (see Appendix II), and would be issued in the United States by Doubleday Page in the autumn.[5] Throughout the summer of 1906 the London trade periodical *The Bookman* described *Set in Authority* as among the six-shilling novels "most in demand," in a list which included Upton Sinclair's *The Jungle*. Other novels of the same year were John Galsworthy's *The Man of Property*, Rudyard Kipling's *Puck of Pook's Hill*, and the American novelist Winston Churchill's best-seller about a local political boss, *Coniston*. It is evident from its conditions of publication and the places where it was reviewed that *Set in Authority* was a book of a specific type, destined for a specific audience: the middle-class one-volume novel intended both for the commercial lending libraries and an intelligent international readership, a type which itself was "modern," having in the 1880s definitively put to death the popular mid-Victorian three-decker which had built that audience.

If Duncan chose to work within the limits of the middle-class novel, it is nevertheless apparent both from the book itself and from several thoughtful reviews it received that in *Set in Authority* she set out to test those limits rigorously. She chose two themes which were then deeply problematic for the class for which she wrote: the manner in which England ought to rule over its colonies, and the solitude and confusion of the woman who chooses to enter the public life of the professions, but as a consequence must renounce the protection automatically accorded her sister who accepts the private domain of "petticoat power." These themes are linked by a single, troubling vision, that of "institutional man" – the man whom society requires to "rule" in the public sphere, but who then negotiates his life in the private sphere in the narrow terms established by his public obligations. In the manner of its Victorian predecessors, *Set in Authority* presents us with a portrait of the network of such institutions within which all its characters live, whether the interwoven gentry families who govern England or the mercantile companies of Calcutta. But the novel's central insight has to do with the institutional mind-set itself, as it is found in two men with pure motives but fatal limitations. One is the able and idealistic Viceroy, whose rigid Liberal principles insist on an application of the law which offends every instinct of the colonial administrators who have to carry it out. The other is his friend Eliot Arden, the literary-minded Chief Commissioner of an unimportant province; in a wrenching paradox his "secretariat mind" so instinctively accepts the autonomy of the woman he secretly loves that when he is freed to marry her, he cannot recognize her tentative overtures in his direction for what they are. Both are examples of a peculiarly Edwardian fictional type, the "detached man" we meet in Henry James's Lambert Strether (*The Ambassadors*, 1903), in Edith Wharton's Lawrence Selden (*The House of Mirth*, 1905), and in Soames Forsyte, Galsworthy's "man of property." In the end this detachment, which Duncan's women can never share, wreaks its havoc; in upholding the equality of the law the Viceroy does the right thing for the wrong reason; in retreating before Ruth's seeming autonomy Arden does the wrong thing for the right reason. It is precisely this kind of ironic chiasmus for which the novel is designed to prepare us from the beginning.

∽ ∽ ∽

E.M. Forster, travelling in India in 1912, was entertained by Duncan and her husband Everard Cotes at their house in Simla; describing the visit in a letter to his mother he shrewdly pointed to the conflicting signals in Duncan's behaviour which hinted at the ambivalence which critics have since had to account for in her writing: "Mrs. Cotes was clever & odd – [at times very (crossed out)] nice to talk to alone, but at times the Social Manner descended like a pall."[6] Duncan's entire career, and in Canada her subsequent critical history, has been coloured by that conflict between intellectual style and social manner, between her desire to forge a notable career as a writer despite her need to conform to social norms, between her novelist's ambition to master an adventurous subject-matter, yet do so on terms still within the range of the unadventurous middle class reader.

Sarah Janet Duncan was born in Brantford, Canada West (now Ontario), on December 22, 1861, the daughter of Charles Duncan, Scottish-born owner of a successful dry goods and furniture store, and Jane (Bell) Duncan, of Irish descent, born in Shediac, New Brunswick.[7] The Brantford of her youth is portrayed as Elgin in *The Imperialist*; in it, looking out upon the Main Street, Dr. Drummond and Lorne's father, John Murchison, see

> a prospect of moderate commercial activity . . . a street of mellow shop-fronts, on both sides, of varying height and importance, wearing that air of marking a period, a definite stop in growth, that so often co-exists with quite a reasonable degree of activity and independence in colonial towns . . . its appearance and demeanour would never have suggested that it was now the chief artery of a thriving manufacturing town, with a collegiate institute, eleven churches, two newspapers, and an asylum for the deaf and dumb. . . . (23-25)

The uneasy co-existence of colonial caution and North American "go-ahead" which this passage conveys defines not only the themes of *The Imperialist* but certain ambiguities of Duncan's own career, and it hints too at her literary method, which as long as she wrote would present her readers with a near-irreconcilable disjunction between what they saw, and what society permitted them to say about it.

What Duncan saw about her as she grew up in her parents' fine Victorian house was a prosperous, self-satisfied society, rich in social nuance but irredeemably narrow. Yet she learned how to view this society from more perspectives than that of the house on West Street. She was educated as the daughter of an important merchant should be (local primary schools, Brantford's excellent Collegiate, and for a brief period Brantford Ladies College). Above all she was a cultivated North American of proudly independent spirit, like Senator Wick's English suit in *A Voyage of Consolation*, "aristocratic in quality but democratic in cut" (30). The career for which a woman of her position was inevitably destined, school-teaching, provided the briefest of early way-stations (1880-84) in a life devoted to seeking the same independence. Duncan set her sights early on becoming a professional writer, and throughout her life almost all her decisions were determined by the managing of that career.

Between 1880 and 1884, teaching part-time in and around Brantford, Duncan began to publish short pieces locally, and to seek newspaper work as far afield as New York. Still without prospects, in the fall of 1884 she resolved on her own to report on the New Orleans Cotton Centennial Fair on behalf of Canadian publications, and persuaded *The Globe* (Toronto) and the *Advertiser* (London, Ontario) to run the material she would send back. Her articles from the fair (under the pseudonym "Garth," December, 1884-March, 1885) appeared in papers in Memphis, New Orleans, and Washington as well as in Canada, and her own horizons were satisfyingly widened by contact with other writers. Returning to Canada she persisted in her attempts to become a professional journalist, working (usually for only a few months) as a columnist for *The Globe*, and then in an editorial position on the *Washington Post*. She also contributed to the important Toronto journal *The Week*, edited by Goldwin Smith, and began to sign her columns "Jeannette Duncan" and then "Sara Jeannette Duncan." In June, 1886 she resigned her position on the *Washington Post* and rejoined the Toronto *Globe* as a full member of the editorial staff, writing the "Women's World" column under the by-line of "Garth Grafton." But by 1887 she had left the *Globe* for the *Montreal Star*, which she served for a brief period in the spring of 1888 as parliamentary correspondent in Ottawa. By the fall of 1888 she had conceived a new project: to travel around the world and write a book about it, and in September, 1888 she set out by train westward from Montreal, accompanied (as a defence against the outrageous idea of an unmarried woman travelling alone) by the Montreal journalist Lily Lewis. The book she wrote about their travels, *A Social Departure: How Orthodocia and I Went Round the World by Ourselves* (1890) was the most successful she ever published. Its impenitent dedication read, "This volume as a slight tribute to the omnipotence of her opinion, and a humble mark of profoundest esteem is respectfully dedicated to Mrs. Grundy."[8]

A Social Departure contains many of the seeds of Duncan's later novels; it is a cheerfully anecdotal source on the progressive Canada of the late-nineteenth century, and its hundred pages on India provide essential background to her later Anglo-Indian novels. In addition, we can see in it the strengths and limitations of Duncan the novelist in gestation: her quick insight into character, her fine descriptive gift, the raw sting of an almost ungovernable irony, and above all her wicked sense of the difference between theory and practice, between the ways people say they behave, and the ways they actually do. In particular, we note how ready she is to exploit popular narrative conventions (often by inverting them), and well-known narrative genres. The set-piece anecdote is already hovering on the brink of becoming a story, and in one or two cases it does, as for example in the Kiplingesque account of the fire-burial of the beggar Chuttersingh, in which the real centre of her attention is the ragged, trembling old friend who must light the pyre, or in Duncan's savagely angry account of her visit to the Towers of Silence outside Bombay, where the Parsee dead are left exposed to the vultures. A Social Departure was written with flair and self-conscious charm; it was written to sell, and sell it did. But there is a symptomatic ruthlessness in Duncan's vision which occasionally asserts itself, as in the moment when she and Orthodocia turn their backs on the Towers of Silence, where the body of a Parsee child has just been offered to the vultures:

So we hurried down the path and through the scarlet hibiscus bushes, putting many steps between it and us. We might have saved ourselves the trouble, for a turn in the road unexpectedly disclosed the towers again, and the vultures were flapping lazily back to their places. (319)

The best of the novels she was to write are defined by their ability to recapture that moment of unavoidable disclosure, the lesser by their strategic decisions to avoid it.

Invited to a reception at the Calcutta mansion of the Viceroy, Lord Lansdowne, whom she had known in Ottawa, Duncan met her future husband Everard Cotes, an entomologist at the Indian Museum; he proposed to her during a visit to the Taj Mahal at Agra in March. This episode was refashioned in *A Social Departure* to fit the person of "Orthodocia"; though Duncan regularly used her own experiences for novelistic matter, they were usually rewritten with a sharp eye for narrative convention, a noteworthy stratagem in a novelist with such a strong personal voice. If Duncan made an early decision to become a writer, she had also been socialized as a woman of the 1880s, and as such she made an equally early decision to be a wife. In that decision two factors must have played a role: the man, and the place. The man was a courtly, mild-mannered civil servant of evident charm and moderate capacity; the place, India, was exotic beyond all her still-provincial experience. The mordantly satirical picture she drew of Anglo-India throughout her life might suggest that she was unhappy with at least that bargain. Yet Duncan published nine books set in India, the largest and most coherent body of her work, and in the end its most mature, apart from *The Imperialist*; Anglo-India was a subject she *chose*, and in writing about it she also chose not to turn out conventional romances like those of such contemporary Anglo-Indian novelists as Alice Perrin and Maud Diver, but to delve successively deeper into Anglo-India's human relationships and eventually its politics. As for the man, it is difficult to know; in publishing her novels Duncan usually styled herself "Sara Jeannette Duncan (Mrs. Everard Cotes)," and was routinely addressed as "Mrs. Cotes" by her agent and publishers; the couple treated each other with dignity and when the war ended quickly resumed their shared life, interrupted for four years when World War I separated Duncan in London and Cotes in Calcutta. Everard certainly liked being a husband, since he married again within months of Duncan's death.[9] In the end it simply may have been one of those marriages in which a difficult woman and a gentle, agreeable man made common cause.[10]

After the world tour was finished and her book published in London, Duncan returned to India for her wedding in December, 1890. In the interval she had written two other books, *An American*

Girl in London, which would be issued to good reviews in March, 1891, and *Two Girls on a Barge*, which appeared under a pseudonym (V. Cecil Cotes) in August of the same year.[11] Both these books, like *A Social Departure*, were serialized before publication in book form, as were most of Duncan's later novels. In the period between 1890 and the early summer of 1914 she established what presented if not a routine, at least a discernable pattern: she would write a novel, sell the serial rights, then arrange for British and American publication. She also wrote regularly for various journals. In pursuit of this evolving career, she travelled regularly between Calcutta and London, often spending several months of the year in some rented Kensington flat writing her next book, reading proof, or making literary contacts.[12] Several times she and Cotes tried to leave India to establish themselves permanently in London, but without success; Cotes could always find work as a journalist on the subcontinent, and in Anglo-India Duncan at least had a subject which she could not let go of, or which would not let go of her.

It was under these conditions that she published twenty-two books in the decades between her tour around the world and her death in 1922. "For almost forty years of her relatively short life," writes George Woodcock, himself a professional to the core,

> she was an industrious and capable journalist (writing for Canadian, American, and eventually Indian papers), and she wrote twenty [sic] books which appeared in her lifetime or shortly afterwards. Most of them were published in both London and New York, and some in Toronto as well. From the beginning of her career they were on the whole well received, and in the latter part of her career she generally gained the respect that is accorded a writer of acknowledged standing.[13]

Much about Duncan is explained if we keep in mind the thorough-going professionalism which she displayed from the moment she sent her first poem to *The Globe* in 1880; her constant travelling from India to England, for example, was the only way she could take care of her interests. And she did take care, as her correspondence with her agents, A. P. Watt and Son, shows.[14] She also managed her money with prudence; royalties went into her bank account in Brantford, which was showing a nice balance when she died in 1922.[15]

This professionalism had its effect on her literary material as well. Without being crass about it, Duncan wanted to write what would sell, and, in selling, make her name; her articles from the New Orleans Cotton Fair and the tour recorded in *A Social Departure* were carefully calculated to achieve that end. In 1900 she was forced to spend seven months outdoors in her Simla garden, then a routine prescription for tuberculosis. She promptly began to write a memoir of her time "on the other side of the latch," pondering how to "observe life from a cane chair under a tree in a garden . . . though a purely vegetable romance would be a novelty, could I get it published?" (*Latch*, 5). Commercial options thus have to be taken into consideration for all her early books; in fact *Set in Authority* may be the only book in which she went against her usual practice, stubbornly writing a deliberately political novel when the political novel she had just published, *The Imperialist*, had been a critical failure. If we assume that her Anglo-Indian novels, beginning with *The Simple Adventures of a Memsahib* (1893), constitute a coherent body of work accumulating over fifteen years, around them and set against them we can see a series of experiments, some successful, some tedious, in currently popular or saleable genres: the "international" novel, *An American Girl in London* (1891) and its sequel *A Voyage of Consolation* (1898); the flawed but fascinating "new woman" novel *A Daughter of To-day* (1894); the thin, over-extended magazine story *Those Delightful Americans* (1902); and late, enervated failures like *The Consort* (1912) or *His Royal Happiness* (1915). Two important mature novels, *The Imperialist* (1904) and the social satire *Cousin Cinderella* (1908), each with its Canadian angle, in their turn drew on the strengths in social observation Duncan accumulated in the long discipline of coming to terms with Anglo-India.

Duncan's willingness to experiment with saleable genres is apparent in some of her Anglo-Indian books as well: the absurd novella *Vernon's Aunt* (1894), for example, or the now almost unreadable pseudo-Jamesian tedium of *The Path of A Star* (1899). But the close observation of the Indian chapters in *A Social Departure* was a harbinger of things to come; when she began *The Simple Adventures of a Memsahib* (1893), exploiting – though with ironic distance – the experiences of her own first months as a bride in India, she entered on the social territory of the great English novelists of the nineteenth century. Though Duncan was early a disciple of Henry James and William Dean Howells, her approach to writing in her maturity was solidly based in the novels of "society" pioneered in the early nineteenth century first by Jane Austen, then by the "silver fork" novelists, and brought to a peak of human and social insight by the great Victorians William Makepeace Thackeray, George Eliot, and Anthony Trollope.[16] These socially knowing, carefully plotted novels, though Duncan's maturest work, are likely to be under-rated by readers hardened to the demands of modernist and post-modern fiction. Yet a reader open to the rich semiotics of Victorian texts will discover that Duncan's route to the modern, if different, is no less demanding, and that she not only probes with unrepentant irony into the life of the tea-table and the social club, but seeks to transform them into metaphorical sites for an initially comic but increasingly more painful investigation of the institutional and personal realities of her age.

In books of increasing complexity, almost all centred on Anglo-Indian life, Duncan began to explore first the social interactions of human beings, as she had done in the popular *Simple Adventures of a Memsahib*, and then the way these social actions become political as they do in *His Honor, and a Lady* (1896). Even the four stories of *The Pool in the Desert* (1903) consider the politics of intimate personal relationships. Though not Anglo-Indian in subject-matter, *The Imperialist* and *Cousin Cinderella* are clearly products of the same learning process; in them mingled themes of private and public politics are translated into the serio-comic mode and to scenes distant from India, but not unrelated to its social complexities. Even later pot-boilers like *The Consort* and *His Royal Happiness*, possibly the victims of ultimately irreconcilable conflicts in her own vision, retain their focus on politics, social interaction, and the problem of legitimate authority. Her last Anglo-Indian novel was *The Burnt Offering* (1909); characteristically, it was written in the midst of the rising agitation for Home Rule which had by then begun to dominate public life in India.

ᴏᴜ   ᴏᴜ   ᴏᴜ

The culmination of Duncan's development as a novelist of Anglo-Indian society is not *The Burnt Offering*, however, but *Set in Authority*, written during 1904-05 at the time of her acute disappointment at the failure of *The Imperialist*; in origin it is the most specifically political of all her novels. At first called *The Viceroy*, a title which Duncan changed while the book was already in Watt's hands, *Set in Authority* is *The Imperialist*'s darker twin. In it that "imperial figure" the taciturn Southern Ontario farm wife Mrs. Crow is replaced by the Viceroy of India, Anthony Andover, fourth Baron Thame, austere and solitary in his castle in Simla, whose five year vice-regency frames the time-scheme of the book, and who like the accused soldier Henry Morgan, with whom he proves mysteriously connected, never appears in the novel either.

Early readers of *Set in Authority* commented on the faint but recognizable resemblance between George Curzon, Baron Curzon of Kedleston, Viceroy of India from 1899 to 1905, and Anthony Andover, and in 1980 T.E. Tausky pointed out the close correspondence between specific events of Curzon's vice-royalty and Duncan's novel.[17] Documents which only recently became publicly available confirm that Curzon's authoritarian style and insensitivity to Anglo-Indian opinion were not only the basis for Duncan's portrayal of Andover (if we can call it a portrayal, since he never appears) but that his actions provided the central incident of the novel itself. In the early summer of 1900 Duncan sent an essay to her agent, A. P. Watt, asking him to obtain publication in an English periodical, but insisting that under no circumstances should it be published over her name. This was "A Progressive Viceroy" (reprinted in Appendix I) which appeared in *The Contemporary Review* in August, 1900. Watt told Duncan he had only been able to obtain £7.7.0 for it, but that he could see that in this case publication was more important to her than remuneration.[18] In "A Progressive Viceroy" Duncan sharply arraigns what the Anglo-Indian world

Lord and Lady Curzon reviewing troops at the 1903 "Coronation Durbar" in Delhi, which Duncan attended. (By permission of the British Library. Mss. Eur. F.111/270/xi (dup. 7.)

considered Curzon's vanity, his expediency, his intellectual pretensions, and his insensitivity to local feeling.[19]

But the essay was an attack not only on Curzon's personality (that "very superior person" enraged more than the Anglo-Indians[20]); it constituted a clear statement of contrasting values. Duncan argued "that the maximum of superintendence may very well reside in the minimum of interference," and maintained that "in the easy old garment of custom, behind the shield of tradition, we have kept the place and the pace in the world's progress that best suited us." Looked at one way, these are the cautious, self-protective values represented in her evocation of the main street of Elgin in *The Imperialist*. Yet they also express one of Duncan's most rooted convictions: that no matter how benevolent the regime they live under, the people on the spot know best how to manage their own affairs. Throughout her writings this conflict between authority and autonomy occurs on a small as well as a large scale; we see it in the drunken bargee Mrs. Bradshaw in *Two Girls on a Barge*, who rails at the noble-spirited Mr. Gershom because her children have been taken away to be educated (134-36), in Ganendra Thakore's speech of self-justification in *The Burnt Offering* (242), in Prince Alfred's need to outflank the court in *His Royal Happiness*, even in the enraged robin who is the victim of her own good intentions in *On the Other Side of the Latch* (214-15). Repeatedly Duncan pits the voices of those who do not quite fit the system against the system itself, even when the system appears to be in the right (or, in the case of the Simla robin, at least well-intentioned).

Duncan and her husband were acquainted, in the way of many minor figures in Anglo-Indian society, with the Viceroy. They had toured, probably in a journalistic capacity, with the Vice-Regal party, and Duncan appears to have been fond of Lady Curzon, an internationally famed American beauty who had been presented at court in the same London season as Duncan herself.[21] A decade after Lady Curzon's early death in 1906 Duncan dedicated to her memory *His Royal Happiness*, the plot of which hinges in part on the tale of the Curzons' lengthy secret engagement. In *On the Other Side of the Latch*, written only months after "A Progressive Viceroy" but before its publication, Lord and Lady Curzon appear, in the rather sugary manner of that memoir, as "the Roy-Regent" and "the Princess" (122-35). The only touch of lemon is in Duncan's shrewd awareness of the isolation of the Princess, and the observation that like most people, including the author herself, the Roy-Regent does not like to be "kindly rebuked" (241). Curzon apparently never found out who wrote "A Progressive Viceroy"; he complained to C. E. Dawkins in London about the "quaint and spiteful" article, saying "in some respects it was rather amusing" but that he could not think of a single person clever enough to have done it. A defence (also pseudonymous) duly appeared in *The Contemporary Review* (see Appendix I), but Dawkins was unable to discover the author of the original attack, and could only commiserate with Curzon on its "vulgar impertinence." Clearly, however, Curzon had been gored; he was still seething six months later.[22] Duncan's motives for writing "A Progressive Viceroy" remain murky, and the anonymity of its publication uncomfortably mirrors the anonymous attack on John Church which Lewis Ancram had made in *His Honor, and a Lady,* and which proves his downfall in Judith Church's eyes. In the end it may be that Duncan was writing, if not as a "hired pen," then at the request of Anglo-Indian colleagues who needed her sharp satiric gift to make their case. But the figure of the "idealist in a hurry" we meet with in her evisceration of Curzon would, much transformed, provide her first with a central motif of *The Imperialist,* and then with the zealous Viceroy of *Set in Authority.*

The plot of *Set in Authority* emerges from Curzon's actions (angrily attacked in "A Progressive Viceroy") during what became known as "the Rangoon assault case." In April, 1899, at the beginning of Curzon's tenure in India, twenty men of the West Kent Regiment gang-raped an old Burmese woman; a court martial occurred, but ended with the soldiers' acquittal because the native witnesses were frightened into withdrawing their evidence. The matter was hushed up by the military and civil authorities, but when Curzon heard of it nearly two months later he was outraged, and, supported by officials in England, resolved on firm punishment, the consequences of which among the colonial English he well understood. "The culprits were dismissed from the army," relates Lord Ronaldshay, "high military officers were severely censured, and in certain cases relieved from their commands; the regiment was banished for two years to Aden [a hardship posting], where all leave and indulgences were stopped."[23] Curzon's biographers agree in attributing his rage not only to the offence itself but to his frustration at the attempts of the military and the local government to keep the story quiet. Local opinion took another view, as Duncan makes clear in "A Progressive Viceroy." Without in any way condoning the original offence, she observes that "the point which claims our interest is that Lord Curzon was not content with the severity of the sentence which his influence was counting for so much in bringing about. That might do − I hope we do not too rashly conclude − for the abstract ends of justice, but Lord Curzon must also be vindicated." What galls her is Curzon's self-righteousness.

Set in Authority thus has its beginning not only in the situation itself − an injustice perpetrated by English soldiery on a native, for which the English would have to be punished − but in the conflict between justice in theory and justice in practice. Duncan transforms the historical incident to suit her purposes: the case of the Black Dragoons over which Colonel Vetchley and General Lemon argue in Chapter V actually parallels the circumstances of the Rangoon assault incident more strictly than the "Morgan case". Similarly, she transforms the rage apparent in "A Progressive Viceroy" into something cooler and more self-consciously structured. Andover's sense that he alone knows what is best definitely grows out of Duncan's earlier criticism of Curzon, but, unable for obvious reasons to portray him directly, she keeps the Viceroy of her novel off-stage, and instead brings to the fore that problem of "abstract justice" which had been a central value of the Liberalism she still prized. One of the great tenets of Liberalism − fought for with tenacity since the 1865 case of Governor Eyre's repression of the Morant Bay revolt in Jamaica − had been to ensure that the law was applied equally to white and brown.[24] How then, she asks, this time not with the essayist's fury but with the novelist's impartially, is this to be done, given the conflicting claims of authority and autonomy? The conflict may have been one she could not resolve, but in it was generated a serious meditation on the illusions required to sustain both.

∾   ∾   ∾

Set in Authority is a novel about illusions: the imperial illusions of those who rule – and those who are ruled; of families about their members; of men and women about each other. The setting moves between the political drawing rooms of London and the verandahs and tennis courts of the English station at Pilaghur in the obscurity of the fictive Indian province of Ghoom. The action is initiated in London, in the Cavendish Square house of Lady Thame, redoubtable Liberal political hostess and mother of the bachelor Radical peer Anthony Andover; she and her daughters are giving tea to Mrs. Lawrence Lenox, visiting from India and the wife of "a judge somewhere out there." The news of the day is Andover's appointment as Viceroy of India, and Mrs. Lenox is in a flutter; her husband fagged[25] for Lord Thame at Eton, and this social connection with the man who for the next five years will, in effect, stand in the King-Emperor's place is going to change the Lenoxes' lives. We are meant to remember this moment when, near the end of the book, it proves to be Lawrence Lenox who obligingly passes the sentence of death on Henry Morgan which the Viceroy then refuses to commute.

The party is joined by Lady Thame's half-niece Victoria Tring, whose refusal of Andover's proposal of marriage has not impaired their intellectual friendship. Victoria's mother is the widowed Deirdre Tring who, when not being a parent,

> fulfilled the law of her being, to which she often said that maternity was an accident. She absorbed London and the time, consumed much social philosophy, became a Fabian as strenuously as she might have become a Mahomedan, threw off her convictions in essays and her impressions in poems, rode in the very van of progress, was, I have no doubt, the first woman who smoked a cigarette in a public restaurant. (73)

Egerton Crescent, London (Photo: Andrew Lamb)

There is another Tring, Victoria's brother Herbert, an embryo "decadent" essayist, but he has mysteriously disappeared from England. At the same time as these first scenes introduce us to the imperial allure with which Andover's new appointment surrounds him, we watch Victoria and Lady Thames's daughter Lavinia lay a secret plot to finance an Irish-American political adventurer, James Kelly. He reports that he has news of Herbert and has volunteered to track him down for the family in the Yukon, which like other distant locations of high adventure the contemporary popular press had succeeded in making almost banal.[26]

Duncan's amused satire of the self-consciously avante-garde "new woman" in her portrait of Deirdre Tring is evident. Less so, at least to a reader of the 1990s, is the way her technique in these early chapters relies absolutely on the ability of her audience to interpret the social semiotics of her narrative. She assumes both her characters and her readers are like Galsworthy's Forsytes, suspiciously "reading" Philip Bosinney's bohemian soft grey hat as the threat to their well-ordered existence it indeed represents. Likewise we are meant to take as necessary and eloquent circumstances of life the obscure family trusts which finance the young women's various degrees of independence, to know what it means for that heiress of the Whig aristocracy Lady Thame to live "in an old-fashioned way in Cavendish Square" (now in 1906 perhaps a bit too close to Oxford Circus), or for Mrs. Tring, however advanced her views, to take a house in prosperous Egerton Crescent. We are meant to take for granted the naturalness of bonds between men who have been at school and sat in Parliament together, and between mothers whose daughters have married the sons of the girls with whom they themselves were once presented at court.

In particular we are meant to recognize the common language spoken by families who for several generations have "gone out" to India, not only their social language but the actual verbal texture of their lives. The "Anglo-Indian" of *Set in Authority* is occasionally (though for the modern reader not sufficiently) annotated by Duncan herself, but it has been memorialized in that wonder of historical lexicography known as *Hobson-Jobson*. Quite as much as the hundreds of Anglo-Indian memoirs of the period, *Hobson-Jobson* opens out to us the daily world of the English in India, a world which almost more than England has shaped the characters in the novel, many of whose families are shown to have deep roots there.[27] The eponymous "Mother in India" of Duncan's 1903 short story, travelling back to the sub-continent by steamer, muses

> It was a Bombay ship, full of returning Anglo-Indians. I looked up and down the long saloon tables with a sense of relief and solace; I was again among my own people. They belonged to Bengal and to Burma, to Madras and to the Punjab, but they were all my people. I could pick out a score that I knew in fact, and there were none that in imagination I didn't know.[28]

Thus in addition to its intense deployment of English social nuance, *Set in Authority* demands that we possess something of this same knowledge of all things Anglo-Indian acquired by so many of the novelist's readers before they themselves "came home." If Duncan wrote *The Imperialist* for "her people" in the Canada from which she had started out and which – as *On the Other Side of the Latch* shows – she still loved, *Set In Authority* addresses itself to, and memorializes, the world of the "people" Duncan had perforce to make her own, the Anglo-Indians.

Yet whether in England or in India, Duncan's cool gaze impels us to recognize what separates her characters from each other as well as from themselves: the social tone of the ambitious Mrs. Lenox is not *quite* that of the aristocratic drawing-room in which she is being received; Lady Thame would willingly see her son immolated for a principle; the girls are eager to take a confidence man at his face value; Deirdre's bohemianism is confined to her artfully disordered appearance; and the hearty convention of northern adventure-narrative is invoked only to be rendered improbable by Kelly's grimmer affiliation with the Irish revolutionary movement.

Then, with the secure structural hand of the professional novelist, Duncan repeats her opening chapters, but this time in the setting of Pilaghur, where the appointment of a new Viceroy is not a family matter but one of surpassing public interest:

Pilaghur is the capital of the province of Ghoom, which is
ruled by a Chief Commissioner, under the Government of
India, under the Parliament of Great Britain and Ireland, under the King. (76)

"Ghoom is in fact very far under," Duncan continues drily. Ghoom
itself is a hill town in Bengal; Duncan makes it a province in the
plains. Its name has ironic nuances; the word *jhoom* was "used on the
eastern frontiers of Bengal for that kind of cultivation which is prac-
tised in the hill forests of India and Indo-China, under which a tract
is cleared by fire, cultivated for a year or two, and then abandoned
for another tract."[29] This psychically impermanent territory contains, Duncan shows us, two Pilaghurs. The first is the quasi-English
one which the people of the station have built, with its cathedral, its
club, and its public gardens, with its Chief Commissioner's wife (the
charming and hard-working Jessica Arden), its careful social distinc-
tions, its English regiment (the Barfordshires), and its myriad of colonial officials, greater and less. From one point of view this is the "3
or 4 Families in a Country Village . . . the very thing to work on,"
which Jane Austen recommended as ideal subject-matter for the
novelist in a letter of 1814 to her niece Anna.[30] But the ironic regard
Duncan bends on the friends assembled in the Ardens' dining room
in Chapter V shows that she is not likely to spare even family, a lesson
already foreshadowed in the much more amiable *The Imperialist*.

The other Pilaghur "crowds upon the skirts of this, a thick embroidery." Perhaps because of the intense presence of travel narrative in her early writing, Duncan is expert at pictorial scene-paint-
ing, though the important things we learn about Elgin or London
more often come from the ways people behave in them. In her
writing about India she deliberately exploits visual detail: the subtle
shades of ochre and apricot, the cloud cast up by a passing cart, the
heat, the dryness, the "grey-green cactuses, many-armed and dusty"
(77). Yet inevitably it is the city "spreading imperceptibly out into
the mustard-fields" which interests her the most:

In the narrow ways of the crowded city by the river the
houses jostle each other to express themselves. The upper

stories crane over the lower ones, and all resent their neighbours. They have indeed something to say with their carved balconies of wood and even of stone, with the dark-stained arches, pointed and scalloped of their shop fronts, their gods in effigy, their climbing, crumbling ochres and magentas. (78)

What the city has to "say" we eventually learn when the English doctor, Ruth Pearce, discovers the revenge of the *munshi*, Afzul Aziz, who has taught everyone in the English colony at Pilaghur their Hindustani while harbouring at the same time a bitter grief from the past.

In the meantime, what we notice is less the difference between the two Pilaghurs than their resemblance. In one, there is the Commissioner and Mrs. Arden, and all who depend on them. In the other there is

> Ganeshi Lal, who wires a price to London for half the seed crops of Ghoom, looking out indifferently from his second-story window upon all. Ganeshi sits on the floor; he wears a gold-embroidered velvet cap, and the scalloped window frames him to the waist. . . . Down below squat his kinsmen round the hills of yellow meal in the shop window, and sell a measure for a copper; up above Ganeshi with a rusty pen and purple ink writes off half a lakh of profits on a piece of brown paper. (78-9)

Though Ghoom may be "very far under" in that Imperial structure which rises up through its institutional levels until it reaches the King-Emperor on his throne, it constitutes a world in many ways parallel to the Imperial one, with multiple layers of society reaching from figures of undoubted rank like the Anglophile judge, Sir Ahmed Hossein, downward to Ganeshi Lal sitting at his accounts, to minor officials, teachers, household servants, and stall-holders in the bazaar, and finally to the leper-woman, "that no-fingered one" sitting at the corner of Krishna Ghat Lane (108). Even the jackals, calling out to each other "Hum Maharajah *hai*!" "Ha *hai*!" ("I am a Maharajah!" "Yes you are!") (238), confirm the hierarchical order of things. Duncan thus presents us with two societies of great complexity and antiquity, with some common interests and many parallel institutions. Yet at the same time as they are fatally entangled by history there are large areas in which they are disguised from each other, as Ruth Pearce eventually discovers.

Set in Authority develops two plots in parallel with each other, linked by the themes of knowledge and judgement, faculties which operating at their best are supposed to penetrate such disguisings. In both cases it is "judgement" — in the varying senses of that word — which determines the course of events: rebellious judgement in the case of Herbert Morgan, who chooses to be tried initially by a native judge; legal judgement as exercised by Sir Ahmed Hossein and Lawrence Lenox; unformed judgement in the case of Lavinia and Victoria in London and Charles Cox in Pilaghur; emotional judgement in the case of Ruth Pearce, who with Arden's own passionate complicity pits her assessment of the Morgan case against the Chief Commissioner and loses. In the Vice-Regal Lodge at Simla the Viceroy too sits in judgement, a good man but a remorseless one. Like all trials, that of Henry Morgan is supposed to reveal the truth of what really happened, and bring justice to bear on the result. But as everywhere in Duncan's novels, theory and practice, the ideal and the real, are in conflict with each other. Complex and ironic human circumstances interfere to baffle judgement, in this instance a trumped-up story carefully stage-managed by Afzul Aziz and the family of Gobind, the alleged victim. The initial judgement of Sir Ahmed Hossein — that "Morgan" should not suffer the death penalty — is partly the result of Hossein's misguided attempt to act in the cultural terms which he believes are those of the English whom he has been educated to imitate. When the case is reviewed, the trumped-up story (which everyone at this point still believes, including the reader) is less the issue than the struggle between the English of India and their Liberal Viceroy over whether justice should be meted out equally to brown and white; again, it is subservience which determines the result, but this time it is the social subservience evident in Lawrence Lenox's desire to cultivate the patronage of the Viceroy.

Anthony Andover's substitution of abstract rigour for informed judgement links the "Morgan case" to the story of Eliot Arden and Ruth Pearce. Arden has slowly but inexorably lost contact with his wife Jessica, that "good woman" who survived with him "that progress from isolation with a policeman and a native magistrate to desolation with a salt inspector, two missionaries, and no doctor, which makes the early stages of the civilian's career" (81). Once one of the keen little *chota-mems* Duncan so evidently loves, Jessica now tries earnestly to make her way through the difficult books Arden reads, while she manages with modest grace the complex social life of a Chief Commissioner. But her husband has ceased to "see" her, a fact which he sometimes guiltily acknowledges; his passion, about which he understands almost nothing, is centred on their gentle friend Ruth, whose apparently detached power of moral and ethical judgement he believes provides a world of values above the constant compromise required of a Chief Commissioner.

As with Hugh and Advena in the sub-plot of *The Imperialist*, Arden and Ruth are paradoxically divided by their shared principles. But though Arden at first takes the side of the Anglo-Indian residents against the Viceroy, in the end, and to Ruth's extreme dismay, he gives in to the pressure exerted on him by his old friend. In *The Imperialist* Duncan's management of her sub-plot is comic, and we enjoy the spectacle of two philosophical lovers inexorably brought together in defiance of their mistaken ideals by a *deus ex machina* in the form of Dr. Drummond, the Presbyterian minister. In *Set in Authority* Arden and Ruth are divided by his submission to the will of the Viceroy, and even the death of Jessica cannot bring them together. More fundamental yet is Ruth's illusion that Arden sees and understands her ambivalences and hesitations, that when she writes, after burning two long, emotional drafts, a reserved letter condoling with him on Jessica's death he will respond with some shadow of that directness and spiritual intimacy which they had once shared. But again, Arden does not "see"; his illusion is that her letter is just that, a letter:

the little note that came seemed kind and formal. If she had not written at all it would have been more significant, would perhaps have roused a doubt in him; but these careful phrases proclaimed her withdrawal with certainty. I cannot insist too much that he was a "senior" official, accustomed to accept decisions and file them. His relation with Ruth was a matter fully noted on, dealt with, and filed. The finality with which he believed this had not even been disturbed by his new freedom.(234)

This conviction causes a ripple of surprise among the observant in Pilaghur society, who in their turn have noted and filed away the attraction between the two which Arden and Ruth thought they had disguised even from each other.

It is Ruth's capacity for judgement which both attracts Arden, and which he at the same time fears. "Behind the kindness of your regard," he says to her at one point, "I see the charnel-house where you will presently be tearing me to pieces." (208). And in the end with precisely this detachment the narrator sits in judgement on Ruth, that "conscientious woman," when she burns in the grate of her Bloomsbury lodging-house the letter from "Henry Morgan" which is a weapon pointed at the heads of the returning Viceroy and Victoria Tring, who has finally accepted his proposal. Duncan grants Ruth a victory when she renounces the retribution coincidence has put into her hand. But she also ensures we see her not as a model of self-sacrifice, but as a confused woman dealing with a situation in the limited way which is the only one known to her. In one of the concluding ironies of the novel, we are left to ponder the resemblance between the lady doctor and her ayah Hiria, who also concealed what she knew at a critical juncture.

∿   ∿   ∿

The voices of Pilhagur society dominate *Set in Authority*. Duncan, who later in life tried her hand at writing plays, was capable of devising bright, vigorous society dialogue with a keen sense of the possibilities of type-characters and a sharp satiric edge. Her ability to catch social nuance through dialogue means that throughout the book we are kept aware of the modalities of language, whether we are listening to the amiable banter of "other ranks," the blusterings of Colonel Vetchley, or the discreet upward maneuverings of figures like the Biscuits and Charles Cox. Significantly, Mrs. Lemon, who is completely disdainful of the tyranny of institutions in English Pilaghur, is also the only completely outspoken character in the book. Duncan has a good ear for the usage of Indian servants speaking the language of their masters – for example, the ayah Hiria's monologues, with their implication of quite other linguistic and social worlds – but readers today will flinch at her frequent satire of the speech of her Indian characters; like many of her contemporaries, she impenitently mocks the mixed metaphors of "Babu English."[31] Yet the problem of language remains one of the defining metaphors of *Set in Authority*; of all Duncan's books it is the one most full of images of the word: language learning, institutional files, cables, and letters provide a continuing metaphor which reaches its culmination in the last pages when Ruth incinerates "Henry Morgan's" letter, and Eliot on the Bombay wharf receives a missive from the Viceroy. It is not by chance that the vengeful Afzul Aziz is a *munshi*, a language teacher.

If dialogue was a gift, however, the handling of point of view was not, and throughout her career Duncan had to struggle to achieve a narrative poise which would reveal her characters as they inhabited their lives, yet make apparent with sufficient subtlety the vantage point from which she viewed them. This task was complicated by her almost compulsive irony, which by laying bare the differences between theory and practice seems constantly to undercut her own position. How, it has been asked, can she appear to side with Lorne Murchison politically, yet allow him to lose the election in the way he does? How can she recognize the creative energy of Elfrida Bell in her "New Woman" novel *A Daughter of To-day* yet allow her to commit suicide? Critics have sometimes attempted to unravel this problem by turning to Duncan's ideas, and pointing out either her consistent "liberalism" or her apparent ambivalences.[32] The reason, however, may lie just as much in her search for adequate technical skills to attempt an increasingly serious subject-matter. Satire and the "social manner" could provide her with the barely-disguised autobiographical first person of *A Social*

Departure and the farcical narrative of Vernon's aunt in the early novella of that name, but they would not lead to the more comprehensive vision she was attempting to achieve in novels like *His Honor, and a Lady*.

Duncan occasionally sought a more sophisticated method in the example of Howells, and especially James, but, as a comparison of *The Path of a Star* and *Set in Authority* shows, her most secure vantage point as a narrator was not inside her characters evoking infinitely discriminated shades of meaning, but outside looking in. She was a social novelist to the core. It is only when she uses the social manner, rather than either being used by it (or attempting to shake it off), that she achieves the narrative poise the topics of her maturity demand. In *The Imperialist* this new poise produces the illusion of a third-person narrative which at the same time hints at the presence of a voice which speaks the language of the community itself. In *Set in Authority*, this knowing voice occurs as well, but almost always in those chapters in which the Anglo-Indian community of Pilaghur is being satirized; elsewhere it is mute, and the characters are locked absolutely into the situations they devise for themselves.

Set in Authority is an expertly plotted novel, and moves with an almost cinematic flow towards its dénouement. Yet the revelation of the identity of Henry Morgan is one of a number of plot twists which to varying degrees unnerve the reader as the novel progresses. At the beginning of a February, 1907 survey of "plot" in contemporary fiction which included, among other novels, a warm appreciation of *Set in Authority*, the American reviewer Frederic Taber Cooper wrote, "it is the commonest experience for the critic to find an unhackneyed plot spoiled by unskilful development, and a threadbare theme skilfully worked over into the most engrossing novel of the month."[33] Like other novelists of her era Duncan freely exploited the available conventions, usually by reversing, inverting, or otherwise mocking them. In *A Voyage of Consolation* the enabling conventions of the modern travel narrative – and their possible variations – are cheerfully laid bare by Mamie as she begins her story. And well before E.M. Forster's ironic "burlesque" of Anglo-Indian romance conventions in *A Passage to India* Duncan seems to have been aware that this was a society for which parody and ironic inversion were singularly appropriate modes.[34] In *The Imperialist* she managed the reversal of plot conventions expertly; that novel is full of conventional types freshly re-written: the promising youth, the condescending Englishman, the prudent beauty, the blighted lovers, and, above all, the widower Dr. Drummond, that most tempting of current popular-romance characters, the unmarried minister.

In *Set in Authority* there are several "threadbare schemes": the seemingly convenient death of Jessica Arden; the murder of Gobind which turns out to be no murder; and most of all the concluding revelation that the prisoner Henry Morgan is actually Herbert Tring. Surprisingly, the first critical response to the last twist, that of the book's eventual American publisher, Doubleday Page, was that the ending was too low-key. Doubleday's H. W. Lanier suggested to Duncan as early as April, 1905 that she had been afraid of making the novel a melodrama:

> You have led up to a highly dramatic and (properly) sensational situation, and then simply dropped the whole thing, so that the reader has a sort of defrauded feeling at the end. If you were to take this missing brother and make him a little more real at the start, so that the reader would get interested in him − it would require only a scene at most − and later make use of the tremendous chance which the Viceroy's unbending following of his conscience produces, you would surely make the book more acceptable to thousands of readers. When all is said and done, you have in the present form run any risks of inherent improbability which such a strange development might bring − and you don't get the advantage of it! Something big and dramatic, that would sweep the reader right off his feet, ought to happen about the time when "Henry Morgan" is to be executed. Of course, this might mean rather a radical change of the finish of your story.[35]

However, as the English reviewers' mixed responses indicate, Morgan's identity was not likely to have been entirely secret to a socially-alert reader of 1906, who might well seize the hint given by the description of him as a gentleman-ranker. If we are meant to realize early on that Henry Morgan and Herbert Tring are the same man, then the currently popular fictional motif of "the young hero's flight to the wilds" with which the adventurer Kelly plays on the innocence of Victoria and Lavinia is also swiftly ironized, and with it the girls are pitilessly seen as the dupes of their own illusions. In the same way, Jessica Arden's death from a minor operation in distant Germany – plausible enough in the context of a less hygienic time – may be sentimentally convenient, but it too is ironized, in this case by the fumbling emotions with which Arden and Ruth respond to it.

But Duncan's unmasking of Morgan as Tring is less skilful. In *The Imperialist* the reader's late realization of Dr. Drummond's "eligibility" is a true comic revelation; we do not need to be the dowagers of a Presbyterian congregation of 1904 to appreciate that every manse needs a mistress. In *Set in Authority* it is only those who can read the social codes speaking through Tring's disguise who are really prepared for the ending; it is almost as if Duncan were contemptuously rewarding those readers who had refused the subtlety of *The Imperialist* with a coincidence blatant enough to satisfy the least demanding taste. The conclusion of *Set in Authority* in every way fulfils the theory behind the novel, but in practice it was achieved at a very high cost.

∾ ∾ ∾

In writing about the colonial scene she knew so intimately, Duncan plunged herself in book after book into an interpretative issue which was already troubling her contemporaries. "To represent Africa is to enter the battle over Africa," writes Edward Said,[36] in commenting on how throughout the eighteenth- and nineteenth-century efflorescence of the English novel, "the domestic order was tied to, located in, even illuminated by a specifically *English* order abroad" (Said, 76). This was particularly the case with the middle-class audience for which Duncan was writing, for whom the identification of English with colonial interests had only five years earlier been celebrated in Kipling's magnificent imperial fantasy *Kim* (1901). Yet Conrad's 1902 novella *Heart of Darkness* questioned everything *Kim* seemed to represent, while inevitably remaining implicated in the discursive structures that made possible even its resistant stance. E.M. Forster's verdict on the English in India had yet to be rendered, in *A Passage to India* (1924), but by that time the foundations of European confidence would be badly shaken on home territory. Duncan's depiction of the two Pilaghurs, Anglo-Indian and Indian, reproduces the dualism inherent in the colonial situation as she experienced it, and raises questions about her point of view or – as James Clifford has helpfully called it, the "styles of comprehension" of the colonial writer.[37] Is a "contrapuntal reading" – one which attends to themes both of imperialism and resistance (Said, 66) – possible in the case of *Set in Authority*, or is the book a straightforward example of what Said elsewhere terms "orientalism," that "Western style for dominating, restructuring, and having authority over the Orient" which he has identified as a powerful hidden determinant in the history of the novel?[38]

Duncan's India was the complex historical product of the interaction over several hundred years of a number of rich civilizations, of which England was only the most recently dominant. Like the Muslim Moghul empire (1526-1761) which it succeeded, England – first through the East India Company and from 1859 directly – ruled a collection of South Asian states and princedoms which were sometimes more willing to trust an external power than to combine to rule the sub-continent themselves. In defiance of the Portuguese and Dutch who laid claim to the trade of the east, the East India Company had been founded in 1600, and when the Moghul empire weakened in the eighteenth century English traders flooded into every part of India. After a period of struggle with the rival French, the British, through the East India Company, effectively ruled much of India from 1760 to 1858. "John Company," as it was colloquially known, was primarily a society of men, the "nabobs" who consorted with and sometimes married Indian women, acquired vast riches in the east, and came to lord it over (and be mocked by) eighteenth-century London. But throughout the nineteenth century the gap between British and Indians widened, in part because educated Indians were pressing for admittance into the administration, in part because more and more British women were living in India, and their presence had begun to transform the social texture of the nabobs' world. Particularly after the Indian Mutiny of 1857 (usually known today as the First War of Independence) the social barrier between white and brown became almost impassable, as the British asserted the need to "protect" the memsahibs from contact with natives. In 1858 the British parliament passed the Government of India Act, and the rule of the East India Company was replaced by a secretary of state and council responsible to the crown; Lord Canning (known bitterly as "Clemency" Canning for his even-handed restoration of order after the Mutiny) became the first Viceroy. In 1876 Queen Victoria was proclaimed Empress of India; her Viceroys governed with the near-autocratic authority of emperors.

Writing to Lord Curzon in 1900, C. E. Dawkins speaks with awe of "the aureole of the great Viceroyalty" floating around the head of his old friend,[39] and Duncan's description of one of Lord Lansdowne's investitures (quoted in Appendix I) is simply the first of her many references to the extreme degree of ceremonial which surrounded the Vice-Regal court and maintained, at every level, the same exclusivity. The Anglo-Indian society into which her "Mother in India" relaxes on the ship to Calcutta is the hothouse product of this history. That society's experience of India – military, commercial, social, familial – stretched back many generations. Eliot Arden has Anglo-Indian relatives, as does Ruth Pearce; one of the most sharply observed moments in the novel occurs when Mrs. Arden asks whether Ruth's great-grandmother was the wife of a planter, and is told gently that she was the wife of a Chief Justice of Bengal. Despite the history of British mercantile and military force in India, the British from the time of Warren Hastings (Governor-General, 1774-85) had concerned themselves not only with the rewards of rule, but the welfare of the governed. Their concepts of what constituted that welfare varied, however, from generation to generation; the idealistic "westernization" enforced by administrators influenced by Utilitarianism, and the horrified distaste for Indian religions evident even among well-meaning missionaries, do not impress us today as "progressive." The portrait of Anglo-India Duncan draws for us is thus not only of a world severely self-delineated, but of one even further marked off by our own repudiation of its values. The question is, to what extent was Duncan aware of such over-lapping perspectives?

Anglo-India occupied the problematic space between two powers, British and Indian, one still imperial in its behaviour, the other colonized and yet already signalling its emergence from dependency. As a Canadian and as a woman Duncan herself occupied such an interstitial space; as Misao Dean has observed, she "presents a view from the margin of Anglo-American ideology, writing against the developing aesthetic and ideological traditions of imperialist patriarchy while fully implicated in them."[40] Duncan put it another way in an interview of 1895: "one sees oneself projected like a shadow against the strenuous mass of the real people, a shadow with a pair of eyes. There is such intensity and colour and mystery to see, that life is hardly more than looking on . . . "[41] But partly because of the varying conventions of the books she wrote for commercial gain, and partly because of her own developing attitudes, "India" – which for her meant chiefly Bengal – shifts its possible meanings in the course of her career.

In *A Social Departure* India is treated with a journalist's enthusiasm and detail, but the travelling ladies remain fairly confident of imperial certitudes. *Vernon's Aunt* (trivial in every way except this) turns the "uninformed traveller" motif on its head, but significantly its comic inversions are not between the Aunt and India but between the Aunt and her Anglo-Indian nephew. And it is that world of interstitial figures, English-bred but no longer English, Indian in experience but never Indian, which slowly emerges as Duncan's fated subject. She is well aware that such figures exist among the Indians as well; in *Set in Authority* Sir Ahmed Hossein negotiates his way carefully through Mrs. Lemon's garden party, and Duncan observes,

> Those among whom he had come were not his people; his ways were not their ways nor his thoughts their thoughts. Yet he had to take his place and find his comfort among them. The drift and change in the tide of events had brought him there, and he had to make the best appeal he could. In every

eye he saw the barrier of race, forbidding natural motions. . . .
He acquitted himself with every propriety, but relief came
when he moved away, and perhaps he knew it; he walked
about curiously alone. (115)

Sir Ahmed cannot "commend himself," as Duncan so delicately puts
it; he is "forced to take the task upon the high and sterile ground of
pure intelligence," and in doing so adopts not the substance of British
principle which he admires, but the superficial codes of appropriate
"British" behaviour. Duncan's attempt to move even partly across
the barrier of race has to await her portrayal of Ganendra Thakore in
The Burnt Offering. Even there, her sense of the automatic merit of
English institutions prevails; she is aware that a new class has arisen
to represent them, but she still sees that class as Anglo-Indian, rather
than Indian. As her husband Everard Cotes stated forthrightly in
1907, "the East is best dealt with by the East, and Great Britain is
alone amongst the nations of Europe in owning the means to turn
this fact to account."[42] But the "East" he had in mind was the East
of the now-denizened colonial administrators, and the "means" he
spoke of was the membership of that class, the Anglo-Indians who
constitute the "we" constantly invoked in his chapter on "India as a
Lever in the Far East."

In Duncan's Anglo-Indian novels the vulnerable status of the society she is writing about is both represented and sustained by the
social codes which govern the lives of all her characters, and are
rarely successfully over-ruled. Her British characters can erase the
boundary line which separates white and brown only by being
"good governors," and her Indian characters only by becoming, as
does Sir Ahmed Hossein, imitation Englishmen. But if we set aside
the early and semi-autobiographical *The Simple Adventures of a Mem-
sahib* we can see that her three major Anglo-Indian novels represent
a genuine response to the changing historical situation with which,
in the decade 1896-1906, Anglo-Indian society was confronted, as
Indian agitation for home rule became a major public issue, and the
Congress Party began its rise. In *His Honor, and a Lady* (1896) the
"good governor," for all his imperfections, is John Church, and his
values are sustained when his impoverished widow Judith, who had

quietly accepted the limitations of her first marriage, courageously repudiates the longed-for suit of Lewis Ancram, who has succeeded her late husband as Lieutenant-Governor of Bengal, but whom she now recognises as a ruthless opportunist. In *Set in Authority*, as we have seen, Curzonian imperialism is deeply questioned, though not yet from an Indian point of view. In *The Burnt Offering* (1909) we finally meet with Indians who have tested the boundary-line, and are beginning to make their own decisions about crossing it.

This last of Duncan's Anglo-Indian novels brings to India an English member of Parliament, based on the respected figure of the labour leader Keir Hardie (in the novel, "Vulcan Mills"), but in *The Burnt Offering* seen from the censorious perspective with which Anglo-Indians usually disposed of the touring English who were so very certain how India could be changed for the better. Vernon's ghastly but irrepressible maiden aunt has become Vulcan's ghastly but idealistic daughter Joan, who has dedicated herself to improving the "dormant intelligence" of the sequestered women of India's *zenanas*, but who is speedily sent home by those unexpectedly well-informed and prudent ladies when serious political trouble looms; her well-meaning but politically inconvenient father had already been deported to Aden, under British guard. But *The Burnt Offering* is also the only novel in which Duncan attempts to see events even partly from an Indian point of view. Still, as with Sir Ahmed Hossein, she does so partly through the examination of interstitial figures – the Oxford-educated Rani Janaki and her Anglophilic, liberal father Sir Kristodas Mukerji, Knight Commander of the Indian Empire. The Rani silently loves the administrator John Game, sees him fall in love with Joan Mills, and endures his death as the grotesquely accidental aftermath of an assassination attempt on the Viceroy made by another of Joan's suitors, the revolutionary Bepin Dey. Duncan's treatment in this novel of a high-caste Indian woman and her dilemmas indicates her awareness that it is no longer possible to speak for the colonized on their behalf. Yet this cannot be done solely by adding to her metaphors of the Anglo-Indian tea-table and dinner-party that of the *zenana* (the rooms of a house in which high-caste Bengali women were secluded); Sir Kristodas and his daughter remain, like the Anglo-Indians whom they have abandoned their caste rules to emulate, figures caught between two realities. Throughout the novel they move through the social scene of mingled English and Indian political life, but in the end they can never return to the upper-caste Indian society they have abandoned. Rather, they leave their palace in Calcutta's Park Street to wander through India, like the lama in Kipling's *Kim*, as pilgrims seeking The Way.

Duncan's Anglo-Indian novels do not leave us entirely in this impasse, however, for if social codes cannot be transcended, at least the voice of autonomy will manifest itself in resistance to authority. In *His Honor, and a Lady* it appears in Judith's ultimate refusal to accept Ancram's proposal, and with it her return to the socially powerful position of Lieutenant-Governor's lady. In *The Burnt Offering* autonomy manifests itself not in figures like the Mukerjis (the Rani Janaki admits to Joan Mills, "I have lost my voice") but in the speech of the agitator Ganendra Thakore at his trial for sedition. Boldly, Thakore tells his judge, Sir Kristodas,

> I am accused of exciting to hatred and disaffection; but I submit that these harsh words do not truly describe the new emotion which is beginning to thrill the hearts of my countrymen. . . . I do not ask you to believe that it is yet very sane or well-regulated. But I do ask a hearing when I maintain that it is the only one they have; and that before they found it they were dead. I know that before I found it I was dead. I ate and drank complacently, in agreement with the world as it had produced me; but I did not know my own spirit. In my fortieth year came the misfortune which awakened me, my Lord, to what your law calls hatred and disaffection; and while I cannot even yet bless that misfortune, there is no moment of the life of the soul into which it ushered me that I would exchange for all the forty dead years that went before. . . . (242)

Duncan presents Thakore as a convinced revolutionary, yet, significantly, she endows him with a name of great prestige in Bengali culture; "Thakoor" is a Hindu idol or diety, and in Bengal the name "Tagore" is that of a Brahmin family of great repute.[43]

In *Set in Authority* the voice of autonomy is almost silenced, but it emerges at last in the hard lesson of history which is represented in Duncan's fictionalized version of "the Rangoon assault case," the story of the *munshi*'s revenge for an offence long past. In several of Duncan's novels it is events from the unperceived present or past which decisively affect the outcome of the narrative; at such moments the stability of the centre (whether imperial or domestic) is faintly but critically impinged on by an event originating in the "other" which determines the ultimate fate of the characters. In *His Honor, and a Lady* it is the critical discovery of a tell-tale newspaper article in the pocket of Philip Doyle's old coat, and a dutiful Indian clerk's accidental posting of it to Judith Church in London, where it decides her matrimonial dilemma. In *The Imperialist*, it is the intricacies of the patronage system on the Indian reserve near Elgin which trap Lorne; Duncan ensures that we take note of the crucial significance of the natives' vote when his brother Alec is sarcastic about their confusing names: "'Chief Joseph Fry,' exclaimed Alec. 'They make me tired with their Chief Josephs and Chief Henrys. White Clam Shell – that's the name he got when he wasn't christened.'" To which Advena (the novel's "truth-teller") pointedly replies, "'That's the name . . . that he probably votes under.'"[44] In *Set in Authority* the same voice from the "other" determines the direction of the action, but it is a voice hidden until Ruth Pearce is allowed to peel away its disguises. Behind the tale told to the police is the tale Hiria really knows but conceals; behind that is grizzled Gobind himself, glimpsed in the market and interrogated; and behind his story that of the language teacher Afzul Aziz.

From a point of view situated at the centre of the imperial fiction, the *munshi* appears as an ordinary villain, venting a wicked grievance against his proper rulers. But Duncan does not tell his story this way; rather, we hear it in the ayah's words when she tells the truth at last. During what Hiria calls "the Great Folly," the Mutiny of 1857, the Indians of Cawnpore massacred the entire British population of the city, a tragedy which later made the city a pilgrimage site for Anglo-Indian and British visitors. Hiria's version, however, is a story of the aftermath, when English forces returned to the city on their way to the relief of Lucknow. The Barfordshires, bent on vengeance, begin shooting all the sepoys (Indian soldiers uniformed in British military garb rather than native dress):

> The father of Afzul Aziz was not a sepoy, miss-sahib. He was a teaching man like this one – and the two older sons were writers [clerks] under the sahibs, good men, of poor spirit, miss-sahib. When the soldiers found them they said, "We are not sepoys!" but the soldiers said, "Look at your feet. You have corns on them. Therefore you wear shoes. Therefore, you are sepoys"; and killed all three. Only Afzul they did not kill because he was so little. But he saw it, miss-sahib, and he has always *zid* against the regiment. So he went to great expense.(263)

In thus situating the originary moment of her plot in the events of 1857-8, Duncan could not have chosen without design.[45] As Bernard S. Cohn writes,

> To the English from 1859 to the early part of the twentieth century, the Mutiny was seen as a heroic myth embodying and expressing their central values which explained their rule in India to themselves – sacrifice, duty, fortitude; above all it symbolized the ultimate triumph over those Indians who had threatened properly constituted authority and order.[46]

Had Duncan wished to exculpate the English it would have been sufficient to point out (as she does) that the actual murderer – of a cultivator, not Gobind's wife, though the issue was indeed a woman – was a Guzerati, a soldier from the native regiment. Instead, the primal moment of disorder in the novel is caused by a manifest injustice done by the Barfordshires, one inflicted not on other soldiers, but – significantly, in view of the themes of language and writing in the novel – upon scribes. The *munshi*'s revenge thus returns us to Duncan's recurrent motif of the autonomous or resistant voice, and in doing so not only strikes at, but attempts to erase, the heroic mythos of English hegemony in India which had underpinned imperial authority throughout his lifetime. The houses bending over the streets of

Pilaghur have indeed, as Duncan earlier observed, "something to say," and it does not appear that she judges them for saying it.

∾   ∾   ∾

A marriage is forecast at the end of *Set in Authority*, though it is not the one we expect, but that offered by the novel's other "love story" – Victoria Tring and the Viceroy himself. Ruth's possession of the letter gives her "a very pretty and convenient weapon" (271) to point at the Viceroy and all his works, though she renounces the vengeance Herbert Tring clearly intended to wreak. What then are those works? Earlier in the novel, in what appears to be a passage of intense imperialist idealism, Duncan writes,

> Whatever happens elsewhere in these days of triumphant democracies, in India the Ruler survives. He is the shadow of the king, but the substance of kingship is curiously and pathetically his; and his sovereignty is most real with those who represent him. The city and the hamlet stare apathetic; they have always had a conqueror. But in lonely places which the Viceroy's foot never presses and his eye never sees, men of his own race find in his person the authority for the purpose of their whole lives. He is the judge of all they do, and the symbol by which they do it. Reward and censure are in his hand, and he stands for whatever there is in the task of men that is sweeter than praise and more bitter than blame. He stands for the idea, the scheme, and the intention to which they are all pledged; and through the long sacrifice of the arid years something of their loyalty and devotion and submission to the idea gathers in the human way about the sign of it.(84)

The impersonality of the prose makes it easy to read this passage as a statement of Duncan's own views, and there is no doubt that, as Misao Dean writes, throughout her life "she depicted the Empire as an ideal of human striving."[47] Yet the passage above concludes, pointedly, "the Viceroy may be a simple fellow, but his effigy is a wonderful accretion," and it is to this effigy, the image of authority, that Arden eventually has to submit.

Thame himself comes to India convinced he can re-define British rule; "he practically repudiates all that we hold by the sword," says Victoria, "and confines us, in the world, to the parts we can plough"(71), a concern confirmed by his interest in the Finns' struggle to recapture their ancient constitution. Victoria predicts that when he comes back, he will burn the book, *The Real Empire*, in which he argues that Britain's destiny is to rule by moral force, and though they remain the best of friends, she rejects him for his views. Yet in the last chapter her mother, the new Mrs. Sambourne, tells us, "'it was his Viceroyalty that did it. Such a splendid range for his genius and character! Victoria has simply gone down before it. She says as much. Especially that wonderful Morgan tragedy, that I have built my play on'" (205). And the Viceroy's mother is proud, as Victoria herself tells us, of having been able to influence him in the right direction at last. Lady Thame's view of the correct action in the Morgan case is not at issue here; from the beginning her real concern has been her son's willingness to rule, to become in fact that effigy of imperial order which Duncan reflects on as Eliot Arden watches the Viceroy's train steam out of the station at Pilaghur. By the end of the novel Thame's decisions, not least in the Morgan case, have turned him into precisely the kind of Viceroy he did not wish to be. It is marriage to this effigy to which Victoria at last so joyously consents.

Yet it may be that in the long run, whatever her practical politics, Duncan's real concern is not with what sides human beings take in the interminable rivalry of political orders and social codes, but with those who perceive what is going on and those who do not. This capacity can be both a strength and a limitation; in *The Imperialist* it is Lorne's ability to "see" the Elgin market-place in all its social plenitude which marks him off from the less imaginative voters of South Fox constituency and leads to his ill-judged political speech. In *Set in Authority* the unperceived hand of history has its psychological counterpart in the Viceroy's (and Victoria's) refusal to "see" the reality of the world he governs, in Eliot Arden's inability to "see" either of the women he loves, or indeed in Ruth Pearce's inability to "see" Hiria when in Chapter XXVIII the ayah tentatively offers to find out the truth for her mistress. Thus, in so far as Duncan is a novelist of the colonial period, it may be less India that is the focus of her attention, than the way India is seen by the Anglo-Indians who are her chosen subject. In *The Simple Adventures of a Memsahib* Mrs. Perth Macintyre observes of the transformation of Helen Browne, the young bride whose early months in India she describes:

> She sees no more the supple savagery of the Pathan in the market-place, the bowed reverence of the Mussulman praying in the sunset, the early morning mists lifting among the domes and palms of the city. (310)

Nevertheless the experience of India has matured Helen Browne herself; by the end of the novel her eyes "have looked too straight into life to lower themselves as readily as they did before" (108).

This process affects Sir Kristodas in *The Burnt Offering* as well; convinced of Britain's advances at the beginning, he "would have laughed at the idea that such achievement could withdraw itself, or even question itself." (45-6). But the novel's last words tell us,

> in the Foreign Office at Calcutta, which has the care of all matters of ceremonial, there is a safe, and in the safe a small morocco box, and in the box a rather pretty enamelled bauble on a ribbon. It is the decoration of the Order of the Indian Empire, returned on behalf of Kristodas Mukerji when he retired from occasions upon which it would be suitable. I believe the Foreign Secretary does not quite know what to do with it. (317)

The bafflement of the Foreign Secretary is that of all governors when faced with an uninterpretable gesture, one which something in "the files" will not help them deal with. Sir Kristodas's decoration would not normally have been returned until his death, and his renunciation of it to take up the staff and begging-bowl of a pilgrim seeking The Way marks Duncan's acknowledgement, at the symbolic level, of what she had already recognized in the historic origins of the *mun-shi*'s revenge: the final and decisive authority of the autonomous gesture, and the impercipience of those who cannot "see" it.

In *A Voyage of Consolation* Mamie Wick's father relies on "the distractions of change" to divert his daughter after a broken engagement; they embark for Europe, and she resolves to write a book about her trip. But it will be a travel book that challenges the conventions, she points out to her father:

> . . . the best heroines never have recourse to such measures now. They are simply obsolete. Except for my literary intention, I should be ashamed to go to Europe at all – under the circumstances. But that, you see, brings the situation up to date. I transmit my European impressions through the prism of damaged affection. Nothing could be more modern. (18)

Re-envisioned through a prism of darker glass and more complex cut, this is where we find ourselves at the conclusion of *Set in Authority*, when Eliot Arden is handed the letter which raises him from the limited sphere of a provincial commissioner to a knighthood, and the authority of Lieutenant-Governor of Bengal. The society gathered on the wharf at Bombay in the final chapter of the novel perceives itself to be triumphant, but the reader is under no illusion as to the nature of that triumph. And this impression is particularly reinforced by the damaged affections of Eliot Arden and Ruth Pearce, isolated from one another in their respective misapprehensions. In this isolation Duncan views them from the standpoint of one "infected with the easily recognizable, ironic awareness of the post-realist modernist sensibility" which Edward Said argues the critique of imperialism actually produced in Conrad and Malraux, Forster and T.E. Lawrence.[48] As such, *Set in Authority* concludes in that condition of modern solitude which the ending of *The Imperialist* only hints at, but which is here represented in all its bleakness.

∾   ∾   ∾

Set in Authority was published in London on May 18, 1906, for an audience which had been prepared by its serialization in the *Times* weekly edition throughout the spring, and was much more warmly greeted than its immediate predecessor, *The Imperialist* (see Appendix II). At the end of May, 1906, *The Outlook* chose *Set in Authority* as its "book of the week,"[49] and throughout the summer of 1906 the novel remained popular; it appeared for three successive months (July, August, and September) in *The Bookman*'s list of six shilling novels most in demand. Doubleday published it in the United States in November, there was a Tauchnitz edition on the Continent in the same year which remained in the firm's catalogue until the 1930s, and the book was re-issued in cheap editions by Thomas Nelson and Company in 1910 and again in 1919.[50]

The seriousness of Duncan's novel was evident to the anonymous reviewer in the *Times Literary Supplement* who wrote that *Set in Authority* "is not a novel of passion or of incident, though it contains both. It is a political, or a philosophical novel, not intended to excite strong anxiety and emotion, but to rouse thought."[51] This was a sophisticated view, however; though the reviewer in *The Academy* seconded this opinion, *The Athenaeum* treated the book as just another Anglo-Indian novel (of the sort the Viceroy's sisters Lavinia and Frances are well acquainted with) and *The Spectator* murmured frigidly, "there is too often a sub-flavour of the disagreeable about the love stories which she introduces, and the love story in this book is no exception to the rule."[52] In the U.S. the *New York Times Saturday Review of Books* said, "'Set in Authority' shows a marked broadening, deepening, and enriching of [Duncan's] intellectual powers . . . she is very clearly a disciple of Henry James. But she no longer boggles, as she used to do, over everlasting attempts to express shades of meaning that are not worth differentiation."[53] So far as is known, there were no Canadian reviews of *Set in Authority* beyond a few perfunctory lines in *The Canadian Magazine*, even though the same issue carried a substantial piece in its "Current Events Abroad" section on the rise of India's Congress Party. Ironically, the concluding lines of that article epitomize the complacent attitude to imperial culture which Duncan scrutinizes so mercilessly: "but it is comforting to British subjects in the self-governing colonies to reflect that England has seldom lacked the far-visioned statesman who knows when and how 'to make the bounds of freedom wider yet.'"[54]

To Duncan's audience in the "self-governing colonies" *Set in Authority*, of course, offered no comfort at all. And though in England it was among the best-known of her books, it slipped into oblivion after her death, lost in the gulf between the simplistic Anglo-Indian romances it so ironically mocks and the more subtle and thoughtful meditation on colonized relationships which by 1924 Forster (not, it has been argued, uninfluenced by Duncan[55]) produced in *A Passage to India*. *The Burnt Offering* was Duncan's last novel set in the world she had made central to her work. In *His Royal Happiness* (1915), a propagandistic political allegory about the marriage of a British king and the daughter of an American president, she produced a fundamentally silly but symptomatic analysis of the conflict between authority (represented by the English court and its rigid customs) and autonomy (represented by the democratizing King Alfred with his passion for America). The novel, which as a plot device employs the lengthy secret engagement inflicted by Lord Curzon on his American wife, was dedicated to Lady Curzon's memory. But the irreconcilable conflict caused by Duncan's refusal to over-ride the rule of social codes requires the ludicrous intervention of a heavily allegorized Canadian fairy godfather to bring the lovers together. Commercial necessity and the social manner had combined to curb Duncan's gift. Yet in *On the Other Side of the Latch* she speaks of the ghost of Cousin Christina, a relative whom she had never met. This gentle and reflective wraith seems to have visited her in the garden at Simla, and of her Duncan writes, "among our poor chances there is one which is supreme, and she had it. Within her radius she *saw*" (250). When Duncan ceased trying to "see" Anglo-India, she never produced another genuinely good book, though she would not lay down her valiant pen until shortly before her death in 1922.

Notes:

Editions of Duncan's works directly cited above:

A Social Departure: How Orthodocia and I Went Round the World by Ourselves.
New York: D. Appleton and Company, 1890.

Two Girls on a Barge. "V. Cecil Cotes," London: Chatto and Windus,
1891.

The Simple Adventures of a Memsahib. New York: D. Appleton and Company, 1893.

His Honor, and a Lady. London: Macmillan and Co., 1896. ["Honor," *sic* in
first London edition.]

A Voyage of Consolation. London: Methuen and Co., 1898.

On the Other Side of the Latch. London: Methuen and Co., 1901.

The Imperialist (1904), with an afterword by Janette Turner Hospital.
Toronto: McClelland and Stewart, 1990.

The Burnt Offering. New York: John Lane, 1910.

1 Duncan's actual travelling companion was the Montreal journalist Lily
   Lewis; "Orthodocia," who is English, was devised at the behest of the
   editor of the *Ladies Pictorial* of London, where the work was first serialized, and is really Duncan's first fictional character. See "Mrs. Everard
   Cotes," *The Bookman* (London) 14 (June 1898): 66.

2 Misao Dean considers Duncan's exploitation of "decadent" culture in
   "The Paintbrush and the Scalpel: Sara Jeannette Duncan Representing
   India," *Canadian Literature* 132 (Spring 1992): 82-93.

3 "True as this novel was, it was not a popular success," Archibald
   MacMechan wrote of *The Imperialist* two years after Duncan's death.
   "The appearance in *The Globe* of a tale preaching that salvation for the
   Empire could only come by Joseph Chamberlain was something of a
   joke; and perhaps Mrs. Cotes had been too long out of Canada. Perhaps
   the book was too true." Archibald MacMechan, *Headwaters of Canadian
   Literature* (Toronto: McClelland and Stewart, 1924) 139.

4 Bhupal Singh's *A Survey of Anglo-Indian Fiction* (1934; reprinted London: Curzon Press, 1975) makes a brief reference to *The Burnt Offering*, and B. J. Moore-Gilbert, *Kipling and "Orientalism"* (London: Croom Helm, 1986), though quoting Duncan frequently, cites only *A Social Departure* and *The Simple Adventures of a Memsahib*. Duncan's Anglo-Indian novels are not mentioned in such standard works on the genre as Susanne Howe, *Novels of Empire* (New York: Columbia University Press, 1949), Alan Sandison, *The Wheel of Empire* (London: Macmillan, 1967), Allen J. Greenberger, *The British Image of India; a Study in the Literature of Imperialism 1890-1960* (London: Oxford University Press, 1969), Benita Parry, *Delusions and Discoveries: Studies on India in the British Imagination 1880-1930* (London: Allen Lane The Penguin Press, 1972), or Sara Suleri, *The Rhetoric of British India* (Chicago: University of Chicago Press, 1992).

5 For full details of publication, see A Note on the Text.

6 Letter 112, to Alice Clara Forster, from Agra, 21 November 1912, in *Selected Letters of E. M. Forster*, Vol. I, 1879-1920, ed. Mary Lago and P. N. Furbank (London: Collins, 1983) 159. Duncan herself had noticed the same social deportment in others; in *A Voyage of Consolation* (49) Mamie Wick observes, "Momma has a great deal of manner towards strangers."

7 Duncan's career has been traced by Thomas E. Tausky in *Sara Jeannette Duncan: Novelist of Empire* (Port Credit: P. D. Meany, 1980) and with some revised opinions in *Sara Jeannette Duncan and Her Works* (Toronto, ECW Press, 1988). Marian Fowler's biography *Redney: A Life of Sara Jeannette Duncan* (Toronto: Anansi, 1983) is rich in useful detail and very informative about Duncan's early years but compresses her later professional history as a writer into the last third of the book. Her view that Duncan was a restless wanderer with an unhappy marriage has not been widely accepted.

8 Sara Jeannette Duncan, *A Social Departure: How Orthodocia and I Went Round the World by Ourselves* (New York: D. Appleton and Company, 1890) [v].

9 Everard Cotes, born in 1862, married Duncan in 1890; Duncan died in 1922 and he married Phoebe Violet Delaforce in 1923. Duncan left her estate to Cotes, and during his second marriage he regularly renewed her copyrights (A. P. Watt and Company papers, *passim*; for the Watt papers, see further below). Everard and Phoebe had two children; he died in 1944, after a long career as Parliamentary correspondent for the *Christian Science Monitor*.

10 In *Redney: A Life of Sara Jeannette Duncan* (Toronto: Anansi, 1983), Marian Fowler argues that the marriage was an unhappy one. This view has been generally rejected by writers on Duncan; for a critique of Fowler's evidence see Judith Skelton Grant's review, "Letters in Canada 1983," *University of Toronto Quarterly* 53 (1983-4): 114-18.

11 Duncan's use of a pseudonym in *Two Girls on a Barge* and in the later *Two in a Flat* (by "Jane Wintergreen"; London: Hodder and Stoughton, 1908) may have been commercial prudence; both books exploit plotting devices uncomfortably close to the "paired travellers" of *A Social Departure*.

12 "Mrs. Cotes works hard, and she works steadily, no matter in what part of the world she may be," wrote her friend Marjory MacMurchy in 1915. "In India, England, or Canada her work is her close companion. It is a lesson in authorship to see the infinite pains with which she revises." "Mrs. Everard Cotes (Sara Jeannette Duncan)," *The Bookman* (London) 48 (May 1918): 40.

13 George Woodcock, "The Changing Masks of Empire: Notes on Some Novels by Sara Jeannette Duncan," *The Year's Work in English Studies* 13 (1983): 210. (This perceptive article on Duncan's Anglo-Indian novels, by some strange chance, does not mention *Set in Authority*.)

14 This previously unknown material on Duncan is in the A. P. Watt & Company Records, Southern Historical Collection, Library of the University of North Carolina at Chapel Hill. I am grateful to Carole Gerson and Elaine Zinkhan for drawing it to my attention shortly be-

fore this introduction was completed, and to the University of North Carolina at Chapel Hill, for permission to refer to it.

15 "By the bye, I presume any money I collect on your behalf is to be paid into your bank at Brantwood [sic], Canada, as before." A. P. Watt to SJD, London, March 14, 1905 (A. P. Watt Papers, 85.8). On the relative value of Duncan's Canadian and British assets on her death, see Fowler, *Redney*, 303.

16 Her "garden book," she eventually decides in *On the Other Side of the Latch* (6), will be a novel of manners, though its characters must chiefly be flowers.

17 See reviews in *The Saturday Review* and *The Bookman* (Appendix II); S. J. Nagarajan acknowledged the Curzonian context of the novel in "The Anglo-Indian Novels of Sara Jeannette Duncan," *Journal of Canadian Fiction* 3, no. 4 (1975): 74-84; see especially note 8; for the resemblance to the Rangoon assault case see especially Thomas E. Tausky, *Sara Jeannette Duncan, Novelist of Empire*, 236.

18 A. P. Watt to SJD, July 11, 1900 (A. P. Watt Papers, 51.18).

19 For Curzon's unpopularity among the Anglo-Indians see for example a contemporary attack which expands in detail on Duncan's precise charges, *The Failure of Lord Curzon: An Open Letter to the Earl of Rosebery* by "28 Years in India" (London: T. Fisher Unwin, 1903), especially Chapter I, "The New Efficiency – 'Dismally Belied'." See also Peter King, *The Viceroy's Fall: How Kitchener Destroyed Curzon* (London: Sidgwick and Jackson, 1986) 44-5.

20 Kenneth Rose, in *Curzon: A Most Superior Person* (London: Macmillan, 1985) 49, quotes the widely-circulated quatrain from "The Masque of Balliol" for 1881; Curzon was then an undergraduate at that college; "My name is George Nathaniel Curzon,/ I am a most superior person,/ My cheek is pink, my hair is sleek,/ I dine at Blenheim once a week."

21 In December, 1901, Duncan travelled with the Curzons on their state visit to Upper Burma and sold two articles about the trip, "The Little Widows of a Dynasty" (*Harper's Monthly Magazine*, December, 1902: 115-21) and "In Burma with the Viceroy," (*Scribner's Magazine*, July, 1902: 58-72). See also her "The Home Life of Lady Curzon" in the March, 1903 edition of *Harper's Bazar* (222-24).

22 London: India Office Library, Mss. Eur. F.111/181: Curzon Papers: Letters and Telegrams 1899-June 1901. No. 143 to C. E. Dawkins (August 29, 1900); No. 187a, from Dawkins to the Viceroy (October 5, 1900); No. 191, to Dr. E. J. Dillon (February 2, 1901). Curzon suspected the attack might have been written by S. S. Thorburn, a recently-retired member of the Bengal Civil Service and minor novelist. Duncan's essay is not mentioned by Curzon's recent biographers, but was quoted extensively by Lord Ronaldshay in his official biography of 1928; referring to an unnamed "scribe with a grievance and a clever and satirical pen" he observed that the attack was made "from the safe shelter of anonymity – which it is now perhaps unnecessary to tear aside," which suggests he knew, or thought he knew, who the author was; see The Earl of Ronaldshay, *The Life of Lord Curzon*, II: *Viceroy of India* (London: Ernest Benn, 1928) 71.

23 For accounts of (and various viewpoints on) the Rangoon Assault case and its aftermath see, besides the response of "Calcutta" in the *Contemporary Review* (in Appendix I): Ronaldshay, *Life of Curzon* II 71-3; David Dilks, *Curzon in India* (London: Rupert Hart Davis, 1969), I 198-201; Peter King, *The Viceroy's Fall*, 51-2; Nayana Goradia, *Lord Curzon, the Last of the British Moghuls* (Delhi: Oxford University Press, 1993) 161-2; and David Gilmour, *Curzon* (London: John Murray, 1994) 170-74.

24 A revolt of the blacks at Morant Bay on October 11, 1865, was severely repressed by the Governor of Jamaica, Edward Eyre. He was recalled in 1866, and British intellectuals divided sharply over his actions; J. S. Mill and T. H. Huxley were among those who sought his indictment for murder, while Ruskin, Carlyle, and Tennyson took his part. Eyre was

not successfully prosecuted, but the issue determined positions on the punishment of non-whites for years to come.

25 See notes to the text, p. 67.

26 Duncan had already mocked the conventions of northern adventure in *A Voyage of Consolation*, when the intimidating dowager Mrs. Protheris, lost in the Roman catacombs with Dicky Dod and Mamie Wick, decides she has to eat her kid boots (two guineas in the Burlington Arcade), and Mamie is offered a generous slice off the ankle (182). For the popular press's exploitation of exploration narrative, see Beau Riffenburgh, *The Myth of the Explorer: the Press, Sensationalism, and Geographical Discovery* (Belhaven Press, 1993; rpt. Oxford: Oxford University Press, 1994).

27 Col. Henry Yule and A. C. Burnell, *Hobson-Jobson: A Glossary of Anglo-Indian Words and Phrases, and of Kindred Terms, Etymological, Historical, Geographical, and Discursive*. New edition, ed. William Crooke (London: John Murray, 1903). The best introduction to *Hobson-Jobson* is the entry on the book's own name. Annotating Duncan with *Hobson-Jobson* in hand shows that the largest part of her Anglo-Indian vocabulary is from Bengal, which is the area of India she knew best, and the locale in which her books are set. But it also shows how many other Indias there were in Duncan's time. The complexity of Duncan's Anglo-Indian linguistic setting is examined by Jennifer Lawn in "*The Simple Adventures of a Memsahib* and the Prisonhouse of Language," *Canadian Literature* 132 (Spring 1992): 16-32.

28 Sara Jeannette Duncan, "A Mother in India," in *A Pool in the Desert*, intro. Rosemary Sullivan (Harmondsworth: Penguin Books, 1984) 9.

29 *Hobson-Jobson*, 460.

30 "You are now collecting your People delightfully, getting them exactly into such a spot as is the delight of my life; – 3 or 4 Families in a Country Village is the very thing to work on." Letter 107, to Anna Austen, Friday 9 – Sunday 18 September 1814, *Jane Austen's Letters*, collected and

edited by Deirdre Le Faye, third edition (Oxford: Oxford University Press, 1995) 275. Duncan's debt to Austen was pointed out as early as 1924 by Archibald MacMechan (*Headwaters of Canadian Literature*, 138).

31 For an unreflective contemporary view of "Babu English" by another Anglo-Indian novelist, see Alice Perrin, review of William Crooke, *Things Indian*, in *The Bookman* (London), May 1906: 67.

32 To take only one sortie in a debate which has not yet been subjected to a consistent over-view, see Paul Litt, "The Cultivation of Progress: Sara Jeannette Duncan's Social Thought," *Ontario History* 80 (1988): 97-119, and Thomas E. Tausky's response, "In Search of a Canadian Liberal: The Case of Sara Jeannette Duncan," *Ontario History* 83 (1991): 85-108. Among all parties there has been a tendency to generalize Duncan's views from her Canadian journalism of the mid-1880s, partly because so much more is known about the early stages of her career than the later ones, for example the details of her journalism in India. Further study of the A. P. Watt papers may yield other instances of anonymous work like "A Progressive Viceroy," discussed elsewhere in this Introduction.

33 Frederic Taber Cooper, "The Subservience of Plot and Some Recent Novels," *The Bookman* (New York) 24 (1906-7): 587. For an engaging commentary on the many slips and subterfuges of Victorian novelists see John Sutherland, *Is Heathcliff a Murderer? Puzzles in 19th-Century Fiction*. Oxford: Oxford University Press, 1996.

34 For Forster's exploitation of parody in *A Passage to India*, see R. W. Noble, "*A Passage to India*: The Genesis of E.M. Forster's Novel," *Encounter* (February 1980): 51-61, especially 60. For the possible relationship of *A Passage to India* and Duncan's novels, see below.

35 H. W. Lanier to SJD, April 4, 1905; (A. P. Watt Papers 91.4).

36 Edward Said, *Culture and Imperialism* (New York: Alfred A. Knopf, 1993) 68.

37　James Clifford, *The Predicament of Culture: Twentieth-Century Ethnography, Literature and Art* (Cambridge, Mass.: Harvard University Press, 1988) 36.

38　Edward W. Said, *Orientalism* (New York: Vintage Books, 1979) 3.

39　Indian Office Library, Mss. Eur. F.111/181, 187a (October 5th, 1900).

40　Misao Dean, *A Different Point of View: Sara Jeannette Duncan* (Montreal and Kingston: McGill-Queen's University Press, 1991) 6.

41　G. B. Burgin, "A Chat with Sara Jeannette Duncan," *The Idler* 8 (1895) 115.

42　Everard Cotes, *Signs and Portents in the Far East* (London: Methuen, 1907) 258.

43　*Hobson-Jobson*, 915. The Bengali poet, philosopher, educator and social critic Sir Rabindranath Tagore (1861-1941) was well-known in Duncan's Calcutta; in 1913 he would win the Nobel Prize for Literature. Duncan's Ganendra Thakore resembles much more closely the militant nationalist Bal Gangadhar Tilak (1856-1920) but Duncan cannot have been ignorant of the implications of the name she chose for her revolutionary. For an Indian critic's view of Ganendra's speech, see S. Nagarajan, "The Anglo-Indian Novels of Sara Jeannette Duncan," *Journal of Canadian Fiction* 3.4 (1975) 81.

44　Sara Jeannette Duncan, *The Imperialist*, with an afterword by Janette Turner Hospital (Toronto: McClelland and Stewart, 1990) 283.

45　Duncan's 1892 children's tale, *The Story of Sonny Sahib*, also had its origin in a "Mutiny" narrative, told to Duncan by an elderly Indian ayah; see Marian Fowler, *Redney: A Life of Sara Jeannette Duncan* (Toronto: Anansi, 1983) 215.

46 Bernard S. Cohn, "Representing Authority in Victorian India," in *The Invention of Tradition*, ed. Eric Hobsbawm and Terence Ranger (Cambridge: Cambridge University Press, 1983) 179.

47 Dean, *A Different Point of View*, 119.

48 Said, *Culture and Imperialism*, 188.

49 *The Outlook*, May 26, 1906 (see Appendix II).

50 Three of Duncan's books were published by Tauchnitz; besides *Set in Authority* (1906, no. 3915), *Those Delightful Americans* (1902, no. 3590) and *Cousin Cinderella* (1908, no. 4069); see William B. Todd, *Tauchnitz International Editions in English 1841-1955* (New York: Bibliographical Society of America, 1988) 974.

51 *Times Literary Supplement,* May 25, 1906 (see Appendix II).

52 The Academy June 2, 1906; *The Athenaeum* June 30, 1906; *The Spectator* June 23, 1906 (see Appendix II).

53 *New York Times Saturday Review of Books*, November 10, 1906 (see Appendix II).

54 "Current Events Abroad," *The Canadian Magazine* (December, 1906): 188.

55 R.W. Noble, in "*A Passage to India*: The Genesis of E.M. Forster's Novel," *Encounter* (February, 1980) 51-61, senses that there is a connection between Forster's book and *Set in Authority* and *The Burnt Offering*, but because he is writing about the parodic stance exploited by Forster he attributes it to what he calls Duncan's exploitation of the late-Victorian comic sketch (58); he seems to be unaware of her other novels, or the centrality of irony to her writing in general.

SET IN AUTHORITY

BY

MRS. EVERARD COTES

(SARA JEANNETTE DUNCAN)

LONDON
ARCHIBALD CONSTABLE
AND COMPANY, LTD.
1906

SET IN AUTHORITY

CHAPTER I

IT would be hard to contrive a friendly description of Lady Thame's drawing-room. One would be obliged to do it in perpetual fear of the suddenly invidious, the thing said in the real rage of that pain which furniture and ornament can so unintentionally inflict. In the end it would be necessary to deny oneself emotion, and make it a *catalogue raisonné*, or perhaps to abandon it altogether in favour of Lady Thame herself. There would be relief as well as justice in acknowledging that Lady Thame might sit among any surroundings, and they would always be adventitious and trifling, though she had selected them personally and entirely. They spoke for so small a part of her. Her drawing-room referred to Lady Thame in much the same proportion as it referred to Cavendish Square, outside, or as Cavendish Square referred to Great Britain, further outside. It was quite subordinate, and the conviction that it was negligible did much to help one to stay in it.

Lavinia and Frances were both there with her, giving tea to Mrs. Lawrence Lenox, a lady whose manner showed excitement, and as plainly the wish to conceal it. A little excited both Lavinia and Frances were, a little roused Lady Thame was, but none of them betrayed the flutter, half exulting, half apprehensive, of Mrs. Lenox, who kept her elbows well beside her on the sofa, but whose eye, at the least sound from that direction, flew uncontrollably to the door.

'I have not seen him since he was twelve,' said Mrs. Lenox, with half a motion, as the handle turned, to rise; but it was only a footman with scones.

'Your mother,' said Lady Thame, 'was one of the people who used to over-feed him on his half-holidays at school. Strawberries. *I* know.'

Mrs. Lenox flushed with happy gratification.

'He used often to come over to us,' she said timidly. 'We were very fond of him, mother especially. She used always to say that for a little fellow he was so wonderfully well informed. I remember his putting her right on a point of botany once. We *were* so amazed.'

Lady Thame looked critically at her visitor, and Frances begged her to have some more bread and butter. Frances, though so well turned out, was pale and serious, and took her duties with almost an agitated anxiety.

'No, thank you, indeed,' said Mrs. Lenox, 'I've had such heaps of things. Yes, a little more tea, please, if it isn't too greedy,' and she resigned her four-cornered cup. 'Is it in the evening papers?'

'They don't seem to have come,' said Lady Thame. 'Just ring, Lavinia, please, and ask. But here it is in the *Times*.'

Mrs. Lenox took the proffered paper and read aloud. "'The King has been graciously pleased to approve the appointment of Anthony Andover, fourth Baron Thame, to be Viceroy and Governor-General in India, in the place of the Right Honourable Henry Halifax Waycourt, Earl of Druse, resigned." They *have* put it nicely, haven't they? Poor Lord Druse! Wasn't it shocking, that paralysis! Overwork, pure and simple. You *must* warn Lord Thame against overwork, Miss Thame.' She continued to look at the announcement, holding it off a little, admiringly, as if it were something jewelled and lustrous.

'There is a long article, too,' remarked Lavinia. 'Rather over-complimentary, mother thinks it.' Though Lavinia had grey eyes and a firm chin, she blushed easily with strangers. She blushed now, as if she had done something rather daring in quoting her mother.

'Oh, does she?' deprecated Mrs. Lenox, smiling over her fresh cup in the direction indicated.

'I do indeed,' said Lady Thame. 'When he has governed the country for his five years to some good purpose it will be time enough to pat him on the back. He's brought forth nothing wonderful so far in home politics, though he has worked hard enough – what can a Radical peer do? – and I can't see why it's so immensely to his credit that his great-grandfather made a name in Canada. It's quite time, too, that he was allowed to forget that he did well at Oxford. *I* can tell them that he has brains and a conscience. Now we shall see what use he will make of them.'

Mrs. Lenox's eye ranged vaguely down the wide column before her. 'I must read this when I get home,' she said, 'I am sure they don't say a bit too much.'

'Anthony comes honestly by his extraordinary interest in India,' continued Lady Thame. 'My father spent years there looking into the religions of the people – he translated some of the Vedas, and wrote a book called *The Law of God in the East*, which gave great offence in some quarters. I have it still – shall I lend it to you? Much pleasure. Knowing the natives as you do you will appreciate it. My husband, too, was always wildly interested in Orientals. Anything black. Adored them. He made a great collection – of books, I mean, not Easterns, though positively Leighton was simply infested – however, they were well enough in their way; and of course it is a duty to encourage their coming to Oxford, to absorb our civilisation, as my husband used to say, at its fountain-head. The one post in the Government he coveted all his life was the Secretaryship of State for India, and I always understood that Mr. Gladstone practically promised – however, a month before they came in again his health broke down. After that he devoted himself to growing trees and shrubs from that part of the world, with astonishing success. "The jungle," we called it at Leighton. Annoyed Broom, the head gardener, beyond words, to hear his pet plantation called "the jungle."' Lady Thame laughed.

'And mother would ask him, every other day, how his jungle was getting on,' said Frances. 'But Broom had you there, mother. He would say "*Terminalia Tomentosa*'s tryin' to make a bit of leaf, m'lady, but *Ficus Indica* is lookin' pretty sorry for itself."'

'Poor Broom,' said Mrs. Lenox. 'Yes, indeed, it is not surprising that Lord Thame – I suppose one mustn't say "His Excellency" yet – is interested in India.'

'He says there's so much to be done there,' remarked Lavinia.

'One thing he has very much at heart,' said Frances, 'and that is to reconcile the natives and the English out there. He says there is no reason why there shouldn't be a better feeling. He thinks that if we truly were all that we pretend to be to them they would appreciate it. He says Orientals have a great capacity for loyalty. Have they?'

'Oh yes, indeed,' replied Mrs. Lenox. 'He is perfectly right. We have a kitmutgar – that's a tablemaid, you know – who has been with us eleven years, and whenever we go on furlough he cries like a child.'

'How touching!' said Lady Thame. 'Poor creature! Oh, I am sure they are a responsive people. If that can be said of a poor what-did-you-call-him, what may we not expect among the better classes? I shall be glad to see Anthony take hold of that problem of race antagonism. He is very well fitted for it. To mend a thing like that there is nothing like example, nothing. And I am confident that the natives will look up to Anthony.'

'We will all look up to him,' said Mrs. Lenox coquettishly. 'The natives aren't everything in India, you know, Lady Thame.'

'Why, what else is there?' said Lady Thame, and did not wait for an answer. 'George Craybrooke told me a fortnight ago that things are so critical out there, what with over-population and famine and the Amir getting so above himself, that they simply could not afford to send any one but a first-class man. He had Anthony in mind at the time, I suppose, though he gave me no hint of it. Well, I should quite like to be going with him.'

'But you ought, Lady Thame,' said Mrs. Lenox, rising. 'Who will help him with his entertaining? Viceregal entertaining is *such* a tax, even when there is a Vicereine. I can't imagine how a bachelor Viceroy will cope with it.'

'And pray what would my poor Settlement do? And how would my Children of the State get on? And my Political Purity League? No, if necessary one of his sisters may go out, later on, but his mother finds enough to do in England. Parochial, you know,' Lady Thame laughed robustly, 'and insular. Parochial and insular, no doubt. But perhaps you will marry him off!'

'Marry a Viceroy!' cried Mrs. Lenox, honestly aghast. 'Oh no!'

'Will nobody have one?' cried Lavinia, crimsoning.

'Is it so unthinkable?' said Lady Thame. 'Like a Bishop?'

'Oh, much worse!' Mrs. Lenox told them. 'Like an archangel!'

On the success of this Mrs. Lenox achieved her good-bye. 'I hope you don't mind my coming on the very first day like this,' she said; 'I felt I simply had to tell you how charmed I was, and how delighted India will be. It makes such a difference to us all, you know, who comes out. It's everything, socially. And Lawrence having fagged for him at Eton too – it is so delightful. I hope you really don't mind.'

'Most kind of you, I think it,' said Lady Thame. 'If your dear mother had been alive, I am sure I should have had a letter from her, poor Alicia. Such a good heart! Dear me, what a trial it was to her when you ran away to India, the only one! Well, well! You mustn't let it be so long again. I think it most kind. We are supposed to be in the country to-day, or we should have had more visitors. Telegrams and letters since ten this morning. Two banquets proposed already, and photographers wanting sittings. Feed him and photograph him when he comes back, I say. Good-bye. Many thanks. Most kind.'

'Her husband,' Lady Thame told her daughters, as the hansom drove away, 'is a very clever rising man, a judge somewhere out there; I forget the name of the place, but I don't know how much Anthony will have to do with him. I was very much impressed by his ability, and so was your father, once when he and she came down to Leighton together. It was the time the natives were daubing the trees all over the place – the mango trees, you know – and we were all in a great fright. He reassured us completely; said there was nothing in it; and the event, of course, has proved him perfectly right. I hope he and Anthony will come across each other; he could put Anthony up to such a quantity of things.'

'She is like an Anglo-Indian lady in a book,' said Frances. 'She is a great deal too young, and I'm sure she has devotions. I do dislike women with devotions. I wonder if they're all like that?'

'That kind of Anglo-Indian woman in a book,' remarked Lavinia, 'is always heroic in an extremity. They prattle on just to show you how silly they can be; and then they set their teeth and perform miracles of self-sacrifice. Wait till she gets you alone in the jungle with small-pox!'

'I dare say she would do one very well,' responded Frances thoughtfully. 'But I should be interested to know if they're all like that. Mother, how *could* you give her the impression that Anthony was going out heart-free to India!'

Lady Thame stiffened. 'What possible difference can her impression make?' she demanded. 'He is going to rule the country, not to wear his heart upon his sleeve. Besides, if he is not fancy-free when he goes, he may be very shortly. It will be an absorbing task, not a thing to take up like a book.'

Frances shook her head. 'I am sure he will be constant,' she said. 'When a man like Anthony makes up his mind – '

'I shall be delighted to hear that he is wedded to the country,' declared his mother.

'Perhaps,' said Lavinia, 'he will ask her again before he goes.'

'It will make absolutely no difference,' Frances told them.

'Would she refuse the Viceroy of India!' exclaimed Lady Thame.

'Perfectly,' said Frances, 'if she just didn't want him.'

'I can't imagine that,' said Lady Thame decidedly, 'or for that matter that she should refuse Anthony Thame. For my part, I don't see why one should fly to the conclusion that he has ever asked Victoria. Fond of her as he may be, admire her he may – '

'Oh, mother, mother!' exclaimed Lavinia. 'You know in your heart that he adores her.'

'Then,' said Lady Thame, 'it's simple enough. He will marry her before he goes. There will be just time. And an extremely lucky girl I consider Victoria will be. An *extremely* lucky girl.'

'No, mother, you'll see – it won't happen,' Lavinia told her. 'There's something about Anthony Victoria doesn't like.'

'And pray what is it?' bristled their mother.

'Oh, I don't think any of us can tell exactly – we're all chips of the same block, aren't we?' and Lavinia regarded the block with a smile of affection. 'But I shouldn't call Anthony a – well, a very *easily* loveable person myself. You see, he doesn't think of *anything* but the aims of civilisation. And we all know she hates his politics.'

'Rubbish,' said Lady Thame. 'A wife's politics are the same as her husband's.' The late Lord Thame must often have congratulated himself that this had been his own good fortune. 'And it seems to me, if Anthony can swallow Herbert, Victoria can very well swallow *any* shade of Liberalism.'

'That is quite a different thing,' said Lavinia, and had no more to say.

'There is never any news of Herbert?' asked Frances. 'No clue at all?'

'And never will be,' said Lady Thame decidedly. 'Herbert has made away with himself – that's my firm conviction, though one doesn't, of course, say it to his sister.'

'I don't know why you will think that horrible thing,' said Lavinia, crimsoning deeply; and Lady Thame, at an appealing look from Frances, mitigated her reply.

'And I am sincerely sorry for Victoria,' she added. 'Sincerely sorry. She had much better give it up, leave it to Providence, and go out to India to help Anthony to do some good in the world – if she gets the chance.'

Frances, at an approach in the passage, lifted her head. 'Here she comes,' she said, and the footman, with four deliberate steps into the room, announced, 'Miss Tring.'

CHAPTER II

A tall girl followed her name, in a well-cut, shabby jacket, with splashes of mud on the hem of her skirt and not wholly removed from her boots. The hair about her forehead was damp, her eyes were dark and enthusiastic. She had the look of being blown in, and a current did seem to come with her that lifted the atmosphere of the room. They all felt it and were quickened; you could see that, whether they approved of it or not, hers was a happy approach to them. The armed neutrality that sat behind their greeting was the artificial thing; the reality was the way they all kindled to her.

'Where is Anthony?' she demanded. 'I want, as the Americans say, to shake him by the hand. I want to shake you all by the hand. I have been rejoicing steadily since three o'clock, and I should be glad of some tea, Frances. But what a chance! I could have wept – I could weep now, and I will if you don't give me two lumps, Lavinia.'

'We thought you would be pleased,' said Frances.

'*Pleased!* His Majesty the King is pleased. I am much more, I am content, I beat the tom-tom. Why aren't you all beating tom-toms, one in each corner? Or Aunt Pamela might occupy the howdah. That would give it a use; an excuse it can't have.'

They looked at the large object so invidiously designated. It stood, cumbrous, silver-gilt, fringed, tarnished, near the fireplace; from the end of the mantelpiece near it gazed the blind eyes of a bust of Herbert Spencer.

'What a down you always have on it,' said Lavinia. 'It wouldn't do in a small room, but in this great cavern of mother's it's all right.'

'I think it would look better in India.'

'Our grandfather made the pilgrimage to Benares in it,' said Frances defensively. 'He thought it would be valued on that account. And we do. Our grandfather once offered it to the British Museum, but they had one already, they said. We are all very glad they didn't take it.'

'Oh, I know,' Miss Tring responded absently. 'Coming like that, of course you can't help having it. And it does explain a lot in Anthony – ' She checked herself, and looked at the howdah as if it had betrayed her.

'I have just been telling a little person from India, whose mother used to be my dearest friend, how honestly Anthony comes by his great interest in the country,' said Lady Thame, without suspicion, 'but it is an old story to you, Victoria.'

Miss Tring looked prepared for a moment to hear it again, but Lady Thame spared her.

'How does he take it?' she asked curiously. The new interest was vivid in her face, and behind it something personal and undecipherable, something of herself which had touched and caught.

'Quietly, to us,' said Frances.

'But any one can see that he is really very deeply moved,' said his mother. 'He only told us yesterday. Mr. Craybrooke offered it to him on Monday, and he took three days to make up his mind. There were one or two things to consider. His journey to Finland he has had, of course, to give up; and he had very much set his heart on investigating and pressing the Finnish constitutional question –

he thinks it intolerable that England should look calmly on. And his book, I am sorry to say, will have to be set aside for the present.'

'*The Real Empire?*'

'Yes. Anthony at once submitted the sheets to Mr. Craybrooke, and though he entirely agrees with Anthony's views *as* views, apart from immediate exigencies, he considers that the expression of them just now would embarrass him a good deal as Viceroy – and, of course, one can understand it.'

'Well, yes,' said Victoria, 'since he practically repudiates all that we hold by the sword, and confines us, in the world, to the parts we can plough.'

'You have seem them too – the proofs?' Lady Thame concluded rather than inquired.

'Yes, I have seen them too.'

'Well, I don't at all agree with you, Victoria. He thinks, of course, that the only legitimate conquest is the soil, and that we have no permanent business except where we can take root. But the finer, higher, and wider conclusion of the book is that England should govern, and does govern, by moral force.'

Lady Thame drew herself up in a line, as it were, with her adjectives, which she produced with elocutionary emphasis and that British play of the hand which comprises a single gesture. With the other she held her cup at an angle which spilled her tea.

'Oh, Aunt Pamela!' exclaimed Victoria. Her laugh had a little accent of something that was not mirth; and into the eyes of Lavinia and Frances shot simultaneously the conviction, 'She *did* refuse him on account of his politics.'

Miss Tring did not pursue the matter. 'They call us hypocrites in Europe,' she said, 'but we aren't hypocrites – we're only anomalies.'

'So the publishers have agreed,' continued the mother of the last anomaly, 'to postpone it until he comes back. Of course, it has cost him something.'

'When he comes back,' cried Victoria, 'he will burn it.'

'Not while I have a safe,' said Lady Thame. 'It was got for his grandfather's manuscripts. Many of them are in it still. Then you haven't seen Anthony himself, Victoria?'

'Not for days and days,' replied Miss Tring calmly. 'And I read the papers even, without seeing it. Mother heard it at her club, and told me to dash round with her congratulations. She has a meeting somewhere. She said I was to tell you, if you hadn't realised it, that Anthony was going out to preside over the destinies of one-sixth of the human race.'

'I hope he will improve their lot,' said Lady Thame; 'I hear that millions of them live, at present, on three halfpence a day.'

'I should think,' said Victoria Tring slowly, 'that – to rule an alien people must be one of the few things in which there is essential glory. To be a king among one's own is a mere accident, without, as far as I can see, any compensations, unless you count not having to catch trains. But to be imposed that way from above, over strange races, with different joys and sorrows, and ambitions, whose knees really tremble and whose eyes really look up – it is like holding a commission from the gods.'

'It would be, Anthony says, if it weren't for the Secretary of State for India,' interposed Lavinia. 'He says they don't half trust the man on the spot, and he can't practically do anything on his own responsibility. But we think Anthony will do something; at any rate, he's awfully pleased at getting the chance.'

'I should think so,' said Victoria, 'I should think so. Do tell me how it came – the offer. On a gold-emblazoned scroll, I suppose, with the royal arms at the top and the rising sun at the bottom. Carried on a scarlet cushion and escorted by a detachment of Horse Guards.'

The ladies laughed, looking at one another in recognition of her lively fancy, and Lavinia quite rose to the humour of it when she said, 'I can tell you, Victoria. Mr. Craybrooke met him somewhere, directly after a Cabinet Council, and offered it to him. "Anthony, old fellow, how would you like India?" he said.'

'Ah, dear Bishop!' exclaimed Lady Thame, as more congratulations took their chance of finding her, after all, in town. Close upon Bishop Wilmington came Mr. Victor Gabriel, a young man who had undertaken to explain his race to the British people. To try to do anything was a passport to consideration in the Thame family, and Mr. Gabriel found in their friendship a reward of the effort he still made and a token of the success he still hoped for. Before Victoria slipped away Mr. Craybrooke himself had arrived, also a retired Lieutenant-Governor of Bengal, the widow of a Commander-in-Chief, and Lady Deborah Flaxe, who still, at the age of eighty-two, wrote articles in magazines upon all subjects which contained the female interest. Victoria stayed longer than she intended, but the door continued to admit congratulations only. 'I will write to Anthony,' she said finally, and went.

This Victoria Tring was the daughter of the late Lord Thame's half-sister. Her mother was the widow of John Tring, than whom Oxford has not produced a more brilliant biologist, or apart from that a more futile individual. He had proved the first, and was convincing his friends of the second when death cut short the less edifying demonstration. Mrs. Tring had a little money of her own and the tastes which led her to marry her husband. She enshrined his books in a house in Egerton Crescent, where she devoted herself intermittently to the task of bringing up her son Herbert Valentia and her daughter Victoria. For Herbert she trusted to known and expensive methods; he had tutors and crammers. Victoria, Mrs. Tring declared, she could not afford to educate; Victoria might just be about and listen to people talk.

When she was not disposing of Herbert and Victoria, Deirdre Tring fulfilled the law of her being, to which she often said that maternity was an accident. She absorbed London and the time, consumed much social philosophy, became a Fabian as strenuously as she might have become a Mahomedan, threw off her convictions in essays and her impressions in poems, rode in the very van of progress, was, I have no doubt, the first woman who smoked a cigarette in a public restaurant. She could do with or without cigarettes, however; the one stimulant she required was the evening paper. She called it the lyre of London.

One had to believe that Herbert and Victoria were accidents to Mrs. Tring when one saw her interest in life so bravely hold even through and after the tragedy of her son's disappearance in the course of his last term at Oxford. Certainly, it was a virile thing in her, both to conquer her passionate widowhood and to survive not only those visits of too possible identification across the Channel, but the cruel mystery itself. Debt and dissolute habits rose like phantoms where this son had been, but could not point the way he had taken. If the Vice-Chancellor's Court had special theories they did not impart them to his mother. It was six months before the first and only request for money came, and dispelled, for the time being, the idea of suicide. The amount was pathetically small, and suggested to Mrs. Tring with curious pertinacity the cost of a steerage passage to America. It was a country, America, of which Mrs. Tring thought well and optimistically. To America she could resign her son with something like confidence. America would offer him a career whatever he had upon his conscience; and in the relief of this conviction Mrs. Tring's head, as fair and fluffy as ever, was soon bent with its accustomed absorption over the evening paper. America, after all, had been open to him whether he had gone there or not.

So the son; with the brother it was different. Victoria accepted nothing, was resigned to nothing. To her the place Herbert left remained empty. A little lamp of hope burned steadily there; and there, too, were put away the three or four brilliant, irresponsible, erotic sketches which had been applauded in one of those magazines that now and then play with interesting luridity upon the neutral-tinted British consciousness, to be chilled and killed in the end, apparently by the mere steady regard of the eye of virtue. They duly helped to extinguish the venture, but they were thought to point to literature as the young man's hope, to *belles-lettres* as his ladder. They argued now for Mrs. Tring that he was climbing in America by means of the periodicals. Victoria could hardly speak about these efforts. She would look steadily at people who mentioned them, defying the criticism that was naturally enough never uttered. She had her private value for them, her private apology too, perhaps, but she kept both fervently to herself. Victoria, more than any one, was held by her brother's charm. If she magnified it into something more potential one cannot be surprised. He had always shown her his charm, had always found it worth while to be at his best with her. Indeed, to do him justice, she represented something valuable to him; and his sister, at that age – she was twenty-two when he disappeared – was not likely to know more of him than he chose to let her.

Literature, people thought, was his hope. As a matter of fact, there was no hope, there never had been any hope, for Herbert Tring. He had justified his father's scientific contempt for the moral sense by coming into the world as far as possible divested of it. As if that had a look of flippancy he began early to prove its necessity, as commonly accepted, to the welfare of the race. Even at Oxford, he might have illustrated the great plan of salvation by natural selection, since this may also be effectively done by the damned. He was too young and perhaps too simply bad to demonstrate more than an axiom of natural science, but so far as he went he was remarkably convincing. He had gone, as we know, too far; he had been sucked down, with all his capacity for the embroidery of certain emotions, with all his allurements of sympathy and tact, to another plane of activity. That was four years ago.

And it was quite true that Victoria Tring had more than once been asked by her half-cousin Anthony Thame to marry him. This by itself was proof enough that she was completely equipped with the moral sense; Lord Thame could never have been deceived. What we may gather from her unvarying refusal is perhaps not so easy to decipher; she herself had probably never quite deciphered it, since many things and many people interested her more than Victoria Tring. The affair had one feature of which she was secretly, perhaps, a little proud; they remained excellent friends. She admired him for a hundred reasons, and could explain every one of them. She may have seen that it would have been illogical and un-English not to admire Anthony Thame, so completely did he realise a national ideal. There he was, the product of fine principle, almost unalloyed. She would feel for him every appreciation but the desire to marry him. That, as she must often have told him, was such a different thing. But she was very just to him, and her impatience on the whole was kind. She admired him, and, in spite of their differences, he consulted her. This rather conspicuous occasion was almost the first on which he had not done it.

So Anthony Andover, fourth Baron Thame, became in due course Viceroy of India, and ruled alone over many places and principalities, among them the city of Pilaghur.

CHAPTER III

PILAGHUR is the capital of the province of Ghoom, which is ruled by a Chief Commissioner, under the Government of India, under the Parliament of Great Britain and Ireland, under the King. Ghoom is, in fact, very far under. The Chief Commissioner has the glory and the responsibility of power. It is he whose person is decked with tinsel and marigolds, whose feet are kissed by petitioning Ghoomatis; it is also he who is lectured for plague riots and called to account for famine returns by His Excellency the Viceroy. Both the garland and the rein lie upon his neck. But he administers through his Commissioners, and they through their deputies and assistants, and they through their native clerks, their 'baboos,' and adjunct to the baboo through the chuprassie, the herald and messenger of Government, who is dressed in scarlet and gold, and has often been known to collect taxes which were never imposed. The police aiding all. Down beneath the bare feet of the chuprassie and the police we may see dimly the province of Ghoom.

Reflecting, we must call Pilaghur two capitals. There is the Pilaghur which the ladies of the station think of, and which figures – it has a cathedral – in diocesan reports. It has a parade-ground as well as a cathedral, and a station club where are tennis-courts and the English illustrated papers, and public gardens set with palms and pointsettias, where the band plays twice a week in the evenings after polo. Two or three roads lie fairly parallel in Pilaghur, and two or three lie more or less across, broad empty roads named after Indian administrators, bordered with tamarinds and acacias. There are certainly lamp-posts, and infrequent in the distance a bright red letter-box; but the absence of everything else gives a queer, quiet, theatrical look to these highways. You could walk for nearly a mile on some of them before being lost again in the incomprehensible agriculture of Ghoom. You might meet a sowar on a camel carrying an invitation to the District Judge to dine at the mess, or a snake-charmer beating his tom-tom and dragging his mongoose, or a hobbled donkey or two nibbling the short dry grass between the road and the footpath; and you might meet nothing more.

The sun-suffused roads run up into rubbly banks on either side, and these are crowned with grey-green cactuses, many-armed and dusty. Behind them, indeterminately far in, indeterminately far apart, are houses, thick-looking low houses. They stand in the sun as a child might draw them, on a very simple plan and rather crooked, with inexplicable excrescences, made too, as a child might perhaps make them, chiefly of mud, and colour-washed. Some of the roofs are high-pitched and thatched; others are flat, with low balustrades round them like those in Bible pictures. They are all of one substance, from the quarters of the Barfordshires to Government House, the residence of the Chief Commissioner, which, however, has two stories and a flag. The plaster balustrading round the second story of his dwelling gives it an innocent look of being iced all over like a Christmas cake. All new comers notice this with a smile, but the impression soon fades away among the realities of things, which are, after all, very real in Pilaghur.

Most of the other houses, like the Chief Commissioner's, are cream-coloured, but some are pink and some are yellow; there are even blue ones. I cannot conceive why they do not give Pilaghur a more cheerful appearance than it has. Perhaps it is because they stand, behind their cactus hedges and their hibiscus bushes, so remote from one another; they insist upon their approaches, they will have their atmosphere, and do not justify either. Or perhaps Pilaghur is depressed because it has, properly speaking, no shops. In one bungalow, standing in a roomy acre of its own, with three crooked sago palms in a far corner and nothing else, a photographer does business, but does so little that his two terriers bark furiously at any customer. In another, the small discoloured pink one by the tank, Miss Da Costa, from a well-known Calcutta firm, is understood to make very nice blouses; and I could show you where to find Mrs. Burbage, spoken of lamentably as an officer's widow, who ekes out a casual and slipshod existence by making bread and cakes for other people. But all this is hidden away; you have to hunt it up in its domestic seclusion, where perhaps it is having tea, with jam, and biscuits out of a tin box, and half resentful of the opportunity of doing business. The eye rests comforted on a single sign, the sign of Ali Bux, General Stores Dealer, who occupies a fortuitous unfenced triangle, and not only supplies kerosine oil and groceries and children's toys, but crockery and furniture on the hire system, a good deal of which, more or less tumble-down, is exposed outside his premises. It is all disassociated. Ali Bux seems to be permitted rather than encouraged or relied upon; we miss the backbone of life. From a point in mid-air, far enough up, this Pilaghur would have the vagueness of a family wash, spread out, in the manner of the country, to dry upon the ground.

The other Pilaghur crowds upon the skirts of this, a thick embroidery. Far out it spreads imperceptibly into the mustard-fields; but here below Dalhousie Gardens and all along to the old Mosque of Akbar it falls close packed to the river; and beyond the reservoir it hives with indifference round the upright stone finger of an old conquest, that still points to history the way of the Moghuls. Out there the multitudinous mud huts are like an eruption of the baked and liver-coloured earth, low and featureless; but in the narrow ways of the crowded city by the river the houses jostle each other to express themselves. The upper stories crane over the lower ones, and all resent their neighbours. They have indeed something to say with their carved balconies of wood and even of stone, with the dark-stained arches, pointed and scalloped, of their shop fronts, their gods in effigy, their climbing, crumbling ochres and magentas. They have the stamp of the racial, the inevitable, the desperately in earnest, which is the grim sign of cities; there is no vagueness, nothing superimposed, in Pilaghur-by-the-river. Never is there room for the tide of life that beats through it, chaffering and calling, ox-carts pushing, water-carriers trotting, vendors hawking, monkeys thieving, and Ganeshi Lal, who wires a price to London for half the seed crops of Ghoom, looking out indifferently from his second-story window upon all. Ganeshi sits on the floor; he wears a gold-embroidered velvet cap, and the scalloped window frames him to the waist. There are hundreds of such pictures. Down below squat his kinsmen round the hills of yellow meal in the shop window, and sell a measure for a copper; up above, Ganeshi with a rusty pen and purple ink writes off half a lakh of profits on a piece of brown paper. The Oriental gutter runs along the side, the Oriental donkey sniffs at the garbage; there is an all-pervasive Oriental clamour and an all-pervasive Oriental smell. The city by the river trenches hardly anywhere on the station beyond; only the Brass Bazar in one place strays across. You have to drive through it to get to the railway station. Pariahs dash out at bicycles, there are one or two haunting lepers, and cholera usually begins there; but it has a pictorial twist and a little white temple under an old banyan tree, which the ladies of the station always praise and generally sketch. And there is no other way of getting to the railway station. These are Pilaghur.

CHAPTER IV

W HEN Eliot Arden 'got Ghoom,' as the phrase went, the secretariats commented freely. It was one of Lord Thame's first appointments, and it showed the type of man who was likely to appeal to him, a type of man in some ways rather like himself, it was noted. There was little criticism; the promotion of a Secretary in the Home Department to a Chief Commissionership was quite to be expected; but it was by no means the only possible nomination. Several others seemed equally likely. There was Beauchamp, of the Foreign Office, who had just brought off a great *coup* with the Nizam and was a charming fellow socially; there was Godfrey, of the Revenue and Agricultural Department, very sound, who had really accomplished something in Western Indian cotton improvement, to name only two. Arden had, of course, the qualifications that had brought him so brilliantly along to the Home Office. Those were understood. But the Viceroy had been known to say of him that he could read as well as write, which was not so common, and after that, of course, his feeling for literature became part of his reputation.

'It's extraordinary,' the stout Staff colonels would say of him, wiping their foreheads after a hard set of racquets, 'the books that chap finds time to get through.' This brought him short of the standard of practical men, who would use words like 'academic' and 'visionary' in calculating his chances of the big successions; but these terms were also beginning to be used pretty freely about Lord Thame, who was at the very top and far beyond the climbing line. He had a perception of the more interesting aspects of life, which does not draw a man into society; but persons to whom that general cup of satisfaction was very full sometimes said that Arden was not half a bad sort when you knew him, and his few friends held him in great affection. He was more intrigued than most men by the consideration of his own existence; out of office hours he frequently possessed his soul. Careless people gave him the old-fashioned name of atheist because he did not go to church and had been known to imply an irreverence for dogma. No doubt in England this would have attracted small attention; but in India we are far from the clashes and concessions of science and theology. The ark, no doubt, originally rested on a peak of the Himalayas; and it is there still, with no apologising bishop looking from the windows. The charge, however, was a mistake. The Secretary in the Home Department was perhaps more aware than most of them of divinity in the world, but he was shy of cheapening his intuitions for their instruction; and, indeed, they would have been shy, too.

Ghoom was a prize, a plum, a troublesome job and a great compliment; no Viceroy would make the selection in a hurry. That Thame should have given it to Eliot Arden – well, it threw a light on Thame. Rulers of India are not able to permit themselves conspicuous personal friendships; nor was that kind of imputation made; but one man remembered how, in the far round of a long walk upon the hill beyond Government House, he had come upon the Viceroy and his Home Secretary stretched among the pine needles and arguing like a pair of undergraduates; and another had heard His Excellency say, 'For all I know about the Upanishads I am indebted to Arden.' There is no recognised official channel for conveying information about the Upanishads to anybody; Arden had not sent it in the files. The uncomfortable hypothesis under it all seemed to be that this, in His Excellency's view, was the sort of fellow to give things to, the sort of fellow who could talk, and who knew about the Upanishads. Something like a qualm would naturally rise at such a conviction within civil and military uniforms entertaining it; which might easily have been dissipated, however, by the fact that Simla had no more Ardens, civil or military.

Oftener it was said, 'So the Ardens get Ghoom,' 'So the Ardens go to Ghoom.' I suppose nobody in England would say, 'So the Fitzalberts have got the Colonial Office,' or the Mountstuarts the Woolsack; but in India we have a family feeling about these things, and confer them, at least colloquially, in the plural. The Hobsons at last attain to the Bench of the High Court, and the Petersons become Quarter-Master-General. People will tell you that when the O'Haras were Commander-in-Chief the phrase had no idle significance, though generally, of course, it has. It carries, however, a sense of the value, in India, of the sparser feminine, and identifies ladies, however casually, with what their husbands have to do.

And everybody approved unreservedly of Mrs. Arden for Ghoom. Mrs. Arden, it was said, was just the person to 'make it pleasant' in Pilaghur as the wife of a Chief Commissioner is expected to make it pleasant. In this further respect Arden was thought fortunate; his wife would 'make up for' his own social disabilities. He had become engaged to her at Oxford, when she was a fair intelligent girl with a poet's name, Jessica Cowper; and they had come out to India together, with what seemed to be ideals in ideally common stock. From the very first, and all through the progress from isolation with a policeman and a native magistrate to desolation with a salt inspector, two missionaries, and no doctor, which makes the early stages of the civilian's career, Mrs. Arden had been 'liked.' She was felt to be clever, and not too clever; superior, but not too superior, a thing pigstickers were not quite sure of in the Arden of those days when they found him consoling exile with a pocket Horace. She was devoted to her husband to an extent that appealed to those who were least devoted to theirs; and there could have been no more pathetic illustration of the sad Indian choice between husband and children than she offered when the boys had to be sent home.

She went with the boys then, and had been a good deal with them since, but people always felt for her. As the Ardens grew more senior – she had managed to be a good deal with Eliot too – people often described her as 'such an interesting woman'; and the stab of surprise with which he first heard the phrase was one of the things which her husband resented long and could not quite forgive himself. After all, that had also been his experience. Remembering how interesting he had found Jessica Cowper, he should have had no impulse to criticise the phrase. Once the Viceroy had called her 'bright.' 'A bright woman like you,' he said, and Eliot, when she repeated it to him blushing, could only say, 'I am sure he meant no offence.'

'Of course he didn't,' returned Mrs. Arden, astonished.

That was in the second year of their administration of Ghoom, when the Viceroy had stayed with them on tour, as he does stay with Lieutenant-Governors and Chief Commissioners in the course of his yearly progresses. Mrs. Arden had not concealed her anxiety about the visit – it was so nice of her, people thought, not to – but had consulted everybody, and borrowed from several people. The Lemons' Goanese butler, Mrs. Lemon proudly declared, never left the place day or night; the Lenoxes' candelabra shone on the dinner-table each evening; everybody helped with flowers. Mrs. Arden had spared no effort, even to reading His Excellency's book on the Yellow Races, which she had always meant to do before, but had never somehow managed. It was in this connection, perhaps, that she had the reward I have quoted, since no one, and least of all the author, could fail to be impressed with the intelligence and perseverance involved. It was a personal thing, her 'brightness'; she could wear it in her mind like a Kaiser-i-Hind medal, and only her husband would wince at its being of the second class.

Mrs. Arden had also, for more general reference, the Military Secretary's statement as they were going away – he was such a nice fellow, so pleasant to have in the house – that His Excellency had thoroughly enjoyed himself and they had all had an awfully good time. Mrs. Arden gave everybody a share of this, mentioning it particularly to Mrs. Lenox in writing to return the candelabra, which had done so much to illuminate His Excellency's satisfaction. She quite deserved her popularity.

Eliot Arden had also his definite gratification in the viceregal visit, though it was naturally different; it had nothing to do with the quality of the cheroots or the champagne. Indeed, if these were particularly good it was probably owing to somebody else: Arden was no critical judge of such things. He himself would smoke any leaf that grew on the earth's surface, and it would hardly occur to him to ask whether it had been produced in Turkey or in Trichinopoly. He was apt to impute a like indifference to other people. Mrs. Arden came to him early on the second day with the tragedy that there was no cream for the Viceroy's coffee. 'Good heavens, he's much too busy to mind,' said Eliot. 'Give him milk.'

But the Chief Commissioner had his own susceptibilities. For a long time past life had given him one supreme engrossment, his share in the burden of the administration of India, what he would have called his 'job.' He was forty-three years old; his job had taken the best of his brains and his energy since he was twenty-five. The whole worth of the man had gone into it; and for some years the chief value of his life had come out of it. Perhaps it was his nature to idealise anything that he had to do. He would have swept a chimney with a thought of the sparks that made his work; and India lends itself to that trick. Ghoom had been, so far, his widest scope, his most responsible opportunity, and his most conspicuous trial.

And Ghoom, troublesome Ghoom, under Eliot Arden had gone well. An Agricultural Holdings Act, which Government had been five years debating in fear of Ghoom, had slipped quietly into operation because the man who had to put the new shoe on the province had known just where and why it would pinch. Coal in Ghoom had been a long-hidden official speculation; Arden had brought it to the surface and provided half a million people with another industry. In this the man of no great practical turn naturally had a special satisfaction; and Arden had warmed with the appreciation of the chairman at the great commercial dinner of the Calcutta year, the feast of St. Andrew, who candidly congratulated Government upon the enterprise and freedom from red tape of what had been done in Ghoom. Other matters for congratulation there were, more interesting in the resolution embodying them than they would be here; and the Viceroy had shown himself as appreciative a critic over a cigar in Arden's office as he had been in the views communicated by the Home Secretary. Each night the two separated in the small hours, and each day the Chief Commissioner kindled into something more and more different from the rather silent, generally acquiescent, indwelling Arden of whom a fanciful person might say that his only solace lay in his dreams. People remarked that the Chief Commissioner was really exerting himself, making a tremendous effort to entertain His Excellency; that was the station's way of putting it. But it had already been said of Lord Thame that he was the first Viceroy to approach Indian problems with a philosophically interested mind; and Arden was certainly not aware of any special pains as he and the Viceroy breasted the difficulties of the moment together, or shared the outlook upon the irremediable.

'One gets moral support out of that fellow,' he said, half shyly, to his Revenue Secretary, as they stood with their hats off on the beflagged Pilaghur platform while the special steamed out; and, no doubt, out of that particular fellow moral support was to be got. But there was more than moral support in the heart of the Chief Commissioner as he drove back to his frosted official residence with his sowars in blue and khaki cantering and jingling behind. Whatever happens elsewhere in these days of triumphant democracies, in India the Ruler survives. He is the shadow of the King, but the substance of kingship is curiously and pathetically his; and his sovereignty is most real with those who again represent him. The city and the hamlet stare apathetic; they have always had a conqueror. But in lonely places which the Viceroy's foot never presses and his eye never sees, men of his own race find in his person the authority for the purpose of their whole lives. He is the judge of all they do, and the symbol by which they do it. Reward and censure are in his hand, and he stands for whatever there is in the task of men that is sweeter than praise and more bitter than blame. He stands for the idea, the scheme, and the intention to which they are all pledged; and through the long sacrifice of the arid years something of their loyalty and devotion and submission to the idea gathers in the human way about the sign of it. The Viceroy may be a simple fellow, but his effigy is a wonderful accretion.

There is a keen harvest of sensitiveness in this. Perhaps experience is the only thing that should attempt to teach it. No doubt it should be read through the isolation and monotony, the every-lowering vitality, the tyranny of the sun and the prison of the land in which it grows. Eliot Arden had gathered it all. Choice would have made him something quite different, but chance turned him out an Indian Civilian. He had stores of philosophy, but they could not defend him that morning against his delight that what he had done well had been seen to be well done. The moral support he acknowledged was warmed by a gratification he said nothing about, and enhanced by his personal esteem for his Viceroy, the sixth who had asked in the name of England for the best that was in him, and had got it. But the Chief Commissioner's satisfaction was, after all, the ripple of a good day and some time past. At the moment to which I beg your attention, Anthony Andover, fourth Baron Thame, had governed India in the name of his Sovereign, and Eliot Arden had administered the province of Ghoom by the authority of the Viceroy and Governor-General in Council, for three years.

CHAPTER V

A good many people were dining with the Ardens – General and Mrs. Lemon, that rising pair Mr. and Mrs. Lawrence Lenox, Mr. and Mrs. Arthur Poynder Biscuit, Colonel Vetchley commanding the Barfordshires, one or two subalterns, and Miss Ruth Pearce, M.B. Miss Pearce properly comes last, because she had no quotable position. The table of precedence does not provide for demi-official lady-doctors, having been invented before they were. It was sometimes a little embarrassing to dispose of Miss Pearce, and it was thought very kind of the Ardens to place her so often, in that rule-defying way, on the Chief Commissioner's left. It was, in the eyes of Pilaghur, a recognition little short of noble of a friendship little short of morganatic.

General Lemon commanded the district, was responsible to the Commander-in-Chief in India for the troops in Ghoom. Mr. Lawrence Lenox was the District and Sessions Judge. Mr. Arthur

Poynder Biscuit was a junior Civilian, whose wife had not long come out. Colonel Vetchley had no wife, but was much wedded to his opinions. There was, indeed, only one married man in the Barfords, Beaufort, and he was on leave. It was a grave regimental question whether Devine, Major and second in command, would countenance Beaufort by following his example, or whether Beaufort would fix up an exchange. Devine was being closely watched. The subalterns Davidson and Lamb belonged to the Tenth Guzeratis, of the Indian Army, and were, naturally, both family men. Mrs. Davidson was not present for domestic reasons, but Mrs. Lamb was actually at the party. She was a thin little, white little thing, who made no pretence of doing her hair, but put a natural flower in it, and wore for further ornament a necklace of amber beads and a very constant smile – the kind of little thing one was instinctively sorry for until one saw in her eyes that she not only had any amount of pluck, but that she enjoyed life as well as anybody. The 'chota-mem,' the keen little chota-mem of Anglo-India. I would like to write pages about her; but there were other ladies at the party.

As some people can be drawn in three lines, so Mrs. Lemon can be, and always was, described in three words. Mrs. Lemon was 'a good sort.' If we in any way lived up to our reputation in India, Mrs. Lemon would be the leader of the military half of society in Pilaghur, while Mrs. Arden championed the civil half, in hostile camps, with an armed neutrality for garden parties. But Mrs. Lemon had no notion of her responsibilities to fiction; she declared that cliquism was the ruination of small stations, and her greatest friend was the wife of the District Superintendent of Police, with whom she shared the enthusiasms and anxieties involved in raising English fowls. She owned to fourteen stone, but she rode to hounds wherever there were any; with two sons in the services, she played regularly in tennis tournaments, and had even been known, when the General was not looking, to borrow a club from some exhausted girl and rush gloriously into hockey. She had an all-embracing interest in life and a geniality you could warm yourself at. She would sit down to a gossip as if it were a meal, and so absorbed she was in what you were telling her that she would hardly ever let you finish the sentence. She would race your thought to its conclusion and invariably be in ahead. Nobody minded; it was the most spontaneous flattery.

Mrs. Lenox you will perhaps remember already to have met at Lady Thame's. Since then her husband had been able to give her rather a pretty tiara and some appreciable precedence; and she looked younger than ever at the Ardens' dinner-party. Otherwise only her clothes had changed. Again, Mrs. Lenox's appearance should have placed her at once in complications – it complicated her, if you remember, in the opinion of the Hon. Lavinia Thame. The tiara alone – in an Indian plains station – should have involved her; to the sophisticated eye she was full of incriminating signs. I am sorry to disappoint, but I must stick to the ladies of Pilaghur as I know them; Mrs. Lenox was wholly virtuous. She had not an idea disconnected with Lawrence, not a desire that wandered from the path of his preferment. One might as well tell the truth in the beginning.

Mrs. Biscuit, on the other hand, Mrs. Arthur Poynder Biscuit, had come out knowing what was expected of her, and feeling able to meet any ordinary emergency. She had even looked forward, I think, to the many interesting situations from which she should extricate herself within a hair's breadth of compromise; but always with the hair quite visible. Her sense that such things were inevitable suggested to her that she might as well make the most of them. But by this time Mrs. Biscuit had reached the private conclusion that either Pilaghur was far from being a 'typical' Indian station, or the novelists were simply not to be trusted. Somebody asked her once whether she found Anglo-Indian society what she expected.

'In some ways,' Mrs. Biscuit replied, 'I think it has been very much over-rated.'

I am afraid she was thinking of this way. She was considered clever; she was clever. You could find the colonial edition of practically everything on her drawing-room table; but she did not always know how humorous she was.

So you have them: General and Mrs. Lemon, Mr. and Mrs. Lawrence Lenox, Colonel Vetchley, Mr. and Mrs. Arthur Poynder

Biscuit, Mr. and Mrs. Lamb, Mr. Davidson and Miss Pearce, all of Pilaghur.

'Personally,' Colonel Vetchley was saying, 'I can't *stick* him.'

Mr. Biscuit, a small, fair, moderate-looking person, glanced with smiling deprecation at his chief, as if he would say, 'We must excuse a certain freedom of expression in the army.' Young Lamb radiated respectful sympathy and said, 'Hear, hear, sir.' Mr. Lawrence Lenox looked, above all things, discreet.

'Well,' said Mrs. Lenox, 'one takes people as one finds them. I must say, when we were in Simla last year we thought him perfectly charming. Of course we both knew him as a boy – Lawrence was his fag two terms at Eton. But that couldn't have made *much* difference.' And Mrs. Lenox looked round appealingly.

'I've never set eyes on him,' said Colonel Vetchley, 'and I hope I never may. I don't deny his ability as a civil administrator, but he's made more bad blood between the natives of this country and the army than can be wiped out in one generation, or two either.'

'The state of things between the natives of this country and the army wasn't ideal before he came, Vetchley,' said his host.

'I don't say it was; but at all events we knew where we were. Tommy was a better man than the native, and the native jolly well knew it and kept his place – got soundly kicked if he didn't, and served him right. And mind you, in the end it was better for the native.'

'In dealing with such cases,' remarked Mr. Lenox, 'Lord Thame has certainly taken a very definite line.'

'If you said he'd shown a very definite bias,' snorted Colonel Vetchley, 'I'd agree with you. Absolutely unwarrantable interference, with no excuse and with the worst results. In my young days – I was out here more years ago than I care to count – regimental inquiry and the C.O.'s decision were thought good enough. I remember the case of a fellow who shot a Bengali swimming in the Hooghly – meant no harm, took him for a crocodile. Blind drunk, of course. We held an inquiry – perfectly clear the man *was* out after crocodile – got off with confiscation of his shooting pass and a warning. No more of that! It would be the courts for a thing like that nowadays, and as quick as you can get there, and the whole business dragged up to Simla and gabbled over in Council. Ten to one sentence pronounced inadequate and the regiment packed off to Aden, or some grey-headed old boy like me told to go over it.'

'Our notion of our proper relations with these people does change, doesn't it, as time goes on,' remarked Miss Pearce; and the Chief Commissioner, who had been absently playing with a salt-cellar, turned to her with a little pleased start of attention. 'My great-grandmother used to send her ayah to be whipped. We don't have our ayahs whipped much now, do we?'

'It sounds like what might have happened in a plantation,' said Mrs. Arden. 'Was she a planter's wife, Dr. Pearce – indigo or anything?'

'She was the wife of a Chief Justice of Bengal,' said Miss Pearce.

Eliot Arden, beside her, made between his closed lips a little sound of amusement, and his long fingers fell again to twisting the salt-cellar.

'But I always thought the army was in the hands of the Commander-in-Chief – not the Viceroy,' observed Mrs. Biscuit to Mr. Davidson of the Guzeratis.

'So it jolly well ought to be,' Davidson told her; 'but the present Chief's a weak chap, you see, and the present Viceroy's a strong chap. You'd think, to look at the orders, that the Chief did it all off his own bat, but that's all Thomasina – he doesn't.'

'The Viceroy is constitutionally the head of the army in India,' said Mr. Lenox.

'The King is the head of the Church of England,' retorted Colonel Vetchley, 'but he doesn't interfere with the discipline.'

'I don't think you'll find,' pursued Lawrence Lenox, carefully selecting a salted almond, 'that Thame has acted *ultra vires* anywhere in dealing with these cases.'

'I dare say he takes good care of that. But it's pitiable, the way he runs the Chief. I say Robert Waterbrook should have resigned rather than put his name to that tar-and-feathering of the Black Dragoons, a regiment with the best frontier record in the history of this country – and I wonder he didn't. 'Xtraordinary, the way administrative work changes a man. I was with Waterbrook in the second Afghan business – he wouldn't have stood it then! Take a fellow because he's a good fellow in the field, and stick him on an office stool, and it's sickly the way he takes it from fellows who have never sat anything else.'

'I'm afraid the Black Dragoons hadn't a very good record in punkah-coolies,' said General Lemon. 'Three of them, weren't there – one assault and two deaths?'

'Under very different circumstances, sir. And the only case that was proved was severely dealt with by the courts. Accused got five years.'

'And at Thame's insistence the regiment got a new colonel, a new adjutant, and Jacobabad,' said the General meditatively. 'I don't know about the wholesale punishment of the men, but I believe in holding officers responsible. And Tommy's got to be taught, too, that it's a cowardly thing to strike a native of this country. It has gradually soaked into his superiors – perhaps we're a trifle thinner-skinned – and it's got to soak into him. I remember the time when it was the commonest thing in the world for a man to give his syce a good hiding for stealing gram, say. And it wasn't at all out of the way to hear these fellows' – he looked casually round, but the servants were for the moment out of the room – 'to hear these fellows spoken of as "niggers." Well, as Dr. Pearce says, those things simply aren't done now; they've become the mark of the cad. Tommy must learn – approximately, we don't expect miracles – not to do them either.'

'I don't dispute it for a moment; but there are ways of doing things, and I maintain it's rotten bad policy for any Viceroy to identify himself with the natives of this country as against his own countrymen,' returned Colonel Vetchley. 'It's bound to do harm; it's done an uncommon lot of harm already. These villagers think they can knock Tommy about pretty much as they like. If a case comes up they've only got to swear up a lot of false evidence and the "Mulky Lat" will give them protection. It looks well at home, of course, where they know nothing about what's involved. I dare say it's worth a good many votes. Thame is too much of a politician to run this country – that's what's the matter with him.'

Eliot Arden opened his eyes suddenly wider, as if the question for the first time demanded his attention.

'I disagree with you there, Vetchley,' he said. 'Absolutely. When I first came in contact with Thame I wasn't altogether attracted by him. There were things – things belonging to the essence of the man – to become accustomed to.'

'It must be an acquired taste,' interrupted Colonel Vetchley, and looked as if he would like to say more, but finished his champagne instead.

'I was put off like everybody else by a certain affirmativeness he has – he's a bit of a moral despot – and by what still seems to me his queer lack of the human interest, the interest in another fellow. You're very well and very worthy, but you're not his affair, I used to think. It was the abuse or the injustice that was his affair, and for that he wouldn't spare himself.'

'That's all right, but he takes too much on himself,' said Colonel Vetchley. 'He's Viceroy of India, but if he were God Almighty there are some things he couldn't change in this country.'

'Then when one saw the scope and the motive of his undertakings,' continued Arden, 'and the courage and devotion he brought to them, and the way he believed in what he had to do, other considerations – well, vanished. After all, if a man consents to sink his own personality in his work, you can't expect him to waste time playing about with yours. And the notion that he was in any way on the make in what he did became simply impossible to entertain. Whether he's right or wrong in this idea that the British soldier in India can be reformed by Resolutions in the Gazette we shall know better fifty years hence than we do now. Opinion about everything changes and moves – he may be in the forefront of it, and we in the discomfort of dragging after. But there shouldn't be two views, either then or now, about his motive.'

'What a pity it is that some nice woman doesn't marry him,' proposed Mrs. Lemon, as a cheery and final solution of the difficulties presented by His Excellency's temperament.

'Isn't there supposed to be somebody at home?' asked Mrs. Biscuit.

'I don't think so,' Mrs. Lenox told her, 'or we would have known. We have such quantities of mutual friends.'

'It seems to me,' said Mrs. Arden thoughtfully, 'that he would be a difficult person for any woman to feel herself a real companion to. It would be such an effort to keep up.'

Her eyes rested wistfully on her husband as she spoke. One might have thought that her own experience, in its less dramatic mould, had been strenuous. But her sigh, if one escaped her, was lost in the smile she sent to Mrs. Lemon, at which Mrs. Lemon, beaming back, led past subservient chairs to the drawing-room.

There Mrs. Lamb, who had no confidence in the regimental doctor, had something very special to ask Dr. Pearce about the baby's diet while it was teething: for this intrigue they sought a retired sofa. Mrs. Biscuit drifted about with her hands locked behind her and her chin at its best angle, examining engravings, picking up books. The other three made a social group to which Mrs. Lenox explained her plan of a bazaar and *café chantant* in aid of the Pilaghur branch of the Young Women's Christian Association, of which she was President.

'We are going to ask you to open it, dear Mrs. Arden,' she was saying, 'and you're such a kind person, I know you will.'

Mrs. Arden made a little spoiled gesture of deprecation.

'Not if I have to make a speech,' she said.

Mrs. Lenox seized the hand. 'No speech if you'd rather not,' she returned affectionately. 'But you know what a difference your name on the bills will make, dear.'

'We're getting things from everywhere,' she went on. 'My mother-in-law – she *is* such a dear – is sending me out a whole quantity of the latest penny –'

'Toys!' exclaimed Mrs. Lemon breathlessly. 'You'll be able to sell them *easily* at a rupee. I had them for my Zenana Mission Fair – thirty shillings' worth. They were every one gone in half an hour!'

'And a man I know in Muscat has promised me –'

'Dates?' beamed Mrs. Lemon.

'No – curly daggers. And we're getting lots of those lovely, painted leather vases from Bikanir, and dozens of little brass animals from Jeypore – they make the sweetest menu-holders – but we've decided not to have many crushed turquoise things from Cashmere; would you?'

'Perfectly right; people are tired to death of them,' Mrs. Lemon assured her. 'Now what I want to know –'

'O Mrs. Arden,' cut in Mrs. Biscuit, 'is this Herbie? What a *darling*! And *how* like Mr. Arden. The eyes, you know – and the chin. *All* the lower part of the face.'

'No, that's Teddy, the one at Heidelberg, you know. Herbie is up in my room, the best one of him. I take them up there by turns – isn't it silly of me?' appealed Mrs. Arden. 'Poor Tedlums has had such a setback with laryngitis, just as his examinations were coming on too – we don't know how he'll manage, poor darling. He's got my throat, I'm afraid. If only he were as strong as Herbie! *Cleverer* than Herbie he certainly is. Such a contrast, the two boys! Herbie writing of nothing but games, and you wouldn't *believe* the spelling for fifteen. I don't know where he gets that, for both his father and I can *spell*. But after all, as it's to be the Army, it doesn't really matter, does it!'

'Not a bit,' said Mrs. Lemon heartily. 'I wouldn't trust the General *now* without a dictionary. But what I want to know –'

'It *is* a clever face,' agreed Mrs. Biscuit, 'such a splendid brow.'

'That's music, isn't it? We really have *serious* hopes of Teddy's music. As a little, little fellow he would be so rapt and carried away when anybody played – I was often quite frightened. It wasn't normal, you know; it wasn't really. He used to run round the room on his little bare legs, if people talked, saying "Sh! sh!" with his little fat finger up – I can see him now. And such a command of English as he has already. I *must* just read you his last letter –'

'To-morrow,' said Mrs. Lemon authoritatively, 'To-morrow, when I come about the paper roses, dear. Now, what I want to know –'

'Oh!' exclaimed Mrs. Biscuit, approaching with a volume. '*Has* anybody read the other one by this person – Mrs. *Pilkington and the Trinity*? Such a brilliant book! The heroine is engaged to three men at once, and keeps them all going – oh, it *is* brilliantly written! Makes the same appointment with each of them to go off with him in a motor, and they all three meet, and she in the meantime has gone and quietly married a *fourth* man – the one she has really cared for all the time. It's far the cleverest of hers.'

'We must put it down at the club library,' said Mrs. Arden. 'I hadn't even heard of it. How dreadfully one gets out of –'

'Touch in India,' nodded Mrs. Lemon, who had been containing herself with difficulty. 'But what I *must* know is – what *are* you paying for a saddle of mutton? My cook coolly bills me ten rupees for every one we have; and when I object he says the Commissioner's lady-sahib pays fifteen! "Go along with you!" I tell him, "the General-sahib doesn't get half as much pay as the Commissioner-sahib. How can I afford this?" But he makes no end of a fuss. Now *do* you?'

Mrs. Arden took the impeachment with a half-flattered smile.

'Truly, truly, only for the very big ones,' she playfully defended herself.

'But it's monstrous,'cried little Mrs. Lamb, who had pulled a chair in. 'One never pays more than two rupees for the best loin; and a saddle –'

'Oh, I wish there were a *definite* price for mutton,' sighed Mrs. Biscuit, sinking into the circle.

'And a saddle is only –' Mrs. Lamb tried again, but they were all caught up by Mrs. Lemon.

'Well, I've had *this* experience to profit by. There are the Wickhams. Mrs. Wickham gives you the best mutton I know, and the best saddles – and you know what a D.S.P. gets. "Lousia Wickham," I said, "when we were on your pay I never *saw* a saddle. How do you manage it?" And I told her what I'm telling you. "My dear," she said, "it's simple *robbery*. All I ask you to do is to go one day to the market yourself – I'll take you – and we'll get the best saddle in Pilaghur for seven-eight." Well, I suppose I was lazy, but we never went, and my man kept straight on with his ten rupees and the tears in his eyes if I said a word. Him and his tears! He got ill last week, and Louie Wickham sent me her cook for my dinner-party on Wednesday. You were there. Now I ask you, did you ever taste better mutton? Seven rupees was the bill next day, my dear – just seven rupees.'

'I *never* pay more than two rupees for a loin,' repeated Mrs. Lamb courageously, 'and a saddle is–'

'But what are you to do when he threatens to leave?' demanded Mrs. Lemon, subsiding on her triumph, and settling with complacency the bracelets on one fat arm.

'It does seem extortionate. But their ideas of extortion are so different from ours, aren't they?' said Mrs. Arden, rising to welcome the advent of the gentlemen.

'And a saddle,' produced Mrs. Lamb at last to nobody, a little disappointed, 'is only two loins.'

CHAPTER VI

'WE don't find Anthony's letters nearly so interesting as they were,' complained Lavinia Thame to her friend and half-cousin. The two sat behind the glass of Lady Thame's motor-brougham, on its rapid and resistless way from the Albert Hall to the Aganippe Club, where Mrs. Tring was to give them tea. Lady Thame was ever in the forefront of progress. She had been among the first to abandon the horse, with the half-formed expectation of living to see his extinction. Her traction-vehicles had the latest improvements, the most expensive gear, and the most remarkable appearance, and were generously employed in calling to inquire for the victims of the accidents they occasioned.

'They're not, really,' repeated Lavinia.

'I find them more so,' Victoria told her.

'You are so keen about his tiresome problems. Mother is too, in a way, and she says we ought to be. But I loved his impressions so, in the beginning, and all the state and pageantry and guns and salaams, and those delicious native princes hung with emeralds, and the things they said.'

'So did I,' said Miss Tring, 'but after all they are only the trappings of the situation, aren't they? The best letter I've had lately – about his Afghan frontier policy – might have been written by one of his under-secretaries, for all the purple and gold there was in it. Don't you think he soon began to be bored by it – that sort of thing?'

'I shouldn't have been bored,' sighed Lavinia, 'if only I had been allowed to go out. But mother's very annoyed at the line Anthony has taken with the Amir, Victoria. She says he assumed the Viceroyalty with the most definite principles, and now he seems to think of nothing but making the map of Asia redder. Do you know, I sometimes think *she* will go out.'

'Oh,' cried Victoria, with a delighted laugh, 'I *wish* she would.'

'She says she doesn't see how he can possibly publish his *Real Empire* now, in the face of his frontier policies and things – so you'll have your way about that – and she's sorry he went. Victoria, how far *are* you responsible?'

'I?' Miss Tring exclaimed. 'Not a hair's breadth or a feather's weight! Do you think anybody is responsible for anything Anthony Thame does except Anthony Thame himself? Seven times no. India is responsible. Who could rule India for three years and talk about empires of the plough?'

Lavinia looked at her penetratingly. 'I believe if you *could* influence him a little you would like him better, Victoria,' she said, but Victoria, unassailed, sent a calm glance through the glass in front of her into the riven street. 'I like him as much as ever,'she said, 'and I admire him more – that cab was as nearly as possible over. Oh – Lavinia –'

Miss Thame changed colour and looked at her with prescience. A new thing had been conveyed in her cousin's note, with abrupt transition and greater seriousness. 'You have heard – something?' asked Lavinia. Her tone, too, had changed, and the long gloved hand on her knee stiffened.

'I hardly like to tell anybody – even you. There have been so many false hopes. But even a false hope, while it lasts, is better than none.'

'Oh yes.'

'And there does seem to be, this time, a clue. In San Francisco. Mother was right, you see, in her certainty that he had gone to the States. I always thought South Africa and the mines. Do you remember how he used to talk about wanting to sink down, down through all the physical processes that had built him a soul? I thought he would do that in the mines. I used to see him down there in the dark, at the nadir of what was so beautiful in him, and I used to plan the way to bring him back again to the zenith – and if ever his wonderful book came I thought perhaps I could forgive the price of it. Well, it seems I was wrong.'

'Oh, Victoria, I'm glad you were wrong. I know he had sometimes dreadful ideas – or in anybody else they would have been dreadful. He made them harmless somehow, with his charm. Is he,' Lavinia hastened, 'is he *known* to be in San Francisco?'

'Oh, don't make too much of it – don't believe in it all at once, Lavinia, or – or you'll break my heart. It's only this. Three nights ago, after one of mother's meetings at Chiswick, a man came up to her and asked her if she were any relation to H. V. Tring whom he had lately met in San Francisco.'

'Victoria!'

'Mother rushed him into a cab and tore home with him, and when I came in from the Geidts's dance there they were in the dining-room with the siphon on the table and things to eat. I said at once, "You have brought news of my brother" – there was no other way of accounting for him – and then he began all over again to me.'

'Go on, quick – we are nearly there,' said Lavinia.

'His name is Kelly, and he's over here on some Irish-American business – he made a secret of that, but one can imagine the sort of thing. There is no doubt about his having seen Herbert – and in the ghastliest low lodgings. He said he got to know him quite well – that creature – and that Herbert told him he was going to have one more shot at life, was putting all he had on a last throw – the Yukon! Kelly says he saw his kit and tried to persuade him not to go. "You're in no shape for the Yukon," he says he told him, and offered to get him a place – he apologised for it to mother – as something in a hotel instead. But Herbert wouldn't listen, and left by the next steamer for Dawson City.'

Lavinia drew a long breath. 'Then he is there now,' she said. 'He must be there, because it isn't easy to get away.'

'He is there now – with the winter coming on. This Kelly told us such things of the winter! Without money – kicked about by stronger men in some frozen camp – making his last throw.'

'Couldn't he – be got home?' Lavinia faltered.

'Yes, he *could*. Kelly says he would undertake to find him. It seems he took a great fancy to Herbert – you know how he *did* attach people.'

'Yes, I know,' said poor Lavinia.

'But of course it would cost. Kelly is extraordinarily kind. He says he would go for little more than his expenses, and would pay his own way from here to New York, but beyond that – well, how could he?'

'Of course he couldn't.'

'And their expenses, his and Herbert's together, could not, he says, be less than five hundred pounds. Mother met that Alaskan traveller, Brandt, last night and pumped him, and he said he thought it a low estimate, so there is no reason to suspect Kelly of trying to make money out of it.'

'Then how soon does Aunt Deirdre hope to get him off?'

'How soon? I am ashamed to tell you – mother *doesn't see her way*. It wouldn't be easy, but she could if she liked, and she won't. Isn't it incredible? Lavinia, I don't understand mother. She was tremendously excited that night; but by the next day she was certain that Herbert was running a newspaper in Dawson City. In a week she will be quite happy about him. Kelly just looks at her.'

'But she hasn't sent him away altogether – Kelly?'

'On the contrary – she is hugely interested in him. He comes every day and they talk *and talk*. She says she is getting for the first time a conception of the Celt under republican institutions. I hope she will find it valuable. I've written and telegraphed, on the chance, to the Emigration Office out there, but Kelly holds out no hope of reaching him that way. And here is the man who will give the time – and mother simply won't pay. I can get, one way and another, two hundred. Those Cousin Mary Thame Trust Fund dividends of mine are just due, and there are one or two things I can sell; but Kelly says he wouldn't cheat us by attempting it on less than five. He's no fraud, you know – he showed us letters from Herbert, one borrowing twenty pounds and another acknowledging it. Mother will pay *that*, thank heaven.

The motor halted, trembling, behind a policeman's hand, and in the motionless carriage, with the tides of Piccadilly checked and fretting outside, Lavinia Thame encountered one of those decisive moments that come to us all and seem to hold so much for each of us. She took it in silence, appearing to consider only the impassive rear of the liveried servant on the other side of the glass, all that was between her and the void, between a well-brought-up young Englishwoman and plunging initiative.

'Victoria,' she said, and drew herself a little further into her own corner, 'I get about five times as much from that Trust as you do. If I made up the amount, would anybody have to know?'

Victoria caught at her hand. 'You dear old Lavinia,' she cried, and stared with tears in her eyes and compunction in her voice. 'Herbert would never forgive me.'

Lavinia drew away her hand. 'Don't you think he would?'

'At least – I don't know. Oh, I don't care, Lavinia, do. I'll arrange it secretly with Kelly, any way you like, and if ever I can pay it back I will, or Herbert will –'

'Oh no!'

'And I won't pretend to be anything but more glad and grateful than I've ever been before in my life. Lavinia, would you like me to kiss you?'

'No, not now. You see, if Aunt Deirdre knew she might think it something like a criticism –'

'Oh yes.'

'Otherwise there is no reason in the world why any relative, even a half-cousin, shouldn't –'

'No reason in the world, darling Lavinia,' said the other happy girl, 'but not a soul shall know. I'll simply refuse to tell mother how I can do it.'

The harassed hall-porter was expecting them in the office, the shabby little page with the bulbous forehead was expecting them on the stair, the patient head-parlourmaid with the pencil was expecting them at the drawing-room door. Mrs. Tring in the Aganippe Club was at the very centre of her sphere of influence; her visitors were expected by everybody. She herself was there before them, presiding, at one end of the crowded room, over three little tables that subserved the convenience of her party, she and Lady Thame, and Alfred Earle, editor of the *Prospect*, and Frayley Sambourne, Parliamentary Under-Secretary for India, whom people still called young Frayley Sambourne because of a distinguished uncle who had retired and an unquenchable self-confidence which threatened never to mature. The men were conspicuous, as they are beginning to be almost everywhere in England; the room was full of the sight and scent and sound of women. Here and there another man sat carefully, conscious and furtive, and assiduously ministered to, but there were not many. Tea was in great demand. Table-maids hastened from group to group bearing trays, both they and the trays charged with the importance of a function. Here and there a maid hovered, and a lady member pulled out her purse to pay, when her male guest, if she had one, tried elaborately to look the other way.

Mrs. Tring, in somewhat loosely-connected black, looked haggard and happy. Her eyes had the heavy lines under them that London draws, but shone with – well, everything that was in the evening papers. Her vague black hat had vague black strings which knotted somewhere on her opulent bosom. Under it her fair hair seemed to reach out, in its own way, for some truth to cling to. A sort of long light wrap lay upon the chair behind her, with the air of a discarded theory which she might want again, and as the two young ladies joined her she was in the act of entreating Mr. Earle for the third time to say whether he took sugar.

Lady Thame had the word. 'I never could endure coalitions,' she said. 'Never. Nothing can come of them but compromise – blurred principle and weakened vitality. Here are we again in office, we Liberals, not because the kingdom believes in us and sets us there, but because two or three dozen of *you* – and very right, too, as far as that goes – couldn't stand a new departure in economics.'

'Mahomet,' said Mr. Frayley Sambourne, crossing his arms, 'had to come to the mountain, Lady Thame. There was no other way.'

'But what I complain of,' continued Lady Thame, waving her toasted muffin, 'is that we pay altogether too long a price for you. Count it up. Labour legislation marking time, technical education paralysed, Chinese slavery –'

'*Fine*, mother!' exclaimed Lavinia. 'We have been obliged to do it,' she explained to the rest as Lady Thame mechanically produced a shilling, 'about that particular expression, and mother consents, because she is trying to learn a new one. The money goes to the Society for Befriending Indigent Aliens.'

'Quite true,' said Lady Thame. 'The expression has become hackneyed, banal, but, Lavinia — what was the new one? However, never mind. Chinese slavery —'

There was a shout of merriment, and Mr. Earle said, 'Have three for half-a-crown, Lady Thame?'

'Drop the phrase, dear lady, at all costs,' advised Mr. Sambourne. 'There never was any slavery, and now there are no Chinese. They have become the only unimpeachably loyal section of the South Africans.'

'Mr. Sambourne,' retorted Lady Thame, 'you may befool the British public with that sort of thing, but you cannot — believe me, you cannot — befool me. Nor is that all. Leave South Africa to her blasted fortunes. Leave the Britannia Beer Trust to the hands that did not destroy it — and look abroad. What is our attitude in China? Aggressive. What is our attitude in Egypt? Aggressive. What is our attitude on the Red Sea littoral? Highly aggressive. That is what Liberal principles have come to — in coalition. I say it's a great deal to pay, even to save free trade for another five years.'

'On the contrary, dear Lady Thame,' said Frayley Sambourne musingly, with his hands thrust deep in his pockets as if to meet her attack with all his personal concentration, 'our attitude in the directions you have named is so painfully weak that if anything could tempt me back to my allegiance — if I were not convinced,' he said, smiling engagingly, 'that the weight of Empire should not be lightly shifted from one shoulder to the other —'

'Not a bit of it! We shouldn't lose you,' Lady Thame assured him cheerfully.

'I believe that to be as you put it,' said Alfred Earle, with his mordant modesty, addressing Sambourne. 'But Craybrooke hasn't bluffed at all badly. He seems to have quite given the country the notion that Liberal and Imperial are not spelled so very differently.

And in India,' he said, looking with deference at a Viceroy's mother, 'there is, of course, something to point to.'

'Ah, in India,' sighed Lady Thame, 'you have indeed something to answer for. At least, I hope it will not all be put down to the account of my poor son. I do not see, on his return, how he is to recognise his own convictions. But I shall show them to him,' she added firmly. 'Never did I dream that his would be the hand to lay the yoke upon an independent people. I hope it may be long before I meet a Shan Chief at a London dinner-table. I would blush to look him in the face.'

'Please,' protested Frayley Sambourne, 'don't depreciate Lord Thame's consolidation policy in Upper Burma. It's the golden apple of his administration, Lady Thame. He is doing splendid service out there – splendid service. We are most indebted to him – as Earle says, he gives us something tangible to point to. And he has done it at a very small cost.'

'In blood and treasure,' Lady Thame returned weightily, 'they say it is small. But in principle – did you see how one of the Paris reviews described his departures this month? *"Les éclatantes tentatives,"* it said, *"les éclatantes tentatives de Lord Thame."* I marked it and sent it out. "Would your grandfather be flattered?" I wrote on the margin.'

'There is nothing,' Mr. Earle remarked gently, 'like the administration of other people's affairs to make an Englishman recognise his mission in the world. Give the most radical of our politicians a dependency to take care of, and he at once fulfils the law of his being, forgets all principle, and glorifies the God who made him. I wish there were enough dependencies to go round. It would help to bring on the reign of candour, which is coming in any case by force of circumstances. With our colonies dropping like ripe plums into other people's baskets, we become once more a point in the North Sea; we recognise once more that we are what we can conquer. We return to the purely predatory, and continue to salve our consciences by giving our lives to administer the trust we have taken.'

'There is still the empire of the race,' put in Victoria. It had not altogether an original sound; and Lady Thame looked sharply at her.

'Which is not the empire of England,' Earle returned; and she said, 'No – I've always said so.'

Mrs. Tring came out of her colloquy with Lavinia, summoned by the fragment of a phrase. '"What we can conquer,"' she repeated dreamily. 'The sword is the true arbiter; by the sword we question destiny and hardily invite chance. The sword is our proof and our warrant, and the extension, so to speak, of our personality. Maeterlinck has created – rather has disclosed – quite new truth about the sword. And who can escape truth? Not, I hope, the Liberal party. In the end do not the seers dictate to the politicians?' Mrs. Tring appeared to ask the teapot. She would seldom, in her rapter moments, encounter the human eye. 'Feel no alarm, Pamela, about Anthony's principles. He only bends, with his party, before the advance of a wind of revelation.'

'I wish it would blow a little harder,' said Frayley Sambourne with the admiration he always expressed for Mrs. Tring. 'I haven't heard your seer quoted in Council yet, dear lady.' He threw all his common-sense, as it were, at her feet, and invited her to trample on it.

'Ah, well,' she replied, 'you may yet. And now, if nobody will have another cup, I think we could find a corner in the smoking-room. You won't mind, Pamela?'

'I won't smoke,' said Lady Thame decidedly. 'You can't teach an old dog new tricks. But I don't in the least mind watching you perform.'

'I think,' said Lavinia, rising into a blush, 'that if Victoria doesn't mind sacrificing her cigarette, we were – weren't we, Victoria, going on together?'

'I hope you didn't mind my dragging you away,' she said to Victoria as they descended the stairs together. 'I do want to hear so much more about that fascinating Kelly.'

CHAPTER VII

HIRIA, Miss Pearce's ayah, was in her way a woman of the world. She did her best within her scope and had a shrug for fate. She was a mistress of 'bundobust' – arrangement, bargain, working plan – hers was the genius of bundobust. She had a capable hand, a good heart, and a shrewd tongue, her own place in her own community, definite and unquestioned. There are states of life in which respectability is not only a virtue but a distinction. Hiria extracted every satisfaction from being respectable; you could see that by the way she folded her arms. She accepted the world at par, with its customs, its chances, and its wonders; she was a Ghoomati sweeper's wife with four silver rings on her toes, but she took life more importantly than many people from whom it would seem to demand greater attention.

Hiria was in the verandah, by the yellow plaster pillar drooping with its purple bougainvilliers, waiting for her mistress. Miss Pearce was late, and Hiria's arms were folded over matter for communication. She shifted from one foot to the other and stood on the very edge of the verandah, keeping an expectant eye upon the drive; the crisp morning shadows of the creeper, dancing over her, accented her impatience. The miss-sahib had as a rule returned from the hospital to breakfast before this. At last, at the bend of the road under the tamarinds, the dogcart appeared, Miss Pearce driving as usual, the syce as usual behind holding the umbrella over her, and beside her the long, free trot of a big waler and the Chief Commissioner riding, which Hiria marked also as being at least not unusual.

Mr. Arden rode on as Ruth turned in at the entrance; but in a pace or so the waler dropped into a walk, stretched his neck, and took the road contemplatively. Miss Pearce's little country-bred, too, came in a checked and thoughtful manner up the drive. His mistress twisted the reins round the whip-handle and jumped out as automatically as the syce came to the pony's head and led it away. She passed Hiria without seeming to see her, unbuttoning her gloves, without seeming either to hear her, though when the ayah said that the bath was ready she replied, 'Is it, Hiria?' showing that she did. Hiria followed dissatisfied, reflecting. 'She comes always thus, walking in her sleep, from talk with the Burra Sahib.' But she deferred to the accustomed fact, and glanced more than once at the grey eyes that regarded themselves with such disconcerting detachment in the glass, as she stood brushing her mistress's hair, before she ventured to cross that strong inward current. Then she began. She spoke in the vernacular, but loved the vanity of an occasional word of English.

'That Gunga Dass has been here again this morning, miss-sahib. It is the wife this time. "O ayah-ji,"' she whined in imitation, bringing both hands to her forehead, '"implore the doctor miss-sahib to come quickly. She is tormented with a pain all across the body." "Ah!" I said, "she hath been eating too many mangoes" — she is but fourteen, miss-sahib — "but I will give the word." That Gunga Dass would write nothing on the slate, though I told him that your honour, being taught by a pundit, could read the Urdu. "It is always cheaper," he said, "not to write." And that is true talk but shameful, for Gunga Dass has half a lakh and seven houses in the bazaar. Yet has he never paid we-folk for the curing of his mother of the rheumitation last year — and she walks now as straight as a Brahminy cow — and it appears to me that neither will he pay now for his wife. If she die he can get another.'

Ruth smiled, but the smile seemed only half connected with the philosophy of Gunga Dass. 'I will go this afternoon,' she said. 'How do you know, foolish one, whether he has paid or not?'

'I know Gunga Dass, that he never pays. And as to the wife there is no urgency,' Hiria told her cheerfully. 'I myself told him of the castor-oil. "If after that she still cries," I said, "you can come again to-morrow."'

'Hiria,' said her mistress sternly, 'twenty times I have told you you are not to give *any* advice —'

'Na-*ee*, miss-sahib,' wheedled the ayah. 'I spoke but of the castor-oil, which the babies, tiny butchas, drink without harm. And that,' she added self-respectfully, 'I knew of before I came to be with your honour. And,' she went on with increasing self-justification, 'Gopal, syce, who coughs, begged again yesterday for the remaining half-bottle with which we cured my sister's husband of the pain in the back; but I told him there was no order for pains in the

chest, and did not give it him. Besides, who knows how soon I myself may have a pain in the back?' Then, with a sudden lively interest, she broke off. 'Your honour came to-day by the Larrens road?'

'No, by the Dalhousie road, Hiria.'

'Then miss-sahib did not see the taking of the white soldier by
the Larrens road. By that road they took him, and all Pilaghur ran to
see. I also, returning from the washerman – he is now three days
late with your honour's muslin dress with the chicken-work, and it
was necessary to give abuse – I also saw. This way they fastened
him,' Hiria dropped the brush and crossed her hands behind her,
'tight with iron – what name? – padlocks, and here, and here,' she
touched her ankles. Her eyes sparkled. She stood trenchantly, with
her sari over her head, for law and order.

'Go on brushing, Hiria. Some *golmal* in the bazaar, I suppose.'

'*Great* golmal, miss-sahib!' attested the ayah, with a half-tone of
indignation. 'Two persons dead! And cannot be taken to the burning-ghat until the magistrate-sahib gives the order. And the door
now locked, till when the doctor-sahib makes *re*-port, and the police-wallah giving no entrance. *Burra* golmal, miss-sahib!'

'That is very bad news, ayah. Are you sure it is true?'

'With my own eyes I have seen it, miss-sahib. The house locked
– in the beginning of the mustard fields it is, beyond the Lall Bazar
– and the syce holding the horse of Dr. Murray-sahib – and the soldier also.'

'Dr. Murray. Yes, of course. Well, it is a bad business, Hiria.'

The ayah glanced dissatisfied at the face in the glass, was silent a
moment, and tried again.

'How shameful it is, miss-sahib, when these things are because of
a woman.' The manœuvre succeeded; Ruth turned her mind to her
maid.

'Without doubt there is often a woman, Hiria. Have the police
taken her, too?'

'She is dead, miss-sahib! Your honour knows nothing of it?
None had brought the news to the hospital? Thus it was. The police-wallah who forbids the entrance – *now* he is walking up and
down by the door! – the wife of that police-wallah last year was
about to die. Gurdit Singh. There was a coming-one, miss-sahib,

and he ran for me weeping. At first I said "No, no," for every one has great fear of a policeman's house; and then Gurdit Singh came again at night with a lantern and howled like a dog, "Come, ayah-ji, for the sake of God," and I went and gave help; and it was a boy-baba, miss-sahib. And because of that he has told me all. The house was the house of Gobind, watchman. The miss-sahib knows the Delhi-an'-London Bank? By the Cat'lik Church? There was the service of Gobind. Walking up and down in the manner of chowkidars, and making a noise, to frighten thieves. Twice in the day, from little morning till eleven, and from five in the afternoon till eleven. For ten years gone Gobind did this service, and no thieves came — *to the bank.*'

Hiria paused significantly, and her mistress said, 'Ah! But I know that old fellow. Haven't we doctored him, Hiria, you and I, for his elephant leg?'

'Three times, miss-sahib! And God knows why we could do him no good. But what an excellent woman was the first wife of Go-bind! How clever with the spinning and the cooking, and how in-structed she was — like your honour! — in medicines and the stop-ping of blood. She could sew also like a dhurzie, though she had but one eye. But she died, poor t'ing, and Gobind made another marriage. Hoh, huh! This one — the day she was born they came for me. What a smart pritty little g'el! What luvely aiyes! And what a quick-learning one of songs and nautch! So Gobind took that one — Junia. Oh, many days since, miss-sahib. Three children she found, one d'otta, two son. All died but the littlest. *Acchcha*. Then the mother of Gobind died, perhaps five months gone. After that Go-bind had no content. Coming after work, found no good food. What bad meal cakes — t'ick, like leather,' Hiria pulled at an imagi-nary one with hands and teeth. 'And the wife eating sweetmeats in bed. That Gobind had not the strong heart and wept, and said, "Why you don' make my food?" Then that Junia roll in the bed,' Hiria twisted her body expressively, 'and said, "I make good anuff; make yourself."'

'Don't stop brushing, Hiria. Well?'

'Miss-sahib, I found five d'otta, and to all, when they burnt the chupatties, I gave smack-smack. Thus they learned crying, but now their husbands are not thin.'

'Then the talk began about the gorah – the soldier. Not being purdah-'ooman, that day Junia went to the street-stand to bring water for the house; but three soldier men had come before to drink at the stand. Everybody saw she did not go back to her house. Back she went not. Like this she pulled her sari.' Hiria exposed one eye, into which, middle-aged woman as she was, she put coquetry. '"*Dado!*" she said, and held out her dish – impudent! – and they laughed much and gave it full; and when they came behind she ran and shut the door. All this everybody saw, and one told Gobind. "Well," he said, "did she not do well to shut the door? It is because she is pretty," he said. "They desire to find harm of her." He would hear nothing, miss-sahib.

'But everybody was then looking to his house, for the three soldiers to come again. Only one came, miss-sahib. Only one, up and down walking, looking this way, that way –'

'What a long story, Hiria. Do get on. Who was murdered?'

'Yes, miss-sahib, I telling. So he saw what time Gobind came, and what time went. Then, in the time of the second watch of Gobind, he came. The cunning one, miss-sahib! That time everybody cooking food. Nobody to see but the leper-woman at the corner of Krishna Ghat-lane – your honour knows that no-fingered one? Twice a year the Dipty-Commissioner-sahib gives the order to send her away, but always she comes back there. "*Give one pice! Give one pice.*"' Hiria spread out imaginarily mutilated hands whining, but quickly grasped the brush again.

'*Acchcha.* She found profit, sometimes two annas, sometimes four annas, miss-sahib! Always he paid her something not to see. She is very sorry for the *golmal*, that one.'

'He could not come often without being seen by others, Hiria.'

'Many times, miss-sahib! But the last time – they are digging by the house of Gobind for the new water-pipes, and the ground is all oolta-poolta there – coming out, he *lit a match*. Which was a foolish thing,' she philosophised, 'but doubtless, being a white soldier, at that hour he was drunk. *Ari!* Three people saw, and one was the son of Gobind by the other wife, and ran to him next day with the shame. Before, only friend-people and caste-brothers had spoken, and Gobind would hear nothing; but his son he heard. But he was an old man, miss-sahib, and not iss-strong, so he said, "What to do?" But the son is iss-strong. So Gobind made excuse of fever at the bank, and together they went at the hour to his house, Gobind greatly fearing. And the soldier was gone. "I told you," Gobind said, "it was lies." But Surat was looking here, looking there, on the ground. "This thing, what is it?" he said. A *cheroot* it was, miss-sahib, not yet cold! How frightened then was that one, saying the dog had brought it in!'

'Then Gobind killed her?'

'Na, miss-sahib. Gobind was afraid for the hanging. Always now Government gives the hanging for killing the unfaithful ones. But Gobind said, "On this account she shall have a little trouble as the custom is," and he and Surat tied her in the bed and cut off her nose. It is the smallest punishment, but Gobind had a good heart. There are already two noseless in the bazaar, miss-sahib, and one is married again. But without the nose-ring, who can marry?' and Hiria chuckled once more at the familiar query.

'Then, Gobind being frightened, they went away, taking the *butcha*. But next day Gobind said he would go back and make her food, so he went, having done no work that day because of grief. *Acchcha*, he is sitting there weeping, *and the soldier comes back!* Thus he comes,' Hiria made a swaggering, familiar stride. 'And inside what has been! *Ari!* He sees the noseless one, and in one breath – what fear, miss-sahib, in such a thing – quick he takes off his gun and shoots Gobind! How angry are the gorahs when they are angry!'

'No, Hiria, that is not possible. He would not have his gun in the bazaar.'

'True talk, miss-sahib; but he came from shooting in the jungle! Have they not the order to shoot in the jungle, those soldier people?'

'Well – and then?'

'*Acchcha*. And hearing the noise, then comes Surat running and three others, and they make a great fight in the house, and they try to hold the soldier. But how hold these strong ones, miss-sahib? *"Dam soor!"* he said, and tore them like leaves, swearing very bad in English. Also he shot Bundoo in the shoulder, but perhaps he does not die. Surat only took no harm. And Surat is the cunning one, miss-sahib. It appears to him that soldier will get away quick, and he has only a chuckoo. So very quick he cuts the belt of the gorah, miss-sahib, thinking he will have something. This Surat did not know, but inside is the lumbra, that marks all the gorah-log –'

'His equipment number – yes.'

'And runs like a dog to his house. But what a golmal, miss-sahib! And that Junia also dead – from fright. Nobody can look on them, it is said. Three days they are lying there, and half the head of Go-bind is gone –'

'Three days? But why were the police not told at once?'

'God knows, your honour. Who tells anything to the police before it is necessary? Already do they not know too much? But in three days Surat found courage, and went with the others to the magistrate-sahib and told all. Then the magistrate-sahib sent the order and all was as I have said. It is a pity your honour did not come by the Larrens road.

'*Ari!* miss-sahib, how they work evil and *nutkuttie*, the gorah people! Yet I was sorry, too. The driving of the white man like an ox is not a good sight. And it is said in the bazaar that the punishment of this one will be heavy, because the Burra Lat is the enemy of all gorah-log who work evil, though they be of his own village even. And Surat was the cunning one to cut the coat lumbra!'

CHAPTER VIII

HIRIA had the substantial truth. There had been the murder of a man and the death of a woman, both natives, and suspicion pointed strongly to a British private soldier as the author. Evil and wrong were plain, inflicted on a helpless and subject household by one of a particularly obnoxious caste of the ruling race. One more had been added to the long series of offences which seemed the inevitable accidents of British prestige. The thing had happened, moreover, at a time which might have been thought critical. Government, in the hardly disguised person and by the hardly disguised hand of Lord Thame, had been taking stern cognisance and vigorous initiative towards this class of cases, thus raising them, in a manner, out of the plane of common criminality to more conspicuous reprobation and wider publicity. The official attitude had not been taken and held without criticism, and public sentiment was still hot and sore. The Storey case, where a tea-planter had used his revolver upon rioting coolies; the White case, in which a young merchant of Calcutta had kicked a punkha-puller with a diseased spleen, and the man dropped dead; the Mir Bux case of a native forest-ranger, damaged so that he died, by a shooting party of three soldiers to whom he had forbidden certain tracts, were fresh in the minds of all Englishmen, and it might be supposed of all natives too, since the vernacular press rang even louder with the claims of equality than the Anglo-Indian newspapers with other considerations in each instance.

Pilaghur, for these reasons, might be imagined in a state of high excitement over the stain upon her skirts, indignant and inflamed. It might be supposed a subject of vivid concern in both Pilaghurs. Perhaps it did make a day's matter in the bazaar and in the quarters. Little caste-companies of servants talked it over as they ate together: one or two gossiping women, like Hiria, carried the tale. They deplored the murder in the conventional way; but the thing that touched their imaginations was the taking of the soldier by European constables and a regimental escort. The crime was quickly accepted and passed into the book of fate, the women lingering to point the end of an erring sister; but the spectacle of the 'gorah' in handcuffs, submissive to the law – that was a tamasha – they all wished they had seen that. And presently the talk was of pice again, and the price of meal.

In wealthy and instructed Pilaghur, among the grain merchants and the jewel merchants, and the pleaders and the clerks, the event had hardly more than the importance of its victims, for the moment. A night-watchman had let his wife get into trouble of a very disgraceful kind, and they had both lost their lives over it – such people dwelt remoter from Ganeshi Lal in his balconied upper story over the grain shop than they did from the Chief Commissioner himself, to whom, indeed, their affairs were of painful and critical interest. Ganeshi Lal commented with a perfunctory headshake upon the laxity in social customs that had crept in among the common people, and drew his own shutters closer; and so by him the matter was dismissed – for the moment. Later on it might attract his more excited attention. A touchstone for inter-racial justice is one thing, a mere crime is another, and Ganeshi Lal found, at present, no need to rouse himself.

In Pilaghur of cantonments the affair, of course, had its official weight. It was talked of with irritation at the Barfordshires' mess, where 'the old man,' who was absent, was said to be in a poisonous temper about it. Little Tighe-Pender, the adjutant, with his yellow moustache much pulled down at the corners, said it would probably cost him his job, which, in view of the loss of two polo ponies within a month, would be damned inconvenient. Major Devine, who was always fussing about the regiment, remarked that one thing was certain – it meant the stoppage of shooting-passes for the whole cold weather, an infernal shame; he had never known the men so keen. Captain Kemp said, 'Don't be in such a hurry; the thing isn't proved yet.'

'No,' said Devine gloomily, 'it isn't, and maybe it won't be, but we don't wait for anything so silly as proof nowadays. Suspicion's all they want in Simla. Dead rats that don't explain near a bazaar mean plague in the bazaar, and dead natives that don't explain near a regiment mean murder in the regiment, whatever the courts say. I'll bet you fifty dibs the passes are stopped.'

From which the conversation slipped naturally round to the afternoon's polo.

The affair was reported promptly, according to regulations, to the Chief Commissioner, the General Commanding, and the divisional officers. Beyond that it travelled to the Adjutant-General for India and to the Military Secretary to the Viceroy, but we need not follow it at present further than Pilaghur. Eliot Arden received it with heavy concern, but it came in the catalogue of the day's business. He put it in the back of his mind, and did not take it out after office hours. Charles Cox, a young assistant-magistrate, newly arrived from England, whom the country still appealed to and the mosquitoes still bit, drove to the club full of the scandal, but found a languid interest in it; though somebody did say that Vetchley would probably get it hot for not keeping his men in better order, and somebody else suggested a rock in the Red Sea as the probable luck of the regiment. Cox was amazed at the apathy he encountered, and wrote a letter to Oxford that night full of dismayed criticism of the service he had joined. Pilaghur had no newspaper, and it was quite three days before the matter was reported in the public press. Then Cox saw it in a Calcutta journal, under the heading, 'Unfortunate Occurrence at Pilaghur.' Naturally he cut it out, and sent it, with sarcastic comments, to Oxford. Ten years hence Cox will be deploring the necessity of such things getting into the papers at all, and inclined to the conviction that it would much conduce to the good government of India if there were no papers. This will be the work of time, promotion, and responsibility. Meanwhile he may be left to his indignation, which he will enjoy about as long as the mosquitoes enjoy him.

CHAPTER IX

THE Lenoxes were not at Mrs. Lemon's garden-party, which took place, indeed, on the very day on which Mr. Lawrence Lenox became temporarily the Honourable Mr. Justice Lenox, and took his seat upon the bench of the Calcutta High Court. One of their lordships had been invalided home, and the District and Sessions Judge of Ghoom had been selected to fill the acting appointment. It was promotion, but not more distinguished promotion than had always been predicted for Lawrence Lenox. He was one of those who climb with every capacity they possess; his very moral faculties seemed to have been given him to assist him to mount. He owed his post in Pilaghur to the great discretion and ability with which he had handled a case in which Government had prosecuted for corrupt practices; but nature had long before that selected him for preferment in any line along which he saw the chance of it. People said of him, contemplating his unfaltering steps upwards, that he would be a Chief Judge before he was forty-five; he was already, at forty, well on the way to it. They observed Lawrence Lenox without malice, as they would a public event; he excited little feeling of any kind among his contemporaries. The fulfilment of manifest destiny does attract, sometimes, this philosophic regard. Even regret at his departure from Pilaghur, where he certainly gave excellent dinners, was obscured by its inevitableness. Some time or other such men must go.

Sir Ahmed Hossein had succeeded Mr. Lenox as District and Sessions Judge, and he was at Mrs. Lemon's party. He was a Mahomedan civilian, differing, necessarily, in complexion and creed from the rest of official Pilaghur; and he brought with him a social interrogation. His official status was clear, but how far he would expect its recognition was not. Social India is nowhere yet upon Arcadian terms with native gentlemen, however Government may have decked them in the *Gazette*. The crucial question, when Pilaghur heard, with a somewhat fallen countenance, that it was to have a Mahomedan District Judge, was, 'Is there a Lady Ahmed Hossein?' Mrs. Lemon laid down the law.

'The General says,' said she, 'that if there's a Lady Hossein and he lets her go out to dinner, well and good, we will ask them and dine with them. But if he keeps her behind the purdah, I am neither to invite them to our house nor will the General let me set foot in theirs – Judge or no Judge.'

Pilaghur felt an embarrassment lessened when it transpired that although there was a Lady Ahmed Hossein – 'Probably three,' observed Colonel Vetchley – she preferred to live in her own native state, lacking courage to take with her husband his alarming strides of progress. The poor lady would not make a problem anywhere; she would stay where she was normal. She always had stayed there, and Sir Ahmed, between his achievement, had made devoted pilgrimages back into her life.

So, to begin with, Sir Ahmed had come to Mrs. Lemon's garden-party. He was the only native there, and he was distinguished in other ways. His fez marked him out, and his long black coat buttoned tightly from the neck, which gave a queer, clerical masque to a personality clearly very much of this world. His face was highly, keenly, broadly intelligent; a black beard grew well up toward his wide and salient cheek-bones, and his eyes, which looked with searching inquiry at what they encountered, were luminous with that naïve impulse of the mind which Orientals do not yet think it worth while to disguise.

Mrs. Lemon took cheerful charge of the new official, and introduced him freely. It could never be said of Mrs. Lemon that she shirked things; but it was plain enough, behind her smiling activity, that she was tackling a weighty duty. He was received on all sides civilly: there was a general sense of conduct toward him, a general desire to be as polite as any regulation could require. One lady even, in her zeal to back up her hostess, offered him a chair.

Sir Ahmed bowed with dignity and made gratefully appreciative response. It was marked, the note of gratitude, the smile of good-will that came so much more than half-way – marked and full, to the observer, of the under-pathos of things. These among whom he had come were not his people; his ways were not their ways nor his thoughts their thoughts. Yet he had to take his place and find his comfort among them. The drift and change in the tide of events had brought him there, and he had to make the best appeal he could. In every eye he saw the barrier of race, forbidding natural motions. He would commend himself, but could not do it from the heart; he was forced to take the task upon the high and sterile ground of pure intelligence. He acquitted himself with every propriety, but relief came where he moved away, and perhaps he knew it; he walked about curiously alone. The afternoon was half over and Sir Ahmed was discussing the outside of something with Mr. Arthur Poynder Biscuit, who was lending himself to the subject with an exaggerated aspect of consideration, when between the rows of verbenas in pots bordering the path to the lawn appeared Eliot Arden.

'Ah – my friend!' exclaimed the Judge, and made a step forward. Then he hesitated and waited until he caught the Chief Commissioner's eye, when he went rapidly towards Arden, leaving little Biscuit balancing a sentence. The two men greeted cordially; the new comer was here clearly on another footing of acceptance.

'Already to-day I have come,' Sir Ahmed told him with glistening eyes, 'to write my name in your visitors' book; but I know your occupations and could not dream to see you at that hour.'

'No,' said the Chief Commissioner simply, 'I would have been glad to see you. But I hope there will be many more opportunities. Let me think – it is three years, isn't it – more – since you were in Simla keeping the other fellows straight on that Mahomedan Education Commission? What has become of your project for a Chair in Zend at Calcutta? Has it moved at all? I ought to know, but one gets withdrawn in a special job like this – it's hard to see beyond the boundaries of one's own province,' Arden added, with his acknowledging smile. Half regretful, half humorous, and wholly modest, it was a charm of his, this smile; people like to provoke it. Ahmed Hossein seemed literally for the moment to rejoice in it.

'They say to me, "Endow it!"' he said, smiling back. 'Well, I am comparatively poor man; alone I cannot endow anything. But I have some promises – about half a lakh already – and there is always the Nizam!' he jested frankly. 'But we have fallen upon the inevitable difficulty of administration. Only yesterday a friend of mine – Parsee gentleman – said to me, "I will give you twenty-five thousand rupees, but on condition that your Professor of Zend is of this country." Now I am against that. We want a European scholar with a systematic, critical knowledge of the literature, not a pundit with his head stuffed with the precepts of the Yazna.'

'I think I agree with you, but of course it is easy to understand the feeling. You had the Viceroy with you, I believe?'

'Oh yes! Is His Excellency not always with the country – past, present, and future?' replied Sir Ahmed enthusiastically. 'He said to me himself, "I wish I were young enough to attend the first lecture."'

'Then eventually, no doubt it will come through,' Arden observed. They were standing a little apart from Mrs. Lemon's assembly, over which the Chief Commissioner's eye now began to travel with careful negligence. 'He seeks some one,' thought the Oriental beside him, 'for whom he would not look,' and Ahmed Hossein's own gaze rested carefully upon the blossoming verbenas.

'Let me introduce you,' said Arden presently, 'to a lady, a friend of mine, who is sitting alone just now – it is an opportunity. This way.'

They found their way to the lady, who lifted her grey eyes to meet their approach just an instant too late to suggest that she was not aware of their progress across the grass. But her smile was accustomed enough. 'Miss Pearce,' said Mr. Arden, 'I should like to introduce to you my friend Sir Ahmed Hossein. Dr. Pearce, Sir Ahmed.'

'I am very glad indeed,' said Ruth. 'I have heard of you for a long time, Sir Ahmed, through one or two friends of your community here. You are a connection, are you not, of Syed Mahomed Ali? I mean the gentleman who has just received a decoration from the Sultan for his researches in early Islamic history. I know the Syed and his family very well.'

The men placed themselves in chairs beside her, and she bent slightly, with graceful, collected dignity, toward the stranger. He, with perfect respect and even appreciation, saw that she was about thirty, and too pale, her hair too black, the shadows about her face too deep, that she had as a woman no amplitude of charm. He became aware of these things in a detached and impersonal way, because he could not help it; any woman presented herself so to him. This one was of another race, and therefore remote, but she fell at the first glance into his instinctive category of the zenana. Then, as she spoke, he became aware of secondary qualities, which one must consider apart. 'Pundita,' he reflected, as he replied to her question about Syed Mahomed Ali, and lent himself willingly to the satisfactions which a pundita could give. Arden, for the moment, took no part in the conversation. He seemed absorbed in observing the attitude of his friend toward the person whom he had brought to her. That alone perhaps would have been enough to single her out from among the other women, so right it was, so adjusted and considerate; but that alone was hardly enough to account for his absorption in it. He remained for some moments outside their talk, until a word of it reached and wakened him.

'And the reason we now know that there was Greek foolishness,' Sir Ahmed was saying, 'is that two thousand years ago we believed Pythagoras.'

'In heaven's name,' said Arden, astonished, 'how have you got there?'

'I don't know,' Ruth told him. 'We are there. Then you think,' she went on to the other, 'that in passing from existence to existence we forget nothing?'

'Nothing valuable. We have not now to be taught that numbers are not beings. But I think,' he said, with a double modesty drawn from Arden's attention, 'it is not most importantly knowledge that we gather, or even philosophy. It is the soul that grows, and spiritual experience that makes the sum of what we are. We go from plane to plane.'

Arden turned eyes upon Ruth Pearce which said, 'How have you brought this out of him?' and she just answered by a glance, of delight in her own achievement and his understanding of it.

'We go from plane to plane,' she repeated, 'and we are the sum of what we have apprehended and conquered. Then the only real superiority lies there.'

'If we could count our planes we could establish our quarterings,' said Arden smilingly.

'And if we had an archangel at the Heralds' Office,' he added.

'Oh, that is not possible,' jested Sir Ahmed, probing the depth of seriousness in the other's eye.

'I hope you see,' Ruth said to the Chief Commissioner, 'what becomes of merely official rank. But these successive birth-planes are delightful – they explain so much. Our understanding of some people, for instance, and not of others. One understands those who are behind one, I suppose, but not those who are ahead of one.'

'I think so,' said the Judge.

'So that the most arrogant thing in the world to say is, "I know you very well,"' she drew him on.

He went even further than she expected. 'By a kind of cultivation of sympathy, which is memory,' he said, 'we can think ourselves back, not only into planes of other people – that is easy – but of animals as well. We plunge again into the life-current of all things. I can feel the impulse that makes this beetle move its limbs; and that crow cawing – he caws to me across æons of time. I hear his spirit in his cry, bound, far behind, and calling, as best it can. And I understand. You perceive?'

The raucous note struck on the air again. 'I believe I know what you mean,' said Arden, and Ruth, seeming to listen interiorly for the uncouth echo, said, 'I believe I *could* know.'

'But, Sir Ahmed,' said the Chief Commissioner, 'surely this is the kind of theory, isn't it, that we get at the other shop? These things are not written in the Koran.'

'The Koran is a good old fighting book,' replied the Judge, and his smile was a half-regretful mixture of pride and submission, 'but, sir, to which of us in the East is left his religion?' He pulled his beard meditatively. 'I myself am but half believer in my casual creed,' he told them, and Ruth, who was listening again to the crows, cried, 'Oh, don't spoil it.'

A lady left a neighbouring group and came toward them across the grass. It was Mrs. Arden, with a very pretty parasol. She approached with the little significant steps of a person whose motions one way or another are observed, and she said as she joined them, 'What are you all talking about?'

'We were talking about our past lives,' said her husband.

'Some people can remember back to the age of two,' she told them.

'Sir Ahmed Hossein thinks he can remember back to the age of a beetle,' said Arden, smiling; and at her puzzled look Ruth hastened to explain, 'We were talking of previous lives, Mrs. Arden.'

'Oh,' she said. 'Now I understand. The thing Mrs. Besant believes in so tremendously. Did you ever meet Mrs. Besant, Sir Ahmed? I can't say I have, but I have heard her lecture on that subject. Wonderfully eloquent – I shall never forget it. But do go on.'

There was an instant's silence. Then Ahmed Hossein, at whom she was looking, said politely, 'I am afraid I do not remember just where we were in our discussion.'

'Oh, don't let me interrupt you,' begged Mrs. Arden.

Ruth made an effort. 'Do you think we have any ground for supposing previous existences, Mrs. Arden?'

Mrs. Arden looked serious. 'Well, only that feeling of having done something or seen something somewhere before, you know, when you know you haven't – we've all had that, haven't we?'

'I'm sure we have,' said Ruth gently.

'Or of having known some one that you couldn't possibly have ever seen before. When my husband and I were first engaged I used to have that feeling about him most strongly – that we had met in some previous existence. But it wore off.'

'Upon further acquaintance,' laughed Arden, and took out his watch. 'I think we ought to be saying good night,' he suggested, and his wife rose with an effect of punctilio which showed her well aware of the exigencies of public appearances. They made their way to Mrs. Lemon, who advanced genially on her part, holding out a tiny glass.

'Have some pumelo gin,' she advised them. 'It's warming. So cold when the sun goes. Won't you? My own make.'

The sun had gone when the General finally accompanied them across the lawn to their carriage; and the Indian world lay chill about them as they drove along the dusty road in the twilight to the cream-coloured house with the guard at the gate, where the Imperial flag, floating above, told all comers at what an enviable point they had arrived.

CHAPTER X

THE indifference off society in Pilaghur to the offence of Henry Morgan, private in the Fifth Barfordshires, so culpable in the eyes of Mr. Cox, and so noticeable even in ours, did not, naturally, extend to his regiment. No doubt if the crime had been committed by Colonel Vetchley instead of by a person practically non-existent except as a fighting unit and a number, we should not have had to complain with Mr. Cox, at all events not so loudly. But even then the feeling of the station about the affair would have been a poor and faint demonstration compared with the interest aroused by the Morgan case among the friends and fellow units of Morgan. It takes more than India to stamp his robust concern with life out of the British soldier. He may be bored, but he is never *blasé*. The sophistications of the canteen are not enough. Nothing is enough, except beef and beer, and they are too much; perhaps there we find the problem of him.

The Barfords were an average regiment with an average record. General officers had reported of them a hundred times that discipline 'on the whole was good,' the Colonel was popular; and the regimental team held the Northern India football championship. They had put in eighteen months' service in the country, just long enough to give them the usual superficial dislike and contempt for the people, which more than one unlucky incident had aggravated. They were a keen sporting lot, and not one of them held the wild peacock sacred, or in his heart respected the regulation that forbade the shooting of it. They had vague ideas about trespass in a country without hedges or keepers, and to meet the voluble protest of the peasants they had only the *lingua franca* of the fist. In the eyes of a good many of them the villagers existed to show the way to good shooting, to supply country spirit on demand, and such other amenities as the neighbourhood might produce, and generally to take orders. The villagers thought differently. The Sahib might command these things; but the 'gorah' was a man without authority, without money, who frequently extracted that for which he would not pay, a person of no understanding and much offence. They were therefore contumacious to every demand, sullenly, sometimes actively, hostile to everything in uniform; and the Barfordshires were so occupied with the full-tongued expression of their scorn and indignation that they altogether failed to measure how much they themselves were disliked.

One would be foolish to look in the regiment for an unprejudiced view of Morgan's offence. As constated by the regiment, Morgan was 'in trouble' – black trouble. Morgan's trouble was a visitation which might come upon any one at any time. He was widely and picturesquely condemned for foolishness in getting into it, but the general study was as to how he should get out of it. Morgan was not a favourite. He had no intimate friends. His speech betrayed him a 'gentleman ranker,' though never in so many words: and he was thought none the better of for being plainly a gentleman ranker without ambition – not so much as a stripe on him. A deserted wife and family, though that of course was nobody's business, were generally attributed to him; the lady lived in Bournemouth and gave dancing lessons, the colour-sergeant remembered having taken them from her. If Morgan had been liked, this would have been less disgraceful than it was – part simply of that ambiguous fate that draws the British private into enlistment. As it was, it made a thing to quote about him. A man who keeps his personality to himself but cannot disguise his vices provides no charitable reception for them; and Morgan's company would have picked them out with pleasure as the likeliest among them to bring disgrace on his fellows. They had no acquaintance with his past, and as little as he could give them with his present; but the man was among them, and the man was known as 'Scum o' the Earth.'

This had to do with Morgan, but not, it should be understood, with Morgan's case. That became, as fast as sentiment could crystallise, a family affair. Morgan was a sweep, but he wasn't the only one, and whatever he was, he was integral. 6575 comes, apart from all other considerations, between 6574 and 6576; that may not be much of a virtue, but it a considerable claim. Individual offence generally means, in a regiment, corporate discipline. The Barfordshires took the curtailment of their shooting parties with glum philosophy, and bore no special malice to Morgan. But since Morgan's punishment lay upon every man, Morgan's defence was the concern of every man; he was merged in the regiment, and his sin had no more individuality than his uniform. We cannot find it so illogical; the race is thus identified with Adam, suffers for the family likeliness, and makes the best of it.

Sir Ahmed Hossein had taken over his duties from Mr. Lawrence Lenox the day before the police were notified of the murder; and this was recognised, as soon as the sensation of Morgan's arrest had somewhat subsided, to bear heavily on the case. The police investigation took two days and the magisterial inquiry a fortnight: there was plenty of time to discuss the judicial chances, and the general feeling both in the canteen and the 'A. T. A.' was that it was sanguinary rotten luck that the case should come before a sanguinary black nigger.

Thomas Ames, Private, was of opinion that this could not happen. Ames was secretary to the football club, organised the sing-songs, and owned a bicycle. 'Is Henry Morgan a European British subject, or is he not?' demanded Ames.

'Yus, most decidedly,' replied more than one.

'Then I say that no native of this country can try such a European British subject for his life,' said Ames. 'Not if he was Chief Justice, which they aren't and never will be. That's one of the things that gives them the 'ump; the law don't allow 'em to do any hanging – any white hanging, be it understood.'

'That bein',' said Truthful James Symes, sharpening his knife on his boot-heel, 'the only kind calculated to give 'em any pleasure.'

'That may or may not be,' remarked Flynn, known as 'the Mugger' from a saurian aspect he had, extended on a bench, comfortably unbuttoned, with a restful cutty pipe, 'but 'ow do you or I or anybody know that murder's got to be the tune? Why not culpable 'omicide? Why not grievous 'urt?'

'It depends on how the magistrate frames the charge,' said Symes, trying the blade on his little finger-nail. 'And that's as much a matter of prejudice as anything else.'

'Prejudice be blowed,' Ames told them. 'It's a matter of form. He'll go up on all of 'em, and I shouldn't wonder if they'd sling in simple hurt to make certain of lagging 'im on something. The Court that tries him can amend the charges, too. I remember a case –'

'Famb'ly affair?' inquired Symes, with affability.

'You shut your head, you bloomin' illiterate. I remember a case where the High Court down in Calcutta had the remarkable cheek to amend a sentence, let alone a charge. They amended it for the worse, too – seven years instead o' five. The next time that chap's lawyer advises him to appeal, I don't think he'll be taking any.'

'I suppose old Scum's gettin' advice all right,' inquired the Mugger, removing his pipe for the answer.

'Armenian pleader by the name of Agabeg,' Ames told him, spitting with precision to emphasise the point. 'Moses Agabeg. And as sharp as they make 'em. Quite a crimin'l repitation. Been had down to Calcutta an' over to Allahabad, before this, on cases. Lives here. I've seen him drivin' about with his missis, but I'm damned if I can tell an Armenian from a Parsee or either of 'em from a black an' tan, when they wear Europe clothes.'

'Ow's he to be paid?' asked Symes.

'Wait an' you'll find out, my son. Our friend the pris'ner's income is exactly fourteen annas three pies a day, him lookin' down, as we know 'e does, on efficient allowances both first *and* second. An' he don't get *many* remittances, as far as I can judge.'

'Wot I should be pleased to know,' remarked Flynn, 'is wot view Anthony Andover's goin' to take of this business.'

'If he's wise he'll keep his snout out of it,' said Ames, 'an' let justice take its course. Are the courts of this country able to take care of the crime of this country or are they not, that's what I 'umbly ask. But he won't risk it again, not after the Laffan case. He got it between the eyes that time. The Bombay High Court discharged the prisoner "without a stain on 'is character." In so many words. Pretty sickly business for Anthony.'

'You think 'e won't, eh?'

'That's my information.'

'The little tin gods 'aven't bin 'eard from yet?' inquired the Mugger with an air of cynicism.

'Ain't been time,' replied Ames. 'Besides they're on the move just now, from their anyoual summer picnic in Simla to their anyoual winter blow out in Calcutta. They'll be 'eard from all right. Don't you be impatient, sweet'art.'

Flynn knocked the ash out of his pipe and sat up. 'Oh, give us a rest,' he remarked. ''As any one here present seen young James Moon this last day or so?'

'I've had to get along without it,' said Ames.

'James Moon ain't pretty at his best, but his own mother wouldn't know 'im now,' Flynn informed them. 'He's been out after duck.'

'In the bazaar?' asked Symes, with a grin.

'None of your double intenders, my boy. In the jheels. An' he took Black Maria.'

The others chuckled anticipatively.

'I warned 'im. "Wot do y' think y' can do with that old slut of a muzzle-loader?" I said. "She was with the regiment when we was in the Mutiny," I said. "She's bin drawin' pension for years," I said. But James Moon, being a recruity, knows it all an' a bit more. So he borrys Maria an' packs in a fistful of shot and about 'arf a pound o' powder. Jams it all in beautiful. An' w'en 'e gets a look in, lets fly. Well, he did a lot o' murder, but Maria kicked all she knew; an' there ain't anything about a kick that dear old sportin' arm *don't* know. An' Moon's cheek is a treat. Oh, it's a work of art!'

'Well, he'll have time to poultice it now,' responded Ames. 'I hear the Goozies' orficers 'ave been writing in to compline of our shootin' pig in the Serai jungle. Wot's the 'arm, I say, 'an who's the loser by our 'aving the bit o' sport? Them Serai pig never come out o' cover, never have an' never will, not even to oblige those wishin' to stick 'em from ponies in a gentlemanly manner. They can't get 'em with their spears an' we can with our guns — that's wot's eatin' them. But I've good reason to understand the C.O. ain't likely to take any notice of it.'

'Blime gall they've got,' remarked Symes, as the three took their way across the dusty parade-ground. 'Dam lot of kitmugars — an' not here three weeks neither. I'd send their chin back to 'em Value Payable, if I was the old man.'

'A fat lot of difference it makes for the next two months, any-how,' Ames reminded them, 'for which our grateful thanks are due to Henry Morgan, Esquire, now enjoyin' all the luxuries of the sea-son in Pilaghur gaol. *De mortibus* and cetera, which is also etiquette for those in similar circumstances, and I 'ave no communication to make to that muck-rake at present. But when he comes out —'

He finished softly on the refrain of a popular song, which was cut short by the appearance of Colonel Vetchley. He came upon them round an unusual corner, looking irritated and depressed, and scrutinised them at ten paces as if each of them, to partly paraphrase the words of the Mugger, had a bloody mystery concealed about his person. The men saluted, dropping instantly into the redcoated wooden trio, putting one foot before the other, which is their convention all the world over, and went on their way.

Anxiety about the chance that Morgan's case might come before a native Sessions judge was not confined to his comrades. As soon as the possibility was recognised it was canvassed in the Club, where

Mr. Biscuit pointed out to Major Devine and Mr. Charles Cox over short drinks, that this was precisely the contingency which should prevent such an appointment as Sir Ahmed Hossein's.

'Every previous Viceroy since the Mutiny has seen clearly enough,' said Mr. Biscuit, 'that such a case might arise, and that in such a case race feeling might naturally be expected – rightly or wrongly – to interfere with the ends of justice. Consequently, until lately, precious few natives have been put into the billet. You may call it timidity, but where it's a question of putting heavy responsibility into the hands of those gentry, I must say I sympathise. I'm timid, too.'

Mr. Biscuit, though getting on very well, was not an original person; and this opinion of his about judgeships of the first grade was quite widely and commonly held throughout the service, in which such senior appointments are naturally not too many.

'Age of progress,' remarked Mr. Cox, 'I think, you know, Biscuit, that we must expect the people of the country to take an increasing share in its administration as time goes on. We must make the omelet and never mind the eggs.'

Major Devine cast upon the latest addition to the Government of Ghoom a glance of extreme disgust.

'It's what you might expect from a rotter like Thame,' he said. 'Always playing up to the natives.'

'But there are native judges even in the High Courts out here, I take it?' inquired Mr. Cox. 'Calcutta – Bombay. There they must exercise supreme jurisdiction.'

'Yes,' Mr. Biscuit hastened to inform him, 'but such cases as this naturally wouldn't come before them – a European judge would be put on to try them. Though a native, of course, might form one of a revisional bench. But this fellow sits alone, you see.'

'I see,' said Charles Cox, making room for yet another admission likely to modify the ideal view. As he pondered it, up came Egerton Faulkner, Chief Secretary, very warm after racquets, pulling a modish coat over his flannels. Faulkner was known as a wit, a dandy, an incroyable. He loved the cynical, nonsensical appearance. To account for his progress, which had been rapid, he would drop a shy eyeglass and smile ineffably, and say, 'Sometimes I pressed their lily hands, sometimes their ruby lips,' which nobody would take to refer to his official superiors, and which nobody should take to refer to anybody at all, since Mr. Faulkner had got on solely by tact and ability, and Mrs. Faulkner was the rather stout compendium of all the hands and lips he had any acquaintance with. His clever talk was tricked out with the quotations and allusions which belonged to his year at Oxford. Though a rising and experienced member of the most distinguished Service in the world, he still wore intellectually his undergraduate's clothes. There had been no opportunity to change. Socially he was called 'a boon to any station.' I think he was one, the funny fellow. His attitude to life was one of such sustained amusement that he had to summon a long face for a serious question. He summoned it now.

'But for Section Four of the Criminal Procedure Code, or rather a Notification under that Section, the contingency you mention would be a grave one, Biscuit. But it has been legislated – I was Under-Secretary at the time – out of existence. I imagine His Excellency, in making the present appointment, was aware of this. The law provides for the commitment of all such cases as Morgan's to the nearest High Court, irrespective, I may add, of the complexion of the Sessions judge. Faultless – faultless as yours and mine may be, my dear Biscuit, neither you nor I, did we occupy the seat of judgment for this district, would be thought competent any more than our friend Ahmed Hossein, sitting alone, to try Henry Morgan for his life. You and I and Sir Ahmed may hang black men but not white ones. Morgan may claim – and no doubt will – to be tried in Calcutta.

'Really, sir, is that the way it stands?' returned the intelligent Biscuit, wagging an abased tail at the note of correction. 'I hadn't looked into the matter. That, of course, explains to some extent His Excellency's departure from precedent.'

'Lamentable – lamentable, these departures from precedent,' and Mr. Faulkner threw his slight figure into an attitude of comedy, 'though doubtless in the line of fate, Biscuit, prefigured long ago by Lord Canning, Lord Ripon, Lord Curzon, I may even suggest by the Lord of All. You and I, Biscuit, live and administer in the dawn of history. You and I gape and boggle at a native Sessions judge.

But our sons may take instructions from Bengali Heads of Departments, and look for promotion to Madrassi Lieutenant-Governors. It is written among the things that are to be. I do not say that I rejoice in it. I have a father's feelings. I am sure you share them, Biscuit. "What, then, is that which is able to direct a man?" said our dear old friend Marcus Aurelius, with his prophetic eye upon the Indian Civil Service at the beginning of the twentieth century. "One thing and one things only, and that is philosophy."'

Mr. Faulkner's pronouncement upon the trial of Morgan spread through the station, bringing a sense of relief. 'He won't be tried here,' said Mrs. Arden to her friends, 'I'm *so* thankful. I am sure Sir Ahmed wouldn't be biassed; but it would be such a disagreeable incident in Eliot's administration.' Alfred Ames was also quoted in his circle; and the talk in the regiment was of Calcutta juries, their character and predilections. Calcutta juries, on the whole, were held to be sound in the head. Certain verdicts, under certain circumstances, it was believed, could not be wrung from them.

Surprise was general, therefore, when it transpired, in the course of a few days, that the prisoner had waived his claim to be tried by the Superior Court, had elected, in fact, to be tried as a native, and that the case would come, after all, before Sir Ahmed Hossein, in Pilaghur, with a jury. Officials found the decision an incomprehensible whim, and received it with dissatisfaction. Nobody could remember a precedent for it, and that alone was irritating enough. Besides, Morgan promised a centre of disturbance, which is always better at a distance. Calcutta was accustomed to them; but Pilaghur would be shaken to its foundations. The regiment took it with blank amazement. It was said that the Colonel himself interviewed Morgan on the folly of his course, but could get nothing out of him except that he was willing to take his chance, and some unfavourable observations on the judicial climate of Calcutta, clearly communicated. Alfred Ames, Truthful James Symes, and the Mugger washed their hands of concern with the prisoner's fate a dozen times a day.

'If he's such a fool as that shows him,' said Ames with frequency and decision, 'he'll 'ave to take 'is gruel, that's all.'

The only person neither alarmed nor displeased was Sir Ahmed Hossein, K.C.I.E., who, indeed, confided to Eliot Arden, in the course of an evening walk, that he could not disguise his gratification. The incident was a sign of that new and better understanding, based on a completer confidence between the two races, which all good men so ardently desired; and he could not help being proud to figure in it.

It was odd that nobody remembered, in the search for an explanation, the wide reputation for cleverness, perception, and tact attached to the name of Mr. Moses Agabeg, the pleader in charge of the defence.

CHAPTER XI

JAMES Kelly was an Irish patriot by one parent only; but he was a man of business in his own right. He could quote the parent — a mother — to explain his connection with the Clan-na-Gael society for reasons of sentiment; and he could point to a considerable account for services rendered to justify it on other grounds. His sympathies, in fact, brought him a handsome turnover. He had pride in them and profit out of them, and so did well.

It was like that with regard to his enterprise in commission from Mrs. Tring and Miss Victoria Tring. He had a liking for the job; it had the touch of drama that appealed to him. He often thought of the moment when he should walk up to Tring and clap him on the shoulder and say, as the crown of many kindnesses, 'Young man, I'm here to send you home.' Just as he anticipated the telegram which should one day flash Irish-American congratulations to Dublin upon the laying of the foundation-stone of her own House of Parliament. It would be a consummation worth doing something for, at a reasonable figure. The figure he had finally managed to screw Mrs. and Miss Tring up to was a very reasonable one — so much for Mr. Kelly's expenses, so much for his time, and so much for the extraordinary advantage he could offer her in having actually seen and known her son. He had seen him and he had known him; and there would be only as much difficulty in tracing him as justified a fair margin. A little more difficulty than he had hinted to Mrs. Tring there would be, since it was nearly three years, and not six months, since he had last spoken to Herbert in San Francisco; but it was not in a sanguine nature, well supplied with funds, to make much of that.

They had their first letter from Kelly about Christmas. At Victoria's urgent petition Mrs. Tring had agreed to keep his commission a secret, and had, as a matter of fact, told only two people, Lady Thame and Frayley Sambourne. Lady Thame because Mrs. Tring considered that Pamela had a right to know, almost as imperative as her own to impart, and Mr. Sambourne because Mrs. Tring would have felt a stain of insincerity in concealing anything from him. It was not a thing, she would have told you, to argue about; it was simply in their relation. Beyond these she did not go, being compelled to acknowledge Victoria's argument that if she did it would be sure to get into the halfpenny papers. Victoria spoke of this in such a way that Mrs. Tring had to cry out that it would be intolerable; but her secret criticism asked why not, and her private bosom heaved in sympathy with the headline, 'A Mother's Quest for her Son,' which sprang before her on the posters.

Lady Thame was cold, colder than the mother of a young Viceroy earning constant approbation in the press ought perhaps to have been, under the circumstances; but she never had been fond of Herbert.

'It is unsatisfactory,' she said.

Kelly's news was that, although he had made all speed across the Continent, he had just, unfortunately, missed the last steamer that would make the Alaskan connection for the winter. He would therefore be obliged to wait until navigation opened in those regions in the spring. He assured Mrs. Tring that he would wait, whatever the inconvenience to himself; and that she had this to console her, that if he, Kelly, was frozen out, her son was by the same circumstance frozen in.

'He can't get away,' wrote Kelly, 'that's one sure thing; and I'll be on to him with the first boat in April.'

Meanwhile he had been making some inquiries, not without result; Mr. Tring had left one or two articles in the hands of the lady he boarded with – personal items Kelly thought his folks might like to have, among them a seal ring – which he had obtained and was sending therewith, redemption of the same to be charged to account. He had also traced out two articles, Mr. Tring had contributed to a weekly paper called the *Bat*, containing his impressions of San Francisco. The *Bat* had since ceased publication, so these had taken some looking for. Hoping for better luck later, James Kelly was hers respectfully.

'It's unsatisfactory,' said Lady Thame, 'this Kelly in San Francisco the whole winter, eating his head off.'

'I have told him,' said Mrs. Tring, 'to employ his time in tracing Herbert's literary output further. He always signed his initials, "H.V.T.," so there should be no difficulty; though the style would be a perfect identification to any of us who know it. Here is a sentence, for instance: – "This westernisation of the race is a crass and high-coloured experiment from which the eye instinctively shrinks." Could any one mistake it? How strange his fastidious note must have sounded to that great city! Perhaps some soul understood – I hope so. There may be other Englishmen there.'

'I don't know what he means,' said the lady he had always called Aunt Pamela. 'The race has got to go, I suppose, wherever there is room for it and wherever it can strike root. Would he find more to gratify his eye in Spitalfields? The faster we westernise the better I shall be pleased. Anthony always said that the United States was far more our possession than India, for example. I don't know whether he would say it now.' Lady Thame's eye gleamed combatively. 'But we shall get him home in another year, I hope.'

'Dear Pamela, why should you know what my boy means – why should I ask you to know? The world is full of paths which we may safely tread together – why should I tempt you to walk upon a cloud? You are not formed for such excursions. Never mind. We are here only to fulfil the purposes of *our own* existence; isn't it so? And I can imagine how vivid must be your grief with Anthony. He seems to have gone over hand and foot to Jingoism, to earth-hunger, to the bloody tradition of the flag. They say he is out-Heroding Herod in Thibet,' she added, referring to a recent strongly Imperial administrator. 'How do you account for it – subliminally?'

'I don't account for it – I write him letters,' said Lady Thame, as one might say, 'I don't argue – I shoot.' 'But if I did I should put it down to the pernicious influence of the East. When a dog grovels before you –'

'You don't stand it on its hind legs, or offer it a chair, dearest Aunt Pamela,' put in Victoria, looking up from her letters. 'Apropos, I am writing to Anthony this very minute, and I want Herbert's articles to send him, mother. They shall go registered, and I know he will return them promptly.'

The two elder women glanced at one another instinctively. They had few points of agreement, but here was an interest that beckoned them over the heads of their propensities. Victoria was writing to Anthony. They both knew Victoria wrote to Anthony, but that did not rob her calm announcement of any meaning that might lurk in it. What meaning did lurk in it? that was what they sought one another's eyes to find out.

'I think I might have been allowed to keep them a little longer,' said Mrs. Tring, delivering up the cuttings, 'though I know them almost by heart.'

'Sorry, but it's Indian mail day,' replied her daughter.

'I am afraid it will be no consolation to you,' Mrs. Tring went on, 'but Anthony is himself becoming a great influence, a magnetic figure out there against the sunrise. Frayley Sambourne more than approves him – adores him.'

Lady Thame had opened her lips to say how far she was consoled by this when the parlour-maid announced Mr. Frayley Sambourne himself; so we shall never know.

'That isn't your place!' cried Mrs. Tring, as he found a chair. 'No, I cannot have you there – the light disfigures you. Thank you, Pamela – if you wouldn't mind moving. He is such a beatitude in his own corner.'

'I haven't by any chance taken his cup and saucer?' inquired Lady Thame grimly.

'Now don't pretend that I am silly,' cried Mrs. Tring. 'I have the only true wisdom: I know it because it makes me so happy.' She looked out at them confidingly from under her fluffy hair, and Frayley Sambourne gave her the kindest glance in return.

'What did you think of the debate last night?' he asked her.

'Oh, you deserved your victory. I thought Craybrooke's vindication of England's right to economic isolation marvellously convincing. That sentence, "She will make here no alliances, even with her children" – extraordinarily probing. And you, when it came to your turn – you did not disappoint me.'

'Oh, I hadn't much to do,' Sambourne said, thanking her with his eyes for all she had left him to understand. 'It is easy enough,' he turned with deference to Lady Thame, 'to defend the present administration of India; and the charge of coercive recruiting among the Sikhs was too absurd. Might as well talk of coercive conversion among the Santhalis. But I was amazed to be able to hold so full a House. Amazed and gratified. We have somehow managed, our side, to revitalise interest in our great Dependency. I candidly don't think so many Members have been in their places through the discussion of an Indian question since the House listened to Burke.'

'Nothing rouses British feeling like an attempt to undermine the liberties of British subjects,' Lady Thame reminded them. 'It strikes home – it strikes home. I hope there was nothing in it most profoundly. I shall ask Anthony himself.'

'I hesitate to suggest it, Lady Thame, but I know your counsel will have weight with him; and I do wish, and so does Lord Akell, that some good friend would say a wise word to him – *our* wise words all have the official odium, you understand – about his attitude toward these unfortunate affairs between soldiers of British regiments and natives. We – '

'So far,' interrupted Lady Thame uncompromisingly, 'it is the single feature of his administration in which I feel the smallest cause for pride.'

'Pride in the principle, in the unquestionably lofty motive, by all means, dear Lady Thame. But, also, how much more there is to consider! We politicians have to look at things in the rough, you know – in the block. The party system yields a fair average of decent government, that we may concede; but it has no use, as our excellent Transatlantic friends say, for counsels of perfection.'

'I often wonder,' remarked Victoria musingly, 'how so much contempt has got into that phrase.'

'I will not follow you, Frayley!' cried her mother. 'No, I will not. There is something in me that refuses – refuses. I wish I could see your aura at this moment. I am sure it would betray you. What is the spiritual colour of expediency?'

'I don't know,' said Lady Thame, 'but why it should be advisable, in the interests of the Liberal party, to let a great brute of a British soldier knock about a helpless native is by no means plain. Anthony has set his face against it, and quite rightly.'

'It isn't quite so simple as that,' said Mr. Sambourne. 'Of course I sympathise with Anthony absolutely; but it isn't quite so simple as that. There is a question of the Courts, which it would take too long to go into, and I am afraid you would find very boring. I myself was routed by the attempt to master it in half an hour before lunch the other day. And it does not do to antagonise so big a body as the British troops in India. It's not as if they stayed there. Already I've seen two or three letters, highly inflammatory to that class, that have appeared in various quarters – mostly obscure publications, it's true. We're prepared to support old Anthony, of course. Still –'

'Still?' repeated Victoria.

'Well, it's playing with petrol and matches. At any moment a case might crop up with just that quality of sentiment that acts upon the British public – and another army grievance wouldn't do us any good.'

'Personally,' retorted Lady Thame, 'I should be grateful for such a case; I should like to see my old Liberal colours nailed to it. Equal treatment for black and white and no caste privilege. Are we French, that we are afraid of our army? Fiddlesticks, Mr. Sambourne. You're sitting up too late at night.'

'I must say I believe British justice can take care of itself,' he replied. 'Now here, oddly enough, is a case in point.' He took a newspaper from his coat-pocket. 'One of these very wretched instances of collision with natives. I'll spare you the details, but the case happened, rather unusually I fancy, to be tried by a native, a Mahomedan, I imagine, by his name – Sir Ahmed Hossein. Oddly the title goes with it, doesn't it? Well, here we are. "The case of the Emperor *v*. Henry Morgan, which has been going on for the past week before the Hon. Sir Ahmed Hossein, District and Sessions

Judge of Pilaghur, and a special jury, closed to-day. The Court, in charging the jury, clearly indicated the view that the accused, who is a private in the Fifth Barfordshires, had committed culpable homicide only, and the jury accordingly brought in a verdict of guilty upon this count. The judge proceeded to sentence Morgan to two years' rigorous imprisonment. The fact that this is the first case of a European being tried by a native on a capital charge, added to the extreme lightness of the sentence imposed, has excited widespread comment throughout India." There are signs of progress in that, I consider.'

'I hope there are signs of justice,' said Lady Thame. 'Who is this Sir Ahmed Hossein? I never heard of him.'

'Could he have been bribed?' said Mrs. Tring. 'One is always told the native judiciary is very corrupt. I should be anxious to know that.'

'Well, I confess,' said the Under-Secretary for India, 'that our chief anxiety is that our people out there should let it alone.'

'It is a matter in which I should trust Anthony completely,' said his mother.

'It was a crime of passion; there is a play in it,' cried Mrs. Tring, who had been reading the paper. 'Bravo, Henry Morgan! My genius is at my elbow. I believe I could do it! I must keep this paper, Frayley.'

'I see opinion is against me,' said Mr. Sambourne, with resignation, 'unless I can get some backing out of you, Miss Tring.' He called her mother Deirdre; but they were friends.

'I should like to know more about it first,' said Victoria, 'but on the face of it, it looks to me very like one of those matters in which it would be wise to trust the man on the spot.'

Again her mother and Lady Thame exchanged glances, this time with a smile.

'I am glad to find that you agree with me, Victoria,' said her Aunt Pamela, and laid a heavily approving hand upon her shoulder.

CHAPTER XII

THE 'widespread comment' in India upon the result of the Morgan case, reported in the Calcutta telegram, had a touch of journalistic exaggeration. Indian comment was not widespread. Expectation had been. The spectacle of an Englishman on trial before a native for a capital offence against natives was not thought edifying, to put it mildly, by the Anglo-Indian Press. The inevitable consequence was hinted here and there; and more than one editorial pen was dipped and ready to proclaim the impossibility of accepting the decision, and the necessity for instant appeal. One enterprising journal of Calcutta had arranged in advance to receive contributions to enable the case to be carried to the nearest High Court, and was all ready with a preliminary list of subscribers, to be published with the judgment. The native journals were, no doubt, equally ready to defend it; but the event left all parties without a word.

'Our esteemed British contemporaries,' remarked the *Star of Islam*, 'are flabbergasted. This has taken the wind out of their hats.'

But the *Star of Islam* had hardly more to say than its esteemed British contemporaries. It was a kind of victory from the gods, and before the campaign; there would have been greater glory in defeat, and one more historic grievance.

It was a good deal talked of, naturally, in Pilaghur. Especially, and for a particular reason, in the Club. I am sure I have not made it plain that the Club was the nerve-centre of Pilaghur. 'Everybody' belonged to it. Not Miss Da Costa, of course, who made blouses, or Mrs. Burbage, who made cakes, or the photographer, or the young man who had started a bicycle agency from Cawnpore; but everybody else. All the people I have been describing, and the station chaplain, and the doctor, and the men on the staff of the Pilaghur College, and the Army nurses, and even the missionaries. There was no foolish exclusiveness about the Pilaghur Club. The missionaries did not come to the Club dances. As Mrs. Lenox used to point out, they 'never took advantage'; why, then, should they not have the benefit of the library and the tennis courts? They were even admitted, with the Army nurses, at a low subscription; and when Miss Menzies, who never appeared in anything but her white drill uniform with the red collar and cuffs – took a pride in it – but was in every way a lady though very badly off, married the Settlement Officer, whom she would have met nowhere but for Club opportunities, everybody was quite pleased. If Pilaghur had a body the Club was the heart of it, the centre of interest, activity, news, amusement. You drove there every evening – for your tennis, or your bridge, or your gossip, or to look at the day's Reuter, pinned up in the reading-room. If you wanted to study the life of an Indian station, as Mrs. Arden declared, you would only have to sit there and look on. How she wished, she often said, for the pen of the ready writer, to describe what she saw in a novel; at which people always assured her she could do it if she tried, they were certain.

The Pilaghur Club was very liberal, but it had never yet permitted a native of India to be proposed to its membership. The thing had hardly been thought of. When the fat old Maharajah of Pilaghur built them a new ball-room, leaving the old one free for billiards, in obscure gratitude for his C.I.E., somebody had suggested that the generosity should be recognised by an honorary membership, no doubt some Mr. Cox, newly arrived, with sensibilities not yet indurated by the sun. But short work was made of the proposition.

'My dear fellow,' he was told, 'it's simply impossible. When you have been out a year you will understand. He's a good old boy, and we'll give him a gymkhana, all to himself, and get Metapora's fellows over for the tent-pegging. But for Heaven's sake don't talk about letting him *in*!'

And in the face of this conviction, which still reigned undisturbed at the point of history of which I write, the Chief Commissioner had proposed Sir Ahmed Hossein.

Miss Pearce had seconded Mr. Arden's nomination; which was so natural that people wondered at it. 'There *can't* be anything in that affair,' Mrs. Poynder Biscuit observed acutely. 'They behave so exactly as if there were.'

They had hoped, Ruth and Eliot Arden, that her name upon the nomination would suggest that it would not be particularly objectionable to ladies, ladies being always the bugbear to social commerce with Indian gentlemen.

'She undertakes too much,' said Mrs. Biscuit, and perhaps she did. She belonged by nature to the pioneers, who do not always look behind to see whether people are coming along.

There was no special opposition among the ladies. Though so usefully made to serve as special pleading on occasion, they are rather specially one with their husbands in a place like Pilaghur; and their husbands had to remember that it was, after all, the Chief Commissioner's nomination. Some of them had to consider, to put it brutally, that they themselves might any day be the Chief Commissioner's nomination. Arden heartily disliked this phase of his official influence, but here, perhaps, was one of the cases in which it seemed to him less objectionable; in which he might even, with his smile of humorous irony, half count upon it. Little Biscuit, for instance. Arden though apologetically that they might count on little Biscuit's vote, because of his size.

The Morgan case closed while Sir Ahmed's name was still up. Very few votes had been recorded, mostly safe; but opposition threatened the regiments. The Barfords' mess were said to be coming down in a body to register their disapproval; and Davidson and Lamb of the Guzeratis had been seen to ballot the wrong way openly.

The Barfords did come dropping in, four or five of them, to see how matters were going, the afternoon of the day judgment and sentence had been pronounced upon Morgan. They found the place buzzing with it, and drew apart presently for private consultation. The thing was admitted astounding.

'Morgan's own company,' said Devine, 'would have given him a jolly sight more.'

Kemp, Captain, inclined to the view Mrs. Tring was to express a few hours later and six thousand miles further west, that the District and Sessions Judge had been bribed. 'They all do it, those fellows,' he said, 'every man Jack of 'em. It's the only way to account for it.'

'Rot!' said Major Devine. 'Where would the money come from? I hear the men are grumbling uncommonly about the cost of the defence. Besides, this chap Hossein's got enough of his own; and I don't think he's that sort of chap anyhow.'

'Then why don't we want him in the Club?' asked Loftus, subaltern.

'He's a bally native,' replied Lascelles, another subaltern, with shorter views.

'I don't see that it makes much diff to us,' remarked Kemp, 'whether he's in or out. We move along next year, in any case.'

'All I can say is,' Devine told them, 'that by taking the view he did, Hossein, or whatever his name is, did an uncommon good turn to the regiment. I don't see how Government's going to round on us, after this.'

'What'll the C.O. do?' asked Lascelles.

'Abstain from voting if I know him.'

'Let's all abstain from voting,' proposed Lascelles.

'No,' said Devine. 'He's going to get my vote.'

'Damn it, I think so too,' announced Captain Kemp.

'But ain't he finished already?' asked Peter Loftus. 'I was dining with the Guzzies last night, and I heard Lamb bragging that he and Davidson had done the trick all by their little selves.'

'The votes of Mr. Davidson and Mr. Lamb can be neutralised,' their Major told them, with a dignity that was peculiarly Barfordshire in discussing the native regiment. 'There's been no pilling in this place since I've been here, I'm glad to say; but here are the Club rules. I was prepared for you fellows taking a different view, so I brought them along.'

The situation was considered as it appeared under the rules, and thought to offer no difficulty to united action. They separated to whip up votes, inspired by that resolute enthusiasm which will sometimes, with this kind, take the place of pure logic. Lascelles, last from Sandhurst, left with a handspring over an arm-chair which the white ants had eaten interiorly. 'Nevertheless go it!' remarked the light-hearted youth as he sat among the ruins. 'Go it for Albert Hossein – he's an out-and-outer! Good old Albert!'

When, at a meeting of the committee three days later, the fatal box was opened, Sir Ahmed Hossein was declared duly elected a member of the Pilaghur Club. Adverse desires need not be considered; they had been overcome. We need not dwell, either, upon the comments of the committee; they bowed to the inevitable.

'Though if he wants to smoke his hookah here,' said Mrs. Lemon firmly, 'we will take it away from him, that's all. If there is one thing I cannot abide it's the smell of a hookah.'

The Secretary at once advised Sir Ahmed that he had been elected. Two or three times already fortune had favoured this Mahomedan gentleman of birth, wealth, education, and refinement. He had been placed upon an important Commission, had been decorated in recognition of his labours, had been given this superior judgeship. But none of these things, I may safely say, even his Knight Companionship itself, had brought him so happy a thrill as the little printed form of the Pilaghur Club. We who have not been Mahomedan gentlemen newly stamped with the social recognition of another world may easily not quite understand. There is no reason to believe that Lady Ahmed Hossein, sitting with her handmaids on the floor of a tall plastered house in Mirnugger, working yellow birds with green tails on magenta silk coverlets for the marriage of her eldest daughter, understood at all. But the District and Sessions Judge of Pilaghur wiped tears from his eyes as he made his hasty way to the residence of his more than ever friend, the Honourable the Chief Commissioner.

It was Sunday morning. He met Mrs. Arden driving to church, a duty she had to be punctilious about, since Eliot would so seldom go. She was even more careful about her appearance on this account, so subtly do official considerations operate; and she was looking very nice as she leaned forward to give Sir Ahmed, without distinction of race, the slightly more pronounced and gracious bow which she had for senior members of 'the Service.' He felt a throb of admiration for her as she trundled away to her devotions, a welling up of appreciation for all that she represented. Perhaps he even bravely considered the steps necessary to put Lady Ahmed Hossein into a carriage and set her rolling up and down the roads of Pilaghur in imitation. If so, it was only gratitude moving on his soul; he knew quite well that Lady Ahmed Hossein sat in an obscurity deeper than that of any parasol; nor did he wish to bring her out of it.

Arden turned in his revolving office chair as Sir Ahmed was ushered in, and was about to get up when his visitor, approaching him quickly, said, with a look of alarm, 'Please sit perfectly still.' Arden stiffened himself, and Sir Ahmed, stretching out his hand, deftly and gingerly, picked an ugly thing from the Chief Commissioner's shoulder. It was a large, black, hairy scorpion; and it hung in the air, helpless from its own weight and clawing, suspended from its captor's fingers and thumb, which held the creature by the horny poison-bag at the end of its tail.

'By Jove! Drop it, man!' Arden exclaimed; but the District Judge continued to hold it up as it were to indignation for a moment, then walked across the room and threw it out of the window.

'Well, I would have hesitated to take hold of a fellow like that,' said Arden, 'I thought I felt something on my back. Thank you very much. But we ought to have killed the brute.'

'Catch him I can easily do; it is a simple trick. But I could not kill him,' said the Judge smiling. '"Do not destroy the life thou canst not give" – I think the Jains say something like that. I am not a Jain, but by my own hand I cannot kill. I will not subtract from the life of the world and add to the death. It is like subtracting from the good and adding to the evil.'

'I agree with you; but I am an instinctive murderer of things that make for the back of my neck,' said Arden laughing. 'I wish my wife would not insist on so many curtains. Scorpions and centipedes are too much of a concession to the aesthetic. But to kill nothing! I sometimes think you are not a Mussulman at all, Judge.'

'No – perhaps. I am an individual. I take my religion where I can get it – a little here, a little there. This twentieth century permits that. Religion is a world-product; and the time is past, I think, to fight for only one kind.'

'Oh, there I am with you, too.'

'And, sir, the Supreme Source – how unfathomable it is! I can understand that a divinity might make a stone. I could almost' – he laughed apologetically – 'show him how! Or a human being. But who created opportunity? Who made time?'

Arden assented a little uncomfortably, and glanced at his files. There were regions he could not explore at a moment's notice, even in this intelligent company. 'Well, it was uncommonly lucky for me that you – '

'But I have come with my thanks,' interrupted Sir Ahmed. 'Yesterday I was elected to the Club. This is for me great promotion, and it is to your distinguished help and kindness that I owe this thing. Under God,' he added seriously.

'Oh, my dear fellow,' said Arden with a smile he could not repress. 'Well, that's capital.'

'I have been much troubled in the matter,' said the Judge. 'I was already ashamed to have asked membership. I expected refusal – no less. It was keeping me awake almost as much as the Morgan case,' he confessed, laughing.

'No need in the world,' declared Arden. 'I hadn't a doubt of the result.'

'It was the military element that might have been hostile – those young officers. But perhaps they were pleased that I did not hang Morgan, and so did not hang me,' laughed Morgan's benefactor.

The joke was a little unguarded. The Chief Commissioner looked gravely at the paper-cutter he was playing with. 'I hope we are out of that business,' he said.

'Oh, Morgan will not appeal.'

'I should think not, indeed! There isn't another court in the country that would take as lenient a view.'

Sir Ahmed looked as if he would deprecate so generous an appreciation.

'There were many things to consider,' he said. 'Better let one man off too easily than inflame the passions of thousands.'

'I think,' he went on with shining eyes, 'I will give a ball to those young – to the Club. And I will have the music and supper from Calcutta. I will give a good ball.'

Arden was silent for a moment before this proposition. Then he said, 'I think I wouldn't, Sir Ahmed. Perhaps later. Look – I'll give the ball. It will be better. You must consent to be my guest that evening.'

Sir Ahmed rose and made an impulsive step forward. 'I cannot dispute your wish, sir. But my heart melts at your good will. Oh, why are there not more natures like yours among our rulers? Then would all bad feeling between the races disappear.

> "My mother bore me in the southern wild,
> And I am black, but O, my soul is white!"

And you, sir, will well remember that

> "We are put on earth a little space
> That we may learn to bear the beams of love,
> And these black bodies and this sunburnt face
> Are but a cloud, and like a shady grove."

Is it not beautifully said?'

The Chief Commissioner was too well accustomed to Eastern emotion to be deeply embarrassed. He got up, smiling, to end the interview. 'I see you know Blake,' he said.

'Oh yes. The most wonderful of our poets, do you not believe? Shakespeare is perhaps the greatest, or do you say Milton, but that William Blake is surely the most wonderful.'

With this he went. The smile of pleasure and of kindness deepened with a touch of amusement in Arden's eyes. '"Our" poets,' he repeated, half aloud, and turned to his work again.

ONE comment upon the light sentence inflicted upon Private Morgan I have forgotten. It was Hiria's – Hiria who was on such terms of fearful intimacy with Gurdit Singh, the policeman that watched over the house of Gobind and Junia while they still lay waiting for the law and the coroner. She came with infinite circumlocution to the point of asking her mistress what the punishment would be.

'Two years to sit in gaol,' she repeated with approbation. 'Is it not too much, miss-sahib; for, whatever is said, was the gorah not the cause of all?'

'Too much, Hiria!' exclaimed Ruth. 'Many people think it too little.'

'Yes, miss-sahib, very little. Too little, perhaps, but God is merciful. I was much afraid. I said, "You will see, he will be hanged, because of the Lord Sahib." But two year *kaidi* (imprisonment), that is not too much. And now perhaps the gorah-people will give less dick and trouble to the poor.'

CHAPTER XIII

THE Chief Commissioner and Mrs. Arden gave the dance. Mrs. Arden could not help feeling it an extravagance, with such an excellent floor in their own house, and the boys costing such an amount at home, to give it at the Club. One had to think of these things.

'And you know,' she confided to Mrs. Lemon, 'what education is coming to in England nowadays.'

And Mrs. Lemon stoutly backed her up, and scolded the Chief Commissioner. Poor Jessica, she invariably had one eye on Eliot and the other on the boys at home, while he seemed to look straight in front of him always, and see nothing but what he had to do. She gave in easily, as usual, about the dance, and – though Mrs. Lemon quite agreed with her that it was 'enough' to have had the new Judge twice to dinner already – helped the odd word with which Eliot suggested its rather special intention.

'Why didn't he put "To meet Sir Ahmed Hossein, K.C.I.E.," on the cards at once and be done with it?' demanded Mrs. Arthur Poynder Biscuit of Mr. Biscuit when nobody could hear her, with that superior *savoir faire* that came to her so naturally from Ealing.

'I expect that would make it too marked,' said Mr. Biscuit. 'We're all *supposed* to have met him, you see. Well, the Chief has decided to do this thing – he didn't consult me – and there's nothing more to be said. But mind, Lena, no dancing with Hossein. That I will not have. If he asks you, you have no dances left.'

'I danced with the Maharajah of Kala Jong at Government House in Calcutta,' rebutted Mrs. Biscuit, who was provocative always, even to her husband.

'That was quite a different thing. Everybody knows Kala Jong; he's been taken up in England to the most idiotic extent. Marchionesses curtsey to him – disgusting – but he's a sportsman, and as English as he can make himself.'

'And dances like an angel. But as to this man,' Mrs. Biscuit posed the tremendous question, 'what about going in to dinner? At the Chief's the other night, Mrs. Beverly flatly refused – told the Aide she simply wouldn't. Upset everything at the last minute, and the boy had to take her in himself. But of course –'

'She's military and can do as she likes. Still I object – I strongly object – to your being sent in to dinner with a native. Let somebody else go. And I will see that you are not. Anywhere but at Government House, I will protest myself – quietly, you know. No use giving offence, but I'll see that it doesn't happen. Of course if Mrs. Arden does it –'

'We can't make a fuss,' his wife agreed, and so they left the matter.

Whatever its private feelings, Pilaghur sacrificed them and came to the dance.

'On *her* account,' people said, everybody absolutely must turn up, referring to Mrs. Arden. Mrs. Arden was so kind, so charming to everybody, so 'exactly the same' under whatever circumstances you met her, that it was unanimously felt the thing mustn't be 'a frost.' Besides it would really take more than the honoured presence of a single native gentleman to put Pilaghur seriously out of humour with a dance. What was life in Pilaghur? Work, hard work, too, upon the unstimulating interests of an alien race, people to whom you must build the bridge of sympathy. And for all complement to that, one another – one, too, we may whisper, so like another! Was it Egerton Faulkner or somebody else who said that no Anglo-Indian could hope for an individuality until he got home; and then he could never escape that of the Anglo-Indian? For everything that enriches the fabric of life, all the pattern and the colour, they had one another, at the dance, the dinner, and the tennis-party; add the gymkhana, with another nought. It was the merest scaffolding of social life; but they clung to it with a zest curiously born of all that it was not. In spite of its sterility of atmosphere – one has only to consider forty or fifty human souls of the human average, remote and isolated from the borrowed graces and interests of their own world, planted where they can never take root, slowly withering to the point of retirement – 'society' in Pilaghur stood for companionship, intercourse, stimulus such as it was, valuable things even such as they were. For Mr. and Mrs. Biscuit society had importance and something like brilliancy as well. There was the question of precedence worked down to a theory of atoms; there was ceremonial always, and often champagne; there was, indeed, a great deal to intrigue and excite Mr. and Mrs. Biscuit. And even with people to whom it did not quite represent the world it stood for certain worldly values; and it was all there was. The Chief Commissioner's dance at the Club will therefore, I hope, be understood as an event.

'Everybody *is* so kind,' declared Mrs. Arden. Everybody was. Mrs. Lemon lent two small drawing-room sofas and any number of 'drapes.' Mrs. Wickman contributed a standard lamp, with a Liberty tulip shade which she had brought out in her hat-box and loved more than any hat. Spoons were gathered everywhere, and from Mrs. Carter, the Barfordshires' doctor's wife, a dozen Japanese coffee cups, the sweetest things. The decorations were in the capable hands of Mrs. Egerton Faulkner, who always did the church for weddings too – loved doing it, you could not prevent her – and she slaved at them till seven that evening, assisted till three by Mrs. Biscuit; who then went home to put her hair up and lie down. Mrs. Arden, who was so far from strong, had been by general compulsion lying down all day. In the end, with old Afghan weapons from the Barfords' mess, and palms and flags from Government House, and red cloth on hire from Ali Bux, and the Club's own Japanese lanterns, it all looked charming.

It was noticed at once and with relief that Sir Ahmed Hossein did not dance in the 'State' Lancers. The State Lancers strictly deserved their name only where a Viceroy led them, and bowed and chasséed opposite a Commander-in-Chief; but Pilaghur, remember, was a capital, and had its Chief Commissioner and its General Commanding, who had only to exchange wives, and there at once was the microcosm of the greater world. The other six couples had to be rather carefully selected. It always gave Captain Dimmock, A.D.C., some anxiety till it was over – but a man gets accustomed to handling even these delicate matters, and, as a rule, there was no criticism. If it were a question between Forests and Police, he would solve the difficulty by putting in the male of one Department and the female of the other, who would usually dance together. Captain Dimmock was praised for tact by everybody; and Mrs. Arden constantly said she didn't know what on earth she would do without him.

Sir Ahmed did not dance in the State Lancers and Mrs. Biscuit did. Little Biscuit looked on with knit brows until he saw this consummation, and then expressed his relieved conviction to Mr. Cox that Sir Ahmed would not dance at all.

'It's a pity he left Terpischore out of that classical degree of his, which I hear was otherwise good,' remarked Cox with the eye of initiative upon the second Miss Hillyer – Salt Department – the fair one. 'Might just as well have picked up dancing at Oxford; and it would have made him more popular.'

'Do you think so?' returned Mr. Biscuit, with the glance of long suffering dissent which by this time he had in readiness for the robust views of his junior. Then his better feelings overcame him.

'Look here, Cox,' he said, 'let me tell you something. Don't go about saying things like that. They're not understood, you know, out here. Do you harm, you know. If you're not careful you'll be getting identified with the Young India party. Congress-wallah – that sort of thing, you know. Bad for a man officially.'

Charles Cox looked for an instant insubordinate; a spark of the Union stood in his eye. Then his glance fell upon Mr. Egerton Faulkner, elegantly erect, wearing an eye-glass of infinite sophistication, bowing whimsically to his partner with his hand upon his heart, and travelled from him to the Chief Commissioner, marked already by the indefinable writing of distinction, and on over the score of vigorous and qualified-looking men who represented for him, in their different ways, the sum of wisdom and of seniority.

'Thanks,' he said, 'I must remember.'

Mrs. Arden often mentioned to friends how much she and Eliot were to one another, and what a different thing such an understanding made of life. She spoke, I fear, from memory; but I know no one but myself who would have had that fancy, unless, in moments of most private confession, it might have been Ruth Pearce. To others it was plain that Mrs. Arden told only the beautiful truth. She made a point of having an opinion upon everything that interested her husband; and if it was generally his opinion, that might well prove how much they were in accord. All through life, where he had harvested, she came gleaning after. She had a bowing acquaintance with nearly all his books. Sometimes she even managed to read them, doing best in biographies and letters; and in India, where ladies like Mrs. Arden are so involved with social duties, we are fortunately divorced by only a fortnight from the London literary papers. The little woman's innocent reputation for wide reading rested, really, upon a single volume – *Obermann*. Soon after they arrived she asked a great many people, one after another, if they had read *Obermann*. None of them had, and several inquired what else he had written, which necessitated a tactful explanation. She had not read the book herself, as it happened, and, as a matter of fact, never did; but it was lying at the time on Eliot's office table, and she fully meant to.

She had two objects in life. One was the boys at home, the other to 'keep up' with Eliot. 'The worst of having a clever husband,' she would explain, 'is that you *must* keep up.' Eliot was her sun; she circled round him, warmed by her revolutions. Whether she kept up or not, it was plain that she could never keep away. Even in the literal sense she could not; she could hardly leave him to his secretaries. Inevitably she would join his group and add herself to his conversations. Together with her devotion she had a kind of futile flair, poor lady, of the unusual and the interesting, and followed it hungrily, arriving too often to find a spectral banquet.

'Now isn't it a good thing, Sir Ahmed,' she exclaimed playfully, as they sat together on the dais and watched the waltzing, 'that I'm not a jealous woman? There is my husband dancing *again* with Mrs. Lemon!' She knew always where he was, and precisely what he was doing.

'I think the Chief Commissioner could never give cause for jealousy,' replied Sir Ahmed, smiling not quite comfortably. He was here on unsure ground. But the little lady prattled on.

'Now that is just like your sex – you always back one another up! As a matter of fact, he isn't very fond of dancing. I wish he were. It keeps a man young in this country, I think. Nor is he much of a ladies' man, I'm afraid, Sir Ahmed. Of course, he has one great friend – I think you've met her – Dr. Pearce.'

'Oh yes – that not quite young lady. She is very learned, I suppose,' said Mrs. Arden's Oriental guest.

'Oh, she is not *old*, Sir Ahmed. If she is not quite young, dear me, what are all we senior married women! And very clever, very clever indeed in her profession.'

The Mahomedan gentleman turned darkly red and cast down his eyes. He had gone as far as he dared, being not yet emancipated enough to banter with a woman on the terrible subject of age. Lady Ahmed, to the world, was without years, as Queen Elizabeth was without legs.

'So I am already told,' he said awkwardly.

'She is quite a wonderful surgeon – does the most difficult things. She has only been out two years, and operations in her hospital have gone up twenty-five per cent. already. But perhaps,' Mrs. Arden suggested, her eye following her husband as he deposited Mrs. Lemon, red and radiant, under a palm, and left her there, 'you would rather women did not go in for cutting people into little bits. It does jar upon some minds.'

'It is useful,' Sir Ahmed shrugged. 'And in this poor retrograde India, where our ladies are always still behind the curtain –'

'Oh, a great boon – I always say so. But perhaps it makes a woman just a *trifle* hard. Don't you think it might? *Please* don't think I mean to say that Miss Pearce is hard – or if she gives that impression, it is because she has such splendid principles. Really the finest character – my husband and I are proud to know her, truly.'

'That must be very favourable for Miss Pearce.'

'Oh, indeed, it is the other way. She is a great resource to us both. There are so few people in a place of this size that care about anything but promotion and official shop – it's not like Simla, you know. And Miss Pearce is really interested in what I call the higher side of life – books and ideas. Not that she and I always agree by any means in our opinion of an author. But my husband and I both find her, in that way, a true kindred soul. So much so that the moment a package of books comes out from home, off some of them must go to Dr. Pearce – sometimes before I have had time even to look at them,' Mrs. Arden added, with a pretence of grievance. 'You must get to know her, Sir Ahmed.'

'I have had the honour to be introduced by the Chief Commissioner himself. I thought her a lady of very fine intelligence,' replied the Judge, cautiously.

'Oh, but to know her well, as we do. I must ask you to tea to meet her. You, I am sure, such a leader of thought in your own world, would appreciate her. It is *such* a comfort to me that the Chief should have a type of mind like that to turn to when he has an hour to spare from work – he is a monster for work, as you know. And cares so little for ordinary amusements. But I think he has been allowed to monopolise her long enough just now – don't you? Suppose we go and claim a share of her, Sir Ahmed?'

They made their way across the crowded floor, the Mahomedan deferentially escorting, Mrs. Arden caught everywhere by petitions for dances, important communications from ladies neighbouring her own standing, or fluttering approaches from junior civilians' wives who *must* just tell her how beautifully everything was going. Smiling, she gathered their tributes with both hands. Perhaps the flow of her privileged talk was a little too unpausing. It was her way of putting people at their ease never to give them the smallest opening for being anything else. They had simply to stand still under the warm douche which descended upon them, and slip away as best they could when it was over. But it was quite a successful way. It was held to show, as Mrs. Arden meant it to be, how little 'side' she had; and that, where side was so likely, was the great thing. This was her happy little hour. She saw in all their words and glances how successfully she was 'making it pleasant'; she loved making it pleasant. It was a natural motion of her kind heart, and here it had the charm and gilding of Imperial function which made it, perhaps, even more pleasant for the devoted little lady herself. 'In my position' was a phrase often on her lips and always in her heart, a trumpet call to lofty duty, to receiving with a headache, to 'appearing' at gymkhanas when a quiet drive was so much more inviting, to asking tiresome people to dinner because they would expect it of the person in her position. Her position was remote, it was a temporary holding and set about with the prickly cactus, but she had climbed to it under Eliot's glorious lead; and its satisfactions were very real. She tasted them all as she progressed to where he sat on a flowered chintz chair, in the attitude of simple converse with Miss Pearce. It was the tone, too, of common intercourse with which he was saying: –

'How can you know anything about your spiritual force – vibration, or whatever it is? That is for others to measure. I might be wandering, after death, sightless, deaf, and dumb – bereft of all but my very Principle itself, and coming upon your essence in the same trance, my soul would cry in the wonderful shock of it, "Oh, it's you!"'

Ruth's eye fell upon the approaching lady.

'Here is Mrs. Arden,' she said. 'How well she is looking.'

And with Mrs. Arden I fancy the ball-room closed in upon them again, and the lights and the music and the scent of flowers; and they both saw the tragedy of Mrs. Biscuit's spangled chiffon rent by Major Devine's spur, and observed that Miss Hillyer of the Salt Department, the fair one, was dancing for the third time with Mr. Charles Cox.

CHAPTER XIV

THE Government of India had hardly settled down in Calcutta for the cold weather, Members of Council had hardly ceased to grumble at the winter rents of their stucco palaces, or Under-Secretaries to repine at the discomforts of Chowringhee boarding-houses, when word crept into the newspapers that His Excellency the Viceroy was extremely dissatisfied with the verdict and sentence in the Morgan case. The newspapers could hardly believe it. I speak, of course, of the Anglo-Indian ones.

'We should have thought,' wrote the *Calcutta Morning Post*, 'that in this instance, if anywhere, the claims of justice had been conscientiously and conspicuously met. The verdict upon the offence of Henry Morgan was rendered by a jury half composed of natives and entirely drawn from the place in which that offence was committed, and therefore not likely to take a palliated view. Morgan was sentenced, leniently it is true, but by a native civilian judge. Sir Ahmed Hossein's decision places him at all events beyond the suspicion of race prejudice in dealing with such cases, and adds to his already distinguished reputation for probity and fair-mindedness. This case, if any, should be one to allay what we can only call, with all respect, His Excellency's mania for interference with the decisions of the Courts in pursuit of some sublimated adjustment of the scales of justice, which apparently he alone feels capable of balancing; and we profoundly hope that further inquiry will prove the statement that it is to be reopened to be groundless.'

Further inquiry, however, brought forth that the record of the case had been sent for and the Administration of Ghoom asked to furnish a complete report of the circumstances. After careful examination the Government of India would send the papers to its own legal servant for opinion. No action would be taken until the view of the Advocate-General had been received. With so much the newspapers and the public had to be content. The official bow was made; the official curtain fell. 'That fellow takes a lot of teaching,' they said at the Calicut Club, referring to Lord Thame and his recent unsuccessful invitation to the understanding of the High Court of Bombay in the Laffan case. They said many other things at the Calicut Club, which was largely composed of merchants and professional men, with no curb upon their tongues like the official Biscuits of Pilaghur; but they looked with confidence to the Advocate-General, Rivers Finch. 'Finch'll squash it,' they said to one another over their long tumblers.

Just why Finch didn't squash it, if it was so completely in his power, is not easy to determine. To treat such a case like a noxious insect is so simple and obvious a course. He was at once provided by the Calcutta world with motives – he wanted the Legal Membership: he hoped for a 'K': he had fallen under the personal influence of Lord Thame – but I know nothing to prevent our concluding that he simply agreed with the Viceroy in the moral aspect of the case, and performed his function by finding a technical fault in its conduct. At all events he armed his Government with a misdirection to the jury, and the Secretary in the Home Department wrote promptly to the Chief Commissioner of Ghoom.

The letter reached Pilaghur in the morning, and the Ardens were to look in upon Ruth Pearce in the afternoon. Ruth had been away for a fortnight, attending a patient in a neighbouring native State. Mrs. Arden was detained, and the Chief Commissioner went alone. 'Tell her I *was* so sorry,' Mrs. Arden said to him as he left.

Ruth got up quickly to meet him as he entered her drawing-room, with a simplicity that she seemed to enforce. She may have wished to disguise from him, from herself, the truth that her day was culminating in his expected step. She had nothing for him but the commonplaces of welcome – where would he sit, and tea would be there directly – and she seemed to look at him almost unwillingly. When she did, the extraordinary emotion in her eyes was half hidden behind a veil of dignity which covered the rest of her completely, through which she moved and even spoke. It was her protest against their situation, and no one, he least of all, could have ignored it.

'How long you have been away,' he said. 'How is the Rani?'

'Getting on very well, I think. But I was only allowed to see her three days ago. She developed light smallpox the day I arrived, and until she had recovered from that they wouldn't let me go near her. Smallpox is a direct communication of annoyance from the gods; and the only treatment was administered by the priests, who sat outside her door and chanted from their sacred books all day and all night. I would have brought down only more anger. As soon as she was better she went personally to the village shrine to sacrifice a kid and feed the Brahmins – I saw the ceremony; it was very interesting – and the next day they came for me. Her other trouble was not serious. I was able to relieve her immediately, and came flying back yesterday.'

She spoke quickly and rather nervously, as if she feared a wrong word.

'And you have been sitting all this time in some miserable rest-house, with nothing to do. Absurd. You should have come home.'

'Not at all! I had a whole wing of a pink palace with wonderful old Chinese vases in it – I did feel covetous – and a carriage and pair with silver harness, where it wasn't rope, every day, and one evening a little nautch all to myself. I don't think they would have let me come away.'

His eyes smiled at her, and her own fell, as if it had not been quite seemly to provoke the smile.

'Well – by the way, my wife was kept this afternoon. She asked me to bring her excuses, and hopes you will dine on Sunday. We shall be quite alone.'

'Oh – hasn't Mrs. Arden – isn't Mrs. Arden coming? I am very sorry. Give her my love, please, and say I shall be delighted to come on Sunday. I hope she has been quite well. No more neuritis?'

'Quite, thanks. I was going to say that I have been visited like your Rani. I also have had a direct communication of annoyance from the gods.'

She looked at him with sudden gravity. 'Not really?'

'I'm sorry to say yes. It's the Morgan case, of course. We've heard from India.'

'They won't have it?'

'They want me to move the High Court of Calcutta and get the case retried. Sir Ahmed went too far, apparently, in charging the jury, and this gives them a chance.'

'And shall you?'

'I'm not inclined to.'

'Then you don't think that justice – miscarried?'

'I think justice carried rather obliquely. I think culpable homicide, on the evidence, was the right verdict, and not murder; but I also think Morgan should have got a good deal more. It seems plain to me, however, that much bigger issues are involved than the proper punishment of one man. For myself I would rather see him go free than let him incite the storm of race feeling and antagonism that will ravage our relations with these people if the case comes up again.'

Ruth silently considered the matter. Behind her grey eyes she put it to one touch-stone after another.

'You see,' he explained to her, 'during the last ten years there has been something like a recrudescence of the particular crime of which Morgan was guilty. Curzon drew the rein a bit tight, and after him came a reaction. And now Thame wants to take up an unmistakable position. It's his idea, I think, if he can get hold of the white murderer of a black man, to hang him.'

'And you think he should not be hanged?'

'Not by any Viceroy, with any intention of setting up for ever, at such a creature's expense, the lofty integrity of British rule. If his judge hangs him, well and good. But when all is said and done, the high-water mark of British justice is found in the Courts. If it is tempered with mercy here and expediency there, that is because it is human, or perhaps because it is divine. But for Heaven's sake let us leave it to its appointed medium. Nothing could be madder than the attempt to do it violence for its own good. It is like undertaking to add to the pain and discipline of the world. God knows there is enough.'

'But it is still to the Courts that the Government wish to appeal.'

'It is also from the Courts that they wish to appeal. The man has been tried and sentenced. In pushing for a new trial they declare their dissatisfaction with the first Court and their hope, possibly of a different verdict, certainly of a severer sentence. I consider that their very attitude is improperly suggestive and likely to influence a weak judge. It's an extraordinary step. Of course Thame has taken it before, and failed. He might fail again. But it shan't go further, if I can help it.'

'You think you can help it?'

'I hope so. They instruct me to take action "if in my opinion" the circumstances warrant it. That is mere official courtesy, of course; they expect me to go ahead. But I've written them, or Faulkner has for me, a strong letter, stating that in my opinion the circumstances do not warrant it. He has worked the thing up very well, and I hope we may block it.'

'What view does Mr. Faulkner take personally?'

'Oh, he agrees with me. But Faulkner's views' – he smiled whimsically. 'Faulkner is a very good fellow, but he turns out views like a typewriter.'

Ruth thought again seriously for a moment. Her face, in its concentration, unconsciously showed its lack; it had not the grace of leniency.

'I don't know the value of the arguments one way or the other,' she said, 'but it is clear that your instinct against doing this springs from something fundamental in you, just as the Viceroy's instinct for doing it springs from something fundamental in him. Then you *can't* do it, can you?'

In his eyes while he watched her was the whole hunger of the man for understanding; he absorbed what she said rather than listened to it; and as she glanced at him he looked away with an air that betrayed consciousness of his own avidity.

'I *need* not do it,' he said, half to himself.

'And they cannot proceed unless you do?'

'They cannot proceed unless I do – so long as I am Chief Commissioner of Ghoom,' Arden told her. 'They *might* override me – the law provides for it; but practically they couldn't.'

'Then, of course, you won't,' she simplified. 'The Viceroy wanting it makes it the more impossible, doesn't it?'

'In a way,' said Arden. 'Not impossible, but –'

'I sometimes feel very attracted by Lord Thame,' Ruth mused. 'I think if I had been under his influence I might have taken his view of the Morgan case. But you have captured my mind. Yes, I agree with you. I shall think more about it, but I know I shall agree with you. I am against him.'

'He is a man with a violent conscience and rather short perspective,' said Arden.

'I like it in him. I should have despised him if he had not felt compelled to take this matter up,' she declared. 'I believe I would have done it in his place.'

'I believe you would,' he said, criticising her from a distance, but soon drew close again.

'He can't help it – he oughtn't to help it. Isn't it curious,' Ruth went on, 'that Lord Thame should have been predestined to persecute Morgan, and you predestined to protect him, from exactly the same motive – what you believe to be right. The Viceroy's is the more heroic attitude, because it is the more unpleasant. I wish I agreed with him. This will make him more unpopular than ever.'

'I think he rather enjoys his unpopularity,' said Arden, smiling. 'It convinces him that he is right.'

'I should hate being a popular Viceroy,' exclaimed Ruth. 'Think what it means – the winkings, the compromises, the smile for everybody! I should feel as if I had wasted a splendid opportunity of disciplining myself for a principle.'

'You could not even be a popular woman,' he declared; and she took the tribute out of its husk and smiled with keen pleasure.

'I hope Mrs. Arden isn't very much worried about it,' she said presently.

'My wife – oh, I haven't mentioned it to her. She is worried about something else. We heard by to-day's mail that our second boy – the one at Heidelberg – was threatening to develop typhoid. Jessica was for starting for home at once, but she has consented to postpone deciding till we get an answer to my telegram of this morning. I don't approve. She is anything but fit for the voyage.'

'Oh, if it's serious, let her go. She will be ill if she doesn't. We shall have her down with nervous prostration. She is not well enough to bear suspense and inaction.'

'Nothing very serious was anticipated, and Teddy is a strong little chap,' he told her, and set forth the boy's symptoms as he was when the mail left. She agreed that they were not alarming; but her thought returned to the mother.

'Promise me that you won't influence her against what she thinks she ought to do,' she said.

Arden gave her an unwilling glance. 'Always with you, "what one thinks one ought."' He half reproached her. 'Does no one else ever know best?'

'Possibly, but one isn't bound by the beliefs of others. One *is* bound by one's own.'

They came back so constantly, these two, to the question of conscience, duty, right. It seemed always just below the level of their thoughts; the least reference disclosed it. They were for ever inciting one another to this abstract consideration; if it lurked under any aspect of any subject they would have it out, and fling it back and forth between them. One would say they drew a mutual support and encouragement from the exercise; one might go further and say that one offered it to the other.

'Poor Jessica, she has had a bad day,' said Arden. 'There is sickness among the servants too. Old Nubbi Bux has got something like pneumonia, I'm afraid. He wouldn't give in – came crawling up with our early tea this morning as usual; but Jessie saw that he wasn't fit to be about, and ordered him to bed at once. The old fellow has been with us a long time – ever since we were married; and my wife is very fond of him. She has been fussing over him the whole morning.'

'I will run in and see him to-night,' said Ruth promptly. 'I shall be in the direction of Government House early after dinner. I know my way about the quarters, and I won't disturb Mrs. Arden, but I'll leave a note; or, if it's urgent, I'll ask for Captain Dimmock.'

'That's very kind of you. Murray sent a Bengali hospital assistant, much to Jessie's indignation. But ask for me, please. I should like to know what you think of the old fellow.'

For a moment their eyes met in the pleasure of that suggestion. Then Ruth said gently, 'I think Captain Dimmock will do,' and he made no more protest.

'I am sending you back *The Nature of Man*,' she said to him; 'I am glad to have seen it in a translation. I know the German would have had more weight with me; and it isn't the kind of thing one wants to believe. Don't give it to Mrs. Arden; it will make her miserable.'

'She is going through a mild attack of that kind as it is, poor little woman. She told me yesterday that she could no longer avoid the conviction that she had no soul. She didn't know exactly what to do about it, but at all events, she wouldn't conceal it.' He spoke in the kindest way.

'What did you say to her?'

'I told her I thought the probabilities were that she was mistaken.'

'I am sure,' Ruth said, 'when people think they have no souls it only means that they aren't yet aware of them. It took a long time, didn't it, to make even our bodies articulate, even our senses delicate? The soul-perception, either of one's own or another's, must be the very last thing to evolve. She simply hasn't discovered her soul.'

'I'll tell her,' said Arden, smiling. 'By the way, it's her birthday the day after to-morrow. Will you help me to choose something for her at Moti Ram's? He seems to have some rather good sapphires, but I'm no judge.'

'I should be de – no – oh no! She will like you to choose them alone. I'm afraid I have rather a full day to-morrow,' she added formally, and a clumsy moment came between them.

'I have something for her birthday, too,' said Ruth presently, brightening. 'A book. I saw some extracts from it and sent home for it. It is called *Life Beautiful* – by a lady. It is drenched with Christian Science, but it has real charm, and I am counting on its making her happy.'

'Will it repair those shattered foundations, I wonder?' said Arden, smiling as he rose to go. 'How good you are to her!'

'I? But I love her,' Ruth cast at him like a stone. As the door closed she turned upon herself.

'Why did I tell that lie? I don't love her. I am sorry for her, but I don't love her. Why did I say I did?'

Perhaps she did not know, but we do. She loved the man, and must rebuke him. Being as she was.

Yet she relented, and before he had well left her. She ran out upon the verandah.

'Then you'll let me know about Teddy,' she called to him as he rode away.

CHAPTER XV

THE reply from Heidelberg was not altogether reassuring; and Mrs. Arden had just time to catch the mail steamer at Bombay. She left Pilaghur on her birthday, wearing Arden's bracelet because she could not bear to pack it, depending on Ruth's book for the distraction of her journey, supported by Mrs. Wickham's air-cushion, and unable to refuse a small bottle of Mrs. Lemon's pumelo punch because it got so cold at night up towards Delhi. Small kindnesses and attentions poured in upon her all day, and everybody was at the station to cheer her up and see her off, and tell her that Government House wouldn't be the same place without her, and that she must come back as soon as she *possibly* could, but that in any case she was perfectly right to go. She left on her birthday, in a little rain of tears and a little gust of importance, and her husband kissed her affectionately as she went out of his life, and said, 'You'll telegraph from Marseilles, dear?'

Ruth was not there; it was her hour for seeing out-patients; but Mrs. Arden sent her by Eliot a special farewell with her love. 'And I'm *so* glad you'll have somebody to speak to while I'm away,' she told him.

As Arden watched the train out of sight, Mrs. Faulkner murmured to Mrs. Biscuit that he seemed to feel it a good deal. It was noticed that he sent the carriage away and walked back alone; but none of them heard his acknowledgment of her as he strode along in the twilight under the acacias of the Lawrence road. 'She's a dear woman. She has always been a dear woman.'

If they had, who among them would have guessed how little the mist that stood in his eyes was called there by his immediate and present parting with his wife?

She had gone so long before. What lingered, what was now speeding west to the ship by the mail train, was just the dear woman.

CHAPTER XVI

ALL the Official Secrets Acts yet invented failed to prevent the Calcutta newspapers from getting hold of the fact that the Chief Commissioner of Ghoom had replied adversely to the reopening of the Morgan case. Secretaries have their human moments. These kept their lips drawn with care during office hours and hardly glanced an opinion; but they talked at the Club. It was a topic of the warmest human interest, and it involved their overlord in the warmest human way. After office hours they dropped down amongst the Public, the men of jute and tea and indigo, and had opinions, like other people. Naturally the import of Arden's protest got into the papers. It was announced with every variety of appreciative comment, from one end of India to the other. The report went that the Viceroy, in great anger, dismissed two native clerks on suspicion of having communicated it; but if the discipline had been complete it would have included half of the secretariats.

Thus was the extraordinary interest in the Morgan Case enhanced from the beginning. It was the most dramatic and the most disputable of all the attempts the Viceroy had made to induce the Courts to take a literal view of equal justice to black and white; and it came at the end of a series of defeats. The Judges of the land had simply not seen eye to eye with His Excellency in such matters; and if this meant that they suffered from any obliquity of vision, it was a very widespread malady. But Arden's attitude was a new feature. Never before had Lord Thame suffered a check from one of his own lieutenants. Arden's objection, added to all the rest, made a total of strong indignation in the public mind. It isolated the Viceroy and his Home Member, who alone was supposed to sympathise. It made them inquisitors, men of one persecuting idea, men of no common sense. The Press took the issue for granted – the Viceroy simply wouldn't, simply couldn't, go further; but even on the way to that conclusion poured forth columns of hostile comment, set free by the attitude of the Chief Commissioner of Ghoom.

In the midst of the shouting a brief *communiqué* dropped from the Home Department upon every editorial table, announcing that the statement which had found currency as to the views of the Administration of Ghoom, regarding the advisability of moving the High Court of Calcutta in the case of the Emperor *versus* Henry Morgan, was wholly premature. No correspondence of a definite nature had as yet passed between the Government of India and the local administration upon this subject, and Government would very gravely deprecate any attempt to excite the public mind by improper assumptions involving the most serious issues.

In such dignified terms did the fate of Henry Morgan swing to and fro among those who were as gods to him, dealing out the remainder of his concern with this life. He lay in Pilaghur gaol, flesh and blood and a memory, visited by the chaplain and by Mr. Moses Agabeg, a critical intelligence contemplating the universe and his strange share in it; but to the world outside he was a name to bandy, a battle-cry for passionate difference, or a sign for the resolute pursuit of a lofty policy.

Egerton Faulkner saw the *communiqué* in the Calcutta paper, and his eyeglass dropped involuntarily.

'I knew we couldn't pull it off,' he said to Mr. Arthur Poynder Biscuit. 'To the Viceroy in his present state of hunger for capital punishment we were merely inflammatory, Biscuit – inflammatory. Clearly nothing but the rope will satisfy Thame. By the dog of Egypt, I wish we could give it him – for his personal benefit.'

'I respect the Chief's courage in differing,' replied little Biscuit, 'but I think in his place I should *not* have differed.'

'I am sure you wouldn't, Biscuit. I'm afraid I can't flatter myself that I would either. Thame is only human, and Bengal will be going next year. I ventured to hint to the Chief that he was risking a good deal. I regretted it, Biscuit. I received my first cold word from him. But when our action got abroad the other day I said in my private bosom, "There, my dear old boy, goes the Lieutenant-Governorship of Bengal, the Blue Ribbon of the Service, a pyrotechnic sacrifice to an opinion." And I nearly wept, Biscuit – I did, indeed. I nearly broke my heart.'

'Has the Chief seen this?' asked Biscuit.

'I am just going to find out. Quite probably not. Arden may be depended upon to go through any newspaper and miss the only point in it of importance to him personally. I love that man, Biscuit. I feel towards him as Alcibiades did towards Socrates, upon my honour. I could grow old in listening to his talk. The fellow has charm – he's as winning as a woman. Gad, if he doesn't convince me of my own reality. I've always felt, do you know, Biscuit, that if I could not be Socrates I would be Alcibiades. Indeed I have. For the sake of his distinguished acquaintance. And if, like that agreeable fellow, I were not afraid that I am altogether too drunk, I would tell you things about Arden, Biscuit, that would make you long to be a bigger and a better man. Remind me of it another time, and I will.'

The Secretary left the somewhat strained but wide and obedient smile upon the face of Mr. Biscuit which his pleasantries were apt to provoke, and sought his Chief, newspaper in hand, to find that he had seen the paragraph.

'Nothing more from Calcutta?' Arden asked.

'Nothing official. But I've had a private line from Lawson, who has just come in as Deputy in the Home Department, saying that

Thame is going to put his back into this. He's been heard to say that Morgan's case is the blackest and most disgraceful since that Madras business five years ago, that the verdict was rotten and the sentence inexplicable, and that if the thing is allowed to pass he will consider it an indelible stain upon his administration of the country.'

'That's Thame, isn't it?' said Arden smiling. 'The thing must be identified with *him*. The rest of us lay it, too easily perhaps, to the charge of a star.'

'His Excellency himself possesses every virtue yet invented for the inconvenience of the human race. If he found one missing overnight he would send to the Stores for it in the morning,' said Faulkner. 'And he is annoyed if any one connected with his administration is less conspicuously adorned.'

Arden laughed. 'Thame always irritates you, Faulkner.'

'He does, by God! His determination to play Providence to a country he only *saw* three years ago – it's ludicrous.'

'Four years. It's redeemed though, by his straight hitting. You remember that pompous old ass Conybeare in the Foreign Department? I happened to see Thame's marginal note on a paper of his relating to the trucial chiefs of the Gulf Coast. "Six pages of pure nonsense and seven mistakes in spelling!"'

'Hectoring beast!' laughed Faulkner, catching at his eyeglass. 'Well, sir, I suppose this will be returned for our more impartial consideration.'

'I thought you explained our views with the utmost clearness. I don't know on what ground we can be asked to change them.'

'They may have something up their sleeve. There's a meeting of Council on Friday. We shall hear early next week – probably from the Hon. the Home Member; Sir Peter never says anything but Amen to Thame. But for that matter none of them do. They ought to be painted in a ring like mediæval saints in their mediæval nightshirts, offering adoration. Or an allegorical subject, "Anthony Andover Thame, Viceroy of India, and his marionettes."'

'Thame is a man of extraordinary personal influence, certainly,' said the Chief Commissioner, twisting in his chair with a motion of discomfort. 'By the way, what's the meaning of that?'

He pushed across the table a sumptuous envelope, and Faulkner drew from it an equally sumptuous card. It bore the arms of the regiment in gilt; it was elaborately engraved; and it mentioned a date upon which Colonel Vetchley and the officers of the Second North Barfordshires requested the honour of the Hon. the Chief Commissioner's company to dinner, rather more than a fortnight in advance.

'The Barfords seem anxious that you should dine with them,' said Faulkner.

'I dine with them often enough. I'm an honorary member of their mess – I'm always dropping in there. Why all this flummery? It has an air of intention.'

'Oh, I believe it's to be a great affair. I hear they're asking fellows from every regiment in the Command; but you are to be the only civilian. They mean to toast you in recognition of your recent uncompromising attitude towards tyranny, I understand.'

'Good heavens! Can they imagine that I would permit such a thing?'

'They are carried away emotionally, sir. A regiment is a corporate ass. The other day when you came in from Guruband they proposed in their happy hearts to take the horses out of your carriage and drag you home. I heard of it and met you with my dog-cart.

'Good heavens!' said Arden again. 'Well, I shall decline this at once. I can go out into the District. And when you see Vetchley,' he added with irritation, 'give him a hint, please, that we have all left school.'

CHAPTER XVII

PILAGHUR saw itself daily, dined with itself most evenings, drifted in and out of the Club every afternoon except Sunday. On Sundays the Club had an air of premeditated abandonment. The home papers lay scattered about, the chintz-covered armchairs stood empty. Only the odd people and the new comers went to the Club on Sundays; the type observed the tradition that the seventh day should be spent somehow differently from the other six. The dear people of England change so little with place or circumstance. Any one who knew the island would have felt at home and uncomfortable in Pilaghur Club on Sunday afternoon.

Ruth Pearce, however, was one of the odd people, the people who liked to look over the *Saturday* or the *Fortnightly* undisturbed by shrieks from the Badminton courts or Mrs. Lemon's last triumph over her cook; and Mr. Cox was one of the new comers. Mr. Cox had to learn so many things. It was pathetic to look at him in his interest and enthusiasm and his exuberant complexion, and think how many. He liked Miss Pearce; she reminded him of a friend of his mother's at Oxford. 'Most people light up from the outside,' he said about her, 'she lights up from the inside,' like his mother's friend at Oxford. When he, too, dropped into the Club on Sunday afternoon they always talked.

'You are in magnificent training,' she was telling him, 'but you will soon learn that it doesn't pay to walk twenty miles in one day anywhere in the plains of India to keep it up. And you are bathed in perspiration. Do you know that the temperature will drop fifteen degrees in the next half-hour?'

'I'll go and get a rub. I sent a change over here – my fellow ought to be waiting about somewhere now. Don't you think it would be a good thing to have some tea?'

And in ten short minutes he had reappeared redder than ever, but, as he assured her, 'dry as a chip.' He sat down solidly to the curls of bread and butter. 'They do cut it thin, don't they?' he said. 'What are you laughing at, Dr. Pearce?'

'Oh, just at you,' she told him. 'You're so nice and new. You don't belong to India yet. Do you still read the *Times*?'

'Naturally.'

'Still take a beer at lunch?'

The young man laughed. He had an explosive laugh, as yet uncontrolled, like his other emotions. Already it had earned him a nickname, and a little quiet dislike.

'When I can get it. Best drink going, Dr. Pearce.'

'You won't always think so. And, of course, you still bleed with sympathy for the down-trodden natives?'

'Oh, now you're chaffing. But – I say, Dr. Pearce. Isn't the Chief a thoroughly good fellow?'

'A thoroughly good fellow.'

'The sort of fellow you could implicitly follow?'

'Quite.'

'Then why doesn't he back up the Viceroy in this Morgan business?'

'For the only reason – because he believes Lord Thame to be wrong.'

'Do you agree?'

'Yes, I do, wholly.'

Charles Cox having finished his tea, leaned back with folded arms.

'It amazes me,' he said, with knitted brows. 'Justice was not done.'

'Justice was not done. It does happen so, sometimes, in this imperfect world. But something was done, and for reasons a good deal more important than the adequate punishment of any man, it ought to be considered done finally.'

'Morgan wasn't properly convicted. They didn't half exhaust the evidence.'

'How do you know?'

'I've heard a lot about it from my munshi, Afzul Aziz – the old boy who is teaching me Hindustani, you know. He knows the bazaar like his pocket, and he says he can produce men who will testify that the poor old chap that was murdered begged for mercy on his knees, kissing Morgan's feet, and that the brute shot him through the head deliberately. You know, of course, that he got off on a plea of self-defence.'

'I wouldn't place much reliance upon any talk of Afzul Aziz,' said Ruth. 'I know him – he taught me Hindustani too. He's very good at teaching Hindustani. But he's an excitable, malevolent old fellow. And remember, the bazaar will be full of evidence the moment it is understood that the Viceroy wants it. That is a handicap His Excellency must submit to.'

'I think I know when a chap's telling the truth,' said young Cox, with masculine reserve. 'And I confess to you, Dr. Pearce, that in my opinion the honour of every Englishman in Pilaghur is pledged to assist the effort Lord Thame is making in this thing. It seems to me heroic.'

Ruth smiled. 'I suppose it does,' she said.

'And I belief the Chief will come round,' said Cox sanguinely.

Ruth lifted her chin ever so slightly. 'I know he will not,' she said. 'When a decision like that crystallises with him into a matter of conscience he simply *can't* "come round." Nothing any of them could say —'

She stopped abruptly. Arden's head, looking oddly boyish under a tweed cap, thrust itself in at the door inquiringly, and making them out in their corner, his body followed it.

'Have you a cup left?' he asked. 'What a blessed peace there is in here. The crows are making night hideous about my place. They fairly drove me out.'

Charles Cox got up in deference to the Government of Pilaghur, and sat down again respectfully in a less comfortable chair. Presently, as the Chief Commissioner continued to talk plaintively about the crows, and nothing but the crows, Mr. Cox slipped away, and they heard the wheels of his dogcart go out from under the porch.

'Nice boy that,' said Arden.

'Very nice. What is troubling you?'

'You are a wonderful woman. Let me think — which of my various complications may properly be described as "troubling"? The famine belt is spreading in Southern Ghoom — I suppose you know? and the ecclesiastics are fighting like mad at Guruband. The Anglican Padre there has fallen out with the Scotch one, and won't lend his blessed church for Presbyterian services. Seems it's too blessed. They both suggest that I should build them a new one as a solution. I've also had a tremendous letter from headquarters — Sir Peter Hichens this time.'

'Ah,' she said. 'Does he bring out anything new?'

'Nothing whatever. The familiar arguments — they're quite good enough to worry a man with.'

'Are they very angry with you?'

'According to dear old Peter, not at all angry. But "grieved" –
deeply grieved.' He looked at her with his charming smile, and she
saw him whimsically ill-treated by fate. This lighter, sweeter side of
him always made a slave of her, and for an instant she just smiled
back. Then she flew again to the matter in hand.

'But to you – that can make no difference?' Her expectancy had
an eager stress in it. She looked a shadow sunk in her chair, with a
pale face and luminous eyes, something over-emphasised.

'None whatever. Isn't it rather stuffy in here? Shall we take a
turn? I should like, if I may, to walk home with you.'

All the way he unconsciously talked to fortify the opinion he
had conceived; and he left her at her own gate more convinced
than before that he had taken the right course, more proudly certain than ever that nothing would turn him from it.

CHAPTER XVIII

'PLEASE be at Mrs. Sannaway's at six; must see you this afternoon,'
wired Mrs. Tring to Mr. Frayley Sambourne, and sent out the cook
with it. The cook was always having to go with a telegram, because
Annie had always already gone with one; but they did it cheerfully,
or anything else that was out of the way, for Mrs. Tring; Mrs. Tring
was so out of the way herself. Their mistress was the drama and the
wonder of their lives, their constant entertainment; and she sometimes called them "dear." Annie said the fact was she was more like
a 'uman being than anything else, a thing you didn't often find. Annie was wrong, of course; it was just the other thing in their mistress
that charmed them – her expanded eyes, and the way she would call
a messenger at midnight to take an article to Southampton Street.
They flew with the telegrams, feeling as if they were on the stage of
journalistic achievement, too, in small parts.

Mrs. Sannaway's Sundays were probably the pleasantest in
Bloomsbury. She was the most generous soul, Mrs. Sannaway, with
herself and her teapot, and her two little drawing-rooms on Sunday
afternoons. She asked everybody to come to her then, although she
might really have asked as few as possible and they would gladly

have turned up. They all came, the few and the many, the assured and the frightened; people who had written as many novels as Mrs. Sannaway had, and people who thought that some day they would like to write just one. Mrs. Sannaway's memory was not as good as her hospitality, and Mr. Sannaway was often too much involved with the muffins to help her with her slightly nonplussed welcome of shy young persons who said guiltily, 'I'm afraid you don't remember me, Mrs. Sannaway. I met you at the Women Writers' Dinner and you asked me to come,' or 'I interviewed you a little while ago for M.A.P. and you were kind enough to say you were at home on Sundays.' The ambiguity with which she would place them on convenient sofas and invite Mr. Sannaway to provide them with tea was always kind, however, and nearly always she contrived to convince herself about them before they went away, often saying, with a warm parting hand-clasp, 'Now I remember all about you!'

The room was full when Frayley Sambourne arrived, but Mrs. Tring was not in it. He was promptly introduced by Mrs. Sannaway to Miss Maskin, 'who ballooned across Lake Baikal – you must know. And do get her something to eat, she must be starving.' When he had appeased Miss Maskin's hunger for tea-cake and gratified her thirst for adventure, he found himself on the crest of an emotion with a Celtic Revivalist, one of the most earnest; and after that Mrs. Sannaway talked to him for a long time herself; she was an old friend.

'Is Deirdre coming?' she asked. 'It's nice of her to be late and give me a chance. I know you will whip off together.'

That was the way their relation was understood among people who knew them; they could be depended on to whip off together. Sambourne's devotion was smiled at for its whimsical futility; Mrs. Tring's intentions were not thought to be serious. The Under-Secretary was a feather in her cap and a prop for some of her moods, not more. People looked after them with amusement as they whipped off together.

When Mrs. Tring's cab at last dashed up, the door that let her in let out almost the last of Mrs. Sannaway's other guests. She passed the Celtic Revivalist, who always stayed late, and was inclined to come back with her, on the stairs, and in the drawing-room she found only Frayley and Alfred Earle remaining.

'How late I am,' she cried. 'And I meant to be so early, Kate; but Victoria and I became involved in a discussion: and I had to take a little Pater before starting, to regain my tone.'

'Very late,' Mrs. Sannaway assured her. 'But you find us all faithfully waiting.'

'I like coming into a room,' Mrs. Tring told them, 'when everybody has just gone. People leave so much suggestion behind them. Their breath, their words, the psychic emanations remain. I know you have had an interesting afternoon, Kate, by the disposition of the furniture.'

'The Sally Lunn is stone cold. I do not advise it,' said Mr. Sannaway, hovering with plates; but Mrs. Tring took a double slice and ate it hungrily, explaining that she had forgotten to lunch and was in a fainting condition.

'And oh, my dear Catharine – my play! I've burnt my play!'

'Burnt "The Fever of the Gods"?' demanded at least two of the other four together, in amazed unbelief.

'And I kept Viola Vansittart here for two mortal hours this afternoon to talk it over with you! She loved what I told her of it,' declared Mrs. Sannaway.

'Ah, Viola would have been splendid for me. But isn't it true that she has bound herself body and soul to play only Arthur Haflin's things? I *was* so hoping it was true. The English drama is perishing for a breath of the ideal – and she does truly care for him, doesn't she?'

'One hopes it isn't all expressed in the brougham and the sables,' said Mr. Earle.

Mrs. Tring looked at him with disfavour and sudden gloom.

'Harsh and bitter?' she exclaimed, gazing before her sadly. 'Why will men of the world say such things? My soul shivers before you, dear Mr. Earle.'

'I'm so sorry,' said the Editor of the *Prospect*. 'But tell us why you burned your play, Mrs. Tring.'

'It is burned – burned – burned,' said Mrs. Tring, while Frayley Sambourne watched her. 'It is a heap of grey ashes in my bedroom grate. It took a long time, but when it was quite dead out it had about as much vitality in it as it had before. Oh, I want to write something round real passion – something human and throbbing and cruel. Suddenly, the other day out of a newspaper, my situation leaped at me – a soldier tragedy from India, one of those "Without Benefit of Clergy" things, you know –'

'The Morgan case?' asked Mr. Earle.

'Don't – don't give it a name. It is present to me still nebulously, potentially. *I* must give it all the signs; it must take body and form from *me*. But yes – but yes! The Morgan case! You have named my play – you and Circumstance, who is the godmother of all plays! But I could do nothing till I had burned the other poor anæmic thing, so I offered it a sacrifice to Life, in the hope that she will now let me come near her.'

'You will have to give it another name, I am afraid,' said Alfred Earle. 'The Morgan case will be as familiar to the British public as the Tichborne case before the winter is over, unless I am very much mistaken.'

'I don't think so,' put in Frayley Sambourne. 'At one time we thought something of that sort might be anticipated, but the probability now is that very little more will be heard of the matter. No use going into detail; but Thame is encountering opposition from the local Government, and our notion is that he will be obliged to accept their view. Very good for him if he will – Thame is a trifle over-fond of centralisation.'

'I sometimes wish we didn't exist in India,' said Mrs. Sannaway, with a sigh as uncompromising as the sentiment. 'Nobody can deny that we ought to be wildly interested in it; but none of us are. Except you and Lord Akell, Mr. Sambourne. I have one friend out there who sometimes writes to me, a Dr. Pearce, a clever woman, but it's very hard to keep in touch.'

'I'm afraid I'm horribly ignorant,' said Mr. Sannaway, 'but I never heard of the Morgan case.'

'You will,' Earle insisted. 'I've had several letters about it from Lawrence Lenox, a Judge of one of their High Courts out there. He says Thame isn't the fellow to take opposition from anybody. He's a great admirer of Thame, and considers him in this case perfectly right. He says the judgement was a scandal.'

'If you don't mind,' said Mr. Sambourne to Mrs. Tring, glancing at his watch, 'I think we ought to be off.'

It was half peremptory and half privileged. He looked at her fur boa on the floor, and seemed just to fall short of picking it up and putting it round her neck.

'Always, always, it is poor me who is charged with dawdling,' cried Mrs. Tring. 'I am sure I am the easiest person in the world to get out of a room. Pray, then, sir, come along.'

She took longer than she had yet spent in farewelling; but he finally marshalled her downstairs. They hailed a cab, and sat in it for two minutes in silence, Mrs. Tring gazing out over the bobbing horse's head into some far and exciting vista which her companion could not see.

'When,' Sambourne said at last, 'are you going to remember that you have something to tell me?'

'Oh, I remember,' she assured him. 'My whole being is occupied with it. And I will tell you presently. But I must find the words. While I am looking for them let us talk of something else.'

Mr. Sambourne smiled indulgently. 'When are you coming to the House again?' he asked.

'No, as a subject that won't do. It ministers directly to your egotism, dear Frayley, and at this moment I could not consider even your shadow. Think of something else.'

'Why won't Victoria marry Anthony Thame?'

'Ah, that's better – that ministers to mine. Because she's my daughter. I could never marry Anthony Thame.'

'If Victoria were as much like you as that,' said Frayley Sambourne seriously, 'I would have married her long ago myself.'

Mrs. Tring tossed out a laugh, a laugh with no age, from the very fount at which the gods draw mirth. 'My dear Frayley, she wouldn't have you, either.'

Frayley crossed his arms and knitted his brows. Knitting his brows drew his features together, which were otherwise rather vague.

'What objection do you suppose she has to fellows like Thame and me? We are both well enough, in a way, aren't we? Both have the type of mind that is called strenuous, both –'

'Don't, Frayley. I decline to consider the points in which you are like Anthony. There must be far more in which you differ, or you couldn't live so near me as you do. You're not a prig, and he's a cavernous prig, with those great black eyes. I've sat through a whole dinner beside him and never seen him smile. My soul flies at the approach of Anthony Thame; my body can hardly stay in the same room with him.'

'But why?'

'He has no spiritual curiosity. His soul has nothing to give to another, nothing to take from another. His world is full of people and things, and the people are only other things. He is all for what he must do. I am all for what I must be.'

'And is Victoria like that?'

'I don't know,' said Mrs. Tring forgetfully. 'Victoria isn't the least like me.'

'But you said –'

'Never mind. Listen. I can tell you now. There is the most wonderful definite news of Herbert!'

'Ah.' Mr. Sambourne uncrossed his arms and crossed them again, with a suggestion of self-control. 'Another trace?'

'Indeed, another trace. A woman, Frayley – and a child!'

'Good God!'

'It seems he became enamoured of her very shortly after his arrival in San Francisco and promptly carried her off – you remember his dashing ways. Kelly gives no particulars of her origin, but through the veil of his language I see that she is beautiful and very desolate. I imagine her to be of Spanish blood – who is it who writes so much about the old Spanish days in San Francisco? Some woman. Herbert would be instantly drawn by an old historic sorcery like that. And the child! "The born image," Kelly says in his way, "of H.V.T." Frayley, I *want* that child.'

'Is the woman his wife?'

'Kelly doesn't say. But she is in need – she came to him, hearing of his quest, to tell him so, bringing the child – that is the child of my son.'

'What did Kelly do?'

'He gave her five pounds and charged it to account and wrote to me. Which was perfectly right, except that he ought to have given her fifty and telegraphed.'

'And what do you propose to do?'

'Send for them both. Give them the shelter of my roof until Herbert appears to claim them. Every nerve in me leaps to welcome them. You know what I think of the marriage convention – do you dream that I shall be troubled as to whether it exists or not between them? She is his first and only passion, and its miracle is there with her. We must make room – make room.'

'It is impossible.'

'So Victoria says. I do not understand Victoria. She adores Herbert, and yet she says this is impossible. But I cannot listen. My heart says, "Do it; it is the Only Thing."'

'Oh my dear lady, I must convince you that you are wrong. You have no proof of any sort. What does Kelly know about this woman, and what do we know about Kelly?'

Deirdre looked at him softly – the 'we' touched a responsive chord. 'Don't range yourself against my heart,' she said.

'It is a matter in which I imagine Herbert would wish to exercise sole responsibility.'

'How can he exercise anything, frozen up in the Yukon? *Don't* oppose me, you great strong man.'

'I should like information additional to Kelly's. And I very much prefer that you should take no direct action in the matter for the present. Let me put it in the hands of my solicitors – they will get hold of the facts for us.'

'I know solicitors are useful things. But if you only knew, Frayley, how a woman wants a baby, on which she has a legitimate claim.'

'It is beautiful in you, Deirdre. But that is precisely what I should like first to establish.'

'Ah, if you will only look at it with affection, with the eyes of your real self,' cried Mrs. Tring, 'and not with cold hostility, like Victoria, I will be guided by you, I truly will, in this as in so many matters. And, indeed, I don't want anything *very* absorbing to come into my life until my play is born. I will wait, if you think it best, Frayley.'

'I do think it best,' said Frayley, as he rang her door-bell for her. 'And may I hope that you will be in the Ladies' Gallery on Wednesday?'

The door was opened by Victoria, who almost huddled her mother into the entry.

'You haven't told Aunt Pamela, mother? Or Lavinia?'

'I have seen only the dear Sannaways, in Russell Square – and Frayley.'

'We must absolutely keep it from Lavinia. I don't believe a word of it, but we must absolutely keep even the lie from Lavinia.'

'But why?' demanded Mrs. Tring, gathering up the sheaf of letters and telegrams on the hall table.

'Because it would break her heart,' said Victoria.

CHAPTER XIX

'MR. Vice – The King!' said the Mess President, standing in his place in the Barfordshire's whitewashed mess-room with a glass of port in his raised hand.

'Gentlemen – "The King"!' responded young Dimmock, Vice-President, from the other end of the table.

There was an instant's silence, every man on his feet, every glass raised. Charles Cox, dining at the Mess for the first time, brought his to his lips, then, seeing himself alone in the act, lowered it again, blushing. The mess-sergeant, standing to attention behind the Colonel's chair, eyed him contemptuously. The band struck up the National Anthem, and as the last note sounded, 'The King! God bless him,' said Major Devine. 'The King!' 'The King!' echoed the others, drank, and sat down again.

Charles Cox was emotional. The imperial sacrament thrilled him. He felt as he did when a regiment passed him in the street; the precision, the formality of each marching step combined with its significance to underline it, and make poetry of it. So with the simple function of the King's health, drunk once a week in the Barfordshires' mess, as in every other, by a dozen men in uniform, half of them boys, on their legs and looking serious for the moment, but taking the high sentiment in the simple order of the day. Mr. Cox wondered if they realised what a fine thing they did, and had an instant's regret that he hadn't gone in for Sandhurst.

'Awful sorry we couldn't get your old man to-night,' said Lascelles to Cox.

'The Chief? He's been out in the District for a week.'

'I know. I say, d'you see the Gunner at the other end of the table?'

'Which is he?' asked Mr. Cox.

'Oh well, there's only one Gunner in the room, you know. Next to Dimmock.'

'Yes; what about him?'

'He's had the most extraordinary luck, that f' low. Practically just out, and over here from Bunderabad, to have his first try at pig. Went out yesterday with three or four of our f' lows. Came bang on to a leopard, if you please, jabbed his spear into him and pinned him down. Brute clawed like mad and got in an ugly scratch on his pony's foreleg – drew blood – and the plucky little brute never budged. I offered him five hundred for her this morning – wouldn't look at it.'

'I thought you generally shot leopards,' said Mr. Cox intelligently.

'So you jolly well have to – it was this f' low's extraordinary luck, don't you see? First time out – think of it! Well, I tell you, the other chaps weren't so keen – ponies somehow not staunch – awf' ly unstaunch, you know – but when they saw he was really there to stay they all got a hole in. By Jove, when the skin came in it looked like a tennis net! There were two in his tail!'

'That would spoil it,' said Mr. Cox.

'His luck doesn't hold everywhere, though,' continued Lascelles. 'At bridge, for instance – he's a fearful fool at bridge. You play bridge?'

'I'm afraid not.'

'Well, of course – it's a game where a lot of money *can* change hands, you see, and this Gunner-man – I forget his exact name – was pretty well bled all round night before last at the Club. So last night he was goin' to play again, and old Devine was brought into the game. "Look here," old Devine said to him, "Can you afford to lose a thousand rupees to-night?" "No," says he. "Then if you play, I don't," says Devine, and he didn't – I mean the other chap didn't. Pretty decent of old Devine I call it, don't you? Seems he knew the other chap's people, and they're not well off.'

'I was thinking of learning bridge,' said Charles Cox.

'It'll cost you about five hundred, probably, to learn in this place. Cheap bridge, I call it here.'

'I don't,' said Mr. Cox. 'I only get five hundred at present. Can't you learn without playing for money?'

'Oh, well, you can't expect chaps to teach you for nothing, you know. They've all had to pay for their experience. I had to shell out about seven, but I'm not quick, you know; in fact, I consider myself rather an exceptional duffer. I wish I'd offered that f' low a bit more for the mare. Brandreth – that's his name. Rotten name to remember. He races her, too – she's entered for three events next week. Ridin' himself. He's a clever rider, Brandreth is, but not a good stableman – takes no sort of care of his cattle. Have you done yourself pretty well in a mount this year?'

'Well, no,' said Mr. Cox, 'I bought a nice-looking animal, and paid a good price for it, but it developed a bone disease of some sort the week after I got it, and –'

'Sold you a pup, eh? Hard luck.'

'No – a horse. Oh, I see – yes, I dare say I was done.'

'That was only my elaborate jest,' apologised Lascelles, and, under cover of a crystallised plum, gave up. Charles Cox, on the other hand, thought within himself, that his choice of the Indian Civil was not to be regretted after all. He ran over in his mind the interests Lascelles had mentioned, and said to himself, 'That's this fellow's whole life.'

From the fresh-coloured young gentleman in the immaculate mess-jacket beside him, cutting away at the crystallised plum, his contemptuous thought turned to the rank and file and the substance of existence as they had to lead it, wandered from the feast, and settled sadly upon Henry Morgan. 'What else,' he reflected, 'could be expected?'

Mr. Cox adopted then that regretful and slightly minatory attitude towards the Army which characterises so many civil minds. Henry Morgan, of course, was the predisposing cause; he felt more and more keenly, more and more tragically, about that matter. He saw the Army an institution necessary to the preservation of peace, which he, nevertheless, for ethical reasons, was compelled to criticise. It was an imperfect institution, an unsatisfactory institution, too much given to compromise, and far too much to the protection of Henry Morgans. In fact, it *was* an institution, that was the trouble, and not a simple agency at the disposal of the Civil Arm.

In the affair of Private Morgan, Charles Cox had advanced, and already beheld himself the ally of justice. Justice sitting on high, gave her clasp to the Viceroy. Charles Cox would take Lord Thame's other hand, at present outstretched so vainly; and Afzul Aziz, the munshi who had taught so many Mr. Coxes Hindustani, would hold again by him. Thus, perhaps, Mr. Cox saw the heroic chain complete; and as the adventure was not free of danger to himself, we can only admire him for it, while we pretend to smile.

Lascelles prattled on to his neighbour on the other side.

'Get along with an allowance of a hundred a year? Oh, it can be done – I know f'lows who do it in this regiment. But we're a pretty economical lot, you know. All the same, personally – well I touched exactly thirty-one rupees of my pay last month. Thirty-one dibs! Every blooming copper.'

'I'd be tickled to death,' said Davidson of the Guzeratis, family man, 'to have a hundred a year. But there's one thing to be said, they don't worry us about uniform as they do you.'

'Iniquitous, I call it,' threw in a man on the Staff. 'I went home on leave the other day after putting in a year in the Intelligence, in

Simla, and while there treated myself to a new waistcoat. It wasn't obesity; it was white ants. "What's it goin' to be?" I said to my man. "Six pounds," says he. "O, damn it all," thinks I, "I'll try another shop," an' at the other shop they says seven pounds. Well, it wasn't any use goin' further, was it? There you are. What are you going to do? So I got the thing. First p'rade after I joined, the Colonel looked me up an' down. "'S'pose you know," he said, "they've taken about two inches of gold lace off us this year?" "Where?" says I. "In the waistcoat," says he. So there you are, you see. What are you going to do?'

Young Lascelles bent over to him earnestly.

'You can wear it out, you know. There's that to be said. They let you wear it out.'

Mr. Cox listened with a silently compressed lip, and turned to a gentle-looking young man in the uniform of the Royal Engineers, who sat next him on the other side.

'You're just back from somewhere, aren't you? '

'Yes; S'maliland.'

'Interesting country?'

'Shouldn't say so. Consists too largely of sand.'

'Should you call the dervishes a people worth studying – ethnologically, I mean?'

'We found it worth while to observe them pretty closely. At Imali –'

'I say,' cut in a subaltern from the other side.

'Sir to you,' said the Sapper.

'Were you in that show?'

'Rather – and at Ajjak, too.' For the first time a smile gathered about the lips of the Sapper, the exulting smile of a schoolboy who relates an adventure in which he had no particular title to appear.

'I thought you fellows were thought too valuable –'

'Oh, I know, we're always having that sung at us. But at Imali we wanted all we had, you know. Besides my fellows were in occupation – we'd been digging out the well for three days before the rest came up. They couldn't refuse us a look in under those circumstances.'

'I suppose not,' said the subaltern, with a half-tone of commis-eration.

'And it's all very well to say our chaps are too valuable – that it isn't their business, and so forth. I don't say it's primarily their busi-ness; but I can tell you those two shows made different men of our fellows. Different men. Especially the Punjabis. It's absurd. They like to let off their rifles just as well as anybody else.'

'Of course they do,' said the subaltern pacifically. 'Beastly lot of routine they must have.'

'Well, it's no joke having to march three hundred miles between wells under a tropical sun with no tents, and then to find water for a thousand ponies out of a choked-up hole when you get there,' re-marked the Sapper equably. 'Men rotten with scurvy too, half of 'em.'

'How did you manage to get scurvy?' inquired Charles Cox, with a hint of criticism.

'It was generally attributed to the fact that we were fifty days on half rations, exclusively of flour,' responded the Sapper. 'But after Imali we had the luck to walk into some of the enemy's cattle. I gave my men a sheep to every six or eight of 'em, and they just gorged it. In a fortnight they were practically fit again. Nothing like fresh meat for scurvy – and a fight, if you can get it. Of course, on-ions are all right, too.'

'I believe there was tremendous carnage at Imali,' remarked Mr. Cox.

'We pounded 'em. Naturally. We'd have pounded 'em harder, only the Somali transport with the main lot stampeded. We were all right; our camels were Indian – never budged, just knelt down be-hind us and looked this way an' that way – cool as cucumbers – I didn't even take the ammunition boxes off their backs. But every-thing S'mali bolts – two legs or four, they all know how to use 'em.'

'Levies not much use, eh?' asked the subaltern.

'Not under our management. The Mullah can make soldiers of them, but he takes a different way. In the Mullah's show, of course, the best men get the rifles and the ponies. If a rifleman drops, some-body is supposed to take his rifle so that it shan't be bagged by the other side, and carry on. Well, about four hundred of the Mullah's riflemen, when they came on at us, gave their ponies to spearmen to hold. When these gentry saw how it was going they jumped on the ponies and cleared out. But unwisely, they made for the Mullah's camp, see? The Mullah, being a little out of sorts I dare say, said, "Hello, what are you doing here?" And had them all executed on the spot. That's against our ideas, of course, but it's the only way to make soldiers out of Somalis.'

'It will be a long time, no doubt,' Mr. Cox observed thoughtfully, 'before we exert anything like moral force in a country like Somaliland.'

The Sapper lighted a fresh cigar. 'In my opinion it isn't worth anything of the kind,' he said supremely.

'Then what are we doing there?' demanded Mr. Cox.

'Oh, just keepin' things movin'. Got to keep things movin', you know.'

Mr. Cox retired into his conviction about the Army, and shut the door.

On the other side of the table Colonel Vetchley also deplored the Chief Commissioner's absence. He deplored it to Mr. Biscuit, who was actually the most senior civilian present. The dinner had degenerated into little more than the ordinary guest-night; it had quite lost its special character. After Arden's refusal several other civilians had been asked, but most of them had been unaccountably engaged. Even Sir Ahmed Hossein, who had accepted in the first instance, excused himself on the plea of illness at the last moment.

It was somehow in the air that the Chief was prejudiced against the occasion; and nobody of importance was inclined to take the responsibility of setting that prejudice at naught. Little Biscuit, in fact, had felt it his duty to consult Egerton Faulkner upon the subject, and only when the Chief Secretary had said, 'Go, by all means, my dear chap; it won't matter tuppence,' did he feel that his act of acceptance was officially sanctioned. Charles Cox happened to have heard nothing of the first intention of the dinner, or of Arden's refusal. If he had he would have been embarrassed to choose between the independence of going and the independence of staying away; but after careful examination he would have done what seemed essentially most independent. Mr. Cox, not content with the noble intention I have explained, was kicking generally against the pricks.

'I hope,' said Colonel Vetchley to little Biscuit, 'there's nothing serious in this report that the Government is trying to get round Arden in the Morgan case?'

Mr. Biscuit assumed exactly the proper air of embarrassment, and fiddled responsibly with the nutshells he had made.

'Is there such a report?' he said. 'It's most unsatisfactory, the way these things leak out. Personally, I know nothing about it. Quite unfounded, I should say.'

'O Mary Ann, Biscuit! What the Viceroy wants is common property; and it's not likely he's going to take it lying down from a fellow under him, is it? The question is, will Arden hold out?'

'I may tell you in confidence,' said little Biscuit, lowering his voice, 'that the Chief reported strongly against the Viceroy's view in that matter.'

'Thanks, my dear chap,' laughed Colonel Vetchley, rather irritably. 'That was in the *Administrator* three weeks ago.'

Mr. Biscuit frowned upon journalistic enterprise. 'I believe it was. Now what a thing like that tempts one to ask is: Have we an Official Secrets Act in India or have we not?'

'Oh, well – Service paper. Interested in a case like that. I needn't say where my sympathies are. And I don't look at it from a purely regimental point of view, by any means. On any practical ground Thame's notions are absurd. I tell you you can't hang a white man for killing a black one in this country. It isn't in nature. It hasn't been done for two generations out here, and it's not likely to be done for ten. The scales don't balance that way. If Thame should get this case carried up to the High Court – I don't say there's the least likelihood, but if he should, and by any chance Morgan was convicted of murder, do you know under what name Thame would go down to history? "The Hanging Viceroy," sir – "the Hanging Viceroy."'

Colonel Vetchley swallowed his glass of Kummel as if this prediction proved the uselessness of further argument.

'His Excellency is a little disposed to be what might be called visionary,' agreed Mr. Biscuit. 'And obstinate. Very obstinate.'

'Call it what you like, it won't work. And as for British troops in India, he simply knows nothing whatever about them. Any ordinary man would make some allowance. Seventy thousand of them there are – think of the dulness for them, poor devils. To men of Thame's stamp the common soldier is a brute, neither more or less, a brute that kicks punkah coolies with his great heavy ammunition boots! Well, why does he do it with his great heavy ammunition boots? Because they're the only ones he's got to wear! Regulations don't provide troops with carpet slippers.'

Mr. Biscuit received this impartially, with an air of reserving his opinion against further evidence. 'I don't suppose the men get many luxuries of any sort,' he said.

'You're quite right there. But apart from all that' – Colonel Vetchley came to the point he had made out to his own satisfaction that very morning in the course of shaving – 'this notion of putting the native on an absolute equality with the European is all Tommyrot; and I'll prove it to you. Man for man he isn't an equal. Take the most fundamental instinct – the sporting instinct – and what do we find? We find he hasn't got it. Do you call a chap like Kala Jong a sportsman? Now I'll tell you something. Six years ago, when we were stationed in Calcutta, that fellow asked me to a shoot. As we started we were given to understand that we were to shoot everything – does, butchas, everything, every head we saw – to beat Dharmsala's bag of the week before.'

'Really?' said Biscuit, to the Colonel's horrified earnestness.

'The absolute truth. When it came to getting does, Devine and I put up our rifles – wouldn't even stand up to it. Did no good; those fellows went on with their slaughter. Afterwards on one island we counted nineteen wild buffalo, left lying, females an' all – hadn't taken a horn or a skin. Sickening. Wonderful sporting country it was then. I remember we put up eleven rhino in one beat. But they massacred the lot. Different matter now, of course. The Commander-in-Chief went down there last March; and they made a fearful fuss about getting one for him. What else could you expect? Kala Jong exterminates everything, the swine. And that's your native – that's the fellow Thame would like to murder a decent white man for killing – in self-defence. I've no patience with the man.'

'I believe His Excellency considers that self-defence was by no means established in the Morgan case,' said Mr. Biscuit.

'Oh – is that his line? But no doubt, as you say, the whole thing is confidential as yet, and hasn't come your way. Perhaps I shouldn't have mentioned it; but Faulkner – of course I know Faulkner very well – told me the other day that the Home Member – what's the fellow's name? Hichens – had written, pressing Arden strongly to change his base about the thing. So far, however, he said, Arden didn't see his way.'

'I was aware of that,' said little Biscuit. 'Of course. And – don't mention it; it's not a thing we want talked of – but matters have gone even further. The Viceroy himself has written to the Chief.'

'Confound him!'

'Written to him privately. That's going very far, I consider.'

'Deuced far. But will he bring Arden round?'

The anxiety of the Colonel's tone flattered little Biscuit. These military fellows were apt to be overbearing in their independence.

'Oh, there's no reason to suppose that – none whatever. But, of course, Thame may have got hold of some new aspect of the case – and the Viceroy is always the Viceroy, you know.'

Colonel Vetchley looked at Mr. Biscuit in a manner that conveyed, without precisely meaning to, an unflattering estimate. Then he finished his port.

'Damn the Viceroy,' he said warmly.

CHAPTER XX

'HAS this shaken you at all?' asked Ruth Pearce, handing Lord Thame's letter back to Arden.

He made a motion of denial. 'No,' he said. 'I see nothing differently. I suppose one might call it a notable presentation of the case, but –'

'I should call it a notable piece of special pleading by Lord Thame for his conscience,' she told him.

'Well, you will admit his conscience, I suppose, as a factor in the situation.'

'I will admit only yours – in the situation as you have to deal with it.'

She spoke very fearlessly, with that disregard of everything but the issue, that he had so happily perceived in her in the beginning. It was one of the things which had singled Ruth Pearce out to him then, absurd as it may stand in eyes unfamiliar with that small arbitrary world, the way in which she ignored the perpetual petty impediment of official position that seemed to tangle all his intercourse with other people – that sometimes stood, when she addressed him at their dinner parties, even in the eye of his wife. From the first he had felt himself with Miss Pearce essentially the man and but incidentally the Chief Commissioner; he who was so universally the Chief Commissioner that he might hardly have claimed any other identity.

After that he was Ruth's friend on terms of detachment from everything else he was; and after that he had become the central figure of her life, always with the same intense reference to that which was most virtually himself and his own. He knew it, and it was the new flame by which he at once lived and watched the spectacle of his own existence; yet at times there was in it a subtle dissatisfaction. She had taken him, all human as he was, and had enshrined him; she knew him mortal, but she would not have him less divine. Her possession of him exacted this; her eye ravaged him for a flaw. When she found one she must have it away. Loving him, she was compelled to find her ideal in him: loving him unlawfully he must be the more transcendently worthy. The necessity arose, no doubt, in the moral egotism of the woman, but need not be the less edifying for that. Her task of illusion was noble and pitiful; it held the chance of tragedy. Arden, vaguely rasped, felt it irrational; and he, from whom she would ward off for ever the falling of a fleck, had sometimes the wilful impulse to cover himself with the common dust.

He was silent for a moment under her final establishing of him.

'You think there is no room for the speculation how far one is entitled to come between the ruler and his conscience?' he meditated aloud.

'None at all,' she said swiftly.

'It has given me a new sympathy,' he said, smiling at the apprehension in her glance. 'For the stumbling-block. The stumbling-block and the rock of offence.'

'I won't be drawn into Lord Thame's point of view. I do not care for that. He is nothing to me,' she added inadvertently.

'It is decent in him – fair-minded – to expostulate in these terms and at this length.'

'You are flattered!' she cried, almost fiercely. She would pierce him to guard him, without a qualm.

'Am I?' he said humbly. 'I don't know. I am – touched.'

She learned forward toward him, putting out her hand, his passionate monitor. 'You mustn't be touched,' she said. 'Don't you see you mustn't?'

'Oh, I have hardened my heart. Unluckily, I can't close my eyes at the same time; and we have to consider a complication. It is offered to us by your ingenuous young friend Cox.'

'I *thought* it was not impossible that he would come muddling in!' she exclaimed, all alight. 'What? How?'

'He has collected a quantity of evidence, or what he calls evidence, with the assistance of an old fellow –'

'Afzul Aziz,' she cried. 'I know him very well.'

'Do you know anything against him?'

'I'm afraid not,' she said, with so fallen a countenance that they both laughed.

'Nor I, unluckily. He's a capital munshi – passes all his men – seems to have borne a respectable character always, and is generally looked up to, as far as I can make out, by the Mahomedans here. All this Cox points out, and it can't be gainsaid. Morgan's offence was against Hindoos; so there is no room for a race motive.'

'Is the evidence Mahomedan?'

'Some of it. Not all. There are two sweepers and a Sikh policeman, who declares he was threatened before the trial by soldiers –'

'And Mr. Cox has sent it up through the ordinary channels?'

'Oh yes – most straightforwardly.'

'So that it was bound to come before you; and you are –'

'Bound to send it on to the Government of India. Exactly.'

She saw the boy's courage, caught at the thing implied, and smiled. 'I like that in Cox, don't you?'

'Of course I do,' he said, and waited for her to go on with the 'but.'

'But *how* exasperating! How discourteous to experience! He has barely been out a year. Oh dear, how *priggish*! Though that will wear off – he's really a good fellow. You must snub him, I suppose?'

'No, I haven't snubbed him. I confess I have hardly thought of him.'

'Of course,' she said, quickly self-accusing, 'the personal aspect is nothing. Do you find anything in it – in what he has got together?'

'Well, it's in the loosest form, and some of it, no doubt, would fail to come to the scratch, and some would fall to pieces under cross-examination; but as far as one can read what would probably be got out of it –' he paused. 'It's the usual thing – a little truth and a great deal of lying, constructive lying, after the event, it seems to me. It's cleverly put together.'

'Does the truth in it bear at all importantly?'

'Not importantly enough to justify a second trial. But you mustn't pin me down like that. I speak only of what I conceive to be the truth. Thame, no doubt, will believe much more of it; because it is in the line of what he wants to prove, and has been constructed precisely with that intention.'

'It seems to me,' she said wildly, 'that you ought not to send it up.'

He took with some eagerness the moral upper hand. 'You can't mean that,' he said. 'It went on at once.'

'No – perhaps I don't.'

'I let them know, of course, exactly what value I attach to it; and the Viceroy's view would carry no weight with the Court, you know, even in the event of a re-trial.'

'But there can be no re-trial. You have pledged your conscience, your authority, yourself, against it.'

'I have placed my opinion on record against it; and I have not changed my opinion.'

'You are pledged,' she repeated. Her eyes darkened on him, insisting, as she believed, upon a principle; but the thing that leapt to him was the passion in them.

'To whom am I pledged?' he asked, though his thought had followed his heart, and he hardly cared for an answer.

Ruth reflected for an instant. 'If there is nobody else, you are pledged to me,' she said.

It brought him foolishly nearer, and he was near before. He sat looking at her, with his hand dropped upon his knee. It was a middle-aged attitude, and he was a middle-aged man, with a film of grey on his hair, a wife and sons in another part of the world, and a post of heavy public responsibility. His honourable past sat there with him, was plain in every line of him. It seemed to lift him into security from irregular impulse, to fortify him against what might happen to men of meaner mould and less distinguished experience. Yet it failed him; and he failed himself.

'There is no way of telling you how deeply I am pledged to you,' he said, speaking as a lover speaks, and will speak always.

'Please say "how loftily?"' she begged. 'That is how I feel it.'

'Oh, as loftily as you like,' he answered with a touch of roughness, 'but more deeply. Down among the sources and mysterious roots of things –'

She met his look with a half-frightened start, and plainly stiffened herself, as she sat awkwardly in her chair, against some great tide of passion from him; she knew the dykes were down. If it had come, and especially if it had swept her for an instant away, I think she might have forgiven him, not so much for the rapturous moment, as because she had a natural lenience for everything that came crashing over barriers, showing itself greatly. She made a class and a category for such things; she set them aside and bowed to them. Perhaps she had an instinct for acquiescence in the supreme; perhaps, being a woman, she was only cowed; there seems something of the essential feminine in it. If Arden had yielded to his pulses she would have sat before him dumb and overcome. But no torrent came. The man struggled with it, suffering the inhibitions of honour and conscience; and so his opportunity passed. Her soul, within a hair's-breadth of capitulation, of some irrevocable word, fell back upon its forces; and she mistook her sudden angry tears, which welled not because of his shortcomings, but because he had not gone far enough. With a great effort she held them back, ignored everything, and smiled at him.

'I like the heights best,' she said.

He would have none of her pleasant interpretations.

'I can't have the heights so insisted upon,' he told her. 'You want to be forever there. Let us recognise the whole of our claim upon one another. Why should we conspire to ignore it? We are not children or cowards. The truth will not damage us. You know what it is.'

She looked at him calmly and fully; and within, far within, beyond tenderness and forgiving and extenuation, sat her soul always in judgement, an eye that never closed, a scale that never trembled. He knew it perfectly, and in his rebellion a bitter word escaped him.

'Behind the kindness of your regard,' he said, 'I see the charnel-house where you will presently be tearing me to pieces.'

'Shall I?' she said. 'I dare say. But it will be something new. I have always torn things to pieces, my whole world sometimes. It is my bane – it spoils my life. But so far, not you. So far I have felt differently about you. Otherwise, how could we have gone on? Your ideals were my bread of life, and – I thought – mine were yours. Wasn't that happiness enough for us both?'

'It was a fool's paradise,' he told her; 'but I see that I have turned myself out.'

He got up to go, but she put out her hand. 'For a moment,' she said. 'I have not told you, have I, that I intend to ask for leave immediately?'

'No,' he said. 'You have only just thought of it.'

'I have always wanted the M.D. of London. One must practise for two years first, you know. I have done that.'

'Do you really think it well to go? Because I leave myself tomorrow for camp. I shall be away a long time.'

'You must come and go as is necessary. Yes, I do really want my M.D. And I want,' she added fervently, her conscience grasping wildly at any straw, 'to see Mrs. Arden. If she is still at Heidelberg I shall go there to see her. I want to – be with her.'

This was intended at least to pierce her own bosom on its way to his; but he took it to himself alone.

'Then,' he said, 'I may not see you again before you go.' He held out his hand, and she took it with a startled look.

'Good-bye,' she said timidly.

'Good-bye. You will take six months?'

'A year if I can get it.'

'I dare say you would be the better for a year. I hope it will be profitable in every way. Good-bye.'

His tongue felt dull with every one of his forty-three years. He even seemed to move from her presence heavily. He was aware of a loss of significance; a familiar deadly conviction overcame him that he was a convention of the Indian Civil Service, and nothing more. She had given him shame to drink and it had made him conscious in every unhappy way.

Ruth stood with her hands on the back of her chair. Her hands looked nerveless, unconscious, frozen to the chair. She heard her heart crying aloud that she had hurt him too much; yet even at that moment something else in her flung down her heart, rushed to the front with a flag. She saw him in disaster, but there was something to be saved.

'You will not forget one thing,' she said. 'You are pledged.'

'Oh that!' he said indifferently. 'Yes, I quite hope we shall be able to hold our own.'

He looked back once from the door to add a final, formal 'Good-bye,' and saw her still standing beside the chair with her rigid hands upon it. She contrived something like a bow of ac-knowledgement and a smile that was in a ghostly way polite; but her farewell to him was in her eyes, her lips by this time refusing to say it. She formed the word, but he heard nothing.

It was an ambiguous trifle; and if it had not touched his life it might have appealed to his imagination. Had she or had she not bidden him a final farewell? However, he made his way home thinking nothing of the form of her severance from him. He had to carry the fact.

THE following day the Staff and establishment were informed that the Hon. the Chief Commissioner had postponed going to camp for the present. This he did unavoidably, owing to a command from His Excellency the Viceroy. It was in appearance an invitation, by the hand of the Military Secretary, to Government House, Calcutta; but Lord Thame no less required than requested the pleasure of a visit from the Hon. the Chief Commissioner of Ghoom at as early a date as he should find convenient, when His Excellency would confer with him upon various important matters now pending. It took this gracious form, but it was as unbending as an order could be.

'I suppose I have no alternative?' said Arden to Egerton Faulkner.

'I imagine not, sir,' replied Faulkner, disguising the shock he received from the question. 'You must go, I fancy. Upon my soul I believe the fellow would come here if you didn't. But in sending for you of course he's within his prerogative. I'm afraid you have no alternative.'

'Oh well, there's some relief in that.'

CHAPTER XXI

OUR haughty snubs to Fate are not always successful. She throws us into a passion we cannot approve; we loftily propose to remove ourselves from its scene and object; we will teach her. And it so happens that we cannot go. Fate thus remains undiscouraged, with the added amusement of seeing us disconcerted. Ruth Pearce sustained herself the whole of the next day upon her intention of taking leave. She saw her out-patients, gave clinical instruction to her dozen Eurasian girl-students, did her routine hospital work, and dismissed a sweeper for an unsavoury drain, voyaging always away toward her purpose. The Red Sea piled blue on the Indian Ocean, the waves of the Mediterranean succeeded these; and they all carried her to London lodgings where she would know how to take the aggressive toward the threatenings of her heart. She went upliftedly about her work and did it unusually well. Our heroic intentions have this way of rewarding us beforehand. Then she came home and found a letter from the Secretary of the Central Committee informing her that she had been appointed to the charge of the Fund's Hospital in Calcutta during the absence on sick leave of its present Superintendent. Dr. Elizabeth Garrens, now at Bijli, would relieve her at Pilaghur, and she would be expected to take over at Calcutta on the 24th instant – in exactly a week's time.

She read the letter twice, remembering, the second time, that she ought to be flattered. Then she felt the desire to give it immediately the reality of a spoken statement, to proclaim that the thing had been taken out of her hands. She looked round for Hiria, but Hiria was not in the room. To talk to Hiria was like communicating without telling anybody. Involuntarily she opened her lips to call her, checked the impulse, and sat thinking, but consciously waiting for the ayah to come in.

Presently she came. Ruth watched her for a moment as she bustled about the room, picking up a handkerchief with a disciplinary shake, hanging up and putting in order, as important a Mistress of the Robes as ever held practical office.

'Hiria,' she said in the language, 'I do not go to England. There is another order. I go to Calcutta.'

'To *Calcutta*, miss-sahib! Good talk! England is too far, miss-sahib; and everybody is very sick in those ships. Three times my grandmother went to England: seven times my mother went. I never going yet. My mem-sahib wanted me many times, and many times my mother said to me, "Hiria, you go, silly gell. You get big wages and you sleep in a bed, and sit on chair, and eat off china plates, like the sahib-folk." But I fear too much.'

'I will go later, Hiria. Without doubt I will go later, only this order has come from the Sirkar for the present.'

'And who can refuse to hear the order of the Sirkar, miss-sahib? Even the Burra Sahib, it is said, must obey when the Lord Sahib speaks. And for me, what order, your honour?'

'Oh, you will go to Calcutta too, Hiria – unless you object.'

'Very good, miss-sahib. In Calcutta rice is fifteen seers for a rupee, and cotton *saris* very cheap also, in the New Market. Your honour has never yet seen the New Market? *Everything* they are selling there, miss-sahib – woolling cloth, glass box, flour, feather, gol' ring – very nice hat too, miss-sahib, *very* nice hat. It is said the sahib-log go always once to Calcutta to see the New Market.'

'Well, Hiria, I shall see it now.'

'But, your honour, what sort of women are those jungly ones at Calcutta! They wear but one garment, those! That first time I went, coming very early morning from the station, my mem-sahib said, "You sit by the coachman, Hiria, so you see everything!" T'ank you, mem-sahib – I see too much! In the tanks bathing, miss-sahib, ten, twenty together – and only one cloth for each – what a sight! And when I pulled my *sari* over my face they laughed – impudents! One day I spoke – "What shame," I said, "to wear only one garment."'

'And what did they say?'

'They said, "It costs as much as all of yours" – which was false talk, miss-sahib – "and if you don't want to see, shut your eyes." They have no respect, those coolie women. And what dress am I now to put out?'

'Whatever you like, Hiria – anything. It is a tennis-party,' said Ruth, with her eyes on the Secretary's letter.

The ayah opened the wardrobe door and hesitated. 'Perhaps,' she ventured, 'the party is at the General mem-sahib's – Lemon mem-sahib's?'

'No, Hiria; it's in the Guzerati lines, where is always much dust, you know.'

'Then there is no need for the new one with the large spots – you will stay there.' She nodded to the new one arbitrarily, and debated again. 'Perhaps it is the Colonel mem-sahib of the black regiment who is giving the *kail* to-day?'

'No,' her mistress told her absently; 'it is Mrs. Lamb's party.'

Hiria, with brisk decision, took down a dress that bespoke her estimate of the social importance of a subaltern's wife.

'Then the cream-wallah of yesterday will be abundantly enough, miss-sahib. I mended the sleeve – and it can go to the wash to-morrow.'

Mrs. Lamb's tennis party was something to count on in Pilaghur, a permanent amenity. If Mrs. Lamb was not giving it somebody else was; and there were certain constant features whoever gave it. Always the refreshments were grouped on little tables under a tree, always cane chairs were grouped near the refreshments; always red and blue striped dhurries from Cawnpore lay stretched upon the grass against the early dew. Withdrawn a little way as if to excuse itself, stood always a special table with whisky and cheroots for the men, the former in a Tantalus stand which was invariably a wedding present. Overhead the crows kept up so constant an interruption that nobody minded them; round about, hibiscus bushes nodded sleepily, always in flower and always unregarded. Not far away a line of ragged coleas and a bunch of marigolds made a vain attempt to disguise the stables or the kitchen.

Of course circumstances differ, and at the General's or the Judge's the tennis-court wasn't jammed up against the back of the house in such a way that you had to ignore the mosquito curtains of your host's bed, the door being necessarily open for ventilation. Or his boots, which stood in a row in the back verandah, or his saddlery, which occupied one end of it, or the family durzie, who sat cross-legged at the other, snipping and sewing in the midst of white things for the mem-sahib. But as everybody knew that circumstances differed, and exactly to what extent, nobody in the least minded Lamb's boots or Mrs. Lamb's petticoats. Rather not. The party sat in a row of oblivious backs and made cheerful conversation, while one kitmutgar, with three buttons off his cotton livery, hastily washed tea-cups in relays behind a bush, and the other, who was pock-marked and had but one eye, again and yet again made solemn offers of cocoa-nut toffee in triangles.

Mrs. Lemon was there of course. Mrs. Lemon made a particular point of going to the parties of subalterns' wives, especially those in native regiments: it was her good heart. The Faulkners were also there, Mrs. Faulkner just a little composed and distant. Also the Davidsons and the Wickhams and Charles Cox, and both the Misses Hillyer, and the doctor, and a pair of new railway people, and practically everybody except the Barfordshires, with whom Mrs. Lamb, and indeed all the Guzerati ladies, sustained for the moment strained relations. We need not go into it, but it does seem more than possible that a bachelor mess might exert an undue influence in a mutton club. I know Mrs. Lemon, without taking sides, heartily endorsed this view.

The Biscuits were not there either. It must be confessed that Mrs. ap-Williams Lamb and Mrs. Arthur Poynder Biscuit were not on speaking terms. That was a much more serious matter, involving a Biscuit terrier which had worried the goat that supplied nourishment to a Lamb baby – the kind of matter that is not likely to be healed either in this world or the next. Unfortunately, there is time only in the smaller Indian plains stations to do justice to such complications; but one is inclined to agree off-hand with Mrs. Lemon – it is phenomenal the number of times one agrees with Mrs. Lemon – who said to Mrs. Davidson, in discussing it, that to charge the goat with temper was at all events absurd.

Mrs. Lemon and Mr. Egerton Faulkner were having the liveliest possible conversation a little apart, in two of Mrs. Lamb's wicker chairs. Egerton Faulkner was always happy with Mrs. Lemon. She helped him more than anybody, with her comfortable twinkle, to the delicious exercise of producing himself. He did it somehow for her benefit and yet at her expense; and Mrs. Lemon enjoyed nothing more than Mr. Faulkner, except Mr. Faulkner and a strawberry ice.

Mrs. Lemon, sipping her ice, was saying, apropos of the goat, that Mrs. Biscuit, though a pretty woman and a well-dressed woman, was too clever for *her*. She supposed it was a good thing to be clever, indeed people said that nowadays a girl had no chance unless she *was* clever, but why – ?

'Why not sometimes conceal it?' Mr. Faulkner cut in with agility. He was the only person in the station who could successfully interrupt Mrs. Lemon. 'I entirely agree. Mrs. Biscuit might conceal the quality of her mind with advantage oftener than she does. She ought to think even more about her clothes, which are so rewarding, or more about Biscuit's future. I confess to you, dear Mrs. Lemon, I sometimes look upon that excellent little man's career with apprehension, wondering whether Mrs. Biscuit feels herself sufficiently involved – sufficiently responsible.'

'Oh, she's a model wife.'

'I'm sure she is — I'm sure she is. One might almost say a French model, and not admire too much. But would she, at a critical moment, sink all for Biscuit? She reminds me fatally at times of a lady I once knew at Simla — in the days, you understand, when Simla was winning the renown that helped so importantly to make Mr. Kipling's. She was a beautiful woman, more beautiful even than Mrs. Biscuit, and there was one who loved her much. It wasn't me. I loved her too, but I wasn't senior enough. And on one occasion this other person — he was *very* senior, of course, to dare such a thing — gently took the hand of the lady, the beautiful lady whom Mrs. Biscuit so strikingly reminds me of. On the spur of the moment, yielding, you see, to untutored impulse, she drew it away. The next instant she thought of her husband's future, and *put it back again*. But it wasn't the same thing. He didn't get on.' And Mr. Faulkner, with a seraph's smile, screwed his eyeglass in to observe arriving guests.

'Simla is better behaved nowadays,' chuckled Mrs. Lemon.

'Simla has lost all the reputation it ever had. I am told that the most conspicuous object on the Mall to-day is the parlour, or whatever they call it, of the Young Women's Christian Association. Dear Mrs. Lemon, Simla has gone irretrievably downhill. And we have let it happen under our very noses. Among the fresh masses of meddling and often mischievous legislation that yearly disfigure our statute–books, no one has ever paused to bring in a bill for — . You are about to tell me, Mrs. Lemon, that I am talking nonsense.'

'No, go on. I like it. Here comes Dr. Pearce. Now *there's* a clever woman, if you like.'

'Oh, consumedly! If she wasn't always dying to tell you what you *really* ought to do to be saved. Which is stupid,' observed the Chief Secretary, dropping his eyeglass.

His face changed as Ruth approached; its look of banter seemed to fall with the eye-glass. She always had this effect upon Egerton Faulkner. He was robbed, at her approach, of his whims and affectations; she made him serious, threw him back upon himself and reality. He very nearly disliked her for it.

It was a passing shadow on this occasion. Ruth responded to his ceremonious bow with a pleasant nod and went on to the railway couple, who were sitting together, new and uncertain, not yet quite accepted and plainly a little black. The railway man often said he hated talking shop, a superior sort of thing to believe, which is usually quite without foundation; but he was presently giving Miss Pearce a quantity of information about the pilgrim traffic to Hurdwar, which she found very nearly as interesting as he did. People always told Ruth about what most closely concerned them, because that was what she always wanted to know. She sat hearing the number of pilgrims who died on the threshold of the sanctity they coveted, pointing out the pathos while the railway man dwelt on the percentage, and accepted tea from the pock-marked kitmutgar, and noted now and then the progress of the tennis. Charles Cox was playing with Mrs. Davidson, once more in form, against Mr. Davidson and the fair Miss Hillyer; it was a tremendous sett, and vied with the badminton for noise.

'How long have they been playing?' asked Ruth.

She was longing for a talk with Charles Cox, for an opportunity of telling him how inexcusably he had behaved. But they had just begun.

'Play up, old man,' cried Mrs. Davidson to her husband from the other side, and Davidson, sending her a hard service, which she missed, remarked gaily –

'If I go on doing that I shall get myself disliked.'

'That's healthy,' observed Miss Hillyer disgustedly, making a second fault. 'Well tried!' 'Well played, partner!' 'Liner, liner!' 'Half a mile out!' 'Buck up, your side!!' The air was full of these battle cries and much laughter. Charles Cox, valiant and threatening at the net, received a ball in his person just above the line, and it bounded back to a shout of 'Well defended!' They indulged in searching sarcasm, splendid boasts, appalling personalities, abject apology, all the high words and bywords that come of doing in excellent spirits the same thing every day. Davidson, when a swift return overtook him somewhere in the legs, spun round twice, and made as if to fall upon the field.

And after all, they were nothing to the badminton, where the quicker play made wilder shrieks, and the 'chirria,' the 'bird,' lent itself to more exuberant humour. General Lemon was generally conceded the best badminton-player in Pilaghur. He played seven times a week, which, I am afraid, was only once a day; but his execution was wonderful. It almost justified the constancy of the practice, especially as he never missed morning service. And here I am only quoting Mr. Biddow, the station chaplain, who ran him very close. It would have been hard to invent more innocent amusements for elderly people, or even for their juniors.

At last the game was over. Ruth paused in the story she was telling the railway man's wife, and her eyes followed Charles Cox, whose own were too clearly fixed upon the pursuit of Miss Hillyer to the neglect of his lawful partner, upon whom, by all the traditions of the game, he should have been pressing tea or claret cup.

'And when you took the stethoscope out of your pocket, Dr. Pearce – ?'

'Oh, she ran away,' said Ruth, rising.

'She was afraid of it?'

'I beg your pardon? Afraid? Yes, I suppose she was afraid. They told me afterwards that she said I pulled snakes out of my clothes. I never saw her again,' said Ruth. 'I think I must go now. There is somebody that I want to speak to.'

Mrs. Lamb had seized upon Miss Hillyer to play again, and Miss Hillyer was protesting that Mrs. Lamb should really play herself this time; and Mr. Lamb had joined the altercation with the statement that the other three players were waiting and the light was going. Mr. Cox, finding that the dispute gave him no opportunity, turned away to see Miss Pearce standing near him. Something in her eyes drew and compelled him; he went up to her at once.

'Well?' he said, smiling as he lifted his cap.

'Well – I have heard what you have done.'

Mr. Cox glanced once again at the contending group, saw that Miss Hillyer was about to be reabsorbed, and postponed further hope in that direction.

'I'm afraid you don't approve,' he said.

'No, I don't approve. You have made a mistake in judgement, I think; and you have added to the difficulties of a man in a very hard place.'

'I can't help that. I feel a jolly sight better now that it's done.'

'Of course you do. You've given your conscience a cathartic,' Ruth told him. She did not always choose her phrases. 'Lord Thame, also, would feel a jolly sight better if he could hang Morgan; but there are more important considerations.'

'Not to us! And – excuse me, Dr. Pearce, but that's just like a woman. The Viceroy doesn't want necessarily to "hang" Morgan; he only wants to get him adequately punished. And it isn't only his rectitude that's involved – it's the honour of England.'

Ruth winced for an instant at the thought of how much more deeply she was concerned with the honour of one man.

'An irritable conscience in a position of authority ought to be very well informed,' she said stiffly. 'I'm afraid I doubt the value of your contribution to Lord Thame's information, Mr. Cox.'

Her tone was inexcusably hostile, but her soul was in confusion for the man she loved, half shrinking from any test of him except her own; and her heart was full of displeasure towards this young Cox, who had stepped in at so wrong a time to darken counsel and perhaps to weaken resolution. He took it very well.

'I suppose there is always the possibility of being deceived,' he said; 'but I have done my best to sift and verify it.'

'It will make no difference. I am sure it will make no difference.'

'I don't know. Perhaps not. But the Chief and the Viceroy together are pretty sure to get at the value of it, whatever it is.'

'The Chief and the Viceroy together? I don't understand.'

The young fellow spoke a little shamefacedly. He had no wish to exult over her.

'Oh – I supposed you knew Lord Thame had sent for Mr. Arden.'

'Upon this matter? No. When does he go?' The thought flew from her mind to her heart and back again, 'If I could only see him first!'

'He starts by the Calcutta mail this afternoon, I believe, at six. There are the guns now.'

It was, in effect, the first gun, and twelve more made formal announcement that the Chief Commissioner of Ghoom was leaving his administrative territory. Ruth listened intently, and neither of them spoke until the thirteenth had boomed and shaken itself into silence. Then a flock of sparrows, settling into some bushes for the night and silenced by the unusual sound began again their storm of squealing chirps, and Charles Cox, eyeing her curiously, said –

'It is impressive, isn't it – the salute?'

'Oh yes,' she replied, 'it is. Especially when you don't – exactly – know what it means.'

'Oh, I fancy it has no very deep significance,' he began to tell her; but at that moment the players were seen to be leaving the courts and Miss Hillyer to come again within the region of the possible. Mr. Cox found an excusing word and left his companion, and she, still listening interiorly to the vibrations of the last gun, hardly knew that he was gone.

She turned and looked at Mrs. Lamb's tennis party, searching the groups in the cane chairs and round the little tables for some one who would say to her confidently, with a serious knowledge of what was involved: 'There is no danger – he will stand firm. You need not be afraid.'

They were all drawn from Arden's world; some of them were his counsellors and lieutenants; she felt strongly that some at least should have this business very deeply at heart. Yet her instinct told her that there was not one to whom she could speak of it and expect a reply that was neither perfunctory, nor indifferent, nor frivolous. She felt with resentment that they had no measure for the man, not stopping to consider how rare and strange a thing it was that she should have a measure for him. The result was that for the moment she had no measure for them; she thought them, in her indignation, a collection of puppet-people.

They drank more tea and ate more ices. The pock-marked kitmutgar circulated among them with feverish activity. They chattered as hard as the sparrows, and laughed, which the sparrows couldn't do; Mr. Cox's explosion was heard at regular intervals with an unmistakable note of excitement. They were occupied with whisky and soda and iced coffee and fifty different things. Ruth Pearce felt it possible to be occupied with only one thing, and went home.

CHAPTER XXII

So Eliot Arden went to Calcutta.

Later in Lord Thame's political career it was constantly said of him that, whatever he was, he was no opportunist. Knowing very well what he wanted, he often appeared to take the most difficult means of getting it — a trait which was more admired outside his party than in it. Biographers of his administration of India might have testified to the same effect in considering his dealing with the Chief Commissioner of Ghoom over the Morgan case. To order a man of Arden's type into his presence like a schoolboy, the historian might point out, was not tactful: to arm him with the expectation of being put upon his mettle was not wise. There was a publicity about the thing, too, that made against its chances of success. Senior officials of Bengal, asked to dinner to meet the Chief Commissioner of Ghoom, must have been aware that there was a subject which, without invitation, it would be better not to enter upon. Anybody might guess, meeting the Viceregal carriage, with its red and gold escort of Sikh cavalrymen in front and behind, what the two men with concentrated looks and folded arms who sat in it, were talking about. A change of opinion, like a change of clothes, is most happily accomplished, one supposes, in privacy.

Lord Thame's assault upon the views of his Chief Commissioner appeared to take nothing of the sort into account. It involved damage to Arden's dignity, to his sense of propriety, and to long settled convictions upon certain questions, not to count his belief in his own experience and so small a matter as his popularity. Perhaps these considerations, once they fully appeared to Arden's mind, rather helped the Viceroy's appeal; and perhaps Lord Thame knew they would. A smaller man might have fortified himself with such things. Eliot Arden, the moment he believed himself depending on them, was capable of making a present of them to the enemy.

I am afraid the matter could hardly have occupied for Arden quite the high ground upon which Ruth Pearce saw it. This is borne out by the fact that she never entered, even to preside, into his heavy deliberations. He saw it in as lofty a light as may shine upon a question of serious expediency — and those may criticise expediency in a theory of Oriental administration who feel qualified to do so — but he did not see it to be a doubt in which his conscience was sole and predestined arbiter, with results gravely critical to himself. Ruth never came in. The matter did not mingle with his thoughts of her, which would have surprised and not pleased her. She believed herself always there, urging and compelling him; it was in that way that she identified herself with him. But he only thought of her before or after. This does, I think, show where it stood for him. If he had recognised it with his soul it would have come to him always with her face.

I am glad to be able to declare that he arrived at his decision without her. Otherwise there would have been a temptation to ferret among the influences that finally tipped the balance, and to make some sort of comparison between the two emotions deepest in him — his feeling for her and this other passion for the ruler. One can imagine them in opposition, tearing him, in so far as he felt them to bear upon his problem, in different directions; but it is a speculation which it is pleasanter to abandon. I feel happier in contemplating him simply the prey to his loyalty, in so far as his mind listened to his heart. If he was pulled by the strings there was only one string. The woman did not come in until afterwards. Then she had her turn.

They took a week over it. Public attention was invited to the statement that further large discoveries of coal in Ghoom and certain difficulties in working the labour regulations there, were receiving the close personal attention of the Viceroy. Public attention was not for a moment diverted from the real question; but the papers observed a certain decency. Nothing appeared that might embarrass either the Viceroy or his guest. People talked, and watched, and waited for the event; varying degrees of confidence in Arden were expressed; but bets were made at the Calicut Club, which had always a pessimistic tone about officials, three to one against him.

Then, one morning, thirteen more guns spoke from Fort William, and any one in Calcutta who happened to be paying attention knew that the Chief Commissioner, who had been for some days the guest of His Excellency at Government House, was starting back to Ghoom. Also the papers mentioned it.

That same morning Arden had a letter from Ruth. It was handed to him by a panting messenger in the red and gold livery of the Viceroy, as he was stepping into the train. The letter seemed, therefore, to have the futility of attempts that are made too late; yet Arden put it in his pocket with an instinct to postpone it until some miles of his journey should add to the inevitableness of what he had done. He had a thought of somewhat cynical congratulation that she had not written before, telling himself that it could have made no difference — and the thing was complicated enough without bringing feeling into it. He waited alone in his special carriage, as the train hurried him through the palm-fringed rice-fields of Lower Bengal, until he began to feel, instead of any apprehension, the simple happiness of having a letter from her to read. He sat in the warmth of that for a while, and then he opened it.

It was neither an appeal nor an expostulation. There was nothing in it to make him, in view of what he had done, sorry for her, though once or twice, as he read it, he felt rather poignantly sorry for himself. It was not the cry of an impulse that could no longer be held down, but the formulation, thought out at pains and at length, of an argument. It had not arrived too late, but precisely in the nick of time. She had watched his movements in the newspapers; and she knew that by the time he received it there would be no further question.

She had no desire, Ruth told him — and she believed it when she wrote it — to thrust herself into his councils. In a way, not in the truest way or the highest way, but in a way, whatever action he took, even what she most feared, would be right *for him*. She would admit that. But no sophistry in the world — Arden's smile ran into a frown at the unconscious rough emphasis which, blotted and underlined, was so like her — no sophistry in the world could make it right *for her*. Whatever he did, he would find in it justification enough; the insuperable difficulty was that she couldn't. And if the worst had happened, it would be to her the kind of blow under which all that was most beautiful and worth saving in their relations would finally perish. She knew no way of keeping it alive. She would be glad always to have had the ideal which he, as it were, had lent her for a little while; but henceforth the room would be empty in her soul where it used to come and go. That, the ideal, was all that there was of it, she certified, all that there ever had been of it; and to deface that was to destroy everything. She told him this in so many vague yet violent ways that he might have read in her insistence the necessity for convincing herself; but he only thought her curiously austere.

Simply said, it came to this, that she could not – and would not if she could – withstand the shock of another disappointment in him. We may not think the first one very shattering; but then the idol was not ours. There was a kind of suffering that she found unbearable. It was implied that he alone could provoke it; but among the plainer terms of the letter I am afraid he failed to grasp this hidden consolation also. His head was not so much wilier than his heart as that would show it. And to everything that had grown up between them, of what was more exquisite and true than what people called the realities of life, there should be a definite end. That was the clear thing; and he grasped it as lucidly as he had grasped any other issue that had been presented to him during the last week.

If he had yielded to the Viceroy – well, he *had* yielded to the Viceroy – Ruth Pearce took herself out of his life. Well, then, she was gone. It seemed to come to him with queer naturalness, as part of the discipline of his long service, something that was laid down by authority not to be questioned, something that was merely to be accepted and obeyed. He folded up the letter and put it in his pocket, as he might have folded up a refusal of furlough or a distasteful transfer – with the same sense that it was part of a scheme of things in which his was the simple duty of loyal co-operation. He had made it a point of honour for twenty years never to protest, and he did not protest now. This was more than ever to be accepted, because it was a legitimate consequence of a thing he had thought proper to do. It was no unjust or arbitrary infliction, such as will sometimes fly from the machinery of even the best oiled bureaucracy, but a direct issue of his own administrative act. He took it up without a thought of rejection, as he would have taken up a lighter penalty, which had not to be poised upon his heart.

He had come, besides, to the point in life when the eager heart has learned how much it must do without; when it knows acquiescence and shrewdly guesses the certainty of denial by the depth of desire. It would go cowled like a monk among the ways of the world if it could, the heart of middle age; so wise it has grown, and so humble. Or perhaps it is like a dog that has been beaten often but still would serve its master, trying to learn indifference to every other foolish wish. Yes, it is most like that; since the poor dog pants and bounds in his allegiance much longer, sometimes, than we have any need of him.

Arden never denied himself, notwithstanding, his right of private criticism; and as he sat there in his corner while the hours and the train went on, he took what lean satisfaction there was in trying his charge, and pulling the logic of his sentence to pieces. As he saw it, she wished to command his political conscience. She would condemn its obedience to the ruler, or even to himself; what she forbade, therefore, that she exacted. It was not a view to be upheld, no doubt; but the man was on his defence against the woman he loved. Perhaps this invalidates all his arguments; I will quote no more of them. Only let me tell how he thought it supreme and characteristic in her that she could thus debate and decide about anything so certified in itself as what they were to one another, a thing which, to his simpler mind, having come into existence, should just be and remain. We know her letter was nothing of the kind, but a mere subtle refuge of hers, tangled and defended with inscrutable woman's ethics; but again we are not in his situation. He sat there, indeed, did the Chief Commissioner of Ghoom, making one mistake after another. His traffic had truly and wonderfully been with Ruth Pearce's soul; and it was perhaps natural that he should refer this decision of hers to what was finest and noblest and least to be disputed in her, and should receive it simply as absolute and irrevocable – which was the greatest mistake of all.

Yet he was her lover. Night came, early night, with its tenderness of stars and its humanity of village fires, the Indian night, in its vague travelling darkness and warm breathing of the expanded earth. Suddenly, as the train fled along, his blood awoke and murmured in him. He leaned with excitement towards the window where the soft air rushed in and brought him nothing. He seemed to have a bond with the night in his veins, which burned with

mounting possession of her, as if imagination cast a sweet fiction after everything else that departed. He sat seized and wondering, for
it was a palpable thing like a visitation; and across his vision, nailed
to the darkness, shot the lights of another train side-tracked to let
him pass. It was the Calcutta mail, and Ruth Pearce was in it, on
her way to her new appointment, a chained slave to the rebel
thought of him, fighting with her longing to know what her letter
would bring back.

Next day she found out by the Calcutta papers.

CHAPTER XXIII

THE individual human lot, how practically it disengages itself from
the mass! We talk of campaigns and revolutions, and it is all paper
theory, less important to our instincts than the single case, anywhere
on the round of the world, that has managed to become detached,
and to rise, like a microcosm of misery, out of the depths. There is
the picture and the drama; and we stare fascinated at the bubble we
see, while the fate of anonymous thousands sleeps in the next paragraph.

Well, the sun rose one morning to throw the shadow of the gallows across the history of India in a new significance, and even in
London they saw it. The earlier telegrams announcing the reopening of the Morgan case in Calcutta had been dry and brief, so dry
and brief as to hint discretion in the wording, and a sense of grave
issues at the Indian end. But nobody thought of finding that in
them, except perhaps the India Office and one or two members of
the Government. The great British gallery passed them by, and they
were presently wrapping up herrings and cheese as if by pre-desti-
nation. In a week or two, however, another note crept into them, a
note that could not be subdued; and the centre of the Empire became vaguely aware that far out upon those circling boundaries
which she manages with such magnificent unconcern something
was happening. 'They seem to be rather upset in Calcutta over that
chap Morgan,' said the breakfast-tables of the City of Westminster.
An imperfect acquaintance with the facts crept even into the subur-

ban trains. Then in the course of time and the progress of the morning deliveries the thing that came throbbing over the cables finally conquered the fogs and grasped the imagination of the island. Henry Morgan emerged from the welter of the world, and his name became the tag of an idea. London – even England – became aware of how and why Calcutta was upset, and naturally, feeling that she had a voice in the matter, became upset herself, and lifted it.

It is easy to hear her. When a subject arrives at editorial importance her tones sound round the world. Henry Morgan became in a moment a touchstone for the character and feelings, the principles, prejudices, and politics of the British nation, as reflected in the metropolitan Press. He made a channel for them all down the fourth page.

The *Daily Flash*, a revolving light which, it was now recognised, could never be extinguished, gave him a brief lyrical setting, with a crisp notice to Lord Thame that his 'great constituency' had an eye upon his vagaries, the last paragraph reminding its readers – comprising one quarter of the literate population of Great Britain – that the *Flash* had been two days ahead of its contemporaries in publishing the original account of Morgan's crime. 'First you see the *Flash* and then you hear the report,' said punning readers of this journal. The *Morning Remembrancer* turned from its daily labour to keep the Anglo-Saxon race within the kingdom of Great Britain, to bestow warm appreciation and applause upon the Viceroy of India, who, in spite of a threatening tradition and a clamouring bureaucracy, was calling down reluctant justice upon a criminal of his own race from a sky which should not shelter them both. The journal referred to with affectionate deference by its contributors as 'the Organ' went dispassionately back over the matter from the beginning, laid a calm restraining hand upon its emotional significance, and finished with an expression of fatherly confidence in Lord Thame, whose course and conduct in India the Organ and the nation had so frequently found occasion to approve. The weeklies joined the chorus, singing second but in perfect tune. *Fireside Comment* spared its readers the unhappy details of Morgan's offence, led them in a serious circle round what it described as a standard of ethics, and implored them to be on their guard against the noxious bacteria of race feeling which might presently be in the air, against which even the balanced mind of the English people could not hope to be absolutely proof. Alfred Earle, in the *Prospect*, pointed out that this was a matter in which a Conservative Opposition might well find its account, as well as one of possible grave reckoning to the nation, certainly a matter to be regarded with the utmost concern in every aspect. After which he congratulated Lord Thame upon his courage in adding the intolerable to the burdens of his administration, and closed with some reflections upon the obvious inconvenience, in an Oriental country, of an Early Victorian cast of mind. People often wondered why the *Prospect*, which was really so clever, did not make more of a mark.

Lady Thame went about with the face and figure of triumph. Anthony stood a fair chance of immolation for a principle at last, and whether the pyre was lighted in England or in India she did not much care. He had gone consistently after false gods for so long, mostly by tortuous paths leading over frontiers, that she had almost given up the hope of reclaiming him. But the affair of Henry Morgan was proving him her own son – 'a Thame,' as the Bishop remarked, 'of the first water.'

She fanned the flame.

'I wish they would drag him from his seat,' she said to the Bishop, who was dining with her.

Deirdre and Victoria Tring were there, and Lady Akell with her husband's excuses. The Secretary of State for India had cried off at the last moment. Lord Arthur Perth, editor of the last monthly review – independent of everything but Ireland – was also present; Jasper Dabchick, proprietor of *Fireside Comment*; an odd man from the Home Office, other London items, large and small.

The Bishop of Battersea smiled along an inclined plane at the chandelier, and the pendants twinkled back.

'I hope they won't do that,' he replied; 'but a friend of mine in Calcutta, a brother-priest of the Oxford Mission, writes to me that feeling is rising very high. The prisoner was transferred the other day from this up-country place with the curious name where the crime was committed, to Calcutta; and I believe the demonstration at the station was extraordinary. Extraordinary, I mean, for Calcutta, where, no doubt owing to the climate, the public is somewhat lethargic. And quite unexpected.'

'Anthony gave me a full account of it,' said his mother, 'at least so far as he was informed by the newspapers. He and his Council had left for Simla just two days before, I regret to say. Otherwise I can quite imagine his going out himself among the people to restore order.'

'The moment of heroic opportunity,' observed the Bishop, 'how often it comes when we are not there! And Simla. That is a town in what they call "the Hills," I believe. Now that's an odd fancy to call the vast Himalayas "the Hills." The Viceroy and his Government go every summer to Simla, I have been told. No doubt to escape the terrible Indian heat. Dear me, how much we have heard of Simla!'

'Of course they do, dear Bishop. How could they accomplish anything down in the Plains, from April to November, with their brains frizzling? But Anthony frequently tells me to believe very little of what one hears of Simla, I am thankful to say. "Think of it rather," he says, "as a workshop of Empire." He says I am to organise a crusade – a *crusade* – against the popular idea of the place; so I might as well begin with you.'

The Bishop put up a shapely hand.

'I fall at once,' he protested.

'"Anglo-India," he tells me,' continued Lady Thame, '"may be roughly divided into men who are intelligent and women who are virtuous. As far as I am able to observe," he says, "there are hardly any others." That was his phrase. Rather epigrammatic I call it – epigrammatic, if I am his mother. You are eating nothing, Bishop.'

'I am so excessively fond of – of this excellent roll, dear Lady Thame. But to return to this unsavoury fellow, Morgan. The trial in the Supreme Court is pending, I take it.'

'The first part of it, to do away with the original judgment – quash it, don't they say? – comes on next week, before what they call a Revisional bench. Which will consist of Dick Wimpole – you know Richard Wimpole, their last appointment from England to the Calcutta High Court? He went out in January. Oh yes, Bishop,

I am sure you do. Who did so much to defeat that wicked Canada Loaf Bill last year. Wrote his fingers to the bone and talked himself into spasmodic asthma. Very bad he was, poor fellow.'

'Yes, yes. To be sure I do. Wimpole. Prominent everywhere but at the Bar, perhaps.'

'Possibly. But as he has private means that doesn't matter. A man of the best principle, and most anxious to be of real service somewhere. And we all thought India, you know, would do beautifully for the asthma. Well, he is to be one of these Revisional judges. Another is an Irishman, not at all over-fond of our military despotism out there, and what they call a civilian judge; and the third is very properly a Hindoo, whose name I can't remember, but it ends in "bhai." Anthony writes that he has every hope that the matter may be put right. Nobody knows but me how much he has it at heart. And possibly,' added Lady Thame, who was scrupulously truthful, as her eye fell upon Victoria Tring, 'one other person.'

The dinner-table was informed with the topic. It possessed the hour and the occasion as a shadow thrown by the morning papers will possess it in London. Lady Thame's party fell on it with avidity, exercised their reflection and their wit, their judgment and their imagination upon it. Among the last of Henry Morgan's poor uses was that of a whetstone. Arthur Perth, who looked heavily weighted with the matter of his Review and drank only Apollinaris, expressed his gratitude that there were still opportunities, in the course of history, for Englishmen to make precedents of conduct. Jasper Dabchick agreed profoundly, but trusted, with a bright and perspicacious eye upon consequences, that Morgan's sentence would not be enhanced beyond, say, ten years. He ought to get ten years, certainly.

'I am inclined to think,' said Mrs. Tring, lifting her head like a daughter of Olympus out of some not quite pristine lace foam, 'that he ought to be hanged. I have never had that feeling before – that any one ought to be hanged – but it seems imposed on me. The ideals are gods that demand sacrifices. We must not withhold them.'

The Bishop looked with what one might call averted interest at Mrs. Tring, who always attracted this curious attention from Bishops.

'Is that your view, Lady Akell?' he asked his neighbour on the other side.

The wife of the Secretary of State for India answered with her eyes, and the Bishop smiled with that conscious discretion that persons in these circles have occasion to use so often. Presently, with the safe precision of practice, Lady Thame being engaged upon her left, Lady Akell, so to speak, developed her glance.

'They don't like it at all,' she told him. 'Akell thinks it an odious persecution, and George Craybrooke is quite nervous about it. It must be backed up, I suppose. But of all the pig-headed —'

'Ah,' said the Bishop, giving her an instant's necessary cover.

'Oh, I assure you! As to that little lady —'

'The advocate of the willing sacrifice?'

'Is she quite mad? I hear that she has broken, over this, with her dearest friend.'

'Really? How very sad – how very sad, indeed.'

'He can't and won't see it as she does – in fact, he's furious with certain people, like everybody else – and he's banished! It's too absurd. You perceive he's not here to-night.'

'And is that remarkable?'

'Oh, she won't go anywhere without him. People understand that perfectly, you know. The odd thing is, he began by not liking her at all. Then one day he went down like a shot. It was at our house. She said one of her extraordinary things, and he replied as rudely as possible, "I don't know what you mean." She looked at him as if he were to be pitied. "No, I suppose you don't," she said, "but that doesn't destroy the meaning." You know how Frayley has always been spoiled and flattered, Bishop. I assure you he almost visibly jumped. And capitulated at once.'

'Dear me, how very interesting.' The Bishop's eye now rested, as if by licence, upon Deirdre.

'Yes, but so annoying, Bishop. Frayley has been tripped in the House by that odious Welshman twice in the last three days. I wish she would marry him and be done with it!'

'Perhaps she prefers to keep her privilege to banish him. There is never any news, I suppose, of that poor fellow, the son – most unhappy affair, that.'

'Oh, they've found him, I believe – or are on the point of finding him,' replied Lady Akell, a statement which seemed greatly to reassure and comfort the Bishop.

Lavinia Thame, asking Victoria practically the same question, as the ladies paired into after-dinner talk in the drawing-room, was less completely solaced by the reply, though it was to the same effect.

'It can only be a question of a few weeks now,' said Victoria, 'but Kelly has only just sailed, you know. Tell me, Lavinia, are you all *certain* that George Craybrooke is going to stick to Anthony through this business? I hear the India Office is against him to a man – and why isn't Akell here to-night?'

'He telegraphed influenza, or a threatening. Kelly sailed on the 3rd, Victoria. We ought to hear *something* by the first week in May.'

'I am sure we shall, Lavinia, dear old thing. We must have patience,' said Victoria. 'If Craybrooke fails Anthony over this Morgan business the last *shred* of my respect for a Liberal Government vanishes.'

CHAPTER XXIV

WHAT they thought in London was a matter of great indifference in India. There they were thinking for themselves. When it came to a tea duty or a sugar bounty, attention was paid, however exasperated, to the home view; but in matters intrinsically Indian the home view was felt to be superfluous. Reuter duly cabled the opinions of the Organ and the *Remembrancer* as to the Indian Government's action in the Morgan case; and they said in the Calicut Club that it was sickening. From their point it *was* sickening; but as this is not a study of an Anglo-Saxon group, isolated in a far country under tropical skies and special conditions, but only a story, I cannot stop to explain why. However they put it in India, they felt that here was a matter removed by circumstance and destiny from the British intelligence, and threw the paragraphs of Fleet Street into the waste-paper basket. The fact that they were politically equipped in no way whatever to deal with it only further heated their blood and intensified their conviction. The Viceroy had again over-ridden the Courts – that was the way they put it. The thing was getting beyond bearing.

The hot air of April burned over the Maidan; and the short grass on the glacis of Fort William withered shorter still. The teak-trees uncurled their miracle of young leaves, branch by vivid branch; the gold mohurs waited for no leaves, but threw their scarlet splendour back to the passionate sun along every dusty highway. They were always dramatic, these flags of the hot weather; and the fact that Henry Morgan, already once delivered from the Courts with his life, lay in a suburban gaol waiting for a second jury and a further judgment, seemed to write itself upon them and make them more intense than ever. The thing possessed the place; it stood in the wide, red roads and the uneven lines of the stucco buildings, and throbbed all day upon the traffic. Calcutta lay helpless under it as cities do lie helpless while the Time-Spirit makes history in their streets; helpless, but bitterly angry.

Not especially angry toward Eliot Arden. Here where we might expect sneers and reprobation, there was nothing worse than a half-cynical acquiescence. The public mind had the habit of inter-official dealing, and accepted the practical politics of the machine. Ruth Pearce noted with indignant grief that he was not even given the credit of a struggle and a decision. 'Extraordinary pressure' was generally assumed to have been brought to bear upon the Chief Commissioner of Ghoom, and his original stand, still figuring as courageous and praiseworthy, was thrust endlessly into the indictment of the Viceroy. With that they had done with him. Arden sent the rest of the Government of Ghoom up to its summer headquarters at Gangutri, but made a late tour for himself among some aboriginal tribes inside his boundaries down below. No doubt he wished to be within easy reach of any commotion or any consequences; but in this his courage found no field. He was set aside as a person no longer concerned with the matter; and in what he had done he was treated as the agent of circumstances. He was not given the dignity of an accomplice, nor was he thought deserving of censure. In these pretty ways will fate sometimes make her compliments to the bureaucrat.

But Lord Thame, high in his castle at Simla, became a target. After the comments in London of the Organ and the *Remembrancer*, the shots came thicker and faster. According to his critics there was no longer any shadow of doubt as to the motive of the Viceroy's dealing with the case of Henry Morgan, and others that had gone before. They were making the capital of his political future. Morgan's crime was being distorted before the home public to lift up Anthony Thame as the champion of righteousness and justice. He would step on their ignorant prejudices and enthusiasms into a seat in the Cabinet. His ambition was boundless; and if he had a conscience it was little more than a working theory of sophistries. They made it all very clear, and grew angrier as they explained.

Across the storm no word or sign came from Simla. This behaviour was contrasted with the line that would have been taken by former Viceroys, now gathered back to Britain, who had one after the other added to precedent, but never disputed it. This one, as strenuous a doer as Lord Thame, would at least have justified himself; there would have been a speech in Council or a Resolution in the *Gazette*. That one, ever regardful of the public pulse, would have withdrawn from the attempt long ago. The author of the familiar epigram that Indian justice was a compromise with the police would naturally never have entered upon it. Any of these courses would have been preferable to Lord Thame's, who, withdrawn and impervious on his mountain seat, watched with apparent calm the course of the action he had initiated.

It was recognised that in the meantime nothing could be done. The Viceroy had gained his first point. Since he could make the law carry out his will, the public quite recognised that he had for the moment the whip hand. Nobody wanted to storm the suburban gaol. As they said at the Calicut Club, there was nothing for it but to see the thing through. Perhaps this was a more philosophic view than it would have been if it had not been supported by long-standing confidence in the High Court. That tribunal had already dealt the Viceroy more than one historic snub. More than once it had been pointed out, in high notes of congratulation, that the Judges of that Court were officers and not officials. Its independence was the pride and glory of Calcutta, and it had almost an unbroken tradition of non-compliance with suggestions emanating from what one might call the trans-frontier regions of practical law. The Revisional Bench would refuse to quash the proceedings at the Pilaghur trial.

Then the Viceroy gained his second point. The Revisional Bench ordered the re-trial.

Still, the strength of its old bulwark steadied public opinion. It began to be believed that on this occasion Lord Thame had put the High Court, as they said at the Calicut Club, 'in a hole,' and that the Viceroy would to some extent 'score.' Only very arrogant spirits indeed, persons who still held to brandy-pegs and the theories of John Company, declared the expectation that Morgan's original sentence would be endorsed or diminished. Nevertheless, for the comfort of all, the High Court was the High Court, the arbiter of large commercial uncertainties, and the last stronghold of the conviction that equal justice between man and man in India is subject to interpretations. And nothing to prejudice this view was found in the fact that the case was to come before the Hon. Mr. Justice Lenox, whom fate had hastened to make 'pucca,' in his appointment, as if for the occasion.

The trial has been described as the most sensational in the history of Calcutta. It lasted a fortnight; and the volume and consistency of the evidence that poured through the daily papers astonished even hardened observers of the Indian witness. The Standing Counsel was a man of unusual ability, lately appointed. The native papers remarked, with their quaint appropriation of homely sayings, that he was a new broom and would make a clean sweep of Morgan; which was quoted in the Calicut Club by a facetious tea-taster, who asked whether it was possible to make a clean sweep.

People did not crowd to the trial; it was too hot, too odorous, and airless. Justice in the East entertains hardly anybody. The Court was daily full of natives and reporters, a score of soldiers from the fort, an occasional Chinaman. The people who lived in the pillared chunam houses along Chowringhee did not attend; but they read the evidence with the deepest interest on their verandahs in the cool of the early morning, and speculated between toast and tea how much of it Lenox would believe, how many years it indicated, and whether Morgan would spend them in the Andamans. Little else was thought of as the long hot days went by; nothing else was talked of under the punkahs that whirled above the brokers' tiffin-tables, or across the baked sward of the golf links when the sun sank over the river and the wind came up from the sea.

The event was a wild surprise. It was known in the Bar Library in a quarter of an hour, known and but half-believed in the Clubs by dinner time, rumoured and discredited everywhere the same night; but Calcutta has no evening papers, and the thing had only the carriage of mouth to mouth. Next morning it came with the as-surance of the reported page. In the case of the Emperor *versus* Henry Morgan the jury had brought in the verdict of wilful mur-der, and the prisoner had been sentenced to be hanged.

The jury had been very plainly charged by the Hon. Mr. Justice Lenox. The address, informed as it was by the essential spirit of equity, would have been read with gratification by the public of the *Remembrancer*, if it could have appeared in that journal. The native papers acclaimed it with applauding words – 'fearless,' 'unflinch-ing,' 'impartial.' It was a summing-up of extraordinary vigour, and it conveyed very clearly his lordship's profound sense both of the double duty and the double responsibility involved in the task they had before them. It was marked withal by the nicest care; it left no smallest cranny for the entrance of that disorganising lever known as a point of law. Calcutta's rage and fury with it, the way Calcutta bespattered the man with it, must have been because it was success-ful.

If the verdict was surprising, the sentence was amazing. It seemed a sentence that took advantage of the verdict – to go one better. The prisoner fainted under it, no doubt from sheer astonishment. An American gentleman connected with the Stand-ard Oil Company said it was 'the limit.' That, perhaps, in its brev-ity, was what Calcutta felt. It was not only the limit, but beyond the limit. Hardly any one but the native papers paused to admire the courage, in thus passing the limit, of the Hon. Mr. Justice Lenox. About the Hon. Mr. Justice Lenox things were said in the Bar

Library, and even, I fear, in other precincts of the Court, which I must not report. It was pointed out with excitement on the Exchange that the case was likely to make a most dangerous precedent. The Anglo-Indian community could not accept such a precedent. The sentence must be commuted.

The only road to that lay through His Excellency the Viceroy. There was no legal appeal. Calcutta ground its teeth in the recognition of this, and went to work at what the *Hooghly Pilot* paused between paragraphs to call orderly and legitimate agitation.

The newspapers bayed and bayed; and though they addressed a public without a vote, which is like shouting into a vacuum, they made an astounding noise. The officials were silent, but the commercial world had its committees, and used them. The matter was transferred in a day from the hands of the Courts to those of the jute balers, and the tea-growers, the wheat and seedsmen. The Chamber of Commerce led the way, with the Trades' Association on its heels, and every mail train for a week carried a corporate remonstrance to Simla. The Defence Committee added to its protest an open letter to Lord Thame, published simultaneously over India, and couched in terms so little discreet that the *Star of Islam* named this body imaginatively the Mafia of Viceroys, at which the Defence Committee took action against the proprietor.

If the incredible thing were done, it was fixed for the first of June. June was still three weeks in the future, but to Ruth Pearce, waking in the knowledge of it, it seemed that every dawn brought that day. Dr. Pearce's extraordinary interest in the case was explained in the hospital by the fact that Morgan belonged to the Barfordshires, and the Barfordshires were stationed at Pilaghur, whence Dr. Pearce had come; but even this hardly accounted for the number of hours – practically all her leisure – that Dr. Pearce steadily devoted to the trial. It was thought morbid in her by the staff, who talked a good deal about it. Once, when the matron asked her 'Were there any other ladies?' Ruth had felt herself covered with a hot blush as she answered, 'No.'

She was not there at the dramatic close. Her duties prevented that; and she, for whom only in all seething Calcutta the trial had a heavy personal significance, saw the verdict and the sentence, like the rest of the world, in the morning papers. It struck straight at her heart through Arden's. She saw it printed black in retribution. It had been a long time, I am afraid, since she thought of the abstract justice of the Morgan case, long, too, since even Eliot's failure to keep covenant with his opinion had weighed much with her. Her heart had fled on before in terror to meet the consequence that threatened, to meet it and engage it, and turn it aside. That was all of her great contention that remained with her, the consequence – the consequence to him. And here it was, heavy and black, a thing for him to carry – and she could never help him – all the rest of her days. It simply must not happen.

So, when the Viceroy's 'No' rolled down the Himalayas, and the anti-Government agitations of the next three weeks began in earnest, a prominent part in them was taken by Dr. Ruth Pearce, of the Dufferin Hospital for Women, who wrote and worked continuously on behalf of the condemned soldier, and made at least one effective speech to a large audience gathered in the Town Hall. It was so unusual for ladies in India to interest themselves conspicuously in matters of public importance that Dr. Pearce's devotion to what was called the lofty principle at stake was given a good deal of prominence in the papers. Eliot Arden saw it there. Never guessing it was all for his sake, he forgave her, with rather a bitter smile, for her campaign against his action and the action he had countenanced.

'Dear fanatic,' he murmured privately, 'she is quite entitled to her opinion.'

Thus he added up every word she said, and every line she wrote, putting the total always to the wrong side of the account. In spite of his philosophy, he grew a little more formal and official, a little greyer and sadder. The ladies of his court at Gangutri told him they were quite sure he was over-working, and said among themselves that the Chief no doubt missed dear Mrs. Arden more than might be supposed.

CHAPTER XXV

'No,' said Egerton Faulkner to his chief, 'Thame won't yield. He's got his chance of playing iron arbiter at last, and he'll take it. That's what he was born for – to hang an Englishman for shooting a native of India, and take the glorious consequences.'

They were discussing the Viceroy's reply to Arden's letter urging the exercise of the Crown's prerogative.

The letter was in His Excellency's own hand; it was a long letter. Arden had gathered from it that his appeal was refused with keener pain and a deeper sense of urgency than Lord Thame had felt in dismissing any other of the many that had reached him. But there was no doubt about the refusal.

'I hear,' Faulkner went on, 'that Jack Maconochy – he's President of the Calcutta Chamber of Commerce this year – went up to Simla on his own account, to give Thame some notion of the feeling. Jack's a good chap, and was at school with him. I believe he let him have it straight, after dinner – told him if he made a public entry into Calcutta now he'd be hissed from Howrah Station to Government House – if no worse.'

'Maconochy had better have stayed at home,' remarked Arden. 'He may be a good chap, but I doubt his intelligence.'

'Vetchley sends me some pretty stories too. The Barfords are naturally wild. One of the men was overhead to remark the other day, after kicking a regimental sweeper, "Now go and tell your 'arf-brother, Antony Andover." But most of the things they say are less quotable. Vetchley himself is almost too furious to hold a pen. His handwriting shakes like an old man's.'

'I don't think we shall see the execution. They will put a stop to it from home. The Service journals are at it like wolves, and I see by to-day's telegrams that Grindlay Maple is expected to make a great attack on it in the House.'

'Maple is elected, I believe, by the hedgers and ditchers of Mid-Bloxham, but his real constituency is Anglo-India,' said the Chief Secretary, gathering up his papers. 'We're not altogether represented by gentlemen who think they should have been Lieutenant-Governors, and enter Parliament to get their knives into their old

Administration. Excellent Maple – I wish he had even more coal in Jerriah.'

'How will that group take it?' asked Arden, smiling. 'The little lot that Thame should have given Bengal and Burma to. They won't support Thame, and they can't disavow the native of India who groans under the tyranny of the cast-iron British Raj. They'll be in a hat.'

'They'll fold their arms and shut their mouths,' said Faulkner. 'But if the Home Secretary commutes Morgan's sentence over Thame's head, Thame is perfectly capable of threatening to resign – and resigning. That would look pretty to the people of England, wouldn't it, sir? Intractable brute!'

'I don't think we shall see the execution,' repeated Arden. 'I hear of strong representations in the highest quarters. Why has Lady Waterbrook gone home suddenly this way, through the Red Sea in the middle of May?'

The lady in question was the wife of the Commander-in-Chief.

'Not for her health, or to attend a Drawing-room, we may suppose,' he continued. 'Lady Waterbrook is a clever woman, and she happens to be the King's godchild.'

'Things have come to a deadlock in Simla,' replied Faulkner, rising. 'The Viceroy and Sir Robert are hardly on speaking terms, and at Thame's last dance not a soul on the Headquarters Staff turned up. Well, I suppose Waterbrook will do all he knows. It may be a serious business for him. He has seventy thousand British troops in India to take care of, and nobody could describe them as a happy family who had any acquaintance with the facts.'

'Waterbrook should have made a stand long ago; he was in a position to do it,' said the Chief Commissioner with a note of irritation. 'He had a big theory behind him and a tremendous interest to defend. This demonstration of keeping your people away from dances is puerile.'

'Oh, ridiculous! He was hypnotised, I suppose, like everybody else. My wife hoped I might bring you back to lunch with us, sir,' added Faulkner hastily. 'She commanded me – ah – to tell you we are to have rhubarb tart – and rhubarb tart,' added the Chief Secretary, covering his embarrassment with a whimsical drop of his eyeglass, 'is one of the things that really comfort one in trouble.'

Arden laughed.

'My best thanks to Mrs. Faulkner,' he said, 'and the temptation is great; but I am afraid I must content myself with a sandwich here.'

He turned as his Chief Secretary left him, to preoccupations other than the fate of Henry Morgan, which indeed made only one claim out of many upon his mind. The matter had passed for Arden beyond the sphere of administrative interest; his active concern with it had closed, at all events for the time. He watched the ferment in Calcutta with all India, and kept the eye of careful observation on the symptoms that corresponded in London; but he felt himself now almost as detached as the Governor of Bombay or the man in Piccadilly. Even as a reference in his mind the character of the thing had changed. In his definite official way he had written it off and filed it. The letter to the Viceroy, of which he and Faulkner had been talking, had been his last duty in the matter. He still hoped, as he still looked, for the commutation of the sentence; but Morgan's fate now belonged to the public records, not to him.

While he sat at his work the English mail came in, bringing letters from his wife. Jessica wrote always copiously, and of late her letters had been very cheerful, full of Teddy's convalescence and outrageous appetite, which seemed a gift in his mother's interpretation, like his turn for languages and the genius she so much more than suspected in him for music. Mrs. Arden was now only waiting for the rains to break and make railway travelling possible in India to return to her husband and their hot-weather perch in dear, beautiful Gangutri; where she hoped the sweet-peas wouldn't be *quite* so good this year when she hadn't been there to help them to grow. And would Eliot please carefully remember to tell her when people, as well as sweet-peas, said they missed her; for she liked being missed, and missed everything and everybody, most dreadfully herself. She hoped the Meteorological — was that the way to spell it? — Department would arrange for an early monsoon this year, for she really couldn't wait after the third week in June. Wouldn't he let her take the chance of bringing it with her? And he mustn't forget to give her salaams to Nubbi Bux and the other servants, and tell them the burra mem-sahib would soon be back to scold them now.

It was nearly all like that, and Arden's eye ran over it with pleasant familiarity, the little melody she had played so often. But the last page or two of the last letter he read twice. Mrs. Arden had been 'doing' Nietzsche for two hours, she told him, and she felt completely tired out. Perhaps, although her German was wonderfully brushed up by being in Heidelberg and having to order everything, it was not yet quite equal to philosophy; at all events her brain simply refused to take it in, though it was beautiful print and *Latinischer schrift*. He must write and tell her what he thought of Nietzsche; she couldn't remember. And what Miss Pearce thought too; their united opinions would help her, perhaps, to tackle him again. She was sure they would think alike. How was Dr. Pearce getting on in Calcutta? It was some time since he had mentioned her. Jessica was sure he must be missing Ruth's thoughtful and stimulating companionship, especially as he had not even his poor little wife to fall back on. His poor little wife must hurry home, or she would begin to feel left behind. The worst of having a clever husband was that you always had to think about being left behind in his interests and pursuits.

'But you can say for me, can't you, dear, that I've made a point of keeping up, except when circumstances were too strong for me, like the time you tried to teach me Persian when Teddy was coming – in Thugganugger, the year the rains failed and we so nearly lost Herbie. Oh, that awful Thugganugger! The sight of an Arabic character, even now, is more than I can bear. I'm afraid the Persian was a failure, and I've never translated Omar Khayyam for myself as I always meant to do; but in other ways, though I haven't kept step, I have kept up, haven't I, dear? I think I say this because, though I've never, in our eighteen years of happiness together, felt it before, to-day I feel so far behind that I have to shade my eyes even to see you. It must be that horrid Nietzsche. But – wait for me, dear.'

Arden's lip for an instant trembled. He got up quickly and locked himself in from the corridor, and said to a servant in waiting on the verandah –

'If any come, the door is shut.'

Then he went back and sat down again at his office table, and remained sitting there with the sheets of his wife's letters gathered in his hand for a long time, as if they presented new and complicated matter to his consideration. He ceased reading the pages, but his eye remained fixed on them, engaged with all that they evoked. He did, indeed, remember Thugganugger and that brazen June and their struggles to save Herbie – he did, indeed. And the poor little scholar who sat so late with grammar and dictionary under the cloud of insects that swarmed round the lamp and fell on the curling page, until she literally cried with the heat and weariness, and he had to take the books away, and assure her that Persian could never make her more to him than she was then. He remembered. Once or twice he took up a pen as if to tell her, but laid it down again. His heart would have it out with him first, and forbade his hand. Besides, it is possible to acquire a secretariat way of dealing with every emotion; one shuns the chaotic, one bounds an impulse and waits for ordered conclusions.

Jessica was a dear woman. He more than remembered that. A dear, loving woman. Had always been. Dear and loving, the woman he chose. Wait for her! The sheets grew blurred. How foolish of you, Jessie, to say a thing like that! Was he not always waiting for you, dear little woman, to come back into his life?

If she hadn't kept step she had kept up. Indeed she had kept up, every mile of the way; and the way had been no primrose path. Months of camping, shifting, changing, years of bad climates, loneliness, of desert and jungle – everything a woman should not have. And never to be persuaded to leave him, until she had to go home with the boys. The Hills were for women who were not so keen on keeping up. Through the pain in his heart he felt the truth, that she had been always there, near him there, keeping up.

He would never let her feel like this again. She never did when she was with him. It was being so far away; and no doubt she was a bit run down after her long bout of nursing Teddy. He would tell her she ought to be out in the fresh air, and not poring over Nietzsche. When she came back he would do a little with her every day, until she forgot about it and took up something else – wood-carving or cactus dahlias. And her instinct was perfectly right, there was more happiness in things than in formulas. Wait for her! He could smile by this time, with just a touch of indignation. Where was she now? He wanted her. Oh well, he supposed the boys had claims.

Again he took up his pen; and I wish he might have answered her letter and written out his heart to her. It would have been a thing done, a message sent. It would have stood to him afterward for something, something 'on record'; and if there had been time to post it so much the better. But there was no time for anything. An urgent despatch from the Government of India interrupted him for half an hour; he was still occupied with it when they brought him the yellow telegraph envelope marked 'Foreign.' He broke it with his mind still half upon the business of the despatch from Simla, and read:–

HEIDELBERG, May 20th.

Dear Jessica died here early this morning. Heart failure following slight operation. Mother with her all through. I arrived too late. We are both broken-hearted. Deepest sympathy. – ELINOR.

'Heart failure,' repeated Eliot Arden, and said it again. 'Heart failure.'

Close on the blow came his imagination with its stab – was it Jessica's heart that had failed? But the thought that hurt him most miserably, with her letter still speaking to him, was that it would never matter any more whether his wife could keep up – she had gone so irretrievably on ahead.

CHAPTER XXVI

SIR Ahmed Hossein disappeared from these pages early in April, having been compelled about that time to take leave to England on medical certificate. He had become unfit for his duties. The Oriental mind, under the displeasure of the ruler, takes a peculiar tone of despondency; and the District Judge of Pilaghur was profoundly affected by Lord Thame's attitude toward his action in the case which was to become so celebrated, the more so as he had expected at least the Viceroy's appreciation. To win and keep that I fear he would have enhanced Morgan's or any sentence, doubled it, multiplied it, cheerfully made it capital. To Ahmed Hossein the Viceroy was more than a god – he was a god of dear benignance toward himself; everything he had except his brains and his fortune he owed to Lord Thame. He grew ill with the censure implied in the Viceroy's determined appeal to a higher tribunal; he starved and was sleepless, shrank from society, pondered suicide. This second tragedy might actually have added itself to Morgan's crime, but for an odd coincidence. The ten-year-old son of Sir Ahmed's coachman, slapped by his father for burning the chupatties, threw himself into a tank in the garden and was drowned. Sir Ahmed looked at the little body and turned away, feeling that the racial instinct was absurd.

But when a medical board pronounced upon him, and ordered immediate rest and change of climate, the District Judge escaped gladly from the storm in which he had so unnecessarily involved his friends. He wrote his feelings fully to Arden, who understood – who understood even when Sir Ahmed wept before the clerks in the office in the act of saying good-bye.

'Three months in England will put you right again,' said the Chief Commissioner as they shook hands, and did not smile even to his spirit when his fellow-official replied in the clipped syllables of native English –

'I am sure that is so. Leave home is the great restorative. There is no place like home.'

Sir Ahmed was, therefore, in England when the storm really reached its height in Calcutta, and the odd revolution of sympathy at home showed plain danger-signals to Mr. Craybrooke's Government. He was at home and in town again, enjoying a daily bath in that admiring consideration which the island always has warm and ready for subjects of any complexion but her own. Tipping a waiter, he was again an Asiatic prince; his furled umbrella almost gave him a vote; under a silk hat he was once more happy and himself.

The *Flash* found him out first, and interviewed him. With regard to desirable people to interview, and knowing where they were, the *Flash* should have been called the *Flair*. Sir Ahmed appeared at exactly the right moment for the *Flash*. The House was very stale, civilisation all over the world very dull, nothing doing in barbarism. Sir Ahmed helped the *Flash* enormously to ask the effective question, 'Shall Morgan Hang?' to make an issue, an emergency, almost a crisis out of Morgan. The young man of the *Flash* confessed in quivering sentences his impression of Sir Ahmed's personality, its dignity and charm and touch of 'mystere austerity,' and added his conviction that 'the lofty convention known as British justice' would be for ever safe under any skies in hands like these.

As to Sir Ahmed's views, he had nothing but approval of the conduct of the case from the beginning. On the evidence brought before him, his Court, he considered, could have arrived at no other verdict; and he did not feel called upon to defend the original sentence. Taking into account the Viceroy's conviction of its inadequacy, His Excellency had no other course than to move the Calcutta High Court for revision of the case. With the fresh evidence laid before it, the Calcutta jury could have brought the prisoner in guilty of nothing short of murder. And in accepting that verdict Mr. Justice Lenox only did his duty in sentencing Morgan to be hanged. As to the Viceroy's prerogative of mercy, personally Sir Ahmed hoped His Excellency would exercise it; but if he did not choose to do so, he, Sir Ahmed, could not say that his admiration for Lord Thame would be lessened, while there was no doubt whatever that the confidence of India in British equity would be greatly increased.

The *Flash* had a brief leading article pointing out the generosity and moderation of Sir Ahmed's attitude, but reasserting its original conviction about the case – a conviction arrived at three days before any of its contemporaries – that the public interest demanded the immediate commutation of the sentence of Henry Morgan. Re-enlistment in India, of which so much was expected, had fallen off thirty-five per cent. in the last year of Lord Thame's Viceroyalty. Figures spoke for themselves. The *Flash* gave Lord Thame unbounded credit for nobility of motive and conscientious compulsion, but would point out that His Excellency had here a unique opportunity of sacrificing his conscience to the Empire, and was unable to forbear to add that, if he did not take it, the Empire was extremely likely to sacrifice him to his conscience.

One would think, indeed, during those last ten days of May that the fate of the Empire depended on that of Henry Morgan. If he did not hang, it would totter morally, according to the Liberal Press; if he did hang, it would crumble every other way, according to the Conservative opposition. The Organ sought painfully for a middle course by which Morgan should be hanged and yet not suffer capital punishment, turning from this exercise to point out that the Crown's prerogative of mercy extended to its humblest subject and its furthest dominions, and that this course, if it commended itself to the Sovereign, would at once relieve his representative of all responsibility, and leave the history of India ennobled by a splendid protest. There could be no doubt, added the Organ with just a hint of expiring patience, that if such a solution were offered to the unhappy question, Lord Thame would see the propriety of accepting it as final. Any other course would be to make a doubtful precedent at the cost of an Imperial scandal. Alfred Earle moaned in the *Prospect* that, whether Morgan was hanged or not, we were rotten, rotten, rotten. Jasper Dabchick chirped in *Fireside Comment* that, whether Morgan was hanged or not, nobody could doubt the integrity of British purpose or the zeal of British administration.

In touching public sympathy Morgan had the advantage of being something like an original instance. The first Englishman in forty years to suffer death for the murder of a native of India was a vastly more attractive figure to the popular imagination than the sixth or even the second would have been. Henry Morgan became a sacrifice to the unknown god of that-which-we-are-not-in-the-habit-of-doing, and a thousand voices cried 'Stop!' 'Wait!'

His case as a common soldier touched the common people. They made his cause their own for the whole ten days. It was suggested to them that Morgan would never have been sentenced to be hanged if he had been an officer and a gentleman. He was to suffer in the cause of a new ideal because he was 'only a Tommy,' whereas officers and gentlemen in India, it was hinted, were known to be guilty of worse things.

As the Viceroy's attitude became more clearly understood, his action suffered every distortion. He emerged a despot, who had torn Morgan from the Courts to make an example of at his own pleasure. His name was bracketed with those of Roman Emperors, and he was warned that modern civilisation had no office for even a just tyrant. He was held up as the systematic persecutor of the army, a fanatic, an inquisitor; he was invited to come home and be hounded from public life. An Imperialistic poet made glorious havoc of the situation in ten stanzas, and the *People's Hour* published the Viceroy's portrait with the inscription, 'Bloody Thame.'

The country was on the eve of a general election; and the Craybrooke Administration felt itself to have a list of matters to answer for long enough without the addition of a piece of stupid obstinacy on the part of an outlying Viceroy. Government messages go at special rates; but the India Office bill for cables that week was heavy. However brief the order or expensive the expostulation that went to Simla, the reply left the situation unchanged. If the sentence of the Calcutta High Court upon Henry Morgan was interfered with from England, Lord Thame would place his protest before the country in the only effective way, by immediate resignation. This had not, naturally, been published to the world; it was an alternative upon which Lord Akell and the India Office were sitting secretly, hoping to hatch a compromise; but it was well enough known at Mrs. Tring's Sunday supper-party, where Lady Thame, indeed, loudly proclaimed it. Lady Thame did not often honour Deirdre's Sunday suppers, having as a rule more important things to do; but on hearing that Mrs. Tring expected Sir Ahmed Hossein, she promptly invited herself – if Deirdre would kindly have something plain – as she thought the man might be worth meeting.

So Lady Thame was there, and Sir Ahmed, whom Mrs. Tring had met only the week before at a large tea in his honour at the Aganippe Club, but had seen with enthusiasm three times since. Sir Ahmed was, indeed, the indirect cause of her reconciliation with Frayley Sambourne; she could simply not resist the possibility of bringing them together. Mr. Sambourne was more than pleased, so he also was there, and Alfred Earle, and the young actor who had made such a marvellous interpretation of brutality in the Tolstoi play, and the young actress who simply accomplished the soul of everything in which a soul could be discerned. Mrs. Tring hoped to secure them both for her own play, which was daily being beaten, out of gold and flame, into four acts upstairs.

'There was once a dispute between a Thame and Cromwell,' said Lady Thame; 'My son's ancestor had his conscience behind him, and Cromwell gave in. That good man shortly afterwards emigrated, I am sorry to say, to America, where he thought it his duty to marry a Mohawk; so the strain is practically lost to us, though, no doubt, still influential over there. But in personal matters we have always felt it a point of honour, to put it on no higher ground, to defeat our Cromwells. You will find that my son will neither be persuaded nor intimidated.'

'His Excellency,' said Sir Ahmed, who had just been introduced, 'has always high courage. In matters of foreign policy also he shows it like no other Viceroy. Look at the Ameer – is he not humble now? Five years ago that great man was roaring.'

'Was he?' said Lady Thame. 'Well, why shouldn't he roar?' But Sir Ahmed was intent upon his panegyric.

'We have upon our frontier some troublesome independent tribes,' he went on, glowing, 'and one fellow – a great priest among them – began preaching *jehad* and raiding. It was the third offence, and the last time we had to send a punitive expedition. Lord Thame was very angry with that mullah. He spoke to me about it. "By God, I'll lay him by the heels," he said, and he annexed that bit of country.'

'Yes,' said Lord Thame's mother. 'I was extremely ashamed of that matter. If that sort of thing was all he found to do in India, I thought the sooner he came home the better.'

'You see,' interposed Mrs. Tring naïvely, at Sir Ahmed's look of blank dismay, 'we are all related to him. Lady Thame is his mother, and I am his half-aunt, and my daughter Victoria is his half-cousin – and so is my son Herbert, who is very shortly coming home from Alaska – so, though he is Viceroy, we can be cross with him if we like.'

'With us also,' bowed Sir Ahmed, 'there is freedom of speech among the ladies of the family.'

'But we are not cross with him at present,' said Lady Thame benignly, as to an infant. 'No! Very pleased. Doing right, we think.'

'What is right?' asked Alfred Earle wearily.

'You will have to expand that in a leading article, Mr. Earle,' said Victoria, smiling.

'The Viceroy is right,' contributed Sir Ahmed unconsciously. 'I myself hope that Morgan's sentence will be commuted by the King, but that Lord Thame will not resign.'

'Can't have both. Can't have both,' said Lady Thame.

'Then we must hang that man,' remarked Sir Ahmed, with decision.

'I've no desire that this particular man be hanged. As a matter of fact I shouldn't be sorry to see him let off,' announced Lady Thame. 'I don't feel bloodthirsty toward the poor wretch, and I'm sure Anthony doesn't; but if the law is not allowed to take its course, I clearly see that a great principle is at stake, and that the Viceroy ought to –'

'Light the stake,' put in Mr. Earle.

'Precisely. By resigning. And you coalition gentlemen' – Lady Thame nodded at Frayley Sambourne – 'may make the best of it.'

'I am generally with the people and for the people,' said Deirdre Tring. 'Oh, and with clemency and for clemency. But here I see the great, dim, helpless mass of Anthony's dark subjects – and justice like a star appearing – and their conquerors seem armed brutes beside them, and I think Anthony is right. This man should be hanged. Besides,' she added with a little frivolous laugh, 'he is hanged in my play.'

'Whatever happens must be,' said Sir Ahmed. '"Our acts our angels are, and good or ill, Our fatal shadows that walk by us still,"' he quoted, looking luminously round the table. It was if he had thrown a stone upon it, disconcerting for an instant. Lady Thame was the first to recover.

'Do you refer to my son or to Morgan?' she asked.

'I am afraid I do not know of what I was thinking exactly. It came to me, that is all.'

'There!' cried Mrs. Tring in general appeal. 'Isn't he delightful? He doesn't always know of what he is thinking; but things come to him! Exactly like me! Sometimes I write them down – do you ever write them down, Sir Ahmed? – and then isn't it maddening to look at them afterwards and wonder what one could have meant?'

Her guest from India beamed and nodded.

'Another day, when one is at what we call a lower psychical temperature,' he said.

'"Psychical temperature" – how perfectly that expresses it, though a little, just a little coldly! Only yesterday I found this in my own handwriting. "Everything is possible that it is possible to imagine, since so much is actual that it is not possible to imagine." Oh, *what* could I have meant? Will somebody explain me to myself?'

'Not at all difficult to explain,' said Lady Thame, getting up. 'You've been reading something you haven't understood, Deirdre. Now, may I ask for my motor, please?'

'Going on to the Stage Society, Lady Thame?' asked Frayley Sambourne.

'Not I – I'm going on to the Bishop. Delighted to have met you, Sir Ahmed, I'm sure. I wish you knew what you want done about Morgan – not that it would make any difference to *my* view, I'm afraid. Come and see me. I live in an old-fashioned way in Cavendish Square. The motor *is* there, is it? I hope Thomas has been inside this rainy night. One advantage over a carriage – coachmen never on your mind – always inside. *Good* night.'

They said farewell to her with extreme relief; and they all, as the door closed behind her and they sat down again, began to talk at once, even the young man who did Russian souls from the inside, and the young woman who did souls of any nationality, catching them apparently in her beautiful hair. These two had hitherto been quite silent in contemplation of Lady Thame. The conversation wandered from the Viceroy of India, irresistibly impelled by the presence of an Oriental, to the occultism of the East. Sir Ahmed found himself surrounded by disciples, and talked happily about the seven Kosmic planes of manifestation, until it became plain that what they really wanted to know was whether he had ever seen a Mahatma and whether he could 'do anything.' Mrs. Tring had in the end to isolate him for his protection, to surround him with her own spirit, give him one of her own cigarettes, and tell him about her play. He was so interested that he threatened, at half-past eleven, to outstay everybody else.

'But, Mrs. Tring, London is the great theatre,' he said, with his eyes glistening; and she cried, 'Oh, I *do* agree! The most wonderful ideas come to me in omnibuses.'

They were all far from Lord Thame and his striking situation, and it was growing late, when Victoria turned quietly to Frayley Sambourne.

'What *is* going to be done about it?' she asked.

'I wish I knew. You are supposed to have some influence in that quarter,' he jested. 'Use it. Urge Tony briefly by wire not to be an ass – any longer.'

'I would urge him quite differently, if he wanted urging; but the splendid thing about him is that he doesn't,' she told him. 'I can't tell you how much I admire the stand he has taken. I am absolutely against you all here. Tony is right; we cannot let Morgan off without shame before a whole Empire. Besides, the man is a brute and ought to be hanged. It is you, now, who are persecuting your Viceroy. Let him take his own high course. You have put India in the hands of a Thame and his conscience, and I think you ought to leave it there.'

'I'm afraid we shall have to usurp the functions of Anthony's conscience this time,' he told her indulgently.

'I don't think you'll do that,' replied Miss Tring with emphasis; and then, as everybody else had gone, she too left the Under-Secretary for India to his privilege of a little final uninterrupted chat with her mother.

CHAPTER XXVII

IF the rancour against the Viceroy had left any room for rancour against Eliot Arden, the news of Arden's sudden bereavement would have gone far to soften it. He belonged, in his distinguished Anglo-Indian place, less to a caste than to a family, to a family that lived always on the edge of tragedy like this, that had learned acquiescence in every kind of strange and sudden loss.

'Poor chap,' they said at the Calicut Club. 'She was a nice woman too. Great shock for him, poor chap. Reminds one of that cousin of his, Harry Arden, of the Assam Police, who rode in from a three days' district inspection tour and met his wife's funeral. Horrid thing – he never quite got over it.'

Everybody would quote a parallel, some near and fresh, some already far but unfaded. Sympathy for Arden was wide and sincere while it lasted. It did not last long. Graves in India are quickly made and soon filled; but for the time it removed him further than ever from the scope of public indignation over the Morgan case.

To Ruth Pearce the sudden word came with a strange solemnity – strange in being so simply and only the feeling which rose in her heart to meet it. A bell-stroke from high Heaven it was; and as the sound throbbed through her heart she could do nothing but listen. She felt even a detachment from it, as the observer of an act of fate. The significance in it to herself she almost unconsciously folded away and would not look at. Her imagination, caught and awed, forbade her for the moment to feel; and her passion shut itself from the sun, and sat beside the corpse that was in the house.

Through those first days she had indeed a wonderful exaltation of spirit, and it brought her a sense of cruelty in being separated from Arden – exactly for those first days. Then, above all other times that had come or could come in their lives, she believed he wanted her help; and she could have helped him. Perhaps this was true, or perhaps it was the creation of her simple wish to believe it, one of those large determinations that so characterised her; but she held to it. She wrote him two long letters, which she burned. Written words seemed an intolerable incarnation of what she would say to him. There was so little, after all, that could be said, so much that could be given; she longed to give. She dwelt with him in his contrition of spirit; she soothed his pain; they talked together gently of Jessica.

Good Mrs. Lemon wrote her the details as they came to be known, but there were not many; the simple story had a simple end. Mrs. Arden, completely run down by nursing her son through enteric, had submitted to a slight operation at Heidelberg, hoping to get it over without letting her husband know, as she did not wish to add even a small anxiety to his daily burden. It wasn't true kindness, in Mrs. Lemon's opinion, there was too much risk in any operation; but people had their own ideas about such things. At any rate blood-poisoning set in almost immediately. They suspected the drains, but of course it was too late – and in three days she was dead. Her mother, most fortunately, was staying with her in Heidelberg at the time, otherwise the poor little woman would have been alone, as the sister seemed to have got there only after all was over. Of course it had put a stop to everything in Gangutri, and people were awfully sorry for him. Mrs. Lemon hadn't seen Mr. Arden herself, but the General had gone to him at once, and said he seemed very broken. She heard, however, that it wasn't to make any immediate difference to his plans; he did not intend to take leave, or anything of that sort. After all, what was there to be done? People were feeling dreadfully about it, and not having so much as a tea-party; but nobody had gone as far as Mrs. Biscuit, who appeared in church, the first Sunday after, in mourning! It was all very sad, and Mrs. Lemon begged particularly to know how long Dr. Pearce's acting appointment would last in Calcutta, and very sincerely hoped that in October or November, when they all came down, they would see her back again at Pilaghur.

Ruth waited a week and then wrote to Arden, but briefly and gently. The emotion of her first letters had taken wings with them when the flame licked up the paper. Perhaps it would have lifted and carried him to a height from which he could have seen down into her heart; but the tide never reached him, and the little note that came seemed kind and formal. If she had not written at all it would have been more significant, would perhaps have roused a doubt in him; but these careful phrases proclaimed her withdrawal with certainty. I cannot insist too much that he was a 'senior' official, accustomed to accept decisions and file them. His relation with Ruth was a matter fully noted on, dealt with, and filed. The finality with which he believed this had not even been disturbed by his new freedom; and she must needs write him a 'letter of condolence' to seal his conviction. He answered it in the same spirit and almost in the same words as he had answered many others; and she forgave the reply, which was a thorn to her love, grieving over the pain she believed it had given before it reached her.

Meanwhile she got what comfort she could out of her solicitude for the criminal, Henry Morgan. She threw herself into the agitation on his behalf with such fervour that the hospital matron thought that 'notice' ought to be taken of it. However, nobody seemed to wish to take notice, except the matron. In Ruth's dreams she saw Arden always Morgan's executioner, putting the noose about the man's neck, while he looked the other way. She believed he would wish her to do anything, everything, she could for Morgan. At last, drawn and repelled by it many times a day, she visited him in gaol.

I believe she was allowed to go three times; and it was remembered afterwards that Miss Pearce was the only person the prisoner saw by his own desire. She came away white and ill from these interviews, which, in their pathetic futility, we may leave to be a memory of her own. She felt vaguely that she might have had an impression of Morgan, of his character and his past – he told her a good deal about his life, and some quite remarkable incidents – but for the one unbearable knowledge that filled the cell and blurred out everything, that she talked with a man whom Arden had helped to condemn to die. One small thing only she was able to do for him, on her last visit, small in itself, but she trembled as she promised it. She took a letter addressed to his relatives, whom she would find in London, to be delivered if the sentence was not commuted.

'But wouldn't it be kinder – ?' she faltered, to which he replied that there were 'family reasons' – he brought out the phrase as grotesquely as he might have produced a visiting-card – why they should know. 'Besides,' he added grimly, 'the death of a fellow like me oughtn't to be kept from his people – it's not common justice.' Then when she turned away he asked her to shake hands with him, and said, when the warder gave his permission, that he thought he could promise that she wouldn't be 'altogether' sorry. And that day did come. As she was let out she felt his eyes following her, speculatively, as if she represented a world with which it might after all have been worth while to have had to do.

The execution was to take place at Pilaghur; and the following day the prisoner was quietly removed there. The hospital matron said it was just as well; Dr. Pearce's nerves were going all to pieces. The whole city felt lighter with the departure of Morgan from the suburban gaol, sore but saner, as after the excision of an abscess that sent poison through the blood. There in Alipore he had been very inflammatory. Excitement about him still ran high; but it was moderated by his transfer to the district that produced him; and a splendid thunderstorm, a real 'north-wester,' further relieved the temperature the day after he went.

Everything had been done that could be done. The great commercial societies had shown the Viceroy clearly what their attitude was in the matter; and the Viceroy had so far disregarded them. The Anglo-Indian Press had urged and entreated, oddly backed up, in the last resort, by two or three tender-hearted Bengali journals, who reminded His Excellency that mercy was a quality twice blessed, and compassion was better than revenge. Skits and sneers had begun to follow anger and astonishment. Even the *Administrator*, a Service journal, which had never been known to quarrel with a Viceroy before, grew acrid over Morgan, publishing a very successful parody of another and an earlier Antoninus, sent by a contributor who wrote it in a tent, fifty miles from anywhere, on the frontier of Baluchistan.

After the mass meeting convened by the Sheriff of Calcutta to ask the Viceroy for clemency had been seen to fail, the Defence Committee had circulated a petition to the King, which gathered the signatures of all Calcutta, sending it to Simla with the prayer that His Excellency would forward it to His Majesty. The people had to come to the petition instead of the petition to the people, to get it signed in time, but they came; and the document travelled to Simla black and heavy. The intimation came promptly back that the Government of India was forwarding it by the first mail to England. That would give His Majesty just three days to overrule his Viceroy by telegraph. Calcutta waited. One woman in Calcutta waited more than any. Beyond the teeming cities where they quarrelled about it, all the burning plain of India, rolling far and wide under the Himalayas, seemed to wait also.

They talked bravely in the Calicut Club of what they would do if Morgan were hanged. Certain manifestations of public disfavour were openly discussed. Lord Thame's term of office included one more winter in Calcutta. He would be compelled to arrive; he could not avoid the usual State entry. Persons who shall not be indicated even by classes or professions volunteered to assist at it, in the sense of making it memorable. The escort of mounted Militia would consist of officers only. There would be a conspiracy of absence from Lord Thame's Levee and his Drawing-Room; the ladies talked of taking a pledge not to attend. A public petition to the Home Government for his removal was seriously discussed, and one tea-planter volunteered to gather men in Assam for a masked conspiracy to raid Government House and put the Viceroy bodily on board a steam yacht bound for England, if funds could be found to commission the yacht. She would fly a foreign flag, and His Excellency would be kept under the hatches until she was well out to sea.

'That's all right,' said a Port Commissioner of the sedater sort. 'This is the end of May, and it's very warm just now. The Viceroy doesn't turn up again till December. By that time we shall have stopped talking either indecency or treason, and Thame will come and go quite comfortably; though I'm not prepared to subscribe to a statue to him myself.'

This gentleman had lived a long time in Calcutta.

CHAPTER XXVIII

RUTH found a certain relief in a humble quarter – she could say anything she liked about Morgan to Hiria. It was the simplest emotional outlet; her anxiety and her hope flowed through Hiria, taking the merest reflection of their channel and paying no heed to that. Hiria was curious and intelligent about the trial, and downcast, in her businesslike way, about the result, which she disapproved. She heard of the efforts to move the Viceroy with a shrug.

'Nothing will come, miss-sahib. The Burra Lat has a strong heart,' she said; but the petition to the King filled her with hope;

and she asked incessantly whether word had come from 'Belat,' days before word could possibly come. When Morgan was sent back to Pilaghur she became restless and dissatisfied with Calcutta.

'It is true talk that this is a place of noise and commotion,' she said. 'Kat-*khut*! Phat-*phut*! upstairs, downstairs, all day long. How quiet is Pilaghur, so that one crow in a tree a mile away can be heard! And the jackals at night – here are too many, miss-sahib, no one can sleep. In Pilaghur a few only, so that it is plain what they say. Your honour knows what they say? One big jackal far off cries out very loud' – she lifted her voice in a long plaintive howl – '"Hum Maharajah *hai*! Hum Maharajah *hai*!" and all the others very far off tell that one, "Ha, *hai*! Ha, *hai*! Ha, *hai*!"'

'Yes, they do say that,' said Ruth, smiling. 'Brush gently, Hiria. My head aches.'

'Poor miss-sahib! Again the head aches. I will give the olly-col-lone. In Calcutta is also too much bundobust – head always thinkin', thinkin'. Miss-sahib's head is never aching in Pilaghur, where the air also is good to eat. Here are too many smells.'

'I thought you liked Calcutta, Hiria.'

'Very good place, miss-sahib. But now cheating. By your hon-our's pleasure I bought three days ago calico for a new petticoat, giving full price. There is a small hole eaten in every measure. I gave it to the sewing-man of the head nurse-mem. He stole two yards from the fulness, so I must go as thin as a post! Without doubt rice is cheap – but that is of God. And there is no order to return to Pilaghur, miss-sahib?'

'No, Hiria. And you are not to say you want to go, for I couldn't possibly spare you.'

'Very good, miss-sahib,' said the ayah reluctantly. 'There is no great need. The marriage of my youngest is for the winter, and they dick me to be returning for the clothes, not more. She is nearly fourteen, miss-sahib; it begins to be shameful that she is not yet married.'

'You shall marry her in the winter, Hiria, when we go back to Pilaghur. Yes, we will have the wedding and I will give the feast. When the clematis comes out, and the big yellow honey-suckle over the gate.' Ruth looked at her softly, 'And the roses.'

'T'ank you, miss-sahib. Nor are there any roses in Calcutta like those that came to our house from the Burra Sahib,' added Hiria, and the face of her mistress suddenly burned.

'The marriage of daughters is a heavy business, Hiria.'

'That is very true talk, miss-sahib. Four I have married,' said Hiria with just pride, 'and one of my sister who died; and now only one is to marry.'

'Wasn't that unlucky, to have so many daughters?'

'I found also six sons, miss-sahib,' Hiria justified herself. 'But to me it was always alike – son, d'otta, d'otta, son – from the same pains they come,' she added with stalwart philosophy. 'Only for the marriage the daughter is much more expense. For the son it is nothing – a cake, two three pray's in the Christine church, no more. Christine way very cheap. But for the daughter everything is to give – nose-ring, toe-ring, jewliar, two pair all clothes, silk jacket, woolling petticoat – to every one I gave alike,' said Hiria capably. 'For is it not the command of God, miss-sahib, that all women should marry – rich, poor, Hindustan-people, sahib-people – to all the same order? In Belat doubtless the custom is not so quick,' Hiria added discreetly, 'but even there, in the end all marry also, I think.'

'No, Hiria. Many do something else, like me.'

'Ah, miss-sahib! It will come to your honour also. Why not – it is the order of Houddha. And it is good, for those with the strong heart, like your honour. For me also it was good,' added Hiria simply. 'Shall I plait now?'

'That is foolish talk, Hiria – there is plenty to be done in the world beside marrying,' Ruth said. The dark hair round her shoulders gave her face the touch of imagination that could make it beautiful. She saw it herself and smiled in the content of it. 'And I forbid you to say that I have a strong heart, like the Viceroy. My heart is very, very weak.'

She looked reproach with tender eyes at the other self in the glass.

'Also I have heard,' observed Hiria thoughtfully, 'that since the Afreeka war there are no more sahibs in England. And the soldier will be hanged at Pilaghur on Friday, miss-sahib?'

'Unless word comes from the King,' said Ruth with a sudden shiver.

'It is not justice, miss-sahib.'

'Many people think that, Hiria.'

'If – if your honour will give the order I will go to Pilaghur and tell the Police Inspector-sahib that it is not justice.'

'What nonsense, Hiria. What good would that do? No, there will be plenty of time to make those wedding clothes when we go back. Don't worry. Good-night.'

CHAPTER XXIX

PILAGHUR was at its hottest and emptiest, but the Barfords were all there. So were the Tenth Guzeratis, the District Superintendent of Police, the station doctor, and a few other persons whose work tied them by the leg to the plains, whatever the temperature. Some of their wives were there too – Mrs. Lamb and Mrs. Davidson certainly, and Mrs. Wickham, and others that should be honourably mentioned. And on Thursday afternoon, the thirty-first of May, when the sun withdrew his cruel tooth and the tamarinds threw long shadows across the hard, white roads, and it was possible to drive to the club for the sake of suffering in a different place, behold, the flag shot up from Government House and the guard stood at the gate. So the Chief Commissioner was also there, a sudden and silent appearance from the Hills.

It was too hot to be astonished; besides, Pilaghur that was left knew quickly, too quickly, why he had come. Mrs. Lamb, driving in from the Guzerati lines past the gaol, had heard the hammering. She said it made her sick. The execution, 'Thame's superior show,' as Wickham the policeman called it, was to take place 'as advertised' – I still quote Wickham – next morning at six o'clock. So far the Viceroy had not been over-ruled. Grindlay Maple had made his attack in vain; the Government had lived quite comfortably through his censuring motion. No word of Royal clemency had come. The strong outcry had had too far to travel. Lady Waterbrook had apparently gone home in vain.

One concession had been made to the 'special circumstances' of the case. The execution remained in the hands of the civil authorities. The regiment was not asked to hang Morgan, the gallows was not going up on the parade ground. The Home Department had insisted, however, that the regiment should witness the hanging – 'and we know whose bark that is,' said the Colonel. The moral effect of the prisoner's fate was not to be thrown away upon the chaplain and the coroner and the Gaol Superintendent. Next morning the regiment, after parading as usual, would march to Pilaghur gaol, fall into convenient formation in the prison compound, and there before all eyes Private Morgan would be hanged for the crime of which he had been ultimately found guilty.

These were the arrangements, and in conveying them demi-officially to Arden, the Home Secretary at Simla added that it would be as well if the Chief Commissioner could conveniently arrange to be in Pilaghur on the day of the execution. The presence of the head of the civil administration would tend to preserve order; and if necessity arose he would be able to take immediate action. Nothing serious was anticipated, but the Government of India was informed that there had been bad feeling for some time between the Barfordshires and the Guzerati Regiment over some restriction of the Barfords in the matter of pig-shooting, at the instance of the Guzerati mess; and this might be made an occasion for its demonstration. Arden had better be there. So Arden, with rather a grim feeling of being chained to the criminal, was there.

In the billiard-room of the Barfordshires' mess that night it was as hot as it was anywhere, except perhaps in Pilaghur gaol and other places unprovided with punkahs. Rather than saying the air was hot, one might say that the heat was aired; the heat was the thing you breathed and moved in. Devine and Dimmock had been knocking the balls about, Kemp looking on, charging them indiscriminately and irritably with 'rotting,' as if they were playing for his instruction and entertainment. Finally they put up the cues and dropped with Kemp into those cane chairs with wooden leg-rests which invite such postures of irregular ease in warm countries. They drew around the door for the sake of the fiction that it was cooler outside, and lighted further cigarettes. Somebody mentioned the Commander-in-Chief, and Kemp, who had been on the great man's staff, told a story of him. When it is desirable to talk something has to be said.

'We were gettin' through a field day in the hills round Kadala,' he related, 'and the Chief was riding a mule – the only thing that could keep its feet. Well, you can take it from me that Waterbrook's the worst rider – *of a mule* – you're likely to see. One of the sepoys with us thought so too, I fancy. Anyhow, he came up to the Chief and offered his back! He did, upon my soul.'

'What did the Chief say?' asked Devine languidly.

'Oh, he laughed. That's a thing you notice about Waterbrook; he always sees the comic side.'

Major Devine and young Dimmock laughed then, too, as if for the moment they had forgotten the comic side. Kemp thought of another 'yarn,' but decided to keep it to himself.

'I notice the weather-man up at Simla gives us early rains this year,' he observed instead. As a rule, any reference to the Meteorological Department in May was safe to produce something ironic and more or less cheerful.

'The earlier the better,' responded Devine, and got up to kill a cockroach running impudently near.

'The air's like flannel,' said Dimmock, and the matter dropped.

'The C.O. played a good game yesterday,' Kemp tried again.

'Ripping,' assented Dimmock, slightly roused. Colonel Vetchley's polo was a subject of regimental pride.

'The Colonel always plays for himself, you know,' objected Devine. 'Never sends you a ball. And he ought to stop, I think, before he begins to go off. I do, really. He's getting too old a man.'

It seemed as unanswerable as it was depressing. Kemp threw his cigarette end into the verandah and pulled out a thicker case. For the attempt to turn heavy considerations into smoke there appears to be nothing like a cheroot. For a few minutes they sat in silence while the night sounds fell monotonously through the darkness – a vagrant tom-tom, the sleepy harsh note of birds disturbed and huddling in the branches, the far wail of the jackal crying that he was a Maharajah.

'I see by the papers,' remarked Major Devine at last, 'that Government is issuing a book instructing British soldiers how to treat natives. The *Administrator* wants to know whether we may expect any book instructing natives how to treat British soldiers. Rather neat, that.'

'They want more than books,' said Kemp. 'My wife tells me she saw a gharry-driver in the bazaar lash one of our men across the face the other day in pure wantonness. The man hadn't got out of the way quick enough to suit the brute.'

'By Jove! Was it reported?'

'No. Nothing's been heard of it. The men don't report such things nowadays. They know perfectly well it only means another "case of collision with natives," and they'll get the worst of it. They say there's no justice for the common soldier.'

'Unless he happens to be an officer,' contributed young Dimmock. 'A couple of fellows in the Second Welsh – that's my old regiment – were out after cheetal the other day, and some villagers made a set on them with lathies, taking them for Tommies. They'd have been perfectly justified in shooting, but they didn't; they said they'd see the thing through, and allowed themselves to be hauled before the magistrate and charged with the most infernal tissue of lies. Of course it was dismissed; but it shows what we're comin' to.'

'There's no doubt,' said Kemp, in a tone of heavy conviction, 'Thame's been playin' about too much with the army. The C.O. had a case before him to-day – damn it, when he told me, I could hardly keep a straight face. Sergeant-Major charged a fellow with disrespectful language. "What did he say?" says Vetchley. "He called me a bloody Antony Andover," says the Sergeant-Major. "Apart from gross insubordination, what do you mean?" says Vetchley, "by using the Viceroy's name in this insulting manner?" "Very good, sir," says the fellow, "but, beggin' your pardon, which 'ave I insulted, the Sergeant-Major or 'is Excellency?"'

'What did the old man give him?' asked Devine.

'I didn't ask,' replied Captain Kemp, and blew a circle.

There was another pause, in the midst of which young Dimmock observed quite irrelevantly: 'All the same I call it beastly decent of Lady Waterbrook to go home to have a shot at it, through heat like this.'

'It's about three in the afternoon there, now,' said Devine. 'Perhaps His Majesty is still considering it – after tiffin. It's to be hoped he'll remember the difference in the time, and make up his mind before the business is over.'

'Oh, it never reached him,' said Kemp. 'Those things don't get beyond some permanent official or other. It was folly to send it, anyhow. For such purposes the V. is Home Secretary for India. The King could never round on him like that.'

'It's a let-off, anyhow, that we haven't to do the thing ourselves,' said Devine. 'I'm not fond of walking at the head of a procession alongside the chaplain myself, with the band playin' "The Dead March."'

'Tommy Lascelles,' interrupted Captain Kemp, 'seems remarkably anxious to get lights out to-night. That's about the fifth time it's gone! No, it ain't pleasant, Devine, as you say. To-morrow we're only to provide the gallery. I believe they're hanging a scoundrel, if that's any comfort to you.'

An excited beat of hoofs drawing towards the mess made them all sit up and listen. The pony pulled up at the verandah, and 'Hullo – I say!' came from his back.

'There's Tommy now,' said Devine. 'Hullo, Thomas!'

'Is Kemp in there? Oh – are you there, Kemp? I wish you'd let me speak to you a minute.'

Kemp got up and strolled out. 'What's up, Tommy?'

'There's a row in barracks!'

'What d'you mean by a row?'

'Just what you'd mean by it, old man, if you were there. The men are simply in a mutinous condition. I don't like it at all.'

Kemp took his cigar out of his mouth and turned round.

'Devine,' he called, 'come here a minute, will you?'

'Now, Tommy,' he continued as Major Devine joined them. 'Keep your hair on, and talk in words of one syllable. What d'you mean by a mutinous condition?'

'Oh, damn it, Kemp, don't rot. I can't get lights out, and the men are shouting and singing and playing the fool generally. I thought I knew language, but the stuff they're throwing about the Viceroy's name made me sick. The Sergeant-Major threatened them an' got a boot at his head – it precious nearly hit me! He thought I'd better let you know.'

'Right-O,' said Kemp, and turned to Major Devine.

'Have you dismissed the picket?' asked Devine with excitement.

'I told them to fall in again.'

'Go back and fall in with them. Who is captain of the week? Here – Dimmock! There's a beastly row on in barracks – natural enough. I thought as much – there's been a nasty feeling all day – here, syce! The bay, as quick as the devil!'

'Shall I sound the officers' call?' asked Dimmock breathlessly.

'No – that would startle people. Sound the assembly. We'll parade every man who isn't on leave or in the lock-up. I'll rout out the Colonel. No – your animal's here, Dimmock – you go; and Kemp and I will get down to barracks.'

Already they could hear young Lascelles crossing the bridge over the nullah as the orderly officer galloped back. Kemp threw away his cigar.

'It's too hot a night,' he grumbled, as he got one leg over his pony, 'for business of this kind.'

Twenty minutes later the Barfords were out of barracks, lined and marshalled on the starlit semi-darkness of the parade ground.

'They won't refuse to turn out,' Kemp had calmed Devine. 'They know we're with them, blast it,' and they hadn't. They had moved mechanically to the familiar words of command with a surly appreciation of the unusual sharp ring in them, and its implication that they were men, and had to do with men. They answered with their muscles, and perhaps the thing on the surface of their minds was the chance that half-buttoned coats would escape notice in the darkness. The other thing that was deeper there was for the instant cowed and quelled and put aside by the necessity of response to routine, with its demand upon the attention, subdued by the simple exercise of putting one foot before another. Yet it was there, throbbing in the body of them as they stood in their orderly lines, a thing to be felt, and a thing incalculable at another moment, the strange dangerous thing that runs one man into the mass and melts the mass into one man. They listened to their commanding officer in silence, but the silence was temporary and imposed, the thing stood there with them; in the hot darkness it had almost a tangible existence.

Colonel Vetchley had no gift of words, but he had a big angry voice and a bullying common sense. He did not make a speech, he spoke; and there were no hesitations in what he said. . . . 'You know perfectly well what this kind of thing leads to,' he told them, 'I don't need to tell you anything about that. File o' men and a hole in the ground – and there you are. Pull yourselves together, men; and don't bring disgrace on the regiment. There's no disgrace like insubordination – I don't need to tell you that.' Those were some, and very nearly all, of his brief reminders.

'We're not boys in the Barfords,' he said to them finally, 'and what comes in the day's work's got to be done in the day's work. Dismiss the parade,' he roared to Devine with the last accent of disgust.

The men marched off quietly enough to their private parades, and the Colonel, Devine, and Kemp were left consulting. They made a little group, in their white uniforms under the lamp-post, whose movements and attitudes betokened serious business in hand.

'If that insane programme has got to be gone through with to-morrow,' said Major Devine, 'in my opinion we'd better get some one else here.'

'The Goozies?' inquired Kemp with sarcasm, lighting a cigarette.

'Don't play the goat, Kemp. You know perfectly well what I mean. The men will want steadying. Should we get Arden to send for the battery at Bunderabad, sir? A wire would bring them – it's only ten miles.'

'No, I'm damned,' said the Colonel. 'It would be nothing short of a scandal. If the men have got to go through it, I'll put 'em through it – I would if they shot me, and dash it, I wish they would, if they're going to shoot anybody.'

'The men'll stand,' said Kemp.

'They'll stand in a way that will be difficult to keep out of the papers,' said Devine.

'There are two reporters from Calcutta at the Taj Mahal Hotel already. I saw them. They're probably wiring this business now, if they possess any ears.'

'I expect they're in bed,' said Kemp cheerfully. 'They've got to get up early to-morrow.'

'I don't see why it should be in the papers,' said Colonel Vetchley. 'Go and have a look, Kemp – and prevent it if possible. No use having a thing like this blabbed broadcast about the regiment.'

'I'll square 'em,' said Kemp, mounting. 'I'll point out their duty to the country, if it can be done.'

'And to-morrow?' asked Major Devine, as Kemp cantered off.

'To-morrow' – began Colonel Vetchley with a grim jaw, 'well – in view of the probable consequences to the regiment if the men do play the fool in any way, I conceive it's my business to go now and knock up Arden and get him to take the responsibility of relieving us of parading them.'

'After what's happened to-night he can't refuse,' said Devine.

'It's hard to say. I suppose Lascelles and Dimmock are keeping the picket out.'

'They're patrolling the barracks now. I'll stop on here then, sir, and you –'

'I'll join you on my way back from Government House.'

They nodded and separated; and Colonel Vetchley was presently riding between the garden shrubs, flaunting and theatrical in the rising moon, of the drive to Government House.

It was barely yet eleven. The Chief Commissioner was sitting smoking in a long chair in the upper verandah with all the air of waiting for him. Arden said as much.

'I heard something sound after last post,' he remarked, 'I thought some one might drop in to say what was going on. Lemon's on tour, isn't he?'

'Yes, he is, thank goodness,' said Vetchley, and explained what had been going on.

'Come inside,' said Arden. 'It's cooler under the punkah,' and sent for the iced whisky and soda that attends most business and all pleasure in those parts.

'I'm as thirsty as a horse,' said Vetchley, and demonstrated that he was. Then he made his request.

'I'm sorry,' said Arden, 'but I'm under orders, Vetchley. I can't do it.'

'Anything might happen,' said the Colonel. A rush – an attempt at rescue – any blessed thing. The men are dangerous.'

'I can't change my arrangements.'

'The Viceroy may wish you had.'

'That's his look-out. I was against the thing in the beginning, as you know, but I surrendered to his judgement then, and I surrender now. But this I can tell you – whatever happens he won't wish I had.'

'There's discredit in it to as decent a body of troops as ever mustered – but I won't urge that. There's the seeds of future trouble in it – worse trouble than ever between the soldier and the native. Anything may happen,' repeated Colonel Vetchley.

'We thought of all that last February, Vetchley.'

'Will you send an urgent telegram to Simla, and get authority?' asked the Colonel.

'No. It would be forcing the Viceroy's hand. But I will do this, if you like. On your assurance that the state of the regiment necessitates it, I will wire to Bunderabad and get the battery over.'

'I can't listen to such a proposition,' said Vetchley with a darkening face.

'But I gather from you the men are in a mutinous condition?'

'I don't want any assistance to deal with my men. But we've had a warning to-night, and I considered it my duty to pass it on to you.'

Colonel Vetchley rose. 'If you choose to ignore it, you take your share, at all events, of the responsibility.'

'I will take it,' said Arden.

'But mind you – I expect something to happen. If that damned sweep at Simla –'

'Pray,' said Arden, 'transfer your epithet to your Sovereign. It would be as justifiable.'

'I beg your pardon. But it's folly to insist on the regiment witnessing the execution. If the temper they show to-night increases, I tell you the Duke of Wellington couldn't hold them.'

'Shall I send for the battery?'

'*No* – not with my consent!'

'I offer it as a practicable measure. If you are unable to keep control of your regiment' – Arden flushed, and paused to regain his temper.

'I'll have a shot at it,' replied Vetchley, furious and turning on his heel. 'The whole business is an infamous miscarriage of justice. The men won't take it lying down, and I don't want to command anybody who would.'

'Good-night,' said Arden, as Colonel Vetchley opened the door. 'I shall do my best. Good-night to you,' replied that officer.

CHAPTER XXX

EARLY, very early next morning, Pilaghur emerged, dim and vague, upon the plain, submissive in her sleep to the burden of another day. The sun, strong and cruel, lay just under the horizon; a palm-tree drooped against the tinging sky. Only the silent trees and garden bushes were awake and waited, and perhaps Akbar's finger-post, which would presently throw a shadow. The East might only then have left the hand of God. Suddenly, up from the roof line of the gaol across the river, a kite circled, screaming, and sank back. The long low wall grew yellow, and an object in the courtyard stood distinct.

But the thrushes were hardly stirring in the acacias or the squirrels in the neem trees, and only two or three people were yet awake in cantonments, when a native orderly on a bicycle slipped swiftly out of the gaol gate and made for the other side of the river. He had a note for Surgeon-Major Carter and a quick commission. As he crossed the bridge he met the chaplain in his dogcart, with his surplice rolled in the parcel-net in front. The orderly slackened his wheel and turned his head, but the padre-sahib was already out of respectful calling distance; and they both went on.

The regimental doctor had not been roused quite so early as the chaplain, but he was up and ready too; though not ready for the note, which he read hastily in the verandah, looking, as he replaced it in the envelope, suddenly more alive than people usually look in Pilaghur on the first of June. He went back with it into his wife's room carrying great, triumphant news.

'Ethel,' he said, 'there will be no execution. Morgan was found dead in his cell at four this morning. Suicide, of course – though how he managed it –'

His wife, half awake, sat up in bed under the punkah, and understood him; and the tears of pure excitement started in her eyes. They looked at one another in silence, taking it in; and across all official considerations a smile broke upon the face of Surgeon-Major Carter. Ethel had the first word.

'Oh, Tom,' she cried 'what's the difference – how he managed it – so long as he *did* manage it!'

'It will make a good deal of difference to some people,' her husband told her. 'Me among 'em, I daresay. Don't cry, Ethel. The fellow was a skunk. It's a let-off all the same. Here's the trap. Goodbye, old girl. Don't wait breakfast; and for God's sake stop howling.'

But Mrs. Carter was not to be intimidated. She continued to howl happily and wipe her eyes; and, being of a mercurial temperament, she mingled her tears with a kind of war-dance of triumph, which she executed in her nightdress in the course of helping her husband to look for his pith helmet. The last thing Surgeon-Major Carter heard her say when he drove away was, 'W-w-wouldn't I like to be the person to wire it to the Viceroy!'

As the doctor's cart went rocking behind a canter along the Lawrence Road the sun flashed up and down the shaft of Akbar and three kites sailed above the roof of the gaol of Pilaghur.

The inquest established opium poisoning. Carter declared that Morgan must have swallowed a ball the size of a marble. Justice automatically shifted her centre. Disdaining the corpse, she revolved about the problem of how the prisoner had obtained the means to take this liberty with her. Two European warders – ex-soldiers both – were put under arrest, and a sweeper; but Morgan's transfer to Calcutta and back made connivance difficult to locate – difficult under the circumstances.

'The stuff stinks so, they must have known he had it on him,' said Surgeon-Major Carter; but he only mentioned that to Ethel and nobody else mentioned it at all. It appears from this that persons who could have held no relations with Morgan in his lifetime did not mind conniving with him after he was dead. The Indian journals gave two days to him. Reuter wired his end to every newspaper in England. The *Flash* described it in a special article by cable, which, if the world revolved the other way, would have been before the event. For a week, perhaps, the suicide was mourned by a Parliamentary party, but London forgot it next day. In India the matter travelled to and fro in the files for months; and at long last the Home Department censured the Gaol Superintendent, who was on the eve of retirement and thereby better pleased to go. After that Henry Morgan sank like a stone into the infinite whence he came.

The rains kept their promise of coming early; they fell upon the just and upon the unjust, and all abroad over the land. They channelled down the khudsides at Gangutri, and filled the steaming gutters of Calcutta, and beat upon the huts round Akbar's finger-post in Pilaghur. They brought a new psychological climate. Reported 'cases of collision with natives' dropped off noticeably; and in the certainty of a good harvest the yearly burden of apprehension slipped from the shoulders that carry it. They were 'good rains,' well distributed, honest, punctual, wet rains, rejoicing the heart. Eliot Arden, in his quiet, lonely, settled way, often wished that his wife could have seen the dahlias that year, the single ones, that crowded the khudsides above the public roads and crowned the crests that looked across, when the rain stopped and the sun came out, towards the Snows. They had never been better. He missed Jessica extraordinarily, considering that she had only been a bright woman – more than might have been anticipated by anybody, even himself. Like the rains that came down upon her flowers she used in her lifetime to water his heart, which seemed now to be shrivelling within him past any of its gentler functions. She had been, indeed, his gardener for small wages; and he looked in vain for substitutes in periods before Christ.

So it just rained through to September and little marked the time except the falling water and the files. October brightened over the hills, with reddened creepers and sharp mornings; and in due course the Chief Commissioner of Ghoom, with his Government and his clerks, his cook and his chuprassies, and all that were his, drove down from Gangutri to the Plains and went back by rail to Pilaghur, where the officer commanding the Second Barfordshire Regiment was the first to write his name in the visitors' book at Government House.

Pilaghur had not taken the liberty of any change. The roads were just as empty, the cactus hedgerows just as dusty. Ali Bux, established on the same triangle, advertised the same fresh consignment of Simla hill jams, and exposed the same maroon sofa with several springs sticking up, also four dining-room chairs and a bed, complete with mosquito curtains, which he had bought from the Assistant Magistrate, Mr. Cox, transferred, rather to his annoyance, immediately after his engagement to the second Miss Hillyer of the Salt Department, the fair one. The Club tennis-courts were reported in capital order as always, and the prospects for polo were excellent as ever. In the public gardens the English phloxes, pink and purple, were again coming out. The bougainvilliers trailed as before over the verandah of the house of the lady in charge of the Dufferin Hospital for Women; and I believe Dr. Elizabeth Garrens was entitled to claim that there had been no falling off either in the number of operations or the attendance of out-patients since Dr. Pearce handed over to her. Dr. Elizabeth was a short effective person, well packed into her clothes, who wore spectacles and created no anomaly anywhere, never had and never would. In the city by the river Ganeshi Lal counted his profits over again on his carved window frame; and at the corner of Krishna Ghat Lane the leper woman, that no-fingered one, spread out her hands to public pity as on that other day. Over all the same sun, the same high spirits and dogcarts driving to the Club, the same little world of the centre – of Ghoom.

And it was entirely what might be expected that the Chief Commissioner should be dining, very quietly, with the Lemons, a small party, only the Faulkners and the Biscuits and a Biscuit sister, just out from home – people he knew very well.

'The man must go somewhere and do something,' Mrs. Lemon had declared in justification of asking him; and Mrs. Biscuit agreed with many words.

They were all keyed to the Chief Commissioner, as was natural, to his presence and his late bereavement; it was the first time he had 'gone anywhere.' Mrs. Lemon, in general genial charge of him, gallantly cheered him up; Mrs. Biscuit, placed next to him on the other side, sought subjects above the general line. The others were all ready, with voice and glance, to urge upon him that life was still tremendously worth living.

Perhaps Mrs. Biscuit was less fortunate than her intention.

'I don't think too much can be said for our men in this country,' she told him, with a very unprejudiced air, 'but the women! Oh, Mr. Arden, the Anglo-Indian women! Take a place like Bunderabad – take Kalagunj – take Hatori! I don't say it's altogether their fault, but the women seem to be deplorably narrow. Do they ever read? Do they keep up with science or art in any form? Have they any ideas? What are their lives made up of?'

Mrs. Biscuit poised her question with a levelling look of great candour, and effective play with a wine-glass on the table at the other end of a straight and shapely arm. Her observation, to a widower, she felt to be felicitous and safe.

'I must not compare my knowledge of the sex with yours,' Arden replied quietly, 'but I should be inclined to say that the principal things their lives are made up of are courage and self-sacrifice.'

Mrs. Biscuit blushed – she was intelligent – and covered her retreat.

'Oh, Mr. Arden, how gallantly you defend us! I'm afraid I was too sweeping; but I had a tea-party to-day – mostly military ladies, I will say that – and I was trying to talk home politics. You can't think how difficult it was.'

'Let us listen to Faulkner's story,' said Mr. Arden.

'I hope it isn't a naughty one.'

It was not at all a naughty one, but a simple, almost a nursery story of Mr. Faulkner's district experience.

'The policeman started off with his prisoner,' he was saying, 'to march him in, a dozen miles or so. They halted at a village half-way, and somehow the policeman lost his man. The prisoner arrived punctually that evening and presented himself at the gaol – but the doors were closed against him. They couldn't take him in without a warrant. And there he sat disconsolate, on the doorstep! They came for me, and I gave him shelter, without prejudice, in a bathroom, and at his urgent solicitation locked him in. Perfectly true, I assure you. I convicted the policeman later of gross and culpable negligence.'

'There are endless stories of the police, aren't there?' said Mrs. Biscuit confidentially.

'I'm afraid there are, and not all so innocent as that,' Arden replied, and turned to Mrs. Lemon's difficulties with her quails.

Mrs. Lemon's quails were the fattest to be found on any dinner-table in Pilaghur, and the amount of time, trouble, and anxiety they consumed made it reasonable that they should be.

'There's only one enemy my wife hasn't to contend against,' the General told them, 'but there is one. When I was in West Africa, towards the end of the last century, we were camped one night in a fairly remote spot where there was one white man, trader of sorts, who had a thatched hut with a couple of rooms. He very kindly put me up; and in the middle of the night I began to hear a queer kind of rustling overhead. It went on and on, and at last I woke the fellow up. "Oh," he said, "it's nothing – probably the boa-constrictors after the chickens." My wife has no boa-constrictors after her quails, at all events.'

'What a lovely story,' said Mrs. Biscuit.

'Yes,' said Mrs. Lemon, 'but now we shall never get the conversation away from snakes. If you once begin talking about snakes you go on for ever, in my experience. No more snakes! But, Mr. Faulkner – I'm sure it's your Department – is it or is it not true that monkeys have been dying of plague?'

'Why should we be denied a subject that our first mother made dear to us for all time?' demanded Egerton Faulkner, screwing in his eyeglass. 'What do we know about monkeys? No monkey was concerned with making us what we are.'

'Oh, are you sure?' cried the others in a breath; and Mrs. Biscuit looked at her plate.

'I am no mere evolutionist. We owe no conscious debt to monkeys, and, therefore' – Faulkner dropped his eyeglass – 'if they choose, in their silly way, to borrow plague from us, I should leave them to the uninterrupted enjoyment of it. Seriously, however, living as they do upon fresh air and other people's ideas, I should doubt the possibility of their contracting it.'

'They are getting very troublesome in Simla,' said Arden, 'attacking children and nurses lately. The Viceroy has ordered the destruction of a lot of them. Langurs chiefly.'

'His Excellency had better be careful,' remarked Mr. Faulkner, 'or he will be examined in the House upon the remorseless shooting down of nomadic tribes – the Bundars, a peaceful and innocent people, pursuing their everyday avocations in the forests of the Western Himalayas, which belonged to them long before they did to us.'

'His Excellency must be getting pretty near the end of his tether,' remarked General Lemon.

'He goes in April,' said little Biscuit.

'And thankful he must be,' said Mrs. Lemon. 'I wouldn't be a Viceroy in this country for something.'

'I should be undeterred,' said Egerton Faulkner, 'by anything – wouldn't you, Biscuit? Even the adulation of the Bengali Press would fail entirely to put me off. By the way, has anybody heard of Maconochy's indiscretion the other day? Maconochy was at school with him, and doesn't always think, you know. Besides, he is one of those Calcutta commerce-wallahs that feel they can babble from the heart. He and the Viceroy were talking about Courtney Young, and Maconochy said Young was something unmitigated, and had been pilled three times for the Calicut Club – a fact that all but Viceroys know, of course. "Oh!" said Thame, "I'm sorry to hear that. I've just given him the Kaiser-i-Hind medal." "Serve him jolly well right, too," said Maconochy.'

They all laughed, for the new decoration had not yet outlived its inevitable first stage of ridicule.

'I should be very pleased to get the Kaiser-i-Hind medal,' remarked little Biscuit.

'Nobly said, Biscuit,' applauded Egerton Faulkner. 'If we searched our hearts I'm sure we all would.'

'The *really* furious people,' said Mrs. Faulkner, 'will be the Lawrence Lenoxes, who got it at the same time. He would expect a C.S.I., at least. She will be fearfully disappointed.'

'I don't see,' said Mr. Arden, 'why Lenox should expect anything particularly. His work on the Courts Procedure Code was purely nominal. He was very lucky to be confirmed so early.'

There was the slightest pause, the merest hint of embarrassment, broken decisively by the Chief Secretary.

'I am convinced we need shed nothing for Lenox, nothing at all,' he declared. 'Lenox rises by natural law. No Viceroy, no circumstance, can permanently keep him down. I agree with you, sir, that Lenox has nothing to be surprised at, and much to be grateful for. Conspicuous decoration, at the moment, should have surprised and pained him. I don't say that it would,' Mr. Faulkner put his eyeglass in, and looked round in cheerful interrogation. 'I know very little about Lenox.'

'What a fuss they are making at home over Sir Ahmed Hossein,' remarked Mrs. Lemon, who never inquired into her trains of thought.

'I saw his name in two society paragraphs last week,' Mrs. Biscuit told them. 'At very smart parties. *Isn't* it ridiculous?'

'There would be something ridiculous in Ahmed Hossein at a smart London party,' said Arden, 'but I think it would be the party.'

'They would take him to be a prince, of course, because of his colour,' said Mrs. Faulkner.

'He has very good manners too,' said Arden. 'They are making much of him every way,' he went on smiling. 'Did you see his verses in the *Saturday*? '

'Does he write poetry?' cried Mrs. Biscuit. 'How interesting! What was it about?'

'He writes very good verse. This was about the illness of the King last month; quite good it was. He is fond of esoteric subjects, but the passion for the monarch takes him furthest. It is in the blood in the East.'

'The last story I heard of Sir Ahmed,' said Egerton Faulkner, 'he told me himself; and it was at your expense, sir. "I asked the Chief Commissioner," he said, "which he would rather meet, St. Paul or William Shakespeare. And he went away sorrowful, for he is a great admirer of the English classics." Is it true, sir?'

'I dare say,' laughed Arden. 'It's the sort of thing he *would* ask.'

'Miss Pearce wrote me the other day that she had heard from him,' said Mrs. Lemon to the Chief Commissioner. 'He had been meeting friends of hers – the Sannaways. You know Mrs. Sannaway, the writer.'

Arden nodded attentively. 'How is Miss Pearce?' he asked with solicitude. 'She wrote to me very kindly a few months ago, but I have not heard from her since.'

Mrs. Lemon gave him a look in which she tried hard to disguise the disconcertment.

'Oh, very well indeed, and liking her Calcutta work immensely. You didn't know then that she stays on there till March?'

'No, I didn't know,' replied Arden, with friendly – astonishingly friendly – interest. 'I am very glad to hear she likes it.'

'And your own plans, Mr. Arden? You must be wanting leave soon – you haven't had a rest for ages.'

'Oh, I shall try for six months in the hot weather, I think. I shall have pretty well got to the end of this job; and I must go home and see the boys. After having a look at them I'm promising myself a lounge in Italy,' said Arden.

The ladies went up to the drawing-room, and Mrs. Lemon, in a two minutes' aside with Mrs. Faulkner, repeated the last part of her conversation with the Chief Commissioner, making rapid deductions.

'I never thought there was anything serious in that affair,' she said. 'It was too literary – too literary, my dear.'

'I can't say –'

'You're sorry. Well, I *am*.'

'She's a nice woman, of course, but it doesn't seem *exactly* suitable,' murmured Mrs. Faulkner. 'In his position – '

'He couldn't possibly do better. Go along with you – with your Service airs,' returned Mrs. Lemon robustly. 'She's a great deal too good for him.'

CHAPTER XXXI

'THE Chief Commissioner told me the other night,' wrote Mrs. Lemon nevertheless when next she addressed Miss Pearce, 'that he had heard nothing of you for months. Why don't you write to the poor man? He is looking distinctly older; and they say in the offices that he's keener than ever on the work – a bit too keen, if the truth were told; but I find him just the same dear old thing he always was. He tells me he is going to Italy in April.'

Ruth read it and looked out at the gay Calcutta life of the sun-suffused 'cold weather.' She seemed to find her problem there, painted on the yellow walls and the waving palms, as it was painted everywhere about her. She simply didn't understand it, the way Arden's life went on without her, and seemed likely to go on. She was for ever changing places with him, and deciding how soon she would have entreated a sign from the woman in Calcutta, how long she could have borne to do without it. Just any little common sign, something to live upon; and the limit was already months in the past. She did not forget her letter of decree, written in the crisis she remembered even better; but she thought of it to euphemise it, and smooth the ferocity out of it and despise it.

'He never could have *believed* such a letter,' she told herself, and 'Surely he would balance me against my emotions.'

But the silence grew between them until it looked like a time of years and the space of a continent.

The happy escape of Henry Morgan had made no difference to her; she had forgiven Arden long before that. She heard of it with thankfulness; but she would have heard of his execution with resignation. As soon as she had freedom to look her love in the face she laughed at the idea of binding it with conditions, and knew that they were part of a miserable figment she had built to hide it from herself. Now that she could love him without restraint she simply did; and any criticism of him seemed the merest poor wreckage, swept and tumbling in the tide. How could such things matter?

The thing she attained was the golden opinion of the Calcutta doctors, two of whom frequently asked for her in consultation. She had never worked so well or so subtly. She was driven by a force not herself; and she referred all her successes to Arden, made an offering of them. He came back to his niche in her temple, but now she dusted him less and worshipped him more.

Ruth and Hiria, therefore, lived on in Calcutta and ruled where they lived. The hospital matron said Dr. Pearce spoiled her ayah, who was unbearable in the quarters; and I dare say it was true. Many an ear heard, for example, that when the ayah was to have her cold-weather coat Dr. Pearce had actually brought her patterns to choose from.

'For my part,' said the hospital matron, 'I dress my servants according to my taste, not according to theirs,' which was, of course, most justifiable, as all the ladies of Calcutta would agree. I don't know whether one should apologise, but Ruth's woman-servant was the thing nearest to her, and she had an overflow of affection to spend upon some one. Hiria was its indulgence. In the matter of the coat she went further.

'I could never direct you to the shop,' she said, 'but we will both go and buy it, Hiria, and you shall have the *dusturi.*'

The *dusturi* was the commission on a sahib's purchase paid by the dealer to any servant, a thing discouraged always by the hospital matron and other right-minded persons. Ruth's mind was like the bow unbent. The small immorality seemed delectable and amusing. 'Why shouldn't she have it?' she said, and Hiria had it. It came to eightpence, with sewing-cotton and six buttons thrown in. Fate wrote a postscript the day they went to buy.

The shop was in a crowded, narrow street outside the New Market. Ruth was standing in the door to get what air there was. Her eyes ranged absently the littered thoroughfare, full of Bengalis and ox-carts and obstruction – chickens pecking in the drains, here and there a Chinaman, smells of the sun on food and fodder, every-where strident sound. Suddenly she started forward.

'Hiria!' she cried. 'Here, quick! Good – Who is that sala'aming – there, by the Cabuli's stall?'

She caught the ayah's arm without taking her eyes from the figure of a disreputable-looking old fellow who was making signs of humble and delighted recognition to her from across the road at the widest part. Hiria's glance followed in a flash; then her face jerked back as from a blow, and her eyes became vague.

'I see no one, miss-sahib.'

'Oh yes, Hiria. There, he is looking at us – how does he know us? Who is it? Beside the lamp-post.'

'Some beggar, I think, miss-sahib. Nothing at all. Oh, your honour is pinching.'

'Hiria, I know that man! Is it *possible!*'

'Some mindless one, miss-sahib. God gives leave to many such.'

'Go and bring him instantly. I must speak with him. In one breath, go!'

The ayah hesitated, then took her way across among the shouting drivers to the other side. There she seemed confused, ran this way and that, passed close to the man, but did not seem to speak to him, finally accosted some one else. As Ruth hurried after her the old fellow turned on his heel and slipped away with an amazing quick limp into the bazaar.

Ruth paused for a moment disconcerted, and already he was a rag in a dissolving bundle of rags. Then keeping her eyes steadily on the yellow wisp of his turban she started in pursuit, Hiria following close and breathless.

'What need, miss-sahib, for going? I will catch him. I will bring him. Your honour's feet cannot come in these places. There, he is gone!'

But Ruth kept up the pursuit through crooked lanes and cramped alleys until he did vanish into a black hole, which, when they arrived at it, proved to contain nothing but a hostile cow and a heap of dirty fodder. Then she turned sharply to the ayah.

'You will bring the man at once. I will stay here until he comes. Otherwise I will give this place into the hands of the police.'

The familiar threat had its effect. '*Na*, miss-sahib, there is no need to talk of the police,' said Hiria, 'I will bring him quickly, that *budzat*,' and she disappeared.

She kept her mistress waiting ten minutes, and then returned with the old man, who looked vacant, stupid, and smiling.

'He says he was a sepoy of your honour's sahib's old regiment,' said Hiria. 'I have told him your honour is a miss-sahib, and there is no major-sahib, and he dreams. And now he is content to go away.'

But Ruth had also been reflecting, by flashes and inspirations, and had come to a different conviction, one of those incredible convictions to which, in the East, the mind is so often invited.

'Speak no false words,' she said. 'This, and you know it well, ayah, is Gobind, who was sworn murdered by the soldier last year. Have I not often seen your face?' she asked their captive. 'Have you not often received medicine from me? And your elephant leg – I see it is no better, but worse.'

The old man's eye shifted to Hiria; his face twisted, and he began to cry.

'Many times worse, Protector of the Poor. And it will never be better until I get leave to come back to Pilaghur, where the Protector of the Poor gives good medicine. But I have yet no leave, and when I saw the Presence in the bazaar, my heart said, "Perhaps the miss-sahib is giving medicine in Calcutta, and will again cure this miserable person,"' and he got laboriously down upon the ground and attempted to kiss her feet.

Ruth looked round at the gathering knot of observers.

'Come,' she said, 'I never cured you; but I will give you more medicine.'

She sent him in front of her through the fetid lanes, and Hiria followed downcast and inventive. Although she found herself in no way to blame, this was very much of an emergency to Hiria. She felt that the bottom of all contrivance was falling out.

As they emerged from the bazaar, Ruth took out her watch and saw that there was still an hour before she was due at her lecture. She beckoned a hired victoria, put Gobind in the box by the driver, and took Hiria beside her. They drove quickly to the hospital, where the office was empty.

'It is an old patient,' said Ruth to the matron, whom they met in the hall. 'He's got a bad leg, hasn't he?'

When the door was shut and Hiria set sentry at the window, Ruth got the story. Gobind confessed promptly that he had committed a fault – Hiria had already convinced him of that. He had come to Calcutta. His orders were to remain far south in Chittagong; but in Chittagong life had gone heavily. He had fallen sick, and the money-order did not always come from his sons in Pilaghur. Also he had no caste brothers in Chittagong, 'and how,' he asked, 'is it possible for a poor man to remain apart from his *bhai*?' But they would not allow him to return.

'So they sent you away,' said Ruth. 'Then who was killed?'

'Nobody killed, Protector of the Poor – only this miserable one badly hurt from the gun.'

'He does not know, miss-sahib,' said Hiria from the window. 'He is old and foolish. Another man was killed.'

'What other man? By the soldier? Explain quickly,' said Ruth.

'No, miss-sahib, it was a cultivator, and one of the Guzeratis had killed him the day before, also on account of his wife,' added Hiria cheerfully; 'it was known, but not yet brought to the *thanna*. And it was much desired to punish the white soldier because of the evil and *nutkuttie* which he did. So they took Gobind away the same night, thinking he might not die, and brought the other dead man there, for his face was broken with the shot; and they put on the clothes of Gobind, and said nothing for three days. After that no one could say, "This is not Gobind," the wife being also dead. And the sons say, "Yes, this is Gobind." But Gobind became well in the house of the post-office jemadar, and afterwards, to avoid trouble, he was given money and sent away, the ungrateful one.'

Miss Pearce was silent, silent for so long that her excellent woman-servant began quietly to cry. Gobind had been weeping for some time.

'Did the police know all this?' she said at last.

Hiria looked frightened. 'The police came to know, *Hazur*. And it was necessary to find many rupees, for one said, "Give me five," and another said, "Give me ten," and the sons of Gobind are now very poor, miss-sahib.'

'And how came you to know?'

'By the babbling mouth of the wife of Gurdit Singh, your honour. And many times I wished she had not spoken, for it has been heavy to know.'

Ruth was again dumb. It was useless to ask the ayah why she had kept the secret. The fear of the police was even then in her face; she looked cowed and miserable. Anger was useless; indignation was useless.

'If I had gone back to Pilaghur in May would you have told then?' she asked the woman curiously.

'I would have frightened the wife of Gurdit Singh so that she would have made her man re-port,' said Hiria. 'I knew a way. I had no liking to do it, but your honour was very sorry – all day sitting very sorry – '

'Oh, Hiria, Hiria!'

'How costly, miss-sahib, was this wretched one's trouble!' Gobind blinked assent. 'How many rupees the excellent munshi also spent! Heera Mull has set up a sweet-shop, and Lal Bey – '

'Afzul Aziz!' exclaimed Ruth, 'I always suspected – why, then, did he pay rupees for lies, ayah?'

'Truly, miss-sahib, is he not a quiet, poor-spirited man to look at? Yet he did this at great expense, for *zid*. Great *zid* he has had all his life against this *pulthan*, because of a bad thing at Cawnpore long ago. I was not born then, but my mother saw the Great Folly, your honour. My father was sweeper with this Baffodshi *pulthan*, and the soldiers when they came to Cawnpore were very angry – shooting, killing all sepoys. The father of Afzul Aziz was not a sepoy, miss-sahib. He was a teaching man like this one – and the two older sons were writers under the sahibs, good men, of poor spirit, miss-sahib. When the soldiers found them they said, "We are not sepoys!" but the soldiers said, "Look at your feet. You have corns on them. Therefore, you wear shoes. Therefore, you are sepoys"; and killed all three. Only Afzul they did not kill because he was so little. But he saw it, miss-sahib, and he has always *zid* against the regiment. So he went to great expense.'

'Oh, Hiria!' Ruth could think of nothing else to say. She looked in silence at the woman curling her toes in anxiety, and at the tattered wreck under the yellow turban, with their extraordinary revelation; and standards of justice and right rose ironically beside them.

THE clock pointed the hour of her lecture. She took out her purse and gave the old fellow ten rupees, with a sense that his situation should place him, somehow, above her charity.

'Come to-morrow at this time for your medicine,' she said. 'I will consider what ought to be done,' and Gobind hobbled out, followed with an eye of guardianship by Hiria.

Most of that night she took counsel with herself, but next day at the same hour she had still to write the letter which should put the Chief Commissioner of Ghoom in possession of the facts. She made out Gobind's prescription and gave it to the hospital compounder, but the old man did not come. Hiria persisted that she knew nothing of his whereabouts, and had obstinately little more to say about the matter; but at the end of the third day she offered an opinion. 'I think he will not come, miss-sahib. He is afraid.'

At that Ruth wrote to Arden. Her astonishing discovery gave her a look of triumphing under which she was very unhappy. It seemed wholly adventitious, Gobind's being alive – and Ruth was aware of wishing that he hadn't been alive – to criticise the acumen of two courts and a supreme ruler, and especially of the Chief Commissioner of Ghoom. It was her business, however, to state the facts, and she stated them, to make them clear and undeniable, and she did so. They went baldly; she found comment impossible. There was nothing to say that might not hurt him and did not distress her; but he would see, would know that. She could trust his instinct – I don't know why she thought she could. Ruth added a line about her own plans. She would be relieved early in March, and had already obtained leave to England, where she would go direct by the mail from Calcutta.

Arden read the letter as a vindication of her position from the beginning, very fortuitous, but undeniable. He found implications in the carefully uncoloured sentences to fit everything that had happened to his damage; he had a trained official eye for what lies between such rigid lines. He wrote in reply with the dignity and courtesy that befitted the Government of Ghoom. He thanked Miss Pearce explicitly for the information she had sent, regrettable as were its bearings in more than one direction. It had already received his careful consideration; and it would certainly receive the careful consideration of higher authorities. His own opinion was that, in view of the irrevocableness of what had come about and the painful tension which the re-opening of the matter would produce, it would be advisable to refrain from further prosecution, and handle the connivance of the police departmentally; but he even implied that if she chose to publish her discovery, and so force the hand of Government, that course was also open to her. He noted with interest that she proposed to take leave home in the summer, and wished there were a better chance of their meeting in England; but his own leave, he feared, would be all too inadequate for arrears he had to make up in Italy. And he was, with very kind regards, hers sincerely. . . .

The end came like that. It marked the absolute close of a case under deliberation; and Miss Pearce had lived long enough in India to recognise the touch.

CHAPTER XXXII

THE glistening black twigs of the hedge of Mrs. Sannaway's Bloomsbury plot were full of the indomitable London buds of March when Ruth Pearce one windy afternoon pushed open the iron gate and went up the steps to her friend's house. She had done what she proposed to do, had handed over her charge in Calcutta, accomplished the voyage home, and settled into London lodgings for the purposes of her further degree. The further task she had accepted from herself, to make her profession all of her life, stood also before her, outlined for accomplishment. When her foolish, unconvinced heart clamoured to hope on, that was the scheme she laid before it.

Mrs. Sannaway met and embraced her in the drawing-room. It was delightful to see her again after all these years. She looked tired – that was the journey. Was the climate really as trying as people said? How often this last winter Mrs. Sannaway had envied her the Indian sun.

'Why have you got your things on?' asked Ruth. 'I thought I was coming to tea. In India we never have our things on when people are coming to tea.'

'You have better manners, dear – eh? Now let me break it to you. I'm not going to give you tea, unless you'd like a cup this instant. I'm going to take you somewhere else. You'll forgive me, won't you? – I completely forgot, and you'll like to come, I know you will. It's Mrs. Frayley Sambourne, a very special friend, most interesting woman, and a bride, at least a bride of sorts. We none of us thought it would happen – miles older than he is – but it did, quite suddenly at the end. This is her first At Home – charming house on Tite Street – sure to be amusing. We'll go for just half an hour and then we'll dash back here in a cab and have our talk comfortably. He's Under-Secretary of State for India, you know.'

'I know his name, of course,' said Ruth, rising submissively, 'and I'll go with pleasure. But I can't come back. You must have me another day. I have a rather sad and dreadful commission to execute – a letter to deliver – and I want to get it over.'

'One of those Indian tragedies that are always happening, I suppose. You must tell me about it later. How nice that it has stopped raining. All sorts of people will be there, you know – quite a special lot, and always somebody you see nowhere else,' said Mrs. Sannaway, getting into the hansom. 'Do you find London much changed?'

Ruth looked at her hostess of the cab, and a smile flickered across her face.

'No,' she said, 'I don't.'

'Well, now,' said Mrs. Sannaway, 'tell me all about India.'

The newly and so originally decorated rooms in Tite Street were full of sitting or shifting groups when they arrived; and Deirdre, more Deirdre than ever, was receiving, farewelling, wavering among them.

'From India?' she said, as she clasped Ruth's hand. 'Ah yes, you have a look of solitudes. This house is much occupied with India.

More than you think, Kate – but greatly more than you think,' she turned to Mrs. Sannaway. 'My girl there has just promised to marry the Viceroy of India!'

'Lord Thame!' exclaimed Ruth, and whether she would or not, her heart bounded.

'Then she has at last!' cried Mrs. Sannaway. 'Oh my *darling* Deirdre, I am so glad! And you are announcing it to-day – how *delightful*! You must let me give you another kiss. But the silly monkey not to have done it before – to let all his Viceroyalty pass – '

'My new husband,' said Mrs. Frayley Sambourne, 'declares that she has saved him from a very absurd position. As Under-Secretary to be father-in-law to the Viceroy – how could he survive it? As it is, I don't know how I am to survive it. But dearest Kate – it was his Viceroyalty that did it. Such a splendid range for his genius and character! Victoria has simply gone down before it. She says as much. Especially that wonderful Morgan tragedy, that I have built my play on – oh, my dear, Mortimer Finch has accepted it, and I'm almost too happy to live. It's to be announced for the first week in June. Well, Anthony Thame came out of that very grandly, we all thought. And it won him Victoria.'

'I sometimes think you are the most fortunate woman on the whole earth,' returned Mrs. Sannaway. 'Two such announcements in one afternoon! Now aren't you glad you came?' she said, laughing, to Ruth.

'*I* could never have married him, Kate,' said Mrs. Sambourne. 'To me he is a mere repository of dead men's virtues – does that strike you as good?' she asked Ruth, who smiled, and said honestly–

'Yes – rather. But not quite true. He has excellent virtues of his own.'

'Well, the phrase isn't mine – I borrowed it from one of the characters in my play. But Victoria is of a thicker paste than I. Here she is – let me introduce you. My daughter – Miss Pearce. From India, Victoria.'

Victoria was lost for a moment under the avalanche of Mrs. Sannaway's happy sentiments. She emerged from them brightly enough and turned to Ruth.

'From India?' Then I am sure that you too will congratulate me. Do you know Anthony Thame?'

'I have never seen him,' said Ruth. 'Most of us, you know, have never seen him. And we don't call him – that.'

'No – out there he suffers dreadfully from capital letters, I know. He has to wear them like a permanent magnifying glass – and it's not necessary, for he *is* great, don't you think, to the naked eye?'

'He has great purposes,' said Ruth; 'and he has carried them into history.'

Victoria looked at her frankly.

'I see your reserve,' she said. 'Yes, I know. He isn't what is called "popular" out there – you would all have your reserves. But in the end don't you think he will be vindicated? About that miserable Morgan case, for instance, don't you yourself feel that he was right?'

It was a direct appeal; it came with force and demanded candour. Ruth looked away for an instant, following the track of a velvet train across the room.

'I am afraid I cannot tell you – quickly, or easily, or at all really– what I feel about that case,' she answered. 'I was rather near it.'

'Near Morgan?'

'Well, yes, in a sense,' said Ruth, with a feeling of escape. 'Near Morgan. I saw him in the gaol at Calcutta. I have now in my pocket a letter he gave me to deliver to a relative in London – a sister, I think – if the sentence was not commuted. He was afraid it might get from the post into other hands. And he said he could not bear the thought of its being dropped in at the door, and picked up on the mat.'

Victoria's eyes dilated; she turned a little pale.

'How – how appalling!' she faltered. 'And how strange that you should have brought it here, to-day! But one shouldn't shrink from such things. May I see the handwriting? No, of course I mustn't – it would tell me the name. He was by way of being a gentleman, wasn't he? – it was not Morgan really.'

'I'm sorry,' said Ruth. 'Yes, I believe he was. I ought not to have mentioned it – I don't know why I did. I meant to do my distress-ing commission to-day, but I'm afraid it's too late now. When does His Excellency leave India, Miss Sambourne?'

'Next Saturday. He is coming by the P. and O. mail, not by the usual man-of-war. He says it makes very little difference; but it's a concession to my future mother-in-law, who thinks he ought to save the Indian taxpayer the expense of sending him. She is very proud of having influenced him in the right direction at last – I say it's a late last. But I mustn't let you call me Miss Sambourne. My mother has just married again. My name is Victoria Tring.'

Oh, the tricks of life! Before this one Ruth Pearce stood for an instant rigid. As she turned her head to look at Victoria the muscles of her neck seemed to move with difficulty, grinding against one another.

'May I ask, what did you say it was?'

'Victoria Tring.'

'I am so stupid about surnames. Would you mind spelling it?'

'Oh, but it is so simple! T-r-i-n-g.'

'Yes,' said Ruth. 'Oh yes. Thank you. What a pretty house this is. I think Mrs. Sannaway said you had only just come here to live.'

'Only just. Our old house was in Egerton Crescent. I liked it better in some ways,' said Victoria.

'Oh yes,' replied Ruth. She felt furtively for the letter, in the pocket of her cloak; and kept her hand there, on it, as if it might of its own accord have leapt out upon the floor, searing the air with its address, 'Miss Victoria Tring, 75 Egerton Crescent, S.W.'

'Oh yes,' she repeated, and her eye wandered vaguely over the moving people. What now was to be done? What was to be said? What was even to be thought?

A footman offered her tea. She emptied the cup at a draught, and put it down with a steady hand. Only her mind whirled and refused to obey her. Obstinately her mind would present nothing to her but the whitewashed walls of a cell in the gaol at Alipore, and a man in the clothes of an Indian convict, who sat on the edge of his bed and talked about 'family reasons' why he should let his people know what fate had befallen him, and whose hand – oh, precisely! – whose hand had sped the bolt. Here indeed, and with a vengeance, were the family reasons! Other fragments hurried before her. What had he said about her not being 'sorry' some day that she had shaken hands with him? That must have been because he had had the decency not to make the appeal of disclosing his identity. Well, it was a good deal to have had that decency. But if he *had* – what a situation for the Viceroy! She must settle afterwards what Lord Thame would have done. But in no case – in no case – She stared at the girl before her, who talked pleasantly on about India.

'Oh yes,' she returned again to something Victoria said, who looked curiously at her. Lavinia came up, and was introduced, but was just on the wing, she explained.

'And before I go,' she said to Victoria, 'I hear there's more news.'

'About Herbert,' said Miss Tring. 'Yes. This morning. From Omaha. Kelly has almost caught up with him now – perhaps he'll be home for the wedding.'

'You got my cheque?' murmured Lavinia; and Victoria replied in the affirmative, with a thousand thanks.

'My brother,' she explained to Ruth, 'has been away from home for years. He is just on the point of being – of returning. We are all rather excited about it.'

'Oh yes,' replied Miss Pearce, looking so intently at her that Victoria blushed.

A lady in the group near began to nod at Ruth, who presently perceived that it was Mrs. Sannaway, conveying to her that it was time to go.

'Good-bye,' she said to Victoria, and held out her hand. Victoria kept it for an instant.

'I should like to have your good wishes,' she said.

'Oh *yes*,' said Ruth once more. 'Yes, indeed.'

'Good-bye, Miss Pearce,' said Mrs. Frayley Sambourne. 'Your eyes tell me that India is a tragedy. Your beautiful eyes have suffered. Good-bye. Come and see my play.'

At the door Ruth turned to Mrs. Sannaway. 'I think I will go back with you after all,' she said. 'Do tell me more about Miss Tring and her mother. They seem unusual people. Is that the whole family?'

And Mrs. Sannaway was only too delighted.

Surely, therefore, if Ruth Pearce had desired to strike back at fate, a very pretty and convenient weapon was placed in her hand – a weapon of remarkable precision. The mere drama of the thing might have tempted her, so complete it was; so beautifully automatic, self-justifying, self-reposing. She had only to deliver the letter. Reasons were not lacking either why she ought to deliver it.

Among them came one reason why she should not; and as she looked at it, it began to wear a certain beauty. Through the Viceroy she had lost everything; through her the Viceroy might keep – everything. That, as she thought about it, slowly emerged the only thing that could be saved out of the wreck, if she had the right to save it. And he *was* the Viceroy – she, too, owed something just to that. Owed perhaps the sacrifice of her sense of duty – after all, when one came to compare – was it so much to sacrifice? Far down the street the notes of a band struck upon the air. She listened thrilling, a smile upon her lips and tears standing in her eyes. It played 'God save the King.'. . . If she were quite sure that only her sense of duty were involved, how gladly she would offer it up!

For a very long time she thought about it ever more passionately. After all, Lord Thame had had the enormous disadvantage of being Viceroy. He had made a mistake. Well, there should be a conspiracy to keep him from suffering from his mistakes. She would join the conspiracy. But gladly! She would *be* the conspiracy. She knew, too, what Eliot Arden would have done, and her heart found an instant's sweetness in the humility of following him – her begging heart, that was so humble now. So humble and yet so victorious, carrying her in this moment splendidly past the barriers of reason and of conscience, on such a tide that she wished for more definite scruples, that they might be overwhelmed. The great moment of her life it was, this conscientious woman's, when she threw Herbert Valentia Tring's dying letter to his sister into the fire.

So a very curious little holocaust went up from the grate of a Bloomsbury lodging-house that night, where a tragedy turned into flame and went out in nothingness. To Ruth, watching, passions seemed to burn and punishments, and even people. Her own soul seemed too near that blaze.

On the canopied and decorated wharf at Bombay, five days later, a crowd of people were slowly dispersing. It was a large crowd, with many ladies in it, and a thick border of natives, who also penetrated, more sparsely, into the heart of it, in the form of wealthy and important Parsees. But the gathering was chiefly of officials in frock-coats and ladies in muslins, with parasols, and even in its moments of warm and impeded disintegration it kept its look of function. Tears, indeed, still stood in the eyes of some of the Parsee gentlemen.

The weather was burning April, the crowd broke up slowly; people waited patiently in groups for their carriages. The Governor of Bombay with his staff had been gone some moments, and the Rao of Kutch had also driven off in state, when a hired victoria drove up among the private carriages and a gentleman jumped out of it, looking at his watch. It was the Chief Commissioner of Ghoom.

Arden saw at once that he had not been in time, as he feared. He looked doubtfully and vaguely about him at the muster of Bombay faces, most of which were strange to him, and made his way among them to the edge of the wharf. Some one clapped him on the back. It was Hichens, Home Member.

'How are you, Arden? You're late, my dear fellow.'

'I am, unfortunately. We had a breakdown coming over the Ghats. It delayed us four hours.'

'His Excellency was disappointed. He had counted on seeing you, and making a certain communication himself,' said Sir Peter Hichens, smiling. 'But he knew it was doubtful, so he had written to you. Here is the letter – he gave it to me to post.'

Mr. Arden opened the letter, and learned from its dignified and effective phrases, that in bidding him farewell Lord Thame had the pleasure of informing him of his appointment to the Lieutenant-Governorship of Bengal, and of his selection for the vacant Knight-Commandership of the Star of India, as the Extraordinary Honours List of the following day would officially notify him. He was permitted to understand that Lord Thame had made few appointments and conferred few honours with such definite and sincere satisfaction as attended his act upon this occasion; and that no consideration more effectively tempered the regret with which the outgoing

Viceroy himself laid down the reins of office than the thought that he had been able to leave the administration of the premier province to hands of such tried capacity as those of the Chief Commissioner of Ghoom.

Arden refolded the letter, and his eyes sought the lessening ship, where it dipped on the horizon to the west.

'May I offer my congratulations?' said Sir Peter.

'Many thanks – many thanks indeed. I wish I had been in time.'

'If you will allow me to say so, Thame couldn't have made a sounder selection,' Hichens said, in a very decent spirit, considering that he had been thought well in the running for Bengal himself.

'He writes cordially,' replied Arden, looking old and tired.

Again his eyes, and Sir Peter's also, sought the vanishing ship.

'He seems to have had a decent send-off,' said the Chief Commissioner. 'I'm glad of that. He's had a strenuous term. And now –'

'He's probably having tea,' said Sir Peter, without sentiment. 'He's going home to be married, almost at once, to a cousin of sorts, a Miss Tring – had your heard?'

'I hadn't heard. I'm very glad. I wish him every happiness,' said Eliot Arden.

THE END

Notes

Duncan annotated a few of *Set in Authority*'s Indian terms herself, and I have preserved her notes below; their sparseness indicates how much she assumed her readers would know about India, or at least about Bengal, the scene she was most familiar with.

p. 64: *Radical peer:* a member of the extreme or radical wing of the Liberal party, committed to progressive and democratic political policies. Thame's rank in the peerage is not high; he is a baron, outranked by viscounts, earls, marquesses, and dukes.
the Vedas: the sacred books of Hinduism.
Leighton: the Thame family estate.

p. 66: *kitmutgar:* a Muslim servant who waits at table.

p. 66: *Settlement:* during the late-Victorian settlement movement, members of the middle and upper class moved into the slums of London to establish institutions for improving the lives of the poor. The "Children of the State" (New York edition: "Daughters") and the Political Purity League appear to be inventions of Duncan's.

p. 67: *fagged for him at Eton:* By Etonian custom, junior boys perform minor duties for the most senior.
has devotions: is piously devoted to some cause, usually religious but perhaps now charitable.

p. 70: *howdah:* the framed seat carried by an elephant.
Benares: the holy city on the Ganges.
the Finnish constitutional question: a heated contemporary issue as the novel was being was written; in 1899 Czar Nicholas II began a policy of "Russification" in Finland which united the Finns against their Russian rulers; after massive protests they were granted the right to their traditional constitution in 1905. Finland became independent in 1917.

p. 72: *a young man who had undertaken to explain his race to the British people:* Mr. Gabriel is presumably Jewish, and therefore a problematic figure for the unthinkingly anti-Semitic world of the British upper classes.

p. 73: *Egerton Crescent:* today, as in 1906, a respectable upper middle class address in Kensington; compare the careful siting of other houses in the novel, in Cavendish Square, Bloomsbury, and Tite Street.

Fabianism: the Fabian Society, founded 1883-4, sought the peaceful establishment of a democratic socialist state in Britain; it was a precursor of the British Labour Party, and many noted intellectuals were members.

p. 74: *the Vice-Chancellor's Court:* Oxford students were outside the jurisdiction of the town courts and to recover debts the local merchants had to go to this ancient University court, which was empowered to deal with all actions where one party was a member of the University.

one of those magazines: a *fin de siècle* journal of literature and the arts—perhaps resembling the *Yellow Book*—which published faintly "decadent" stories, poems and drawings.

p. 76: For "Ghoom," see Introduction.

famine returns: statistics of famine deaths; Lord Curzon had to deal with a major famine early in his Viceroyalty.

baboo: clerk, writer, and perhaps scholar; in Bengali originally a term of respect (Afzul Aziz's uncles in Hiria's later account were "writers"); in Anglo-Indian parlance often disdainful, signifying a superficially cultivated Bengali; in general usage, a native clerk who writes English.

chuprassie: in the Bengal Presidency, an office messenger who bears as the badge of his office a cloth or leather belt.

sowar: a native cavalryman.

p. 78: The comparison between the imperial gestures of "Dalhousie Gardens" (named after Lord Dalhousie, Governor-General of India, 1848-56) and the Mosque of Akbar (named after the great sixteenth-century Moghul emperor), is evidently deliberate.

the Moghuls: see Introduction.

p. 79: *lakh:* any unit of 100,000, but in Anglo-Indian parlance specifically 100,000 rupees.

trenches: cuts into.

pariahs: members of a lower caste; by extension, as here, an ownerless dog.

Nizam: the hereditary prince of Hyderabad.

p. 80: *the ark . . . on a peak of the Himalayas:* English intellectual life was gripped in the third quarter of the nineteenth century by a battle between fundamentalists who read the bible literally (i.e., insisting the ark came to rest on Mount Ararat) and the Higher Criticism, which read the bible as a historical creation, and thus seemed dangerously secularizing. For Anglo-Indian society this controversy, dying out at home, is still lively, and Arden is suspected of irreverence. Duncan seems to suggest mockingly that for the self-centred and complacent Anglo-Indians, the ark may just as well have grounded in the Himalayas and remained there, needing no theological explanation.

cheapening his intuitions: setting his thoughts out; marketing them.

Upanishads: The latest parts of the *Vedas*, the sacred books of Hinduism (hence, "end of *Vedas*, or Vedanta"); their central concern is the nature of reality and the relationship between the individual soul and the universal.

p. 81. *Simla:* the Himalayan town which was the seat of the Viceroy during the hot weather in the plains below; the Viceroy resided in Calcutta from December to February, then spent six or seven months in his grand lodge (Duncan several times calls it his "castle") in Simla away from the heat, and perhaps two months "on tour." Duncan lived in Simla for long periods and wrote about it often; it was famed for its claustrophobic social atmosphere.

Woolsack: the wool-stuffed cushion upon which the Lord Chancellor sits in the House of Lords (it represents England's medieval primacy in the wool trade); hence, by extension the office of Lord Chancellor.

salt inspector: salt is valuable and from ancient times has been taxed by many regimes, including the Moghul empire; from the eighteenth century the British government in India held a monopoly on salt, one which Gandhi strongly opposed during the independence movement.

pigstickers: hunting wild pigs with spears on horseback; Ames later expresses the attitude of lower ranks to this gentlemanly inefficiency.

a pocket Horace: a small portable edition of the Roman poet; this would specifically characterize Arden as one of those civil servants whose ideals were shaped by a classical literary education which they never left behind, a type which recurs in the memoirs of British public figures even into the period of the second world war.

She went with the boys then: Anglo-Indians preferred to educate their children in England, and this often meant a hard decision for their mother: to go "home" with them, or stay with her husband. See Duncan's short story "A Mother in India."

p. 82: *Goanese:* from Goa, capital of the Portuguese possessions in India.

Kaiser-i-Hind medal: the "Emperor of India" medal; in Chapter XXX the characters joke about it, and Duncan observes that "the new decoration had not yet outlived its inevitable first stage of ridicule."

p. 83: *cheroots:* the distinctive cigar, tapered at both ends, in use in India and Manila; a cheroot becomes a clue in Chapter VII.

p. 85: *an Indian Civilian:* a member of the Indian Civil Service.
Miss Ruth Pearce, M. B.: Bachelor of Medicine.
table of precedence: the list of titles, in descending order of importance, according to which all formal functions, and informal ones like dinner parties, were arranged.
morganatic: a marriage between a man of high rank and a woman of lower social position; the wife retains her lower social status and her children do not inherit either the title or estates of their father.

p. 86: *the Tenth Guzeratis:* this is an Indian Army regiment of native soldiers with English senior officers; unlike the Barfordshires (an all-English regiment with only one married officer, Beaufort) the Guzeratis' English officers would ordinarily be married.
chota-mem: "mem-sahib" (Madam Sahib) was a hybrid term of respect denoting a European married lady in the Bengal Presidency; a "chota-mem" or "little lady" was an English lady of junior status.
our reputation in India: that is, in Anglo-Indian romantic fiction.
fourteen stone: a stone is fourteen pounds, so Mrs. Lemon weighed nearly 200 pounds.

p. 87: *some appreciable precedence:* Mr. Lenox has been moving up in the Anglo-Indian hierarchy, though Pilaghur society thinks he is rushing matters a bit by providing his wife with a tiara.
the tiara . . . wholly virtuous: more mockery of the intrigues of popular Anglo-Indian fiction, which Mrs. Biscuit, as the following passage shows, has thoroughly absorbed.

p. 88: *Tommy:* "Tommy Atkins" was the conventional name for the archetypal British soldier.

p. 89: *Aden:* very much a hardship posting, as Lord Curzon knew when he banished the West Kent Regiment to Aden in 1899 (see Introduction); in Chapter VIII Duncan refers to it as a "rock in the Red Sea."

Ayah: a native lady's-maid or nursemaid.

all Thomasina: all nonsense.

ultra vires: outside his jurisdiction; beyond his powers.

Black Dragoons: the eighteenth-century nickname of the 6th (Inniskilling) Dragoons, a Scots regiment, allied to the 25th Brant Dragoons of Brantford; it is not clear why Duncan attached this version of the "Rangoon assault case" to a regiment whose name she must have been so familiar with.

the second Afghan business: the British invasion of Afghanistan in 1878-80, caused in part by British concern over Russian pressure on the Afghans from the north.

p. 90: *Punkah-coolies:* a punkah was a hanging frame covered with cloth; the low-status "coolie" pulled it for hours on end to create a breeze in the hot weather.

Jacobabad: in present-day Pakistan, and known for its intense heat; the record is 52° C in the shade.

syce: groom.

gram: grain; specifically the species of vetch fed to horses.

Mulky Lat: "great sahib": the Viceroy.

p. 91: *the Gazette:* the regular government publication which lists announcements, appointments and legal notices.

p. 92: *Mrs. Lemon led . . . to the drawing-room:* the ladies leave the gentlemen in the dining-room to enjoy their port and cigars for a period after dinner.

café chantant: a café-style entertainment with songs.

rupee: the standard coin of the Anglo-Indian monetary system.

Zenana: the rooms of the house in which Muslim and higher-caste Hindu women "in purdah" (literally, "behind the curtain") live in seclusion; the Zenana Medical Missionary Society was dedicated to bringing Christianity to them.

p. 93: Since he is interested in music in the age of Brahms and Wagner, Teddy may have been sent to Heidelberg for the sake of his German; young Jarvis Portheris also goes there to learn German in *A Voyage of Consolation* (292-3).

Mrs. Pilkington and the Trinity: an unidentifiable title; presumably Duncan is satirizing the contemporary popular novel and its conventions.

p. 94: *sahib:* specifically, a European gentleman; "Sir" or "Master."
D.S.P.: Deputy or District Superintendent of Police.

p. 95: *Aganippe Club:* though the Aganippe Club is fictional it typifies the clubs being founded by middle and upper class women to provide themselves with a social setting outside the home.
salaams: Muslim salutation, "peace!"

p. 96: *Amir:* commander or lord, often the title of Muslim princes.

p. 97: *some Irish-American business:* Kelly is (profitably) involved in the movement to liberate Ireland from the British; see Deirdre's response to his conception of "the Celt under republican institutions", and the reference to the "Clan-na-Gael" society at the beginning of Chapter XI.

p. 98: *Trust fund dividends:* like other unmarried young women with a social position to keep up, Victoria has a private income from a family trust fund; interestingly Duncan describes the income as derived from funds provided by a woman, "Cousin Mary Thame."

p. 100: *the men were conspicuous:* in a strictly masculine social world, men do not stand out; Duncan is referring to the new "public" society of women and their clubs, where the occasional male visitor is very noticeable.
Mahomet had to come to the mountain: proverbial, but originates in Francis Bacon's essay "Of Boldness" (1625), "If the hill will not come to Mahomet, Mahomet will go to the hill."

p. 101: *"Fine, mother":* a family joke; Lady Thame has to pay a forfeit whenever she is carried away in conversation about one of her pet causes.

p. 102: *a Shan chief:* the Shan are the people of Thailand or Laos; in general the Indo-Chinese.
Upper Burma: the kingdom of Ava, independent of British India after 1852 but open to intervention by the French, was annexed in 1886 after military intervention by Lord Dufferin (the Third Anglo-Burmese War, 1885). Burmese policy was an important issue with subsequent Viceroys; see for example Everard Cotes's article "With Lord Curzon in Burma," *The National Review* 39, no. 229 (March, 1902) 122-132; Duncan and Cotes travelled with the Curzons on the trip reported there.

p. 103: *Maeterlinck:* a reference to Maurice Maeterlinck's *La Sagesse et la destinée* (1898); number 47 of this series of brief philosophical essays observes that Destiny can easily master the ordinary man, but to master the hero and saint "Destiny can only attack with one irresistible sword, the gleaming sword of duty and truth."

p. 104: *a Ghoomati sweeper's wife with four silver rings on her toes:* Hiria is of a very low caste, but her silver toe-rings confirm her prudence and ability to amass resources.
waler: a colonial-bred horse, especially one from New South Wales in Australia.

p. 105: *Burra Sahib:* great or important Sahib.
in the vernacular: probably in Hindustani, one of the two major languages understood by most people in India (the other being English); based on a dialect of Hindi, it was developed as a *lingua franca* in the Mughal empire and was promoted by the British during the colonial period.
ayah-ji: the suffix "ji" denotes respect.
pundit: a learned man, especially in Sanskrit lore.
Urdu: the language of the Muslim inhabitants of India; it employs Arabic and Persian words but has a grammatical structure identical with Hindi.
Brahminy cow: to Hindus, the cow is sacred; a Brahmin cow (of the highest caste) would be very sacred indeed.

p. 106: *Larrens:* Lawrence (named after Sir John Lawrence, a nineteenth-century military hero of British India).
golmal: [Duncan's note: disorder]
burning-ghat: the low river shore where dead bodies are burned.
wallah: from a Hindu suffix denoting "agent" or "doer"; an all-purpose word usually meaning "fellow" (though see "cream-wallah," below).
a coming-one: the policeman's wife was in labour.

p. 107: *chowkidars:* "chowkidar" is a prison, thus by extension, a guard.
dhurzie: tailor.
nautch: a women's dance; also, a stage entertainment.
acchcha: [Duncan's note: "very good"].

p. 108: *chupatties:* unleavened wheat cakes.
I found five d'otta: I had five daughters.
gorah: someone with fair skin; any European not a sahib, e.g. a soldier.

purdah-'ooman: Junia, being of a lower caste, does not live in seclusion in the Zenana as higher-caste Hindu women did (see "Zenana," above, note to p. 92).

Dado: [Duncan's note: "Give!"]

pice: (plural, pies): a small copper coin, 1/4 anna; "pice" is slang for money in general.

anna: not a specific coin, but simply the value of 1/16 of a rupee.

p. 109: *caste-brothers:* the strongest of all social bonds, in a society organized according to caste-boundaries which cannot be crossed.

"But without the nose-ring, who can marry?": a Bengali bride wearing customary garb has a thin golden chain running from her head-dress to an earring, and then to a nose-ring.

butcha: [Duncan's note: child]

p. 110: *"Dam soor!":* "Damn sewer!", pig, scoundrel. This curious word, thought to have first occurred in Nancy Mitford's fictional portrait of her father, Lord Redesdale, as "Uncle Matthew" in *The Pursuit of Love* (1945), may be obscure military slang of Tamil origin (Tamil "soona" means "devil"); according to Mitford's biographer Selina Hastings, Lord Redesdale spent a brief period as a tea-planter in Ceylon, where he picked up the epithet he used freely for the rest of his life. Duncan's use appears in fact to be the earlier.

chuckoo: [Duncan's note: clasp-knife]

gorah-log: English soldier.

lumbra: number.

nutkuttie: [Duncan's note: naughtiness]

Burra Lat: the "great sahib" or Viceroy.

p. 111: *Storey case; White case; Mir Bux case:* not traceable. Duncan seems to have devised these incidents to suit her narrative; in them responsibility for attacks on natives is distributed evenhandedly among planters, merchants, and the military.

tamasha: a spectacle; a popular excitement.

pleaders: barristers.

p. 112: *"Pilaghur of cantonments":* in the British enclaves or "cantonments" surrounding Indian Pilaghur.

dibs: slang for rupees.

p. 114: *Arcadian terms:* the equality of status conventional in pastoral or Arcadian literature.
fez: a hat worn by Muslim men.

p. 115: *under-pathos:* the pathos underlying existence.

p. 116: *Zend:* the dialect of ancient Iranian in which the sacred Zoroastrian books are written.
Parsee: an Indian descendant of ancient Persian stock; Zoroastrian.
Yazna: the *Yasna* is one of the five parts of the *Avesta*, the sacred book of Zoroastrianism; it is liturgical in content.

p. 117: *Syed:* one who claims to be a descendant of Mohammed; also, a man of the pen as opposed to a Sharif, a man of the sword.
pundita: a learned lady.

p. 118: *Pythagoras:* Greek philosopher, c. 580 BCE–c. 500 BCE; in the following lines Ruth's remark about "passing from existence to existence" refers to the Pythagorean doctrine of the transmigration of souls, a principle also characteristic of all the major Indian religions.
quarterings: the divisions on a heraldic shield denoting familial descent; English heraldry is strictly regulated by the College of Heralds.

p. 119: *Mrs. Besant:* the contemporary popular reformer Annie Besant, who began as a Fabian but shortly embraced Theosophy; she lived and worked in India much of her life. Mrs. Arden's reference to this current celebrity puts a chill on the philosophical conversation.

p. 120: *pumelo gin:* gin flavoured with a large citrus fruit called pumelo or shaddock.

p. 121: *lingua franca:* common or shared language.
gentleman-ranker: a man of higher social status (that is, officer class) whose circumstances have compelled him to enlist as a private.

p. 122: *a sweep:* a scoundrel (literally, a chimney-sweep).
magisterial: magistrate's inquiry.
A.T.A.: the Army Temperance Association, established in 1888 and very active in India; it provided coffee shops and meeting places for the men and was strongly supported by the higher officers.

p. 123: *sanguinary:* "bloody" (very rude profanity, thus the euphemism).
gives them the 'ump: galls them.
Mugger: a mugger is a crocodile (thus "saurian").

cutty pipe: a short pipe.

lagging 'im: catching him.

p. 124: *black an' tan:* contemptuously, a dog (terrier or setter).

efficient allowances: extra allowances.

remittances: money sent from his family at home.

the Laffan case: not identified; possibly devised by Duncan to suit her narrative.

jheels: stagnant lagoons.

Black Maria: presumably an old muzzle-loading gun.

p. 125: *the Mutiny:* the "Indian Mutiny" of 1857; see Introduction.

Goozies: Guzeratis.

Value Payable: cash on delivery.

De mortibus: correctly "*de mortuis nil nisi bonum*", "say nothing of the dead except what is good."

muck-rake: literally, manure-raker.

p. 126: *put into the billet:* given the appointment.

rotter: slang; literally, an idle fellow; generally, a contemptible person.

the High Courts out here: one of the features of British India was its complex and highly developed legal system, the various jurisdictions of which provide the subject of the ensuing conversation.

a native might, of course, form one of a revisional bench: as in fact a Hindu does when Morgan's case is reopened in Chapter XXIII.

p. 125: *"sometimes I pressed their lily hands, sometimes their ruby lips":* an untraced allusion; possibly a music-hall song?

his year at Oxford: the class of his year.

p. 128: *Canning, Ripon, Curzon:* all Viceroys of India who in various ways initiated more liberal policies.

Marcus Aurelius: (121-180 A.D.): Roman emperor and Stoic philosopher, whose *Meditations* were widely read in subsequent centuries, not least by the classically-educated civil servants of Duncan's time.

Alfred: Duncan earlier calls this character *Thomas* Ames.

p. 129: *K.C.I.E.:* King's Counsel Indian Empire.

Clan-na-Gael society: the "Gaelic Clan", a semi-secret society of prosperous Irish-Americans who sympathized with the Fenian objective of creating a military force which would oust Britain from Ireland.

p. 130: *half-penny papers:* the popular press, then (as today) eager for scandalous or sentimental stories.

p. 131: *eating his head off:* i.e., living at their expense.

Spitalfields: the area around present-day Brick Lane market in the east end of London; a slum redeveloped in the mid-nineteenth century, it was always full of poor workers, from the 1880s onwards immigrant Jews in particular.

p. 131: *westernise:* to move westward, by means of colonial expansion.

Jingoism: holding blustering and aggressive patriotic views.

pp. 131-2: *out-Heroding Herod: Hamlet* III, ii, 14.

p. 132: *Indian mail day:* the day on which mail must reach the P. and O. (Peninsular and Orient) ships which travelled on a regular schedule to India.

p. 133: *the debate last night:* in the House of Commons.

Sikhs: the Sikhs are famed military men; their large and well-disciplined army was as impressive as the forces of the British.

Santhalis: one of the peoples of West Bengal, whose religion centres on the worship of spirits.

since the house listened to Burke: the great Whig parliamentarian Edmund Burke's speeches of the late 1780s advocating the impeachment of Warren Hastings, the first Governor-General of India; Hastings was ultimately acquitted.

Transatlantic friends. . . counsels of perfection: Americans, who are presumably more practical.

p. 134: *another Army grievance:* for Army conflicts with colonial peoples at this time, see the Introduction.

Are we French, that we are afraid of our army?: Another example of Duncan's absorption in current public issues: in 1894 Captain Alfred Dreyfus of the French army, a Jew, was accused of selling military secrets to the Germans. His sentence and imprisonment on Devil's Island split France into two fiercely antagonistic camps: nationalists, authoritarians and anti-Semites against those who stood for individual freedom and a democratic civil authority. Émile Zola's famous letter in *Aurore*, "J'accuse" (1898) accused the army of a cover-up; Zola was found guilty of libel and imprisoned, but Dreyfus was cleared in July, 1906.

p. 135:   *he called her mother Deirdre:* a clear social signal that their intimacy is growing (though society carefully still categorizes them as "friends").

p. 136:   *the wind out of their hats:* Anglo-Indians (including Duncan) habitually mocked the mixed metaphors that sometimes occurred as Indian writing in English evolved towards the "Indian English" which is a respected subject of study today.

p. 137:   *Settlement Officer:* especially in Bengal, an administrator occupied with the tax (known as a "settlement") on revenues from agriculture.
the day's Reuter: a print-out of the news from the Reuter's wire-service agency.
C.I.E.: Companion of the Indian Empire.
gymkhana: an athletic event, especially with horses.
Metapora's fellows: possibly the rissaldar-major (Indian cavalry captain) of the Guzeratis, with his men.
tent-pegging: a popular military sport in which a mounted lancer attempts to ring a series of "tent-pegs."

p. 138:   *the men are grumbling:* "Morgan's" fellow-soldiers are apparently bearing the cost of Mr. Moses Agabeg's services.

p. 139:   *pilling:* black-balling.
Sandhurst: the English officers' academy.

p. 140:   *hookah:* a water-pipe or "hubble-bubble."

p. 141:   *Jains:* an ascetic sect; the earliest group to break off from Buddhism, and opposed to the taking of life in any way.
Mussulman: Muslim.

p. 143:   *"My mother bore me . . . " and "We are put on earth . . . ":* both from William Blake's "The Little Black Boy," *Songs of Innocence* (1789).
less dick: trouble, worry, bother.

p. 144:   *Ealing:* a neighbourhood in west London, developed for the middle classes in the 1870s and 80s, and known for its amenities as "the Queen of Suburbs"; by 1906 it was being flooded with cheaper housing.

going in to dinner: the ritual of the English dinner party required each gentleman to escort one of the ladies into the dining-room, in pairings which the hostess organized carefully to accommodate the rules of precedence and avoid the kind of social *contretemps* alluded to here; the host led off with the senior (or most prestigious lady), and the hostess with the senior gentleman.

Aide: aide-de-camp: an officer attending on the Viceroy or Chief Commissioner; see Captain Dimmock and his functions later in the chapter.

p. 146: *Liberty tulip shade:* in the currently very fashionable "arts and crafts" style of Liberty and Company in Regent Street, London.

State Lancers: an elaborate late nineteenth-century ceremonial version of a dance ("the Lancers") originally derived from the aristocratic quadrille of Parisian ballrooms; an important social symbol for Duncan, who with extreme contrivance imports it into a ball at the White House in *His Royal Happiness.*

p. 147: *Terpsichore:* the muse of choral dance and song; Sir Ahmed, as Mr. Cox observes, took a "good" Oxford degree in Classics; this was a notoriously demanding field and had he been English would have led to a promising career for the brilliant young man.

Young India party: in the aftermath of the Mutiny many associations of educated and nationalistic young Indians were founded; in 1885 the first Indian National Congress was held in Bombay; this was the origin of the Congress Party, which was to lead India to independence.

a spark of the Union: the Oxford Union, the university's noted undergraduate debating forum.

p. 148: *Obermann:* a novel (1804) by Étienne Pivert de Senancourt, chronicling in letters the hero's acute melancholy and frustration, and widely read in the nineteenth century by those who shared his sentiments. Mrs. Arden has not read it, but her husband clearly has.

p. 151: *Chowringhee:* the European quarter of Calcutta.

p. 152: *the Legal Membership:* the member of the Viceroy's council responsible for legal affairs.

a "K": a knighthood.

the Rani: "princess" (the feminine of Rajah).

p. 153: *a little nautch all to myself:* an entertainment with songs.

p. 154: *We've heard from India:* the Government of India, i.e., the Viceroy.

p. 158: *The Nature of Man:* possibly a reference to Elie Metchnikoff, *The Nature of Man: Studies in Optimistic Philosophy* (English trans. 1903); despite its title the book was concerned with the deep pessimism afflicting contemporary life, and its possible biological remedies. It was originally published in French, not German.

p. 159: *Life Beautiful:* an unlocatable title, probably fictive.

p. 161: *the Emperor:* i.e., Edward VII in his capacity as Emperor of India.

p. 162: *Bengal will be going next year:* the Viceroy will be appointing a Lieutenant-Governor of Bengal next year (as he indeed does at the end of the novel).
as Alcibiades did towards Socrates: the brilliant and unscrupulous Athenian general was close friends with the philosopher Socrates; each had saved the other's life in battle. He appears in several of the Platonic dialogues, most famously in the *Symposium*.

p. 163: *to the charge of a star:* to fortune.
trucial chiefs of the Gulf Coast: representing the coastal peoples of the Persian Gulf (now the United Arab Emirates); they signed a truce with Britain in 1853, but Britain retained Aden and ruled it from India.
the Home member: member of the Viceroy's Council appointed from London to be responsible for Home (i.e., English) affairs.

p. 164: *the Second North Barfordshires:* a slip on Duncan's part, which she continues (see Chapter XXX and "A Note on the Text"); earlier the regiment is called the Fifth Barfordshires.
the type: the regulars; the typical members.
the Saturday and the Fortnightly: the *Saturday Review* and the *Fortnightly Review*, contemporary London periodicals.

p. 166: *munshi:* a secretary, writer or interpreter; specifically applied by Europeans to a teacher of native languages, or a scribe.

p. 168: *call a messenger:* one of the hundreds of messenger boys who kept London business and journalism functioning before the second world war.

Mrs. Sannaway's Sundays: ladies of the upper classes regularly received guests "at home" on a specific day of the week; Mrs. Sannaway's choice of Sunday shows she wants her "at home" to function as a literary salon.

Bloomsbury: in central London near the British Museum; a self-consciously literary milieu in contrast to the Trings' respectable Kensington.

p. 169: *M.A.P.:* possibly the little-known periodical *The "Music and Poetry" "Art and Language" Society*, which issued twelve numbers in London in 1902.

"do get her something to eat": old-fashioned tea-party manners require that though the hostess or a lady of suitable dignity is enthroned behind the tea-pot, the women guests are waited upon by the men.

Celtic Revival: the revival of Irish arts and letters in the last decades of the nineteenth century.

p. 170: *take a little Pater:* Walter Pater (1839-94), an associate of the Pre-Raphaelites; Deirdre may have calmed her nerves with his *Marius the Epicurean* (1885).

Sally Lunn: a yeast bread served with jam at tea-time.

p. 171: *one of those "Without Benefit of Clergy" things:* Kipling's story of that name (1890) concerns an English administrator's tragic love for the Indian girl who has borne his son.

the Tichborne case: a long-lasting *cause célèbre* in Victorian England; the "Tichborne Claimant" was an Australian who in 1865 attempted to lay claim to the Tichborne baronetcy by asserting he was the just heir, who it was thought had been lost at sea; he was eventually charged with perjury.

p. 175: *the Ladies' Gallery:* reserved for lady visitors to the House of Commons.

p. 177: *the Indian Civil:* the Indian Civil Service, which Cox has chosen in preference to the army.

p. 179: *S'maliland:* in 1900 Sayed Mohammed Abdul Hassan rebelled against British influence in Somalia; the Sapper has just emerged from this conflict, which continued until 1920.

dervishes: strictly speaking, the members of Sufi Muslim religious brotherhoods, but since the Somalis were Sunni Muslims, Cox must be using the term vaguely.

"Sir to you": the subaltern is an officer, the Sapper, that "gentle looking young man in the uniform of the Royal Engineers" is a technician, but the latter's experience and military value effectively out-rank the former.

p. 180: *Mullah:* a Muslim learned man, teacher, or doctor in the law.

p. 182: *Kummel:* a liqueur.

p. 183: *does, butchas, everything:* in Col. Vetchley's view, a good huntsman does not shoot female or infant animals; it would prejudice subsequent years' shooting.

p. 192: *"in the language":* in Hindustani.
Sirkar: in Bengal, the house-steward, an office Hiria is familiar with; Ruth means the Secretary of the Central Committee in London.
seers: a measure of weight varying between 1/2 and 3 lbs.

p. 193: *sahib-log:* English officers.
the Guzerati lines: encampment of the Guzerati regiment.
Kail: [Duncan's note: play]
cream-wallah: dismissively, "that cream-coloured thing."

p. 194: *dhurries:* carpets.
Tantalus stand: a stand with decanters which cannot be lifted out until the bar holding the stoppers is raised.

pp. 194-5: *a bachelor mess exercising undue influence in a mutton club:* the cost of mutton must have encouraged the wives of the Guzeratis' English officers to combine financial resources, an arrangement in which the bachelor mess of the Barfordshires presumably had economic weight beyond its numbers.

p. 196: *Simla and Kipling:* probably a reference to Kipling's early stories, some of which evoke the scandals of Simla.

p. 197: *plainly a little black:* possibly of mixed blood.

p. 207: *all down the fourth page:* the most important news in an English paper was not always in the headlines; the *Times* front page was actually devoted to advertisements.

p. 210:   *Canada Loaf Bill:* there is no bill by this name in the statutes of either
Britain or Canada; Duncan seems to have invented it to make a point
about British interference in the conduct of colonial affairs.
Apollinaris: mineral water.
a daughter of Olympus: in Hesiod's *Works and Days* Aphrodite (the
Roman Venus) is described as arising from the sea-foam about the
severed male organ of Uranus, castrated by his son Chronos.

p. 213:   *the Maidan:* esplanade, parade-ground.
glacis: a parapet with a long slope on one side.

p. 215:   *"officers, not officials":* officers of the court, not officials of the government.
brandy pegs: a tot or measure of brandy; an old-fashioned habit in a
whiskey and gin society.
John Company: old-fashioned slang for the East India Company.
pucca: literally, ripe or cooked; thus substantial, permanent.
Standing Counsel: equivalent of Crown Counsel.
clean sweep: punning here on "chimney sweep" (see note to p. 122).
chunam: plastered, stuccoed.

p. 216:   *Andamans:* the Andaman Islands in the Bay of Bengal; a British penal
colony between 1858 and 1945.
tiffin-tables: lunch-tables.
equity: fairness, impartiality; in English law the legal recourse to general principles of justice to remedy the limitations of written law.

p. 218:   *made at least one effective speech:* for a lady to speak before a general
audience was still unusual, even in England where the suffragettes had
created a public space for women.

p. 220:   *even more coal in Jerriah:* an obscure reference. There is a Jeria south of
Allahabad with coal in the region; the ensuing passage about "the little
lot that Thame should have given Bengal and Burma to" may imply
that Maple is connected with industrialists or investors with an interest
in Indian mining.
in a hat: very upset.

p. 222:   *"doing Nietzsche":* Mrs. Arden is attempting to master one of the phi-
losophers of the hour.
Latinischer schrift: in Roman letters rather than the *fraktur* (Gothic
black letter) almost universal in German printing before 1945.
the sight of an Arabic character: Thugganugger was presumably Muslim
and public signs would have been in Arabic script.

p. 226: *'mystere austerity'*: this not very grammatical phrase is the same in the New York edition; a touch of *fin de siècle preciousness?*

p. 228: *an Imperialistic poet . . . stanzas*: a poem like Kipling's eerie and very well-known "Danny Deever".

p. 229: *jehad*: jihad; a Muslim holy war against infidels.

p. 230: *"Our acts our angels are, and good or ill, Our fatal shadows that walk by us still"*: John Fletcher (1579-1625), "Upon an Honest Man's Face."

p. 231: *seven Kosmic planes*: possibly an allusion to Zoroastrian ideas. *Mahatma*: a "great soul"; someone with more than natural powers; also a title of respect.

p. 233: *enteric*: typhoid.
suspected the drains: thought the infection emanated from ill-kept sewers.
it had put a stop to everything in Gangutri: social activity ceases for a time in mourning (though Mrs. Biscuit goes too far in wearing black, which would be the family's prerogative).

p. 236: *Antoninus*: Mark Antony; possibly Shakespeare's, but given the classical education of civil servants, perhaps the actual historical figure.

p. 238: *Belat*: England.
olly-collone: eau de cologne.
"Hum Maharajah hai! . . . " [Duncan's note: "I am a Maharajah! I am a Maharajah! Yes, you *are*! Yes, you *are*! Yes, you *are*!].

p. 239: *Houddha*: possibly Hiria's pronunciation of Buddha?
the Afreeka war: the Boer war (1899-1902).

p. 241: *rotting*: fooling about, wasting time.

p. 242: *sepoy*: a native soldier in English-style uniform and under English discipline; a sepoy thus wore shoes, and in the narrative of Afzul Aziz's vengeance in Chapter XXXI the British soldiers make the corns on his uncles' feet an excuse for calling them sepoys and killing them.

p. 243: *gharry*: cart or carriage.

cheetal: leopards.
lathies: a solid bamboo bludgeon with iron rings.

p. 244: *the gallery:* the spectators in the balcony.

p. 245: *picket:* the guard.
the bridge over the nullah: the original text has "mullah", which is ridiculous; the correct word is "nullah," meaning a small watercourse.

p. 246: *to their private parades:* to be inspected by their own officers.

p. 249: *Akbar's finger-post:* the muezzin's tower of the mosque of Akbar.
kite: a bird of prey.

p. 250: *trap:* dog-cart.

p. 251: *khudsides:* in the Himalayas, a precipitous slope; a deep valley.
the Snows: the distant snow-covered peaks of the Himalayas.

p. 252: *His gardener for small wages ... periods before Christ:* possibly a literary allusion?

p. 256: *C.S.I.:* Companion of the Star of India.

p. 260: *the Cabuli:* the man from Kabul, in Afghanistan.

p. 261: *budzat:* scoundrel; low-born one.
the Presence: Ruth, whom Gobind respectfully addresses in the third person.

p. 262: *bhai:* brother, friend.
thanna: [Duncan's note: police station].
jemadar: a native officer; also the supervisor of servants in a household.
Hazur: " Huzoor", "the Presence."

p. 263: *zid:* [Duncan's note: grudge N.Y.: malice].
pulthan: [Duncan's note: regiment].
a bad thing at Cawnpore long ago: in June, 1857, during the Indian Mutiny (the First War of Independence, 1857-59) Indians massacred the entire British population of Cawnpore (present-day Kanpur). In subsequent decades Cawnpore, with its Memorial Gardens, became an important point on the pilgrimage of British visitors to Mutiny sites. The murder of the *munshi's* uncles is described as an act of retribution by British troops, and Duncan's audience would have assumed it took

place during the summer of 1857 when Sir Henry Havelock's army fought back through Cawnpore to the relief of Lucknow to the north, often engaging in fierce reprisals against the native population.

writers: clerks.

p. 266: *Tite Street:* then as now, upper Bohemia; Oscar Wilde once lived there.

p. 272: *the Rao of Kutch:* the ruler of Cutch, a Native State (that is, not under British administration) in the west of India.

the Ghats: generally, a mountain pass, but sometimes (as here) the coastal mountains themselves.

Appendix I: Viceroys

A) From Chapter XXVII of *A Social Departure: How Orthodocia and I Went Round the World by Ourselves* (1890).

(In Calcutta on March 1, 1889, Duncan and Lily Lewis attended a "Durbar" or court at which the then Viceroy, Lord Lansdowne, whom Duncan had met in Ottawa the previous year, invested various Indian dignitaries with awards.)

. . . an A.D.C. handed us a large double sheet, with the order of the Ceremonial imposingly printed on it in letters of red and of blue; and there seemed, indeed, to be something in the heavy perfumed air like the suppressed excitement in a theatre before the curtain goes up. It was what the newspapers next day probably called "a brilliantly representative assembly" that picked its satin-shod way over the carpeting across the grass, and gathered under the great *shamiana* [tent] in the grounds of Government House, to see Imperial honours done that night. The Lotus-eyed was there, waving her fan, the Heaven-born flashing his medals, nobles from Upper India, an envoy from Cabul, a dignitary from Nepaul, princes from Burmah, from Oudh and Mysore, and from Hyderabad Mr. Furdoonji Jamsedji.

And the Aide-de-Camp-in-Waiting, no longer a chrysalis of blue lapels, but winged in scarlet and gold, hovered over all.

An expectant instant, as the band outside struck up the National Anthem, and then all the people stood up, for the Viceroy and Grand Master of the Order of the Star of India, preceded by all his Secretaries and Knights-Commanders and Aides, was walking up the aisle. One thinks a Governor-General in the full panoply of his office rather well-dressed, until one has seen a Viceroy of India in the mantle and insignia of the Most Exalted Order of the Star of India. I am afraid I cannot be trusted for details, but the general effect was of gold-glowing, sword-flashing, ribbon-crossing, white silk knee-breeches and buckled shoes, three-cornered hat, and long pale blue silk mantle floating out behind, the ends carried by two tiny pages, all in pink and blue, with powdered heads and silk stockings. The procession walked as far as the throne chair, on a dais under the Royal Arms, draped with the British flag, and parted, making reverent obeisance as the Grand Master passed through and took his seat. Then an Under-Secretary said something to the Grand Master, which purported, I believe, to tell him the purpose of the occasion, and at a given signal the first gentleman to be decorated came forward three steps, with a Knight-Commander on either side of him and the Under-Secretary in front. Then they all four stopped and bowed, not to each other but to the Grand Master, who looked pleasant, but, naturally, said nothing. The necessity of bowing at every three steps prolonged the process of getting within speaking distance of the Grand Master, but they all finally accomplished it. Then the two friendly Knights-Commanders who had supported the unfortunate gentleman to be decorated thus far, withdrew, and left him alone in his glory in the awful and immediate viceregal presence, under the analytic eye of all Calcutta. One would have needed a heart of stone not to feel sorry for that man.

Then the Grand Master did it with a very collected manner, and I thought in an extremely friendly and considerate way, but the unhappy old gentleman who had knelt plain "Mr." and arose "Sir Knight" looked round him as helplessly as if he had just been given notice of his execution, until the other two friendly Knights-Commanders stepped forth again, one on each side of him, and together they retraced their steps backwards, pausing at every three to bow to the Grand Master on the throne, who could not show commiseration, though he must have felt it. It was agonising to look at, that backward progress, in its awful indetermination, its varying slips, and its terror-stricken sidelong glances at the politely-repressed audience. The ceremony was then performed for another gentleman, who was made Companion, and then the audience came to its feet again as the procession went forth to the robing-tent, where his excellency changed his Star of India robes of insignia for those of the Order of the Indian Empire, not obviously less gorgeous, but representing a lower rank. Then I learned for the first time how that a C.S.I. and C.I.E. differ, not as one star differeth from another in glory, but as the sun and the moon in India. Not that C.I.E.'s are regarded the less, but that C.S.I.'s are regarded the more. For good works many "natives" are exalted to be C.I.E.'s for one thing, whereas C.S.I. is not so easily attainable by drains and hospitals in the capital of the aspiring Rajah. The Rajah's possession of it does not appear to enhance an honour in Anglo-Indian eyes. Half a dozen Indian dignitaries sat expectant opposite at that moment, and presently it was our fortune to see the pleasure of the Queen towards them.

Up they came, the stately subjects, pacing with far more composure than their British fellows-in-honour. One wore a rose-coloured silk cap, with an aigrette in it of the hair-like tail-feathers of a bird of paradise, every one of which dropped heavy with a diamond. Round his swarthy neck hung seven rows of pearls like berries, clasped with an emerald the size of an egg. Another wore robes of pale blue silk with strings of twisted jewels hanging about his forehead. His eyes were limpid and beautiful under their drooping lids, but his face was fat and sensual, and under his little foppish, waxed moustache lurked a foolish, supercilious smile. We asked the name of this one, and were told it was the great visiting Maharajah – the Maharajah of Jeypoor.

The band played again; again his excellency the Grand Master, this time at the head of the procession, went forth, and all the people stood up for the last time, and the guard presented arms. The spectacle was over: Her Majesty the Queen of Great Britain and Ireland and Empress of India had played another trump card. There was no denying its grandeur, its state, its impressiveness, and we were most glad we had seen it. My last glimpse I shall remember longest – of the trooping out through the great entrance-gates, under the Imperial arms, of His Excellency the Viceroy's mounted body-guard, tall, majestic, turbaned Sikhs, on splendid animals. Two by two they passed out of the nearer darkness through the lighted gate, and away into the further darkness, while all the people turned their heads to look, and again, and yet again, the band played "God Save the Queen."

B) From *The Contemporary Review*, v. 78 (August 1900), an essay written by Duncan but published under strict conditions of anonymity; it was signed *Civilis*, "of a citizen," that is, "the views of a citizen."

A PROGRESSIVE VICEROY

On the top of a Himalayan hill, looking one way across the plain of the brimming Sutlej, and the other over shouldering ridges to the Snows, sits George Nathaniel, Lord Curzon of Kedleston, administering from a point immediate and involved the affairs upon which, from the remoter vantage of Downing Street, he had for so long turned an interested and effective eye. The place is extremely isolated, and it is inhabited solely by bureaucrats and monkeys, but it has an altitude of seven thousand feet, and is thus a suitable perch — a very suitable perch. When we understood that Mr. George Curzon wished to take advantage of it, we were, nevertheless, somewhat confounded; it was such a new view; political expediency and Simla was like the association of the *Daily Mail* and hoary tradition. We suspected a flippancy which was not, of course, there; we were filled with doubts and misgivings which we could only explain by the statement that we had never before been given a young man to rule over us on a constructive political record, who wanted us because we were in the line of his ambition, and expected to get us because he had been useful. It was precisely because he had been useful that we did not particularly care about him: the condition which we had been accustomed to consider supreme in our over-lords was that they should be ornamental. We had grown, I fear, through a hundred years, into servile liking for prestige, not the prestige attaching to the sharp retort or the ready figures of an Under-Secretary, but the old indolent kind that belonged to great lineage, passable brains, a good seat on a horse, and that perfection of behaviour upon all occasions which had become, through our long good fortune, part of the spectacle. They used to come out, these former Viceroys, impressed above all things with the idea of the inadequacy of their qualifications for the post; they emerged from their illustrious hereditary past fully aware that none of the accomplishments of their grandfathers particularly fitted them for this Imperial task; humble and docile they landed at Bombay, with an anxious eye in quest of the invariable A.D.C. bequeathed from the outgoing Staff, the A.D.C. who "knew the ropes." Gradually they settled into a very nice perception of the etiquette attaching to the Viceregal Court, into such acquaintance with the country and the people as can be gained in a given time by a survey from the highest point, and, above all, into the conviction that the maximum of superintendence may very well reside in the minimum of interference. It will be imagined how comfortably we have got along, how in the easy old garment of custom, behind the shield of tradition, we have kept the place and the pace in the world's progress that best suited us. It was subversive and alarming to be given to apprehend that India was at last to wheel into line, that the gorgeous East was to be held in another kind of fee, collected on business principles, and applied impartially for the benefit of the ruling race, the Conservative Party, and a superior person. India opened her eyes very widely at this, and she is still staring.

We missed from the beginning the tentative note, the attitude of deprecation, the pathetic desire to be informed. In face of the facts affectation of these things would have been obviously too gross. On the contrary, at one of His Excellency's earliest opportunities, the good people of Bombay were reminded that he had already gazed five times upon their city from its harbour; no doubt upon the occasion of Lord Curzon's introduction to the Waziris and the Mohmunds he will inform their Jagirs that he has long since written a book about them – a perfectly justifiable reference, and one which can hardly fail to inspire confidence. His speech to the Council, the first day on which he did it the honour to preside, was brief, but it contained a suitable allusion to the fact that, as Under-Secretary of State for India, in 1892, he and Lord Cross – I remember he did mention Lord Cross – had in the Indian Councils Bill won the consent of Parliament to the enlarged membership of that body. It was a statement of extreme utility, compelling the gratitude of the enlarged members, felicitating himself upon seeing them before him in the very mould and image which he gave them; and at the same time reminding the British public of the liberal spirit in which he might be expected to enter upon his Imperial duties, though it is impossible to say whether it was telegraphed. From all this it will be seen that the Governor-Generalship of India presented itself to Lord Curzon under none of the aspects of an experiment, that he brought with him no need for the faintest apology, and that his natural function would be rather to impart information than to receive it.

So, indeed, we have found it. The contemporary problems of Government might be supposed to offer scope enough for the activities of any Viceroy, but Lord Curzon's conception of his duty to India appears to include a large proportion of the past, as well, of course, as all the future. Thus the other day we had him enlarging with a savant's feeling, before the Asiatic Society of Bengal, upon the ancient monuments of India. The address ranged with facility from the Sanchi Tope to the Taj Mahal, and implied even more erudition than it imparted. His previous address to the same body capped the investigations of a travelling German archaeologist with his own observation of traces of comparative Buddhism in Ceylon, Nepal and China. The members of the Asiatic Society were scientists, but Lord Curzon was Viceroy. The individual in contact with him, however highly specialized an individual, always feels that, I believe. It is said that none such can come into the presence of our ruler without acquiring some new fact, which he only thought he knew before. The impression is abroad that, given time and a library, it is seldom possible to approach His Excellency with a view to telling him anything. There is a hint, perhaps a warning, of this in most of his speeches. "My own researches have informed me," "I learn from my own reading," have become phrases which we should now miss from any public utterance of His Excellency in which he had forgotten them.

A Viceroy cannot be estimated entirely, of course, by his public utterances; they have so much more to accomplish than ordinary words and sentiments; but to many of us they are the only medium of acquaintance with the august speaker, and in Lord Curzon's we are privileged to discover quite a special measure of individual quality. Chiefly to be noted, perhaps, is their possession, in an exceptional degree, of the admirable quality of the expected. Invariable preparedness, an orderly and masterly marshalling of facts, and then all through the warp and woof of the oration the flash and thrust of just the epigram which we remember to have heard before with a context in which it was not half so useful. From the very beginning, when, at the dinner given to him as Viceroy-Elect by Old Etonians in London, he referred to "that Imperialism which is every day becoming less and less the creed of a party, and more and more the faith of a nation," we know that the Viceregal speeches of the current term would be marked by the happiest and most industrious employment of the apposite. I cannot say that he has beaten this, but he is always trying to do it; his use of the cliche is able, earnest, almost illumined; on his lips it obtains a new value derived from the rest of what he has to say. "One of the defects of the Anglo-Saxon character," he told the students of Calcutta University, "is that it is apt to be a little loud both in self-praise and in self-condemnation," what was, doubtless, a new light to the attentive baboos. Lord Curzon has a nice and unfailing perception of the character of his audiences, and a remarkable adaptability. To the baboo that afternoon he was candid and kind. "Deep down in me," he said, "behind the mask of the official immersed in public affairs, and beneath the uniform of State, there lurks an academic element, ineradicable and strong, connecting me with my old University days." Not everybody, certainly not every Viceroy, would have been willing to turn a ray of revelation deep down in him in that conspicuous way; but Lord Curzon knew that the baboos would love it, and did not hesitate. He seems aware that nothing is more agreeable in a Viceroy than these flashes of private disclosure. In an early speech to the Municipal Corporation of Calcutta he referred to the self-sacrifice which he understood to be imputed to him in his resignation of political life in England to take up the rule of India. "Such," he said plainly, "is far from being my own view of the case." "It was in no spirit of self-denial," he openly confessed, that he had surrendered his seat. There may have been Municipal Commissioners of Calcutta who thought otherwise, certainly nobody else did; but that does not alter the value of the statement. The simple truth, in politics, is sometimes as effective as anything.

It is this aim of wide effectiveness, by no means confined to un-enlightened and un-enfranchised India, that principally operates to place Lord Curzon in another category from his predecessors. Most of these, by comparison, were simple persons of short views, who soon absorbed the limited political gospel of India, and lent themselves to carry out its doctrines as best they could under the endlessly hampering conditions which exist. Some of them, with a natural aptitude for being agreeable, made efforts to achieve popularity, but how naif and futile appear the graceful compliments and sympathetic assurances addressed to the subject people by a Lytton or a Dufferin, compared with the pregnant utterances Lord Curzon sends over their heads to wake an admiring echo in the bosoms of the Nonconformist thousands of England! For a Lansdowne or an Elgin, once acclimatized to our varying political temperatures, accord with the India Office became a lost ideal, and the Secretary of State a natural born antagonist. The desire of a Lansdowne or an Elgin, acquired as soon as his eyes were opened, was as the desire of us all, to govern the natives according to our understanding of them, and to make war upon our borders whenever and wherever it seemed expedient to us. The Secretary of State stands directly in the path of these purposes, and any weapon – expostulation, execration, intimidation – is good enough to persuade him to step aside. It is true that Lord Elgin once created a lasting unpleasantness for himself by speaking, in forcing through the irritating Cotton Duties Bill, of the "mandate" of the Secretary of State: but that was in his first session, before the nine days had elapsed. In the end we find him in direct and violent variance with his own shepherd, Sir Henry Fowler, upon the retention of Chitral, and had not the Liberal Government most opportunely gone out of office before their decision had time to take effect, we should have seen what we should have seen.

In what sharp and admirable contrast is the attitude of Lord Curzon! Those others held the firm's appointment, and kicked up their heels in it none too gratefully, considering the value of the gift; he, Lord Curzon, is a member of the firm, with a concern for the profit and loss on every page of the ledger far beyond his salary. One imagines relations of almost fraternal amity between him and Lord

George Hamilton, while the India Office sit in a row gazing with rapt agreement towards the East. He not only avoids coercion, he creates ground for enthusiastic consent. A happy example lies in the Sugar Duties Bill, one of the first measures of his administration. India had been asked in Lord Elgin's time what she could do to help Mauritius, but the idea of countervailing duties suggested in the despatch from home was "not favourably received," in the reply sent by that Viceroy, and the matter ended. Lord Elgin gave his reasons, but they are not essential here. *Autres rois, autres moeurs.* The request was again made, at the instance of Mr. Secretary Chamberlain, of the present Indian Government, and the point for our appreciation is that what Lord Curzon was asked to do for the benefit of Mauritius, he found himself actually able to do for the benefit of India! "It is in the interest of India, and of India alone, that the legislation has been proposed by us," said he in Council introducing the Bill. He also gave his reasons, but they are as unnecessary to our purpose as were Lord Elgin's. Our amazement lies in the magical capacity to change at a bound, or a nod, or a wink, or what not, a favour besought into a plain advantage. "We are exercising our own legislative competence, of our own initiative, to relieve India from an external competition fortified by an arbitrary advantage," he continued. In view of resources like these, the unreadiness of that pottering person, Lord Elgin, in dealing with the desire of the home Government to relieve Lancashire by the abolition of the India Cotton Duties becomes almost unforgivable. Mark, too, the characteristic promptness of the operation. The first letter from the Colonial Office bringing "to the special notice of Lord Curzon of Kedleston" the desirability of countervailing duties bore date the 7th January, 1899, and on the 20th of March His Excellency was able to telegraph to the Secretary of State "Bill passed Council today." As to cotton Lord Elgin talked injudiciously about a mandate, and came to heel snarling. As to sugar Lord Curzon smells out a useful hint, and leads the way barking rejoicefully that he is only too delighted. The contrast is instructive and illuminative.

The records of the present Viceroyalty are all written large, but I can find nothing among those likely to be seen from a greater distance than the action Lord Curzon was pleased to take upon what was known as the "Rangoon Assault" case. It is unnecessary to describe the disgraceful incident on which this case was based further than to say that the assault was committed by a number of men of a regiment, stationed at Rangoon, upon an old Burmese woman, and that the Civil Courts failed to convict and punish the offenders. This, while deepening the odium of the affair, by no means meant that justice was evaded. The matter was taken up regimentally, the men confessed, and the whole thing was made the subject of departmental discipline. Lord Curzon's indignation at the occurrence was extremely forcible. Officials likely to be informed spoke respectfully of the "measures" which His Excellency proposed to take in connection with it, and intimations were freely made that the matter was to be gone into "very thoroughly." It was certainly an irritating thing to happen in a Viceroyalty of unblemished intention, and apart from this consideration it was a stain upon the skirt of British morality in India, which no decent Englishman could see without anger; but there were many who think the banishment of the whole regiment to Aden, the compulsory retirement of its Colonel and Sergeant-Major, the resignation of its Adjutant, and the summary discharge of the offenders from the Army, a disproportionate retribution. This, however, is no place to plead such extenuation as there may have been for the offence or such unfairness as there must have been in the exemplary punishment of the seven hundred and odd men and their officers who had no share in it. The point which claims our interest is that Lord Curzon was not content with the severity of the sentence which his influence was counting for so much in bringing about. That might do – I hope we do not too rashly conclude – for the abstract ends of justice, but Lord Curzon must also be vindicated. An Order appears in the official *Gazette*, bearing the unmistakable imprint of His Excellency's attitude toward Sin. The order begins by reminding any who may have forgotten it that the Governor-General-in-Council is invested with the Supreme control of the Army in India. Then we learn that he is "unable to pass by, without an formal expression of the opinion of the Government of India, the recent occurrence," etc. We are informed that Lord Curzon does not claim to interfere either with the Courts of Justice or with the Commander-in-Chief in the exercise of their functions, but there will be "delay" in the issue of the disciplinary orders "owing to the necessity of reference to England." This delay, this decent pause of deliberation, is filled by His Excellency's Order in the *Gazette*. "In the meantime," he says, "the Governor-General in Council desires to place upon record the sense of profound horror and repugnance that has been felt by the Government of India at the incident in question." There is a good deal more of it, chiefly admonitory, but that, perhaps, will do; with "profound horror and repugnance" the pen went deepest into the ink. An Order in the *Gazette* is here as elsewhere the most permanent form of fixing the views of the Government which can be devised. There is a black and damnatory emphasis about blame so expressed, and it lasts long after the emotions that inspired it have faded from the mind of the most immaculate Viceroy. The regiment against whose good name now stands for ever the "profound horror and repugnance" of the Government of India is one of the most distinguished in Her Majesty's service. Its colours bear the names of Corunna, Vittoria, Ferozeshah, Sobraon, Alma, Inkerman, Sevastopol, Lucknow, and more than these. Regimental honour is a sensitive thing. The spectator stands amazed at the apparent lack of a sense of proportion implied in this official Order. But Lord Curzon does not suffer, in other transactions, from any such lack. His judgment is, on the contrary, remarkably well balanced and well based. The eye ranges further and further from India, nearer and nearer to England, in search of adequate explanation, until it is arrested in the suburbs of a great city. We keep forgetting out here, so far from civilising influences, that there is a political use even for dirty linen; but Lord Curzon remembers that in Clapham it all depends upon the soap, and resolutely rolls up his shirt sleeves. O Clapham, how grateful you should be!

As to the actual business of administration sent up every day by the Departments, which is, apart from matters of popular interest which get into the newspapers, the real work of a Viceroy, Lord Curzon has made an exceedingly good general impression. The nick-names he quickly earned – "the Young-Man-in-a-Hurry," "George the Fifth," "Imperial George" – hint of the fatherly smiles of his Councillors, most of whom were struggling with the problems of India while Mr. Curzon was rounding his promising periods in the Oxford Debating Society; but while it is generally recognised that he is the kind of person who thinks he can make the world go round a little faster by kicking it, allowance is made for this fallacy, and no doubt a margin left for it in all matters brought to Viceregal notice. His capacity and his inclination for work are prodigious, and his recent tour on the frontier shows him equal to no small feats of physical endurance. He is content with nothing but personal experience, and into districts where the plague was deadliest and the famine sharpest he has gone down himself to see. The quickness of his grasp of complications brought to his notice is matter of general comment; he has a genius for the main point. "Goschen told me that Dizzy had said to him after one of his speeches on University Reform," writes the late Mr. Jowett, "Though I don't agree with you, of course, I congratulate you on having a subject; it is such a good thing for a young man to have a subject." Lord Curzon is an ideal example of a young man with a subject, and he is giving it his very best attention. The subject has presented itself, of course, for a couple of thousand years with such uniformity of paradox that even a young man of signal ability may find a little difficulty in changing many of its aspects. That we shall see later, but, meanwhile the magnificence of the spectacle of Lord Curzon and a subject that really suits him cannot be denied. Always and everywhere he carries himself as the representative of the ruling race, he is more than aware of what is due from him to them, and from all others to himself. The ruling race may congratulate themselves upon a lofty figurehead. Righteousness and equity are ever before him, and if, in his efforts to attain them, we perceive some gestures of the original prig, we are merely reminded of the defects of all qualities. The pity of it is, we must agree with him in thinking, that in spite of the news agencies and the *Times'* special correspondent in Simla, so small an echo of all that he is doing should find its way into the London papers. His term of office as Viceroy of India must have, to this late Under-Secretary, some of the aspects of a temporary retirement into private life. We have, nevertheless, seen that if anybody can stimulate the lagging interest of the British public in their great dependency it is Lord Curzon of Kedleston.

Socially – I hesitate. As a mere member of the social body one fears in some way to express a resentment that His Excellency so obviously regards social functions as a necessary but very unfruitful part of the duty attaching to his post. That consideration apart, however, I do not know that there is anybody who would not agree with Lord Curzon that his great talents are wasted upon the frivolities which he is bound to countenance. He came out to India with the eye of a bishop and the side-whiskers of an under-gardener. The side-whiskers have been sacrificed, doubtless to some end of public utility, but the episcopal vision remains, and one fears that any day it may see too much – too much. I am glad, however, to record that His Excellency does not find us in this connection so black as we are painted – in fact, that he was gratified on early inspection to discover us a very passable white. Explaining his surprise at the comparative dulness and respectability of married people under the deodars, "we thought at first," he is reported to have said, "that they were afraid *of us.*" I am glad to say that we have stood the test of more prolonged observation, but I have no doubt that we keep the breath of scandal from our humble hearths all the more successfully because of a terrifying standard and an illustrious example.

It is very difficult to any one with so profound a sense of his obligations to the Empire to conceal it even at dinner, and some explanation of this kind probably attaches to the complaint, occasionally heard, that His Excellency finds officials and others worthy of his attention at such festivities only so far as they can profit him with the facts of their departments. This tendency cuts, of course, both ways, as it is sometimes said, probably by persons with no facts at their disposal, that the Viceroy, like the newspapers in Mr. Rose's opinion, is too full of public events to be interesting. These, of course, are superficial cavillings, and attach only in the lightest way to the distinguished personality we are considering. The only really graphic blunder in his relations with his fellow men in India Lord Curzon made a few weeks ago in Calcutta, on the occasion of the funeral of His Excellency the late Commander-in-Chief, Sir William Lockhart. In the cortège that followed the body of this great captain and head of the Army in India came Members of Council, officers of all ranks, high officials, merchant princes of

Calcutta. The Lieutenant-Governor of Bengal, Sir John Wood-burn, a man strongly sensitive to all honourable obligation, walked in the dust of the road that hot March afternoon, followed by his A.D.C.'s, behind the gun carriage from the Fort to the cemetery. The Viceroy alone, of all those from whom honour was due, drove separately through the streets of Calcutta, with his A.D.C.'s behind him, in a dog-cart, at a brisk pace, as if to a business appointment, and met the funeral procession at the cemetery gate a minute or two late. Now, Sir William Lockhart was more to India than any mere administrator can ever hope to be, and this scant courtesy on the part of his civilian contemporary was neither kind nor wise. It was a mistake, and one would gladly have omitted to refer to it, but it is the kind of mistake that unmistakably reflects character, and so is valuable to an impression.

Here he sits, on his Himalayan hill top, with his councillors and secretaries round him governing the great India which spreads at his feet, under his eyes, two thousand flat miles to the south. Here he sits, one of the Empire's "coming men," known and proved at home, anxious to be known and proved abroad, to rise upon the things he will do, to leave his mark upon the time. Lord Curzon's is a moving virile figure upon the open page of our history; it commands our interest, and invites our criticism. In the remarkable trinity of the man, the schoolmaster, and the Parliamentarian, one hesitates to predict which will most conspicuously survive – perhaps Mr. Lecky would know – but for any of them the nation, however captious, should be grateful. When every flaw is noted, and every fleck revealed, it is the superior person that carries England's credit furthest; and for the ends of the broad blunt Imperialism we should pray for his increase, even while sending up an aside full of gratitude that he is not too predominant in private life.

CIVILIS

C) From The Contemporary Review, v. 78 (October 1900), a letter to the editor, published under the pseudonym "Calcutta," responding to Duncan's "A Progressive Viceroy."

To the Editor of the CONTEMPORARY REVIEW

SIR,

The article entitled "A Progressive Viceroy," by a writer calling himself "Civilis," in your number of August, contained a number of amusing but rather spiteful remarks about Lord Curzon, the present Viceroy of India, which may be regarded as the special feature or prerogative of anonymous criticism. In so far as these remarks conveyed either the personal impressions of the writer or ingenious distortions of the words and actions of Lord Curzon, they call for no comment or answer from me. In two respects, however, the writer committed gross and palpable errors of fact, the effect of which, if uncorrected, can only be to cause misapprehension, to do serious injustice to the Viceroy, and to give pain to others. It is in the certainty that the Editor of the CONTEMPORARY REVIEW cannot have desired to produce any such result that I write these few words of correction.

The first case is that of the so-called "Rangoon outrage" of last year, in regard to which "Civilis" conveys the impression that after "the matter was taken up regimentally, the men confessed, and the whole thing was made the subject of departmental discipline." The Viceroy nevertheless intervened, in order that "Lord Curzon must also be vindicated," and that "his profound horror and repugnance" must be expressed by His Excellency's Order in the "Gazette."

These remarks betray a most extraordinary ignorance both of the constitutional procedure of the Government of India, and of the facts of the case. The matter is one that I should have thought that few Englishmen would have desired to disinter from the oblivion into which it has now fortunately passed – so unrepeatable are the details (with which I will not sully your pages), so profoundly discreditable was it to the majority of those concerned.

So far from the matter being "taken up regimentally," it was the failure of the regimental officers to bring the culprits to justice, and their apathy in the elucidation of the facts, that brought upon them the severe punishment which "Civilis" has described as "a disproportionate retribution," in apparent ignorance of the fact that the sentences which he condemned were proposed by the very officer whom he has elsewhere described as "more to India than any mere administrator can ever hope to be," namely, the late Sir William Lockhart; and were accepted by the Government of India, by the Secretary of State for India, and the Secretary of State for War.

So far from the men having "confessed," an untrue story was concocted by them, and supported by a conspiracy of falsehood. One soldier alone of the 30 to 40 involved made a sort of confession in a statement to the Court. A few others, less than half a dozen, made a confession to one of the officers of the regiment in circumstances and under inducements which rendered their evidence inadmissible in Court, and insured their acquittal. None of the remainder confessed at all. Upon technical grounds, in spite of the overwhelming evidence of guilt, the accused were found not guilty. Finally, as to "the whole thing being made the subject of departmental discipline" – this discipline, for the character and degree of which the military authorities and the late Commander-in-Chief were primarily responsible, is the very retribution which "Civilis" has designated as disproportionate.

As regards the Order in Council which "Civilis" attributes to "the most immaculate Viceroy," I do not suppose that Lord Curzon would desire in the smallest degree to minimise his responsibility for an act which has done more than any incident during the past 20 years to convince the natives of India that the justice administered by their British rulers is even-handed, and that horrible and revolting crimes shall not be winked at because they have been committed by the soldiers of a regiment with an illustrious record, or because an effort to condone them has been made by highly placed officers. But it requires only the meanest constitutional knowledge to be aware that an Order in Council cannot be passed by the Viceroy alone, but demands the assent of his colleagues, and that no such Order that affected a regiment of the British or Indian Army could possibly emanate from the Council of the Governor-General unless it had secured the assent and support of the two high military authorities who sit upon it.

The second illustration of the ignorance of "Civilis" is even more striking, and effectually proves that he cannot have been in India, or, at least, not in Calcutta, when the incidents which he travesties occurred. The matter is a painful one to all those affected; but inasmuch as "Civilis" has chosen to drag it from the privacy that is ordinarily allowed to overshadow the tragedies of life and death, and to make it the occasion of an attack upon the Viceroy that is little short of offensive, I must claim the privilege of stating the facts. "Civilis" declares that at the funeral in March last of Sir W. Lockhart, while, in the cortège that followed the body, came Members of Council, high officials, and others, and while the Lieutenant-Governor of Bengal walked behind the gun-carriage from the Fort to the Cemetery, "the Viceroy alone, of all those from whom honour was due, drove separately through the streets of Calcutta, with his A.D.C.'s behind him, in a dog-cart, at a brisk pace, as if to a business appointment, and met the funeral procession at the cemetery gate a minute or two late." This "really graphic blunder" "Civilis" "would gladly have omitted to refer to" (why did he not do so?) "but it is the kind of mistake that unmistakably reflects character, and so is valuable to an impression."

Would it be believed, from these quotations, that this Viceroy, who is thus accused of having shown dishonour to "the great captain and head of the Army in India" was one of the latter's most intimate personal friends; and the last of his colleagues who, a few hours before his death, was summoned to the bedside of the dying man? Now, what are the facts of the case? The Viceroy offered to the military authorities who were arranging for the funeral to accompany the procession from the Fort to the cemetery, but was requested by them to meet the body, with the other Members of Council, at the gate of the cemetery. He deferred to and acted upon this advice, which by an accident was not conveyed to the Lieutenant-Governor, who was led to believe that the place of meeting was the Fort. Lord Curzon and his A.D.C.'s could not drive to the funeral in a dog-cart, because he does not possess such a vehicle. He drove in an ordinary landau, but without the bodyguard, having paid to the memory of the deceased Commander the tribute of deputing the entire bodyguard to join in the procession. He and the whole of the Members of Council received the body as agreed upon at the cemetery gate. I am in a position to know; because I was present in Calcutta, I attended the funeral, and I was standing within a few paces of Lord Curzon at the gate when the procession arrived.

These facts will suffice to correct the "really graphic blunder" into which "Civilis" has fallen. Adopting his own language, I "would gladly have omitted to refer to it, but it is the kind of mistake that unmistakably reflects character, and so is valuable to an impression."

CALCUTTA

Appendix II: Contemporary reviews of Set in Authority

England:

Times Literary Supplement, **Friday, May 25, 1906.**

In *Set in Authority* (Constable 6s.), Mrs. Everard Cotes (Sara Jeannette Duncan) shows a Viceroy of India insisting that a private soldier shall be executed for the murder of a native; and the private soldier (who calls himself Morgan) is the brother of the woman with whom the Viceroy is in love and the very man with whom the Viceroy's sister is in love. Again, it is discovered, after the matter has passed out of human hands, that the native is still alive. And, again, the Chief Commissioner of Ghoom, in whose district the murder was supposed to have taken place, has long loved a lady named Ruth Pearce; when a telegram announces the unexpected death of his wife, he and Miss Pearce are separated by his decision to support the Viceroy. There are three situations, out of any one of which a novelist of passion or of incident might make a "strong," exciting story. We can imagine the Viceroy learning the identity of the soldier and torn between private and public claims, or discovering after the execution, but before his marriage, that the murder was never committed; or, again, the Chief Commissioner's efforts to regain Miss Pearce at the expense, if need be, of his principles. Mrs. Cotes shows us none of these things. The Viceroy never learns who the soldier was, never learns that there was no murder; and the Chief Commissioner makes no attempt to recover Miss Pearce. This, in fact, is not a novel of passion or of incident, though it contains both. It is a political, or a philosophical novel, not intended to excite strong anxiety and emotion, but to rouse thought. It regards men and women not as units of passion nor as pieces in a game of circumstance, but as parts, personal and sentient, of a great whole, which they shape and by which they are shaped. The effect upon the government of India of the Viceroy's determination that a principle of Liberalism, the equality of races, shall, at any rate in one matter, be carried into practice; the difficulty of doing justice to native and Briton alike; the effect of the great machine itself on the characters of the men who compose it; the relations between the civil and military sides – these are Mrs. Cotes's chief characters. Her "hero" is not the Viceroy nor the Chief Commissioner, but the "Morgan Case." The course of her story shows clearly on which side her own opinions lie in that matter of equality; but this is no party statement. It is a wise and able exposition of both sides of the question. And that this kind of novel, the novel of principles, can be written with no loss of truth or vividness to the individual characters Mrs. Cotes's lifelike, and often amusing, imaginary portraits of people in India and in London are enough to prove. Here and there it is easy to recognize the "real" man and woman from whom she drew the sketch that was afterwards worked up to more or less finish; but every character in the book is alive and every character has its proper measure of interest.

The Outlook (London) "The Book of the Week", May 26, 1906.

A Novelist of Governance

The creator of a certain great daily once said that the new journalism is the best "school of philosophy" which the world has ever seen. It is a true saying.

I could name a score of novelists, half of them born in Great Britain and all of them trained in matter-of-fact journalism, whose work has this element of vitality. And one and all have the power of thinking Imperially because they could never shut their eyes to the most majestic and most miraculous of modern facts – the growth of the Empire. Three of these novelists have seen this organism enter into its springtide from a standpoint in India which is the logical meeting-point of all our paths of conquest and colonisation. Need I labour to justify this definition of India? Canada is our overland route to India; the aboriginal inhabitants are still called "Indians" to remind us of the ultimate why and how of the finding of North America. South Africa was but the turn in the long, long oversea trail to the East; there the East Indiamen took in water. Australia was the accidental discovery of a seaman whose first ambition was to find the North-West Passage – a short cut through salt-water to India. There and thence the first and clearest vision of the Empire, our first need for an ampler word for kingdom. Disraeli's addition to the (late) Queen's style was not, as many believed at the time, the result of a survival in the statesman of the politician's love of purple patches. It was the finding of the right name for a reality; an instance of the Disraeli touch in meeting a journalistic emergency. No wonder that our three most Imperial-minded novelists have found their best inspiration in the spectacle of the Indian *Imperium et Libertas*. The novelist of the governing race in India is, of course, Rudyard Kipling – the man with the magic words who has shown us the "man who does" at the heart of any workaday deed. Carlyle, who lived through a period when journalism was the merest logomachy, would have seen in him the great man as journalist. Mrs. Steel is the novelist of the governed, the introspective peoples crowded under the pressure of countless centuries into the wedge-shaped Asiatic *cul-de-sac* who are so slowly regaining their objectivity. Each of her novels is a psychological panorama, and her style has something of the first cinematograph's tremulous, wearisome brilliance. Too often she seeks the silken shimmering phrase – a fault due, no doubt, to the lack of a journalistic training. Thirdly there is Mrs. Everard Cotes, the witty and vivacious and slightly cynical Sara Jeanette [sic] Duncan, whose first essays in journalism revealed to a self-isolated and self-conscious Canada the wonders of the Orient at her western sea-gate (the closed "back-door" of those years), and, what has more potency for England's future and Canada's, the very woof and warp of Imperial policy in the East. She is the novelist of Indian governance, for ever following with the mind's eye the swift interplay of volitions (those of the dominant party in Great Britain, of the Raj, and of the amorphous and incoherent native population) which is the equivalent in the higher Imperial politics of the dynamical problem of three solid bodies. She alone of the three Indian novelists really comprehends and can explain in pellucid English how the stability of the system is maintained.

This Laplace of the Mécanique Celeste of our Indian Empire – what an apprenticeship she has served. She knows England, Canada, the United States, Japan and India from the snows to the ocean and through all their breadth and density. Everywhere she has studied politics with the keen imaginative eye of the statesman born *and* made. Her first Indian book, *The Simple Adventures of a Memsahib,* seems at first no more – and no less – than the chronicle of a young Englishwoman's attempt to "make a home" for her husband of small means in an alien land. A strange power of psychical mimicry which is best compared with that of Mr. Douglas Blackburn causes the reader to realise the most casual of her many characters with startling vividness. It has no more "graces" of style than *Prisloo of Prisloosdorp* and it has the same quality of latent satire which distinguished that amazing document. But – there is something more behind it all which puzzles and allures. Presently it dawns upon the reader that the thing is also a study in the science and art of Indian governance. Helen, the young memsahib, is the British Cabinet; at any rate, so long as she keeps the freshness of her insularity. George is the Raj; anyhow for the first six months. The household stands for the unfused native peoples. It is a study in the political problem of three bodies in the small and easily surveyed sphere of domesticity. After all, once you have mastered the way of a wife with her poor husband and with the items of any Indian household, the study of Imperial policy presents no insoluble difficulties. In *The Imperialist,* far and away the best novel of Canadian political life which can yet be written, Mrs. Everard Cotes tackles a somewhat different problem with uncanny success. Two charmingly contrasted love affairs constitute, in the opinion of most readers, its primary motive. But the crucial interest for all who avoid falling in love with Advena (you must give your heart to Rose Jocelyn or her like to be immune, and I have long ago taken that precaution) is the discussion of the Preference v. No Preference question. Here is a searching criticism of the British do-nothing, say-something pose in dealing with the larger issues of politics, which is put into the mouth of the protagonist.

The conservatism of the people – it isn't a name, it's a fact – the hostility and suspicion; natural enough; they know they're stupid, and they half suspect they're fair game. . . . As to a business point of view, I expect the climate's against it. They'll see over a thing – they're fond of doing that – or under it, or round one side of it, but they don't seem to have any way of seeing *through* it. What they just love is a good round catchword; they've only got to hear themselves say it often enough, and they'll take it for gospel. They're convinced out of their own mouths. There was the driver of a 'bus I used to ride on pretty often, and if he felt like talking, he'd always begin "As I was a-sayin' of yesterday"; and it doesn't matter two cents that the rest of the world has changed the subject. They've been always a-sayin' a long time that they object to import duties of any sort or kind, and you won't get them to *see* that the business is changing. If they do this it won't be because they want to, it will be because Wallingham wants them to.

Here is the whole deadly truth – with the one consolatory true saying at the close for those who hope to see the day when the Englishman understands that England must be something more than a belly conscious of nothing save its vacuity. It is this intuitive knowledge of folk-psychology which enables Mrs. Everard Cotes to evaluate the political factors at work on India, and to give us a clearer insight into its governance than may be obtained by reading any of Rudyard Kipling's pungent stories, or looking at Mrs. Steel's enshadowed cinematographs. In *His Honour and a Lady* she goes from the Memsahib's narrow sphere to that of a Lieutenant-Governor, who falls to the "pull" of party opportunism in Great Britain – and is succeeded by an opportunist who has been guilty of an odious act of anonymous treachery. He loses his lover, and with her the last shred of his self-respect; a *coup* of poetic justice described with the upmost power of reticence. But alas! this poetic justice, after all, is but the incorporeal *dea ex machinâ*; and the ending is melodramatic in essence. But *Set in Authority*, with its amazingly complex yet simply presented plot (which persuades one to hope for the long-expected Indian drama from its author), covers the whole ground of Imperial policy in regard to India. It is a complete vivisection of the whole system. Such is the reality of the personages and persons of the tale that one suspects at first that she has perpetrated a *roman à clef*. It is not so. Lord Thame, the Viceroy, with his bias in favour of the subject race and slight taint of self-righteousness which is burnt out of him and his backbone of nickelised steel, may or may not be three historic men in one. On the whole I think not – for the third evades me and can exist only in the future. To unfold the plot with its well-guarded secret would be contrary to the equity of reviewing and could, after all, only be done by one of those abbreviators of evidence of whom, according to Charles Reade, there are only two or three living at one time. As an example of the book's statesmanship let the following excerpt suffice: –

> Whatever happens elsewhere in these days of triumphant democracies, in India the Ruler survives. He is the shadow of the King, but the substance of kingship is curiously and pathetically his; and his sovereignty is most real with those who again represent him. The city and the hamlet stare apathetic; they have always had a conqueror. But in lonely places which the Viceroy's foot never passes and his eye never sees, men of his own race find in his person the authority for the purpose of their whole lives. He is the judge of all they do, and the symbol by which they do it.

Mrs. Cotes has written the novel of the year. (E.B. Osborn)

The Academy, **June 2, 1906.**

A novel which is serious but not dull, philosophic but not dry, full of purpose but not one-sided, is so rare – and especially so among novels written by women – that Mrs. Everard Cotes's new book should be read carefully and intelligently, not tossed aside as soon as the reader discovers that it is about India and the feasibility of carrying our beloved doctrines of Liberalism into practice in that strange land. Mr. Broadbent himself in *John Bull's Other Island* was not so doughty a champion of Liberal principles as Anthony Andover, Baron Thame, the Viceroy in Mrs. Cotes's novel. In one point, at any rate, he was determined that a favourite doctrine of Liberalism – the equality of all men and all races – should be made real and practical in India; and so, when a British private soldier is supposed to have murdered a native, the Viceroy overrides the decision of the Chief Commissioner of the district in which the murder is supposed to have taken place, and, in effect – though the gallows are never used – procures the condemnation of the soldier for murder. And, after all, there was no murder, and the man who is hounded to death by the Viceroy is innocent. A terrible comment on the application of the principles of our glorious Liberalism to other lands than our own! But we must not give a wrong idea of this novel. It is not a political object-lesson only. In with the politics is wound a story of men and women, of love and loss and hopes and fears, which displays a number of very cleverly drawn characters, whose thoughts and feelings are of deep interest. The soldier, by strange bonds that remain concealed till the very end, is united by close ties to the Viceroy himself – and the discovery adds pathos to the wretched muddle which everybody made of things. It is not a comforting or exhilarating story, but it is a clever, mature, and thoughtful piece of work that will increase Mrs. Cotes's already high reputation.

The Daily Telegraph, **Wednesday, June 6, 1906.**

. . . . "Set in Authority," by Mrs. Everard Cotes (Sara Jeannette Duncan), is a serious story of Indian official life, with a tragedy in it which brings out the motives and characters of the persons of the plot, and makes a most enthralling as well as a most instructive piece of reading. It is, in brief, the story of a judicial error, in which an English soldier, accused of murdering a native, is first given a light sentence by a native judge, and then retried by order of the Viceroy and sentenced to be hanged – a sentence which is duly carried out. It is not the story which is remarkable but its treatment. For here we get a real insight into the official mind, its honesty and its limitations, and we have drawn for us not only the possible error but the justification of such an error, and we realise that sometimes suppression of facts is more expedient and more highly wise than an exposure of an error beyond recall. It is a great subject, and demands adequate treatment. That it gets it here makes the book an achievement of which the authoress may be proud. She has managed to present all the sides of the tragedy through her characters without ever making them act contrary to their dispositions, and she has managed to do this without being dull. Although so different in fact and milieu, the story recalls the Dreyfus case with its unsympathetic hero, the key, perhaps, to its tragedy. To us the picture of official India must be of great interest, and with the author one can stand aloof and form a calm and sympathetic judgment on the actions of those whom training, tradition, and political exigencies have fashioned. In this world justice is often hard, and sometimes hideously mistaken, but if it is carried out by honest men with the purest motives, sensible people will realise that they can ask no more of what is only human. Only a Divine intelligence can make all things straight. "Set in Authority" enables us to stand outside, and see the comedy of government and justice going on, and to admire the motives of men who are not always free from error. The end of the book is particularly fine, and, on the whole, probably right. All people who are interested in India, and who like a good story, and who prefer fiction which is about things which matter, which enables them to get a clearer insight into the problem which beset us, will read this book and have a word of hearty praise for the authoress. . . .

The Spectator, June 23, 1906.

There was once a French farce the point of which was that Madame So-and-so, the central figure in the story, never made her appearance at all. Mrs. Cotes has chosen this model for her new novel, *Set in Authority*, which centres in the figure of Lord Thame, Viceroy of India, a gentleman of whom the reader is told a great deal, but who never actually appears upon the scene. When authors introduce such magnificent personages as Viceroys this is probably the wisest way of treating them. The plot of the story deals principally with the trial of an English private soldier for murdering a native. The trial is conducted by a native Judge, who passes so lenient a sentence on the soldier that the Viceroy upsets the decision and insists on having a new trial. Mrs. Cotes is always entertaining when she writes about India, and her accounts of Anglo-Indian official society are extremely interesting and instructive reading; but there is too often a sub-flavour of the disagreeable about the love stories which she introduces, and the love story in this book is no exception to the rule. Readers will find the chapters of which the scene is laid in India very much better reading than the chapters of which the scene is in London. The book is well put together, and the final decision of Ruth Pearse [sic] to conceal the real name of the private soldier – a gentleman ranker – because his sister is going to marry the Viceroy who practically condemned him is finely conceived and executed. Mrs. Cotes is never quite at her best in an ordinary novel, her most delicate work being done in books of the type of "The Simple Adventures of a Memsahib" or "On the Other Side of the Latch." Her present book, though from a literary standpoint not quite in her happiest vein, is, however, well worth reading.

The Athenaeum, June 30, 1906.

Mrs. Cotes has given us of her best in this story of Indian life. The coterie of aunts and cousins who send off the Liberal Indian Viceroy are highly amusing, both in their aspirations, so soulful and so vague, and in their disappointments, when Lord Thame has actually to lend himself to some concrete work of the usual type upon the border. The dialogue and *dramatis personae* are well fancied on the English side, and on the Indian we think no station with its inhabitants was ever reproduced more faithfully than Pilaghur.

The Saturday Review, **June 30, 1906.**

Mrs. Cotes has before now written exceedingly "topical" stories of Anglo-Indian society, but her latest book takes a more daring flight. We are introduced to a Viceroy who had written a book on the problems of the Yellow Races, and another work on Asiatic affairs which his appointment compelled him to cancel. He signalises his rule in India by remarkable activity in the matter of assaults by British soldiers on natives. After this, it is a small matter that the Lord Thame of the book is a radical and a bachelor, or that the name of Lord Curzon is mentioned among his predecessors. There is a strong situation in which a British regiment is to be paraded to witness the execution of one of its privates for the alleged murder of a native, but the author strains coincidence too far in her revelation of the unsuspected identity of this victim of the reforming Viceroy. The book introduces much sensible discussion of this delicate question of collisions between soldiers and natives, but it is weak on its narrative side. Society in the capital of a small Indian province is cleverly sketched, but the ineffective love-story of the chief characters is unconvincing. Mrs. Cotes is remarkably well up in Indian administration, but is wrong in supposing that a death-sentence passed by an Indian court could come before the Home Secretary for revision. The Secretary of State for India is the King's adviser on such matters.

United States:

New York Times Saturday Review of Books, **November 10, 1906.**

Anglo-Indian Folk. Mrs. Everard Cotes's several novels have put her among the first rank of the novelists who deal with the mingling of races and of forces in that blind land. Her successive books have shown a steady growth in her knowledge of life, in her outlook upon it, and in her command of her artistic gifts. Her latest book, "Set in Authority," shows a marked broadening, deepening, and enriching of her intellectual powers. Her artistic method has become better settled, more clear cut. She knows now just what she wants to do and how she wants to do it. She has settled upon her metier.

In her attitude toward her material, her manner of using it, she is very clearly a disciple of Henry James. But she no longer boggles, as she used to do, over everlasting attempts to express shades of meaning that are not worth differentiation. Her artistic method is, briefly, to provide a maximum of atmosphere and a minimum of story. The atmosphere is there, cubic miles of it, clear, convincing, highly artistic. And winding through it is the scarlet thread of a story, tragic, pitiful, ironic in the human cocksureness with which its protagonists, in valiant battle for what they believe to be right, defeat their own most desired ends. Mrs. Cotes makes her atmosphere after the manner in which Mr. James produces his marvelous effects.

The reader is brought into the presence of many people, singly, in groups, in crowds, listens to their talk through endless pages and so comes to know them, their dearest hopes, their secret aims, their outward manifestations, and also the concrete embodiment and the indwelling spirit of the society in which they live. She has treated in this way London drawing rooms, the gatherings of Anglo-Indian society in Pilaghur and to a less extent but very cleverly and convincingly the life of the natives. Out of this atmosphere she has evolved her characters and her thread of story, as spirit pictures seem to form themselves out of an enveloping cloud. And she has done it with a very sure grasp of her method, with an ever-present background of intellectual interest, and with a keen appreciation of the small humors and the large ironies of life. People who like atmosphere, much clever talk, details of life and character, will enjoy her book. Those who prefer much story and less atmosphere will pronounce it tedious.

The Bookman (New York) vol. 24 (1906-7)

. . . . *Kim* would be merely a fantastic and purposeless extravaganza if it did not symbolise and interpret for us the very heart and soul of modern India. And in a more modest, more circumscribed fashion Sara Jeannette Cotes has attempted something of the same sort in her recent story of English life in India, *Set in Authority*. Racial antagonism is her theme, the antagonism that grows out of the open contempt shown by British residents and British soldiers for the natives, and more particularly from the difficulty which the Hindoo experiences in obtaining legal redress for any injustice from the white man. The author projects the epoch of her story somewhat vaguely into the future. Lord Curzon's tenure of office and that of one or more successors has expired, and a new Viceroy with new theories has come upon the scene. Justice, he determines, shall be administered, not according to the established Anglo-Indian methods, but without

distinction of colour or caste. The height of his ambition, so his enemies declare, is to hang an English soldier for murdering a Hindoo.
And before long he has the chance to do this very thing. A private
in the Fifth Barfordshires, having carried on an intrigue with a native
women, is said to have been discovered one day by the husband and
to have killed him – quite wantonly, so the native witnesses testify;
in self-defence, the accused persistently declares. Tried after the usual
methods, he is sentenced to imprisonment for two years. At this
point the new Viceroy intervenes, and by using the whole power of
his personal influence, his authority, the machinery of his office, he
succeeds in having the man retried, convicted of murder and finally
executed – and that, too, in spite of the remonstrance of his friends,
the sneers of his enemies, the storm of denunciation that rises on all
sides from every one, soldier and civilian alike, who understands India and knows the danger of this new radicalism. And when the luck-
less private of the Fifth Barfordshires has died a shameful death to establish a new precedent of racial equality, it turns out that the
Hindoo whose murder he has expiated was not murdered after all.
He was nursed back to life by his friends, who smuggled him out of
the way and cheerfully committed perjury about him to gratify their
private ends. And finally, as a crowning touch of irony, it develops
that the dead private, whose antecedents had baffled the efforts of the
secret service men, was in reality the missing brother of the woman
whom the Viceroy finally marries. But for his own peace of mind,
the Viceroy is spared this knowledge. . . . (Frederic Taber Cooper).

Canada:

The Canadian Magazine, December, 1906

"Set in Authority," by Mrs. Everard Cotes (Sara Jeannette Duncan),
is a novel of Indian life dealing with the trials of an idealistic Viceroy
whose views regarding the natives are opposed to the ideas of all
other Europeans in the state. The book is characterized by the subtle
humour, the quiet fashion of exposing "life's little ironies," which
make Mrs. Cotes' fiction a source of genuine and gentle enjoyment.

A Note on the Text

SARA Jeannette Duncan sent the manuscript of *Set in Authority*, then known as *The Viceroy*, to Doubleday Page in New York late in 1904 or early in 1905, using the literary services of a "Miss McIlwraith," apparently a friend of the novelist. This arrangement was inconsistent with her agreement of 1894 to work exclusively through the literary agents A.P. Watt and Son. It is not clear whether there had been a breach, or whether Duncan had just acted independently, but in a letter of March 13, 1905 (written in London, which she was just leaving), she returned the management of her literary affairs to Watt, apparently dissatisfied with the lack of response from the U.S. (Watt Papers, 85.8).[1] H.W. Lanier of Doubleday would in fact send her his comments on the book on April 4 (Watt Papers, 91.4; see Introduction), but by that time she had returned to the Watt fold.

Watt's response to Duncan of March 14, 1905, established a new agreement between them; it also implied that Methuen had shown an interest in *The Viceroy*; however he did not wish to sell book rights until serial rights were disposed of (Watt Papers, 85.8). The correspondence over proofs described below suggests that at the last minute Duncan changed the title of her new book to *Set in Authority*, and was very anxious to ensure the change was made: "I recently offered *The Viceroy* or as it is now called *Set in Authority* to Mr. Moberly Bell, of *The Times* ... ," Watt wrote to Duncan, October 27, 1905; and to Moberly Bell on October 31, "I have deleted the old title because I understand Mrs. Cotes is very particular that the story should be published under the new one, *Set in Authority* .... " (Watt Papers: 91.4).

Watt attempted to sell the story to at least nine other journals before *The Times Weekly Edition* made an offer for serialization rights on October 23, 1905, and he was never able to dispose of rights for the serialization of this book in the U.S. In making his offer the edi-

---

1   All references are to papers in the A.P. Watt collection, Wilson Library, University of North Carolina, and are cited with permission. It is not always clear from the copy letters on file, which frequently lack signatures, whether Duncan is corresponding with A.P. or A.S. Watt.

tor of the *Times Weekly Edition*, C. Moberly Bell, complained that the manuscript was "abominably typed ... illegible 2/3 and unintelligible 1/3," and that someone must be found to deal with the proofs. In transmitting this offer to Duncan on October 27 Watt told her it would be quite impossible to send her proofs, but the next day in a letter to Bell asked him if the story could be typeset immediately and proofs sent out to Mrs. Cotes so that she might, at least, correct the latest episodes. This letter suggests that he and Bell had conferred in person and arranged to have proof read in the *Times* office. Bell's formal, hand-written offer of October 30, however, said "I take no responsibility for corrections but will do my best and send out what I can next mail. I will send you original and proof next week" (Watt Papers, 91.4).

On November 2, 1905, A.P. Watt wrote to Duncan in Simla that he had sold the British and Colonial book rights of *Set in Authority* to Archibald Constable and Co. for a 175 pound advance, and that in accordance with Duncan's instructions they had agreed to reserve the Canadian book rights, which on her instructions he proposed to offer to Copp Clarke (sic) of Toronto; there is no evidence in the Watt papers, however, that this was done, and Copp Clark has no records from that period. Watt was expecting a cable from Doubleday Page but was not optimistic about selling the book to them, and proposed to approach D. Appleton and Company for American publication (Watt Papers, 91.4). In the event, however, Doubleday decided to publish *Set in Authority*, and it is their involvement in the publication process which gives us such information as we have on the textual state of the book.

On January 18, 1906, Watt wrote to Lanier that Duncan had returned to England; within the next few days she would provide him with "complete corrected 'copy' (in 'Times' proof) of the whole story, and immediately this comes to hand I will post it to you in order that you may at once begin the composition and printing of the American edition of the book" (Watt Papers, 91.4). Doubleday Page thus printed their text from a set of the corrected proofs of the *Times* serialization.

The novel was published by Constable in London in May, but close comparison of that text with the Doubleday Page edition published in the following November shows that after dealing with the *Times* proofs, Duncan had continued to add minor revisions to the text, chiefly clarifying or simplifying phrases, specifying (and sometimes changing) the names of minor characters, and so on. It is evident, therefore, that the sequence of texts is as follows:

[M= manuscript; TW = *Times Weekly* text; TP = *Times* proofs; DP = Doubleday Page; C = Constable]

M (early 1905) ——→ TW (Nov.- Jan. 1906) ——→ TP (Jan. 1906) ——→ DP (Nov. 1906)

└———→ C (May 1906)

Two further editions were published by Thomas Nelson and Company in 1910 and 1919; the text was re-set but the same plates were evidently used for both editions. In them the erroneous numbering from Chapter XX onward is corrected, but there appear to be no further alterations. I have not been able to compare the *Times Weekly* text with that of the American edition, nor have I seen the Tauchnitz edition of late 1906.

If we seek a text which records Duncan's final thoughts on her novel, it is evident that copy-text for any new edition should be that of the London first edition, published by Archibald Constable on May 18, 1906. Constable's editorial preparation of the book was not as careful as it should have been, however. As required by their contract, Doubleday Page included in their edition the notice "This story originally appeared in the Weekly edition of the *Times* and is now issued in book form by arrangement with the proprietors of that journal." This notice was required by the *Times Weekly Edition* as a matter of course to establish the priority of its serialization and had solely legal significance; it carries no specifically textual weight. The Constable text (which on all the evidence is the latest of the three) was supposed to carry the same notice, but the publishers carelessly omitted it on this and another book by one of Watt's authors, and almost became involved in legal action as a result (Watt to Meredith, of Constable and Co., c. Nov. 1, 1905; Archibald Constable to A.P. Watt, September 22, 1906; Watt Papers, 91.4). In addition Constable misnumbered the chapters beginning with Chapter XX (the heading of which repeats no. XIX); in this respect the New York edition is correct, and I have followed its chapter numbering.

This text of *Set in Authority* is therefore that of the first London book publication (Archibald Constable, May 18, 1906), compared with and in a few cases corrected from the New York edition of Doubleday Page (November, 1906). Substantive differences between the two texts are noted, plus those which indicate revision. However, I have not noted alterations in paragraphing, which are numerous.

Variants in the 1906 New York Edition

p.63: to do it] NY: to proceed.

p.66: Children of the State] NY: Daughters of the State.

p.70: near it gazed the blind eyes of a bust] NY: near it gazed with blind eyes a bust.

p.73: upon all subjects which contained the female interest.] NY: on the relation of women to modern questions.
Victoria, Deirdre Tring fulfilled] NY: Victoria, Mrs. Tring fulfilled.

p.81: clever, and not too clever] NY: clever, but not too clever.

p.86: As some people can be drawn in three lines] NY: To go on with the list of them. As some people can be drawn in three lines . . .

p.95: She had been among the first to abandon] NY: She had long abandoned.

p.110: ' . . . the lumbra, that marks all the gorah-log – ' 'His equipment-number – yes.'] NY: ' . . . the nom-lumbra, that stands for the name.' 'His number, yes.'
[At the end of Chapter VII, NY has an additional paragraph, cut from the London edition:]
Thus tragedy entered Ruth Pearce's life. She thought it had come before, with very different features, which she would scan for hours at a time, as if she could put it out of countenance. She was so much occupied with this that Hiria's sordid tale went in at one ear and out at the other. She was very much occupied indeed.

p.114: Ahmed] NY: Ahmet [and *sic* throughout the text].

p.115: do not yet think it worth while] NY: do not think it worth while.

p.118: said the Judge.] NY: said Sir Ahmet.

p.122: the police investigation.] NY: the police examination.

p.123: Thomas Ames, Private] NY: Thomas Ames, Sergeant.

p.126: a revisional bench.] NY: a full Bench.

p.127: commitment] NY: transfer
to try Henry Morgan] NY: to try George Morgan. [But otherwise in NY, "Henry" Morgan.]

p.128: Alfred Ames was also quoted] NY: Sergeant Ames was also
quoted.
in Pilaghur, with a jury.] NY: in Pilaghur, with a special jury.
Nobody could remember a precedent for it, and that alone was
irritating enough. Besides . . .] NY: [not in the text].
Alfred Ames, Truthful James Symes] NY: Sergeant Ames,
Truthful James Symes.

p.130: her own to impart] NY: her desire to impart.

p.133: since the House listened to Burke.] NY: since Burke im-
peached Hastings.

p.135: Fifth Barfordshires] NY: tenth Barfordshires. [And see note to
164, below.]

p.137: some Mr. Cox, newly arrived] NY: some Mr. Henry Cox,
newly arrived. [But otherwise in NY, "Charles" Cox.]

p.138: their husbands had to remember] NY: their husbands had to
consider.

p.145: Was it Egerton Faulkner . . . that of the Anglo-Indian?] NY:
[not in the text].

p.146: Mrs. Carter, the Barfordshires' doctor's wife] NY: Mrs.
Meakin, the doctor's wife.

p.148: divorced by only a fortnight] NY: only divorced by a fortnight.

p.149: 'So I am already told,' he said awkwardly.] NY: "I believe so. I
am sure," he said awkwardly.

p.150: Smiling, she gathered their tributes . . . was the great thing.
This was her happy little hour.] NY: [not in the text; continues: It was her happy . . .].

p.152: Finch.] NY: Fink.

p.158:   Moti Ram's.] NY: Nur Mahomed's.

p.160:   And I'm *so* glad.] NY: [no italics].

p.161:   Arden's objection] NY: Arden's protest.

p.164:   Second North Barfordshires [but see 120 and 135: Fifth Barfordshires, and 252: Second Barfordshire; there is no indication what Duncan finally intended.].

p.171:   *I* must give it all the signs] NY: [no italics].

p.174:   *Don't* oppose me, you great strong man.] NY: [not in text].

p.181:   special character.] NY: special charter.

p.183:   don't provide troops] NY: don't provide Tommy.

p.184:   chapter xix] NY: [correctly] chapter xx. [The ensuing London chapter numbers have been corrected in this edition.]

p.188:   and will speak always.] NY: and will always speak.

p.193:   T'ank you, mem-sahib] NY: T'ank you, hazur.

p.197:   shop, which is a superior sort of thing to believe] NY: a superior sort of thing to believe, which is.

p.201:   London reads "metal." NY: (correctly) mettle.
         could hardly have occupied] NY: could never have occupied.

p.202:   which would have surprised and not pleased her.] NY: [not in text].

p.203:   and if the worst had happened] NY: And if it had happened.

p.209:   of this excellent roll] NY: of these excellent rolls.
         The first part of . . . consist of] NY: The first steps are taken in a fortnight, before what the call a Revisional bench. Which will consist of.

p.210:   Well, he is to be one . . . out there] NY: Well, he is to be one of the judges. Another is a man named Lenox – Lawrence Lenox – a very clever rising fellow.

p.212:   this is not a study] NY: this is not a social study.

p.214: the champion of righteousness and justice.] NY: the champion of righteousness and justice before the people of England.

p.215: practical law. The Revisional Bench would refuse . . . Still, the strength] NY: practical law. The strength of its bulwark steadied public opinion even after the Revisional Bench ordered the retrial. It was generally believed that on this occasion.
'in a hole,' and that the Viceroy] NY: "in a hole," and that Morgan's sentence was bound to be somewhat enhanced, and that the Viceroy.
Nevertheless, for the comfort of all] NY: Still, for the comfort of all.
And nothing to prejudice . . . as if for the occasion.] NY: [not in text].

p.216: how much of it Lenox would believe] NY: [not in text].
the essential spirit of equity.] NY: the very spirit of equity.

p.216-17: Hardly anyone but the native papers . . . such a precedent.] NY: It was pointed out with excitement on the Exchange that the accident of a Revisional Bench consisting of a time-serving civilian, a fool from home, and a Hindoo, was likely to make a most dangerous precedent. The Anglo-Indian community could not accept such a precedent. I must decline to quote what they said of Lenox. But upon one thing they were resolved. The sentence must be commuted.

p.218: Town Hall.] NY: Victoria Memorial Hall.

p.224: But the thought] NY: But perhaps the thought.
whether his wife] NY: whether Jessie.

p.226: And in accepting that verdict Mr. Justice Lenox only did his duty] NY: And in accepting that verdict the Court only did its duty.

p.234: he was a 'senior' official] NY: he was a middle-aged man.

p.235: And that day did come. NY: [not in text].

p.239: Hindustan people, sahib-people] NY: Hindustan-people, miss-sahib.

The dark hair . . . in the content of it.] NY: With her dark hair around her shoulders she saw in the glass that she looked almost beautiful, and smiled.

p.240: Grindlay Maple . . . too far to travel.] NY: No word of Royal clemency had come. The strong outcry had had too far to travel. Grindlay Maple had made his protest to no purpose.

p.245: the bridge over the mullah [*sic* in NY]; amended to "nullah" (see annotation to text).

p. 246: to their private parades] NY: with their officers.

p.247: keeping the picket out.] NY: keeping the guard out.

p.248: A rush . . . dangerous.] NY: [not in text].

p.250: looking, as he replaced it in the envelope, suddenly.] NY: looking, with its news, suddenly.
Me among 'em, I daresay.] NY: [not in text].

p.251: event. For a week, perhaps, the suicide was mourned by a Parliamentary party, but London forgot it next day. In India the matter] NY: event, and London forgot it next day. The matter.

p.252: Second Barfordshire [see note to 164, above].
well packed into her clothes] NY: well packed into grey alpaca.
on his carved window frame] NY: in his carved window frame.

p.259: as all the ladies of Calcutta would agree.] NY: [not in text].
overflow of affection] NY: overflow of whimsical affection.
Fate wrote a postscript the day they went to buy.] NY: [not in text].

p.261: different conviction . . . so often invited.] NY: different conclusion [remainder not in text].

p.262: brought to the *thanna*.] NY: not yet spoken of.
came to know, *Hazur*.] NY: came to know.

p.264: with a sense that his situation . . . above her charity.] NY: with a sharp sense that she was doing him at once a kindness and an indignity.

know that. She could trust his instinct – I don't know why she thought she could. Ruth added a line] NY: know that. She added a line.

He found implications . . . damage. He had a trained] NY: he found his own implications in the carefully uncoloured sentences; he had a trained.

p.270: Victoria kept it] NY: Miss Tring kept it.

p.273: said the Chief Commissioner] NY: said Arden.
a Miss Tring – had you heard?] NY: A Miss Tring. An old affair, I believe – had you heard?

Sara Jeannette Duncan: A Brief Chronology[1]

December 22, 1861

Sarah Janet Duncan born in Brantford, Canada West (Ontario), the daughter of Charles Duncan, Scottish-born owner of a successful dry goods and furniture store, and Jane (Bell) Duncan, of Irish descent, born in Shediac, New Brunswick.

1879

After education at Central School and Brantford Ladies College, graduates from Brantford Collegiate Institute. Earns her third-class teaching certificate at Brant County Model School. Drops the "h" from her name, to become Sara.

1880–82

Teaches school in Brantford area. January-June, 1882: Registered at Toronto Normal School to obtain her second-class teaching certificate.

February 1880

Her first publication is a poem, "My Prayer," under the initials "S.D." in *The Globe* (Toronto).

1883–84

Begins to publish short essays and sketches while teaching in Brantford, and starts looking for a newspaper job.

Fall, 1884

Decides to report on New Orleans Cotton Centennial Fair on behalf of Canadian publications and persuades *The Globe* (Toronto) and the *Advertiser* (London, Ontario) to take her articles.

---

1 Details of the serialization of Duncan's works can be traced in Marian Fowler, *Redney: A Life of Sara Jeannette Duncan* (Toronto: Anansi, 1983), on which the following chronology is based, with additions.

December, 1884–March, 1885

Publishes accounts of the Fair in a number of Canadian and American papers under the pen-name of "Garth"; travels briefly to Florida and British Honduras, and returns to Brantford in April.

May–September, 1885

Writes a weekly column in *The Globe*, "Other People and I," under the pseudonym "Garth Grafton"; also publishes articles in American newspapers.

September, 1885

Joins *Washington Post* as an editorial writer, in charge of book reviews and cultural topics, but without a by-line.

February, 1886

Begins to contribute to the important Toronto journal *The Week*, edited by Goldwin Smith. Signs her columns "Jeannette Duncan" and then "Sara Jeannette Duncan." Becomes friends with William Dean Howells. Attends Women's Suffrage Convention in March.

June, 1886

Resigns her position on the *Washington Post* and moves to the Toronto *Globe*, writing the "Women's World" column with the by-line "Garth Grafton."

April, 1887

Leaves *The Globe*; during the summer publishes columns in the Montreal *Star* and joins that paper full-time in October.

February–June, 1888

Serves as parliamentary reporter in Ottawa for the Montreal *Star*.

September, 1888

Conceives a plan to travel around the world and write a book about her adventures; begins her journey on September 17, accompanied by Lily Lewis, a journalist on the Montreal *Star*, both women sending regular articles to their papers at home. Their itinerary includes Western Canada, Japan, Ceylon, India, and Egypt.

February 28, 1889
Invited to a reception at the Calcutta mansion of the Viceroy, Lord Lansdowne, whom she had known in Ottawa, she meets her future husband, Everard Cotes, an entomologist at the Indian Museum. In March he proposes to her during a visit to the Taj Mahal at Agra.

May 1, 1889
Arrives in England with Lewis and begins to seek serialization for *A Social Departure*.

February, 1890
Duncan stays with Cotes's uncle and his wife in London and participates in her first London "Season"; she is presented at court on March 17.

May 3, 1890
A Social Departure is published simultaneously by Chatto and Windus in London and by D. Appleton in New York, to a warm response.

Late summer, 1890
Returns to Canada. Her engagement to Cotes is announced in *Saturday Night* (Sept. 27, 1890). Duncan is at work on *An American Girl in London* and *Two Girls on a Barge*.

October, 1890
Duncan leaves Canada permanently, travelling via England to India; *An American Girl in London* is serialized between September and November in London and New York.

December 6, 1890
Duncan marries Everard Cotes in St. Thomas's Church, Calcutta.

March 9, 1891
An American Girl in London is published by Chatto and Windus, and is well reviewed.

Spring, 1891

Duncan and Cotes travel in Europe and return to Calcutta in June.

August 14, 1891

Two Girls on a Barge published by Chatto and Windus under the pseudonym V. Cecil Cotes.

May, 1892

Cotes promoted to Deputy Superintendent of the Indian Museum. Duncan is working on *The Simple Adventures of a Memsahib*, which Chatto has agreed to publish, as has Appleton in the U.S.

August, 1892

Duncan is back in England; she begins writing articles for British and American magazines.

December, 1892

Returns to Calcutta; writes *The Story of Sonny Sahib*.

1893

The Simple Adventures of a Memsahib is serialized, and then published on May 18, to very good reviews. Duncan writes both *Vernon's Aunt* and *A Daughter of Today*.

April, 1894.

Cotes resigns from the Museum and the couple prepares to move permanently to England, where, after visiting Paris, they arrive in May. Cotes seeks work as a journalist.

June, 1894.

A Daughter of To-day is published by Chatto and Windus. *Vernon's Aunt* is published by Chatto in England (October) and by Appleton in the U.S.

Fall, 1894

Duncan holidays in Scotland; in November, 1894, the Cotes take a flat in Kensington. But Cotes is offered the editorship of the *Indian Daily News* in

Calcutta and they prepare to return to India. In December Duncan appoints A. P. Watt and Son her literary agents.

January, 1895

Duncan and Cotes return to Calcutta where she assists him on the *Indian Daily News* by writing articles and editorials. Duncan begins work on *His Honor, and a Lady*, her first political novel. In March she is in London but in the fall returns to Simla.

Spring, 1896

His Honor, and a Lady is published by Macmillan (London) and Appleton (New York). During a summer and fall of drought, cholera, and plague, Duncan works on *A Voyage of Consolation*.

March, 1897

Cotes resigns his editorship of the *Indian Daily News* and in June becomes a government press correspondent in Simla. Duncan is at work on *The Path of a Star*.

March, 1898

Duncan travels to England. *A Voyage of Consolation* is published by Methuen (London) and Appleton (New York).

Summer, 1898

Duncan visits Brantford and takes hydropathic treatment for her chronic bronchitis in Dansville, NY; visits New York City in the fall.

April, 1899

In Simla Duncan becomes friends with the wife of the new Viceroy, Mary Curzon, whom she had probably met earlier.

1899

The Path of a Star is published by Methuen in London and (under the title *Hilda*) by Frederick Stokes, New York.

1900

A child may have been born to Duncan (date unknown) but it lived only a few days. Duncan sends the essay "A Progressive Viceroy" to Watt to market, but insists that it be published anonymously. Diagnosed with tuberculosis, she spends the summer in her garden at Simla and writes *On the Other Side of the Latch*. "A Progressive Viceroy" is published by *The Contemporary Review* in August.

1901

Duncan and Cotes move to Calcutta so that he can recruit for the Boer War. Duncan is at work on *Those Delightful Americans*. *On the Other Side of the Latch* is published by Methuen, and as *The Crow's Nest* by Dodd, Mead in New York.

December, 1901

Duncan travels with the Curzons on their state visit to Upper Burma and sells two articles about the tour.

Spring, 1902

Those Delightful Americans is published by Methuen in London and Appleton in New York. Duncan arrives in London in April, 1902.

Summer, 1902

Back in Simla, she is at work on *The Imperialist*, and at the end of the year on the four stories in *The Pool in the Desert*.

January, 1903

Duncan and Cotes attend the 1903 Coronation Durbar in Delhi.

May, 1903

Duncan returns to England, and in the fall visits Brantford. Sends John Willison *The Imperialist* for serialization in the *Toronto News*.

Summer, 1903

The Pool in the Desert is published by Methuen, and by Appleton in New York.

December, 1903

A reception is held for Duncan in Toronto, attended by many well-known literary people of the day; she leaves for London.

October–December, 1903

The Imperialist is serialized in *The Queen*, and between December, 1903–February, 1904 in the *Toronto News*.

March 17, 1904

Duncan leaves London for Simla.

Spring, 1904

The Imperialist appears, to largely unfavourable reviews in London and Canada; Duncan deeply upset, as she regards it as her best book. However, Archibald MacMechan reviews it warmly in the *Halifax Herald*. Around this time Duncan begins *Set in Authority*.

September, 1905

Duncan writes her first play, "Browne with an E" (possibly a dramatized version of *The Simple Adventures of a Memsahib*?), for the Simla Amateur Dramatic Club.

November, 1905

Duncan and Cotes once more prepare to leave India for good.

January, 1906

While Cotes tours the Far East with a group of journalists, Duncan takes up residence in London at 40 Iverna Court, Kensington, and reads proof for *Set in Authority*, which is serialized during the early spring in the *Times Weekly Edition*.

1906

Set in Authority is published by Constable in May, and is a success; the novel is published in New York in November by Doubleday Page. Death of Mary Curzon. Duncan is at work on *Two in a Flat*.

April, 1907

Cotes returns to India and in July Duncan goes back as well. She begins
Cousin Cinderella. Duncan's father dies in October.

January, 1908

Cousin Cinderella is published in the spring by Methuen in London and
Macmillan in New York.

Spring, 1908

Duncan returns to London; is at work on *The Burnt Offering*. Later returns
to India. *Two in a Flat* is published under the pseudonym "Jane Wintergreen."

Spring, 1909

Duncan spends the spring in London. *The Burnt Offering* is published by
Methuen in the fall.

Spring, 1910

Duncan returns to London, but she and Cotes go back to India quickly
when he is offered the position of Managing Director of the Eastern News
Agency; he holds this position until 1919. Duncan establishes their home
in Simla, at "Dormers."

1911

Duncan is working on *The Consort*.

Spring, 1912

Duncan is in England, where *The Consort* is published in May. On her return to India brings her niece Nellie Masterman with her.

November, 1912

E. M. Forster visits Duncan and Cotes at "Dormers." The Cotes and Nellie move to Delhi so Cotes can be nearer the source of news.

1913

In March, another visit from Forster, in Delhi. Duncan spends most of the year at "Dormers," at work on *His Royal Happiness*; she buys four lots of land in Prince Rupert, British Columbia.

1914

His Royal Happiness, dedicated to the memory of Mary Curzon, is published in New York by Appleton at the end of the year. Duncan visits Brantford in the summer of 1914; she is there when war is declared on August 4 and stays on, turning *His Royal Happiness* into a play for production in Toronto.

January, 1915

His Royal Happiness is produced at the Princess Theatre, King Street, Toronto, on January 4, starring Annie Russell; received poorly, it runs for only a week. Duncan leaves for England. *His Royal Happiness* is published by Hodder and Stoughton early in the year.

March, 1915

Duncan returns to "Dormers," with Nellie; writes a play, *The Convalescents*, for the Simla Amateur Dramatic Club, which is successfully produced in October, 1915. In late fall she leaves India, planning to take *The Convalescents* to London's West End. Cotes and Nellie remain in India till 1919.

1916

Duncan resides in London; in March *The Convalescents* opens under the title *Beauchamp and Beecham* at the Lyric Theatre. The play tours for two years but in a vulgarized form; Duncan will eventually try to withdraw it.

1917

Duncan's play *Julyann* is produced by W.G. Fay (of the Abbey Theatre, Dublin) at the Globe, London.

1919

Cotes sells the Eastern News Agency and returns with Nellie to London, where the Cotes lease 17 Paultons Square, Chelsea. In September and October they travel to Canada; Cotes is part of the Press entourage for the Prince of Wales's western tour, and Duncan accompanies him; they are with the Prince when he visits Brantford on October 20. They return to London in November.

1920
Duncan stays in London while Cotes spends seven months touring Australia with the Prince of Wales.

1921 and early 1922
Duncan is working on *Title Clear* and *The Gold Cure*, her first novels since 1914. Makes her will on May 6, 1921, bequeathing everything to Cotes.

Spring, 1922
Duncan and Cotes buy a house in Ashtead, Surrey, which they call "Barnett Wood Lodge." They move in May; *Title Clear* is published in June. Duncan falls ill with pneumonia in June, lingers for five weeks, and dies on July 22. She is buried in the churchyard of St. Giles Anglican Church, Ashtead.

1923
Everard Cotes remarries, and for the next seventeen years he is parliamentary correspondent for the *Christian Science Monitor*.

1924
The Gold Cure is published posthumously.

1944
Everard Cotes dies.